The Ten-Year Nap

MEG WOLITZER

The

TEN-YEAR
NAP

Chatto & Windus
LONDON

This edition published by Chatto & Windus 2008

First published in the United States by Riverhead Books in 2008

2 4 6 8 10 9 7 5 3 1

Copyright © Meg Wolitzer 2008

Meg Wolitzer has asserted her right under the Copyright, Designs
and Patents Act 1988 to be identified as the author of this work

First published in Great Britain in 2008 by
Chatto & Windus
Random House, 20 Vauxhall Bridge Road,
London SW1V 2SA

www.rbooks.co.uk

Addresses for companies within The Random House Group Limited can be found at:
www.randomhouse.co.uk/offices.htm

The Random House Group Limited Reg. No. 954009

A CIP catalogue record for this book
is available from the British Library

Hardback ISBN 9780701182700
Trade paperback ISBN 9780701182717

The Random House Group Limited supports The Forest Stewardship Council (FSC), the leading
international forest certification organisation. All our titles that are printed on Greenpeace approved
FSC certified paper carry the FSC logo. Our paper procurement policy can be found at
www.rbooks.co.uk/environment

Mixed Sources
Product group from well-managed
forests and other controlled sources
www.fsc.org Cert no. TT-COC-2139
© 1996 Forest Stewardship Council

Printed and bound in Great Britain by
CPI Mackays, Chatham, ME5 8TD.

For Peter Smith

ALL AROUND THE COUNTRY, the women were waking up. Their alarm clocks bleated one by one, making soothing sounds or grating sounds or the stirrings of a favorite song. There were hums and beeps and a random burst of radio. There were wind chimes and roaring surf, and the electronic approximation of birdsong and other gentle animal noises. All of it accompanied the passage of time, sliding forward in liquid crystal. Almost everything in these women's homes required a plug. Voltage stuttered through the curls of wire, and if you put your ear to one of the complicated clocks in any of the bedrooms, you could hear the burble of industry deep inside its cavity. Something was quietly happening.

BIP BIP BIP. By a bed on this Monday morning in fall, the first alarm went off in a house with cedar shingles in a small, buffed suburb, and a woman sat up, the prospects of the entire day rising before her. *BOOP BOOP BOOP.* Three towns over, there went another alarm, a full octave lower, and a woman broke the skin of consciousness in her colonial, blinking. "*—A LOOK AT THE TRAFFIC.*

RANDY, WHAT'S HAPPENING OUT THERE?" Throughout the region, and in others not unlike it, in houses broader and more spread apart or else smaller and tightly bunched, the women awakened. Farther away, across unswimmable waters and over a nexus of highway and bridge, in the residential towers of the city, a whole other crop of alarms peeped and chirruped and wailed and beckoned.

They sounded in both suburb and city, on individual night tables beside facedown, broken-spined volumes being read for book group with titles like *Bigfoot Was Here: A Father's Letters to His Newborn Son from Iraq,* and among curling school permission slips ("I, _____, allow my child, _____, to attend the field trip to the recycling plant"). The intensifying chorus of alarms urged the women to get up and go wherever the day would take them. Some would shepherd their children into huge, fully stocked, cornball American family vehicles, adjusting rearview mirrors and backing out into the world, while others would grab their children by their soft little hands and yank them like pull-toys into the mash of urban foot traffic.

One by one the women began their separate and familiar routines. Unlike in the past, there were no presentations to give, no fears of having to keep vast savannahs of information in their heads all morning, and then, at eleven A.M., having to recite it all aloud to a roomful of colleagues. Because now there were no colleagues, just as there were no conference calls or lunches with "a client." All of that was over, and when the alarms sounded in the morning and the women were startled awake, they sometimes took a momentary dip into the memory of what they had left behind, and then, with varying degrees of relief or regret, they let the memory go.

COO COO COO COO COOOOOO. In a light-stippled apartment on Third Avenue in New York City, on the eleventh floor of a newish colossus of a rental building fashioned of glazed brown brick, an alarm called out in Amy Lamb's bedroom. She was alone, as she always was when the alarm went off, for Leo had been awakened by his own Timex over an hour earlier, and had staggered like a newborn monster through the violet shadows to the bathroom and the elevator and the gym and then finally to the office. By the time the doves called to Amy, Leo Buckner was already at his desk in midtown, looking into the eye of a video device that sent a slightly convex version of him to the clients sitting around a platter of pastries in an industrial-park conference room in Pittsburgh.

As Leo went about the start of the workday, Amy slowly woke up. Her clock, which he had bought her as a recent birthday present from the Domestic Edge catalogue, and which, depending on the setting, made a noise like one of a variety of animals, today sounded like a flock of mourning doves. Leo and their son Mason were sent into a shared frenzy by gadgetry. The apartment, because of this, contained objects that blinked and hummed and made animal noises and sometimes actually spoke sentences in flattened android voices, remarking, *Your-keys-are-o-ver-here*, so clearly indifferent to where your keys actually were. But husband and son were content with the impersonal nature of electronics; they didn't need these objects to love and embrace them, because Amy did, and that was enough.

"Mason!" she cried in a dry, fruitless morning voice. "Time to get up!" There was no response. It would have made much more sense if she'd simply gone into his room right away and hung over his bed like a jackal in a tree, the way some mothers did. "MASON!" she cried again, rasping but loud. Still nothing, and so Amy gave it a rest, standing in the middle of her pale bedroom and moving her head from side to side, listening to the internal neck pops and explosions. At age forty her physical self seemed to make much more noise and require so much more attention than it used to. She stretched her arms over her head, her body nicely thin but slightly battered by middle age, tight-nippled inside one of Leo's oversized undershirts, which she wore to bed each night out of habit, because long ago he had said it was an erotic sight. For some reason, men often liked women in some sort of nominal drag, though Amy couldn't remember the last time Leo had been all that excited by her. Maybe she should have had gadgets affixed to her body, she thought. Instead, married for thirteen years and in the middle of their life together, they often lay in bed at night like two tired prehistoric animals that had individually been out in the world for many hours, fighting for survival.

"What a stupid day," Leo had said last night in the dark, and his hand halfheartedly, almost accidentally, bumped against her breast and stayed there. "Stutzman wanted to know when we're going to be ready to go to court. I told him I can only do so much. That I'm not Vishnu. So he said, 'Who's that, a new associate?'"

"Oh God," she said. "I remember that kind of thing."

"It's worse now. You always have to stop and explain what you mean. And you have to appease everyone. It's an onslaught. Corinna and I basically just roll our eyes."

Corinna Berry was his closest friend at the office. Once, long ago, Amy had been Leo's primary work confidante, the one he had rolled his eyes with, but she had lost that tender role. "I'm sorry," she told him.

"Everyone else manages," said Leo. "It's like they're being thrown some bone that no one's throwing me." He added, dolefully, "I keep waiting for the bone."

Whenever Leo expressed unhappiness about his job, Amy tried to find something to say that might be a comfort, even an anecdote about herself that could create a marital symmetry between them. "My day was bad too," she'd said. "The pediatrician's waiting room. Like typhoid central! And we sat there for a full hour."

It was as though they performed small reenactments for each other in bed, depicting the different ways the day had been spent. When he described and acted out scenes from his life at Kenley Shuber, the law firm where she had once worked too and where they had first met, she easily pictured the toast-colored corridors, the conference room with its oak table and recessed lights. But as she began to tell him about her own day, he made polite, generic sounds of sympathy in his throat. She knew he could barely picture Dr. Andrea Wishstein's waiting room with its streppy, fractious children on the floor pushing wooden beads along wire, and its pastels of clowns on unicycles lining the walls, and that he wouldn't really want to picture it even if he could.

The paradox was that Leo adored her but wasn't always interested in how she spent her time. Jill Hamlin, Amy's closest friend since college, who had moved from the city last spring to the suburb of Holly Hills, had recently told her about a woman she'd met there whose husband had admitted that he swallowed their hyperactive son's Ritalin every evening on the commuter train going home so he could actually *pay attention* at night when his wife told him about her day. "He couldn't bear to listen to her without it," Jill had told Amy. "He said he loved her so much, but that whenever she started to speak, he would automatically think about other things. He was so ashamed."

"Are men's stories inherently more interesting?"

"Yes."

"Yes? You're serious?"

"During my two-second career in film," said Jill, "or at least right at the end, they kept emphasizing the idea of *the four quadrants,* like it was an Aristotelian concept. The four quadrants are: older male, younger male, older female, younger female. The fact is that both older and younger men *and* older and younger women—all four quadrants—will go see movies about men, but that only *two* quadrants—women, young and old, will go see movies about women. So right away there's a huge discrepancy. But it's the way it is."

Amy saw herself on a screen, in afternoon light, walking down a city street to the dry cleaner, then sitting on a small chair at her son's school, attending a meeting about the evacuation policies in case of terrorism. There was very little dramatic tension to these scenes; out in the audience, the men would start to rustle, and one by one they would leave the theater.

Mason, in bed, didn't stir yet; the apartment remained still. Amy always left a few minutes' leeway in their morning schedule, so now she picked up her laptop and sat with it on the edge of her bed in the dim morning room, checking e-mail. There were a couple of messages from friends in the city and elsewhere, and one from her son's school with the subject line REMINDER: SAFETY PATROL TODAY, but the only message she opened now was from her mother.

Up in the house in Montreal, Antonia Lamb wrote her daughter free-form e-mails roughly once a week. She was an historical novelist who only recently had made the change from typewriter to computer, and e-mail was still a novelty to her, the way once, decades past, answering machines had been a novelty too, and Antonia had recorded her own voice solemnly reciting the last stanza of Sylvia Plath's poem "Lady Lazarus" as her outgoing message: "'. . . Out of the ash / I rise with my red hair / And I eat men like air.' Please leave a brief message, and remember to wait for the recorded beep tone. Thank you."

Today, even the subject line of her e-mail was provocative and, to a daughter, irritating:

A THOUGHT ABOUT WHAT YOU COULD DO NEXT

Amy opened it, and found:

> A,
> It occurred to me: what about a public defender? Let's discuss. Am making my plans for NAFITAS (my women's conference in NYC) this winter. Cannot wait to come stay on your air mattress and spend time with you and L and, esp., sweet Mason.
> xoxo
> Mom

To her mother's thinking, Amy had apparently once confessed to her: *I am lost in the woods in the middle of my life. You were once lost too, so tell me what to do.* Antonia Lamb remained preoccupied with the fact that her middle daughter no longer had a profession and that perhaps she already was the totality of what she would ever become. Amy's sisters had stayed on in Canada: Jennifer was a gerontological social worker, and Naomi worked for the slow-food movement, promoting agricultural biodiversity. Naomi, in particular, spoke a great deal about her work; she was a bit of a grind, always very literal, but if you were the slow-food movement of Canada you would want her as an advocate, because she would put in long and thoughtful hours among the herring spawn and the red fife wheat, and she would never leave, except briefly to have children, but then, once they were in day care, she'd be back for good.

"You girls will be able to do just about anything you want," Antonia had told her three daughters when they were young, taking a tug on her first cigarette of the day. Feminism had recently landed in Canada; apparently the longing and ability to write historical fiction had always been inside Antonia, but it had taken a political upheaval to disgorge it. Once it was brought out, life in the house changed. Antonia warned that she was no longer going to be able to spend all afternoon with the girls when school let out for the day. She had a job now, she said, and it was no different from anyone else's job. She created an office in what had once been a guest room, and she made sure the girls were set up with their homework or a game or a book, and then she told them, "This is *my* time," and went inside and shut the door.

At first, it was a shock to have their mother so close and yet unavailable. They were stung by her absence, as though it was a personal affront. Together, Amy, Naomi, and Jennifer learned to make no-bake fig bars and toasted cheese sandwiches and to vacuum. They fought, shrieking at one another as they slammed through the house, motherless. They felt so sorry for themselves, and over time they pretended to be blind and wandered the rooms, nearly knocking into furniture, and they sat and sang the saddest songs they knew—including the one about the ghost of the girl who sold cockles and mussels alive alive-o—and they acted out the orphanage scenes from *Jane Eyre*. They were no longer allowed to disturb their mother during the day, Antonia had gently made clear, unless it was a "life or death" emergency. Somehow, they got through the months and the years of this routine, only occasionally interrupting her when something big came up, although each time it happened they were hesitant to knock on her door, because they knew she would be annoyed, at first, to be torn from her moment of concentration.

Amy got her period for the first time late one afternoon when her mother was working. Did that count as "life or death"? She and Naomi and Jennifer had stood out in the hallway in the slant of sunlight through the high single window, debating this point in whispers.

"You could bleed to death," Naomi, one year older than Amy, had said philosophically. "You could exsanguinate. It's happened before. Though it's not really likely. Is your flow heavy?"

But Amy didn't really know what "flow" meant; she was not yet versed in the language of womanhood and didn't want to be. Who would? And she also didn't want her sisters here, assisting her; it felt a little too orphanlike. She imagined Jane Eyre finding blood in her underpants one morning at Lowood School and having to be helped out by tragic little Helen Burns. The girls would have had to crack the ice in the basin in order to get some water for Jane to wash herself. Now the three sisters stood with their fists paused over the surface of their mother's door. Finally, hesitantly, they knocked. There was no answer, so they knocked again, and the knocking soon became a fusillade.

"Who is it?" Antonia asked.

"It's us."

"Yes?"

"We need to talk to you."

Antonia pulled open the door. She had a pencil between her teeth, caught there as though it were a rose and she were dancing the tango. It seemed, in that first, stark moment, as if they had interrupted something sexual in nature. Their mother whisked away the pencil and said, "What is it, girls? You know I'm working. It's the middle of my workday."

"Amy got the curse," Naomi said without preamble.

"What?"

"My period," Amy muttered, looking down at the floor in a kind of obscure shame.

"Her period," Jennifer echoed, pointlessly.

"*Oh.* Well, did you go get the sanitary pads from my bathroom? They're under the counter."

"No," said Amy, and though she was twelve years old, she began to cry. She stood outside the open door of her mother's office with the view of the desk and the typewriter and the empty pink cans of Tab, and the tears dropped. She knew, somehow, that she only wanted her mother to go show her the secret place where the napkins were kept—the kind that women wore back then, as thick as submarine sandwiches—and to sit down with her and say a few corny phrases about maturity that Amy and her sisters could mock later on. She wanted it all, the way it used to be, before all the hypnotized mothers had started disappearing into guest rooms or real-estate offices or travel agencies, telling their children, "This is *my* time."

A sound now caught in Antonia's throat. Her face grew pink, and she softened. "Honey," she said. "Oh, honey. You're upset."

"No I'm not," Amy said, now weeping.

Her mother swiftly pulled her against her. "Look, I didn't realize. I was lost in thought. This is a very, very big deal. I'm glad you interrupted me."

"You are?"

"Absolutely," said her mother. "Congratulations. I should have said that right away."

The three girls and their mother spent the rest of the day going to Loblaw's to buy the big pads as well as the junior tampons that were as thin as swizzle sticks, and then Antonia had simply closed shop for the afternoon and sat around with them making kettle corn and ironing their hair. The following morning, she returned to her study, and the door was shut.

As they grew older, the early experience of having once had a mother who was available all the time—an iconic figure like the Statue of Liberty, raising a glass of milk and serenely handing it over—lost its clarity. Had Antonia ever truly belonged to them? Yes, yes, she had, and the ownership had been extraordinary, though they had taken it for granted. They'd had her during the day, and their father had had her at night; it had been a system that seemed to work well. But now she belonged to everyone: to her "muse," as she said with irony, and to her publisher, and to her earnest friends in her consciousness-raising group. Her daughters never really got her back exclusively. And anyway, as Naomi pointed out, they were more independent themselves now too. The older two had become focused on the habits and particularities of boys, and all three of them could prepare their own snacks and could help check over one another's homework. Still, the pain of the loss had been as real as anything—as startling as blood in the underpants—and then, after a while, it began to fade. It was just like waking up from a dream in tears: You weren't sure what you'd been so upset about, but you were just relieved that it was over.

Now, at age sixty-nine, Antonia Lamb was still prolific, although her mostly female readership had diminished over the past few years, perhaps finally exhausted by her big, historical, unapologetically feminist novels, which over time kept coming and coming, as if somewhere a bookshelf was toppling, its contents relentlessly falling upon everyone's heads. She had won all the significant Canadian literary prizes; her work "spoke to the frustrations and yearnings of women everywhere," according to the judge of an awards committee back in the mid-1970s, describing Antonia's first novel, *Turning Around and Going Home,* from the podium at a book festival in Toronto.

Antonia Lamb had walked onstage that night in a gunmetal-gray crushed-velvet gown, and spoke in her slow, intelligent voice. She'd said, "I'm going to talk tonight about gender, power, and the insidiousness of self-censorship. You might think these subjects have nothing to do with you, but you would be wrong." The women in the seats had listened well, their faces uptilted in devotion. She was a minor heroine to them during a time when feminism seemed like an electrical current that would convulse the world in perpetuity. But in the end, the audience had shuffled out of the dim glow of the auditorium and returned to their lives, some of which would be adequate, some awful, and who knew what had happened to most of them over time.

And here was Antonia Lamb's middle daughter all these years later on a Monday morning in fall, a woman of forty, who, unlike her mother, had never been deeply in love with her work. Becoming a lawyer had made sense to Amy for a long time; she'd been on the debate team in high school and had thrown herself into the excitement and tension of the meets and the internecine drama of the club itself. She'd had a long flirtation with the team captain, a confident goofball from down the street named Alan Bredloe, who had memorized all the lines to *Inherit the Wind*. They mock-debated each other on subjects such as euthanasia and pesticides and the sovereignty of Quebec; they once even debated the topic "Is there a quantifiable thing called 'love'?" ending up in the slippage of a long kiss and with hands moving around under each other's clothes on the Bredloe family couch.

Amy liked the beauty of debate, the way you could bark at another person until you wore them down, which meant you had *won*. "Your reasoning is so faulty it's pathetic, Bredloe," she said to Alan, and he said, "You think so, Lamb? You really think so?" "Yes, as it happens I do," she said. "And in the next two minutes I shall prove it." They were fifteen years old, and they sparred with each other in the way that high school debaters did, but they both felt as though they were also in training for a greater sparring that would take place when they were much older. Whenever Amy debated, her face grew hot, and she felt charged with the same preening vigor that people felt when they exercised or, supposedly, had sex.

Years later, after high school and then college, Amy was among the bloc of English majors in her class who gamely applied to law school. They knew, these English majors, that literature was an open field and law school was an enclosed pasture, but they were practical too. No one would take care of you forever; the world would not love and protect you. You had to know how to *do* something well. This was different from a passion for your work, and while it was always best to have one of those, no one could give it to you or tell you how to acquire it.

Off in law school, the jousting spirit from those long-ago teen-aged debates was mostly absent, and so was the quiet, self-conscious serenity of sitting in a chair reading the great novels. Instead, you had to be passive and accept the idea of the largeness of the law and the smallness of the self. You had to learn how to think like a lawyer. Some people were giddy to do this. A few of the women in Amy's law school class had always wanted to be lawyers; they had felt it when they were six years old and went around making extemporaneous arguments, in response to which their mothers had looked at them with surprise and pride and called them Clarencina Darrow. Maybe the mothers had been lawyers themselves, a pioneer variety that worked in labor law and always seemed aggrieved, because "the system," that Escher drawing of steps and turrets and impossible angles, was rarely manageable. Amy knew a couple of law students who were obviously brilliant, and who loved the intellectual rewards of some legal texts. Their excitement and their brilliance astonished her. She had also met a woman in law school named Maura who was absorbed by the concept of justice. When she was young her father had been given a forty-year sentence for drug trafficking. He was a grizzled con now, unrecognizable. Maura had gone on to clerk for a U.S. Supreme Court justice, and was currently the dean of a midwestern law school. She'd developed her fascination with the law because of the marijuana that her father had stored at home in bales, as though the entire suburban house was a silo.

But without a passion, said one of the other former English majors in Amy's first-year class at Michigan over pizza one night, eventually you were in trouble. The law didn't come with passion already embedded in it, as somehow Amy had thought it would. You needed to develop it and stoke it yourself. Without it, you had to pretend you felt strongly about your profession when really you didn't. But what was an English major supposed to *do* after college, asked another one of those pizza-eating law students: go work for Beowulf? Yes, said someone else, Beowulf, Grendel & Schwartz. They all laughed bitterly, and then they threw around some more literary law-related jokes for a while, trying to protect the fragile sense of superiority that was rapidly abandoning them. "Mr. Kurtz, he dead. He dead from boredom during Contracts class," said Amy. Someone else said, "I had a farm in Africa. I went there after my nervous breakdown during law school."

Oh, they laughed and laughed as their English classes receded like a shoreline, and together they silently grieved the loss. But then law classwork took over fully; snow discharged itself upon the Michigan campus all winter, and the former English majors separated, thinking of themselves only as law students now. They were as exhausted and capable as anyone else, sitting in the law library with wet coats slung over the backs of chairs, their heads bent to read the legal writing that, no matter how hard they studied it, would not sing or attempt metaphor.

Amy worked in trusts and estates for Kenley Shuber—T&E, it was called—an area that women tended to be drawn to more than men, because, she speculated, it had a big personal-relationship aspect to it. In a way it was a relief after three years of law school for Amy to be good at what she'd been trained for, but later, when it was time, she willingly exchanged the law firm for the long and astonishing inhalation of motherhood, which itself, over time, had gradually been exhaled. Her son Mason was ten years old now and in no need of close watching or nursing. She didn't have to be there for him all the time anymore, but she was. And though the mornings could be sluggish and harsh, she still loved the period after the school day ended, when they spent a little time together that wasn't rushed.

"Do you know the story of Achilles and how he was dipped into the River Styx as a baby, except his heel didn't get wet?" Mason might suddenly say as they walked home, and she would say no, please tell me. The chance to hear the story of brave but tragically vulnerable Achilles, as rendered by her son, was hardly a reason not to work, or at least it wasn't meant to be. But the hours between three and six P.M. comprised his clearest, brightest window of time and, by association, hers too.

Increasingly, lately, there were fewer stories about Achilles. There were empty segments of time in the day, and Amy had become highly aware of them. She had only infrequently regretted being at home with Mason when he was little; there had been boring times and maddening times, but there were moments when he wanted only her, and there were also sudden bursts of the extraordinary. There was always so much to *do*: There were lists and plans and schedules that were essential to a well-run household and that were still laughably, almost hysterically, tedious. You, the brainy, restless female, were the one who had to keep your family life rolling forward like a tank. You, of all people, were in charge of *snacks*. Your hands tore apart the cellophane on six-packs of juice boxes, while your head cocked to hold a cordless phone into which you spoke the words "Maureen? Hi, it's Mason Buckner's mom. I'm calling to set up a playdate with Jared."

You had to say "playdate"—that nonword that had been so easily welcomed into the lexicon—and you had to say it without irony. Certainly, you could also focus the thick, keen lens of your intellect on the greater world if you wanted. You could anguish over the war that ground on far away on another continent—and Amy did dwell on it periodically, hopelessly, during the day—but you would have to do this on your own time, between plans. You were the gatekeeper and nerve center and the pulsing, chugging heart of your family, the one whom everyone came to and needed things from. You were the one who had to coax that unconscious child from his bed, day upon day.

She took a breath now, then called, "MASON! I ALREADY TOLD YOU IT'S TIME TO WAKE UP, BUDDY!"

To her surprise, many of the words that she said to her son lately each morning came out in the same slightly irritated voice. "Are you like that too?" Amy had recently asked Jill, who had taken the train into the city. The two of them were sitting in the back booth of the Golden Horn, the place where their group of women had breakfast a couple of times a week and where Amy and Jill often used to sit before Jill defected to Holly Hills.

In the late morning, after the world had settled itself down, the room was steamed and spiced behind its glass front, and the women stayed put for a long time. The owner and the waiters knew their habits and never bothered them or hustled them from the booth. "Do you find yourself shouting at Nadia like some kind of drill sergeant," Amy asked, "even though you hate the sound of yourself, and you don't really know why you're doing it?"

Jill looked up, startled. "Yes, I do. I say to her, 'Nadia, move it.' Or, 'Let's get cracking.' I've been given this entire, terrible vocabulary."

"Me too. What have we *become*?"

"Whenever really young women meet either of us they probably look at our lives and think to themselves that they never, ever want to have kids," said Jill. "We're like a cautionary tale. Why would they possibly want to give up their fun, erotic life of freedom for this bossy, scheduled thing?"

"Ah, fuck them, those hypothetical really young women," said Amy. "They know nothing about anything." They both laughed a little and then were briefly silent as they poked at the eggs on their shining plates.

Out in the world with your child, you were only occasionally complimented or rewarded. Amy remembered how once, years earlier, before Mason was even in preschool, it had rained for days, the city saturated and desolate, all the unworking mothers and young children and nannies forced indoors. She and Mason had been penned into the apartment and the carpeted playroom on the top floor of their building. One morning, desperate, Amy said, "You know what, kiddo? I am taking us to a museum," even though at the time he was the kind of boy who would need to be chased through galleries and clattered after down fire stairs.

But there was a Magritte show there that day, and she loved Magritte. To her surprise Mason had stood and actually stared without moving at *The Son of Man,* the painting of the man with the green apple in front of his face. Fleetingly, insanely, she worried that Mason was autistic. But no, he was just *interested,* so she had started lightly explaining about Surrealism, and Mason had listened closely and asked questions. An old woman who stood nearby came closer

and said to Amy, "Excuse me. I couldn't help but overhear you and
your little boy. He is wonderful, and you are wonderful with him.
What pleasure you must take in each other." Then, the bonus: "You
both look so happy."

It had made Amy's day. No, it had made her life. She had carried these remarks around all these years like an amulet. And now,
this morning, standing in her bedroom and calling to her son across
the length of the apartment, she tried to remember them all over
again, for such moments were rare. She had no office environment
in which everyone saw everything and gave commentary and back-
slaps. Instead, she and Mason were always off on their own, and
except for the stray remarks of strangers or friends or even, once in
a while, the pediatrician, Dr. Andrea Wishstein—"Mason, you were
excellent with that strep test. Lots of kids practically break my wrist
when I try to get a swab"—mostly they had to take pleasure in the
moments that no one else would ever witness.

Amy quietly appreciated her child, not during the precocious
moments, for those seemed prepackaged for anecdote and narcissistic gratification, but during the small, almost unnoticeable ones. She
observed the way he suddenly stopped near a homeless man on the
street and whispered forcefully to Amy, "We have to give him money,
Mom. We *have* to."

So Amy, who had become more and more inured to the tableaus
of poverty and mental illness that appeared on the glittering streets
of the city and who over time had given less to the homeless until
essentially she gave no handouts at all but instead grimly walked on
and just wrote a modest check each year, was uneasily made more
human by her son. He made her give out money, person to person,
and so she gave it. She had no idea whether there was something
awful and knee-jerk reflexive in the act of stopping, giving a small
amount, and then walking on, but she couldn't think it through; with
her son's coaxing, she and Mason just gave out dollar bills to the men
who sat smoking on the grate outside the newsstand by the subway,
and no one saw. Their life together, which had its distinct rhythms
and drama, was generally invisible to everyone else; sometimes she

thought they were like performers in a flea circus between shows, doing their microscopic tricks only for each other.

"MASON!" Amy called now from her bedroom. "ARE YOU UP? YOUR CLOTHES ARE FOLDED OVER YOUR DESK CHAIR! PUT THEM ON!" There was a pause, a serene silence. "ARE YOU PUTTING THEM ON?"

Mason was certainly not dressed yet. He was probably still inert, his skin roasted warm from sleep, the sheets and his torso and his long feet all the same elevated temperature. "MASON, YOU HAD BETTER GET GOING THIS MINUTE!" Amy cried.

While his mother called to him and his father sat in his office and talked to corporate clients in Pittsburgh and gathered up receipts from his travel expenses, Mason slept on in his faraway room. Amy slipped a shirt over her head and pulled on some pants and went to wake him up in person. She walked out of the dark bedroom and down the hallway where the walls, tipped in shadow, held photographs of herself and Leo dazed and pink on their honeymoon. Beside them were pictures of Mason at various ages, and then there was a photo of Amy's parents and one of Leo's parents. Finally there was a photo of brown-haired, sweet-faced, average-looking Amy and tall, blonde, patrician Jill on a spa weekend three years earlier at a place called Wildwood Spur, which had had a last-minute Internet special, and so Leo had said sure, sure, you both should definitely go.

She had been so excited to get away with Jill; it would be like college again, they said. They hadn't known that soon enough Jill would move out of the city and that they would no longer see each other a few times a week. When Jill finally moved, Amy felt the loss in a sickened way that she didn't like to express, because at age forty it was commonly held that as long as you had your family beside you, all would be fine. A family was like a little frontier cabin tossed through the world, caught up in its storms and ravages; but if you all stayed inside together, you would be safe, and contented.

At night at the spa that weekend, in their separate double beds, the two women had lain on their backs and told each other significant details from their lives of long ago that they had somehow neglected to reveal before. Jill told her that once, as a teenager, she had come upon her depressed mother at the kitchen table with her head in her hands, sobbing, and had simply turned and walked out of the room without asking what was wrong or ever referring to it again. Amy said, "You can't blame yourself. It was probably always chemical, but they just didn't have the information back then."

"I know. I just have this image of her. I can't get rid of it; it's always going to be in my brain."

"Maybe it should be," said Amy. "It was who she was. At least, it was part of it."

"You would have really liked my mother," Jill said finally. "I know she was fragile, but she was such a nice person." Then she wiped at her eyes with her fingertips, and said, "Tell me your thing now."

So Amy told her about how she'd once sat in the corner of a party when they were both freshmen at Penn, and a beautiful woman had come over to her, and they'd started talking. Somehow, the woman had ended up sitting on the arm of the chair, and a little while later, she'd leaned down and kissed Amy on the mouth, and Amy had kissed back. The woman was a lesbian who was androgynous and stylish in a man's tuxedo shirt and studs, the sleeves rolled up to reveal long slender wrists, and her hair cut short in back and falling across her eyes in front, making her look a little like James Dean.

"You mean that girl who lived in French House?" Jill asked, astonished. *"Aptly?"*

"Yes."

"Did you like it?"

"Well, yes," Amy said. "It was exciting, actually."

"I can't believe you never told me this."

"I guess I was confused by it then. I didn't know that you could be excited by something you'd never desired before."

"At least not consciously desired."

"I don't think I'm much of a lesbian," said Amy. "But I did like the idea of trying on a life."

"I'd like to do that too," said Jill. "Just try on another life for a few days. Although I guess you could say that that's what we're doing now. And I could get used to it."

But they both knew that this wasn't really true; the siren song of their own lives already quietly urged them back. They had taken their BlackBerries with them up here to this small spa in the Berkshire Mountains of Massachusetts, and both of them had received text and voice messages from husbands and children, asking rudimentary household questions and sending electronic bursts of love and need. The weekend was a relief, but it also began to seem a little long. They had sat at a table in the balsam-paneled dining room, with the mountains visible like a sketch through the windows and the din of other women's voices all around them. Sparse leaves of salad were strewn across plates as though blown there accidentally. A couple of women at a table in the corner were on a juice fast, sitting stoically before a decanter of sea-green fluid.

"There are times," said Jill from her bed that night, "when I feel as though Donald and Nadia are completely helpless. I know it's mostly my fantasy, but I feel as if they can barely survive in my absence. That it's like I'm leaving newborns."

Amy had nodded. In the span of ten years, this was actually the first time that Leo and Mason had ever been alone together for an entire weekend. Whenever they were supposed to go off for a few hours without her, she always dutifully sent them with the things they needed. They had come to understand that whatever they required would just magically appear before them. So when they became thirsty on an outing to the park, they reached into the cooler she had given them and pulled out a bottle of lurid blue or orange sports drink she had placed there. If Mason skidded on the ground and opened a window of skin on a knee, Leo could ferret around in the room-temperature compartment of the cooler and dig out the Band-Aids and the tube of antibiotic ointment that Amy had provided. She would pack provisions for an entire brutal winter if she had to. Always, her husband and her son would find them and use them, and always they would expect to find them.

Now, in the apartment in the morning, the darkness of the hallway ran like a tributary into the living room, becoming a glazed pool of light at this early hour. The apartment was too expensive, but Amy took her cues from Leo, who attended to their finances in the tiny study, the place where her mother would sleep when she came to visit in the winter for her women's conference. Leo often sat at the rudimentary desk that the catalogue called Sven, which housed all the bills and invoices in its pigeonholes. As long as Leo didn't throw his hands up, saying, "We're fucked," then they could keep going on like this. Amy didn't want to know all the specifics about their financial situation, or at least she preferred to clothe herself in a loose understanding of what they could and could not afford. The apartment was "a nightmare," Leo sometimes said, and yet they managed. The spa weekend, however, had been "doable." She often turned to him for such cryptic pronouncements and vague reassurances.

Once she started looking with any depth at their money, she became anxious and quickly backed away from her own curiosity. She knew this was childlike and irresponsible, but it had become a habit. Money was one of the topics that had been quietly worked out over time in their marriage, just the way their sexual life had been too. In the beginning, they had been commendably open with each other, listing all the people they'd ever slept with. "Give me their names, I'll kill them one by one," Leo had told her, and to Amy's surprise this had pleased her. They said what they liked and did not like in bed. Humiliated but brave, he had admitted that he liked his nipples "you know, sucked a little," for starters. "I cannot believe I just used the word 'nipples' and 'sucked' to describe *myself*," he had then said, laughing with a honk of anxiety.

Leo Buckner was a big, blunt, thickset man, a commercial litigator with curling black hair and a slightly flattened, dazed face like a boxer. Right away in the beginning, after they met at the law firm, when they lay together after sex in the wet fluency of love and unalloyed joy, they sometimes wandered into rudimentary conversations about money: how much they each made and how much they hoped to make eventually. Neither came from a family with a great deal of money. Leo's father had run a magazine stand in the lobby of an office building, and his mother had been a housewife. Though this was very different from Amy's own childhood, spent with her sisters and their novelist mother and economics professor father, financially it wasn't really that different at all. There had never been much money in evidence in the Lambs' house, or at least what there had been was buried in plain sight, allowing the family to take annual trips to France, where they stayed in bad hotels and rented a Citroën that Henry Lamb, in a madras shirt, drove tensely along twisting mountain roads. The Lambs had been neither rich nor poor, and their money had quietly moved across their life.

But that was back during a reasonable time. Now, at the start of the twenty-first century, the cost of everything was high and the relative worth of everyone had become public information. Money, unlike in the past, always showed itself in full. Amy Lamb and Leo Buckner lived with their son in this huge, homely rental building with a high turnover rate on the east side of the city. The awning read "The Rivermere," though their avenue was situated near no river. The names of her friends' buildings—the ones whose owners or management companies had had the vanity or energy to name them—mostly made no sense, either. One friend lived in The Cardiff, another in The Chanticleer. The lobby of The Rivermere was a virtual wind tunnel, so that the elevators occasionally had to be pried open, and the apartments were marbled and bright, ringed by big square windows that looked out upon the expanse of the city. The top floor of the building held the playroom where, when Mason was younger, he used to waddle through the carpeted space that, no matter how many air fresheners had been slapped onto the walls, retained an ambient diaper stink. Mothers and nannies sat on the carpeted window ledges, bored, calm, flipping through magazines or children's clothing catalogues from Vermont, or else lightly chatting and trying not to inhale too deeply.

When Amy and Leo had first moved in, the playroom had been a big draw. Of course, back then Amy had imagined in some deluded way that Mason would use that playroom forever. She'd pictured him as an eternal toddler, someone she could sit near and keep an eye on and occasionally take to a museum in the rain to see the Magrittes. She had not really understood that he would get older and tramp off into the world, and that the playroom would eventually go unused by him, taken over instead by a new generation of babies, who waddled and crawled and licked and grabbed and sat stunned in that sunlit, shit-tinged aerie.

New York City was an island unreachable by most people in America, and somehow even the taint of horror and fear that had fallen over it in 2001 had given it a dented, temporary quality that made it seem even more valuable, in the way that fragility always increases the price of a thing of beauty. They had rented their apartment in its bulky, unbeautiful fortress at the height of Leo's flushness as a lawyer. The Rivermere was for young families moving rapidly forward; no one was expected to stay in these overpriced rented apartments for years and years, and yet Amy and Leo weren't able to buy an apartment elsewhere and leave.

There were always alternatives to this kind of draining urban life. If you were determined to stay in the area, you could move to one of the other boroughs, as all the practical or adventurous people did, and you could live there decently. Early on, Amy knew couples who had nosed deep into neighborhoods in Brooklyn. The middle class extended its reach, reconfigured its range of territories. Narrow art galleries and cybercafés grew on patches of street beside check-cashing stores and rundown walk-in dentistry centers. Strollers abounded on craggy sidewalks in the steep shadows of the Brooklyn Bridge. Those neighborhoods were overrun with families now, and if the new residents were incidentally knocking out the low-income dwellers, they couldn't really think too much about it; they would surely become squeamish, and then the whole plan would fall apart. The less game couples Amy knew went to nearby suburbs or to quaint and faraway towns with a single, narrow main street and one not-great restaurant that closed at eight, forcing everyone into their homes for the night, as though desperadoes roamed freely and there were townwide curfews.

You had to love the companionship of your family unambiva-
lently in order to live up there, Amy thought. You had to be willing to
stay put in those dark-wood-trimmed old-house rooms as night fell.
But Amy and Leo would neither go to Brooklyn nor buy a house in
an outlying town. Though it wasn't prudent for them to stay in their
apartment, they stayed anyway.

"We're like the Jews in Berlin before the war," Leo had said, and
Amy told him the analogy was obnoxious, and that his great-aunt
Talia, who had been in Dachau, would have been offended if she'd
heard him. "I only mean that we refuse to see what's happening,"
he added. "We are demented and irrational." But still they did not
leave.

Over the years the steep increases in rent at The Rivermere
were frightening. You had to live for the moment, Amy Lamb understood, treating even real estate as if it had an existential dimension.
The rent battered and shook them; it sucked the money away from
them each month as if it were stored in the wind tunnel of the lobby.
Mason's school tuition drained them too, and Amy still thought
uneasily that he should have gone to public school, like the rest of
the country's children did. They had tried to get him into a public
gifted program. ("It's like winning the lottery, and we won, we won!"
the father of an accepted child had cried, actually jumping up and
down as he spoke.) But Mason had only scored in the ninety-seventh
percentile, not the ninety-eighth, and so he had been knocked out of
the running.

When Amy and Leo went to look at the local public elemen-
tary school, they and a hundred other parents had stood in the low-
ceilinged cafeteria/gymnasium with its exposed pipes and boilers
and flickering lights. There was no money for the arts. Their son
would not paint or throw pots on a wheel or play an instrument. He
would be artless—literally and figuratively. There were no sports to
speak of, either, and the student-teacher ratio was discouraging.

"So, do you think we can do the private-school thing?" she had
hesitantly asked Leo as they walked outside after the tour.

"I don't know." He sounded pinched and sour.

She wished they had liked the school more; it was integrated and democratic. Over the doorways you could read the quaint words that a hundred years ago had been cut into stone: "Girls' Entrance," and "Boys' Entrance," though now girls and boys poured in through either door, watched over by a tough-looking female guard with a nightstick. In theory the school was an enclosed utopia. But this was New York City, where life was impossible and dear and the schools were a splintered mess, except for the ones where the parents banded together and served as substitute teachers and librarians and held one long, perpetual bake sale to rescue a school from a slide into indigence.

"Can we at least figure it out?" Amy asked Leo.

"Now? Right now?"

"No, I don't mean now, obviously. What are you so angry with me about?"

But he ignored her question, and on the corner of First Avenue in a light rain, with his shoulders slumped against the onslaught of the future, Leo pressed the calculator function on his BlackBerry and ran some numbers, then sighed in a dramatic manner and said yes, yes, he thought they could actually do it, at least for a while. "It'll probably be a big mistake," he warned. "And we may have to pull him out later, when it will be much harder."

Leo made a fine income by most American professional standards, and yet as a salaried associate at a small, second-rate firm— not a partner, not a rainmaker—his earnings placed them at the crux of the city's striving and diminishing middle class. The school that Mason eventually attended seemed almost a direct rebuke to the unhappiness of the morning that they had spent in that dark cafeteria. It was beautiful, orderly, all-boy. Close attention was paid by thoughtful teachers. But Amy and Leo were shocked when it came time to pay Mason's tuition twice a year, and when the American Express bill appeared in the mail as thick as a long, torrid novel, its many pages detailing the folly of the previous month. They spent too much at every turn, writing checks and charging meals and purchases, throwing bills and hailstorms of coins at cab drivers and handymen and the tolerant Hispanic waiters at the Golden Horn. *Here,* they seemed to cry, *take it all.* Money was forced away from them in the wind tunnel, but then the wind eventually shifted so it blew the other way, bringing more money with it.

In his own bedroom in the apartment now, Mason slept on obliviously. Over his head, warplanes hung on fishing wire, and on his shelves were stacks of board games that were barely used. By now almost all children had made the transition into games played upon screens, though their parents and grandparents still stubbornly kept buying them the latest editions of Battleship and Stratego, trying to seduce them back toward the last embers of the pre-microchip world.

"Mason, honey," Amy said in the softest voice, as if in penance for all the shouting. "It's time to get up."

She looked into his wide, beautiful face, at the slender nose and deer-brown hair. His eyes batted open and he said, thickly, "Five minutes?"

"No, sweetness, sorry," Amy said. "I already gave them to you."

"Oh." He blinked a few times, then said, "Can you name all the U.S. presidents who were left-handed?"

"What? No, I can't."

"Try."

"I can't try. It's not something you try."

"James Garfield Herbert Hoover Harry Truman Gerald Ford Ronald Reagan George Bush the first one and Bill Clinton," he said in a big release.

"Well. Well. That's very good," she said, and truly she thought it was, though it left her with nothing much to say in response. He sometimes just came at her like this with *facts*; to her they seemed random, but to him they were part of a beautiful system in which an array of presidents sashayed back and forth across his consciousness, grasping pens or quills in their left hands.

He sighed now and lifted himself from the bakery warmth and human smell that churned below his covers. She wanted to pull him back onto the bed and heave him into her lap, though he was ten years old and his legs were long and gangly, and it would have been approaching incest at this point if she had done that. But she longed for him, as well as for the version of herself that had been his mother when he was small. Remember when we saw the Magritte painting of the man with the green apple? Amy wanted to say now, and perhaps he would remember, and inexplicably both of them would begin to cry.

But Mason was finally out of bed, standing and urinating in the tiny slice of a bathroom connected to his bedroom, making a sound as loud as glass being struck with a hammer. He was awake and in no need of cuddling from his mother, and was already thinking about what awaited him at school. Someday, Amy thought with an astonishingly sharp sadness, her little boy—who told her all about the left-handed presidents and about Achilles with his undipped heel, and who until very recently had held her hand while walking along the street, and with whom she experienced fits of closeness that made life seem not just *not pointless* but *pointed*—would likely be sitting in an office behind a sealed window, looking out upon a city or an industrial park. Amy briefly remembered her own view from the window of her office at Kenley Shuber and how sometimes, in the afternoon, she would take a break and stand for a minute with her forehead and the palms of her hands against the glass.

Life in that office, at first, had been crisp and collegial. There was always more work being set before her, and always she could manage it, but eventually a low-grade familiarity set in that Amy tried to ignore, because when you really thought about it, so many elements of life were similar. The tasks at the law firm became at times interchangeable, and even the clients over lunch began to seem as if they could be siblings. The lawyers wore similar gray suits and silky ice-blue ties, or cream-colored tailored blazers. Someone became the "funny" one in the office, and someone else became the "irritable" one, and the firm took on aspects of a small and self-contained village. Amy became one of several female "nice" ones. She didn't mind this role; it meant that everyone came to the door of her office and leaned against the frame and said, "What's up, Amy?"

or "We're all going to Umbrella Sushi tonight," or sat on the edge of her desk, wanting to reap her niceness personally.

Soon, when she and Leo fell in love, the job took on a new quality. She had seen big Leo Buckner in the corridors and at meetings, though the domains of their work rarely overlapped. He'd been there a year longer than she had and was a popular young lawyer, broad-bodied, dark, with an easygoing, sighing quality that appealed to everyone. Women were always flirting with him, practically climbing on him as if he were a genial, napping uncle.

Once Amy and Leo became involved, the other women backed politely away, as if in a formal gavotte. With an office romance, work had a shimmering, exciting aspect, and most days were punctuated by moments when she would see her curly-headed beloved in the corridor, and they would each remember what had happened the night before.

Then, finally, they were married, and there was the pleasure of being newlyweds at the firm. The work itself remained tolerable, even sometimes highly enjoyable. At night, eating take-out food in bed or watching TV together on the spineless futon in their starter apartment, they advised each other on work matters and deconstructed the idiosyncrasies and intentions of their colleagues. When Amy became pregnant, they agreed that she would leave the firm for an allowed twelve weeks and then return. It was raining on the day of her going-away party, and the sky outside the conference room was dark. This room had also been the scene of other going-away parties; one by one over the years, young lawyers were picked off either through opportunity or failure or having been sucked through the widening portal of motherhood.

"I'll definitely be back in twelve weeks," Amy had said in her brief, embarrassed goodbye remarks. "So nobody take my coffee mug."

But twelve weeks proved to be nothing, and when the time was up, it was as though an alarm had suddenly gone off, sending electronic doves cooing, chickens squawking, and horses galloping—the entire rotation of animals in a clamor as if there were a fire in a barn—and yet she could just not get up. She could not leave the apartment, that crazyland of strewn burp rags and unironed miniature outfits and gifts of rattles and soft pillow-books that still lay with the detritus of their wrapping paper all around them. The garbage overflowed, the baby confused day with night, and anyone in her right mind would have wanted to run from that place and return to the sharp corners and fragrant tang of the office climate, with its industrial carpet and stuttering fluorescent lights that forced you awake in the morning like a flask of ammonia passed under the nose.

But a new mother was not in her right mind. Something overcame her, and her entire purpose was to *save that baby*, as though she were a superhero flying with arms outstretched through the metropolitan sky. Even a quick trip to the Korean market for yogurt and juice was interminable, and Amy ran the three short blocks back to The Rivermere. She could not leave Mason yet; she loved him too much for that. But neither could she turn him over to some woman from Jamaica or Guyana or Mount Olympus. She could not turn him over to the kindest, softest woman in the world; even a gigantic, gelatinous, floating human breast would not be good enough. She was the only one who could rescue him; their marrow matched, and everyone else's was imperfect. She was the sole donor, and he drank straight from her tap. The hush of the office and the seduction of all the briefs and the clients and the conferences were worth nothing to her now.

Amy had observed the way lawyers treated other lawyers who had recently returned from maternity leave: They didn't hide their impatience or their occasional distaste. She'd seen a jangled new mother on the phone with a pediatrician right before a meeting, whispering tightly into the receiver, "Last night his fever was 100.1, and before I left for work this morning it was down to 99.9, but our sitter just told me it's back up again and that he's crying a lot. . . ." The other people in the room glanced at their watches, and someone came to the doorway and tried to look casual, smiling in a friendly manner, then mouthed, "Anytime you're ready."

Amy couldn't become like these women yet. A law firm or a

corporation could never give you what your baby did; it didn't need you or love you. It could never flatter you enough. It didn't say *Amy, you are the one.* You were just a tiny cog, and could a cog ever feel gratified? Was a cog ever proud? You were expected to devote your entire self to your job, coming home so late in the evening that you could get only five minutes with your baby, as if he were an over-scheduled CEO. If you were going to miss so much of that tender baby-time, then shouldn't it be for a job that was extraordinary? How, she thought, could you possibly choose a corporate law firm or a company's soullessness, or even choose its bland products or components—its clients or textiles or pharmaceuticals or automobile air bags—over your baby's hopeful, open soul? How could you choose any of this over the place on his head where the bones had not yet fully joined or over his puffed little mouth with the outline as beautiful as calligraphy?

"Please," she said to Leo, "isn't there a way I can put it off? Just until the baby is big?"

"You could go part-time," he said.

"That never works. They call it part-time, but that just means it's nine to six, five days a week, for sixty percent of your salary, instead of having to be available twenty-four hours a day. And very few people with real influence work part-time."

So Leo sat down in the study at the Sven desk they'd put together so poorly that the drawers opened at awkward angles. He stayed in the light of the gooseneck lamp for a long time, and finally he walked back out into the living room, where Amy now sat with Mason fastened onto her nipple, as always. It was midnight. She looked up in anticipation, and Leo, in a Rutgers T-shirt and boxers, unshaven and unwashed, said, "Yeah, all right, for a while longer, if they're okay with extending your leave."

"Really? Oh, great. I just wasn't ready to think about any of that. You are God."

"Yes, that's right. I am God."

So slowly the baby gifts got put away, and several thank you notes actually got written, and there were even some evenings when Amy and Leo watched an entire video and cooked a roast chicken and felt the stirrings of shoots of young, dear, new-family happiness bumping up through soil. She loved the small-animal care that an infant required. Nursing became easier, a perfect example of supply and demand; her economist father would approve. Her baby came to life, became more of a person, and there were times when she could not wait for him to wake up from a nap, because she longed to play with him. Desperation was replaced more frequently by pleasure, and Amy knew that staying home with a baby was her right, and she did not judge it or wonder if it had been a mistake. They didn't discuss exactly when she would return to Kenley Shuber, though once in a while Leo told her that the partners were making noises of unhappiness about her absence or that someone had said, "Too bad Amy L. wasn't here for that whole business with the Genzler estate."

Then it became clear that she would not return at all. Her mother was upset, and even had Amy's sister Naomi call from Edmonton, Alberta, to try to coax Amy into becoming a lawyer for the international slow-food movement. "You know, Jonathan and I have found a good life for ourselves in slow food," Naomi had said, as though reading from a script that Antonia had prepared for her.

When Amy officially left the firm, her position in trusts and estates was immediately filled by a young, unmarried woman who also happened to be a marathon runner. Leo's stories from Kenley Shuber became like folktales, and the landscape in which they took place seemed outdated, as though they were set in Constantinople or Old Bavaria. Amy began to care less about her former life and the work she had done. All her T&E expertise became irrelevant to her. She continued to stay home, and in a kind of postnatal Zeno's paradox, the baby grew bigger and bigger without actually achieving *bigness.*

It had been ten years now since she had stopped working, and for a few of those years she and Leo had had occasional, circular conversations about the possibility of Amy going to another law firm. It would be tough, she knew. Work wasn't like a trolley; you couldn't just jump on and off. Lawyers did their own word processing now, and she would have to learn how. Also, the state bar had a continuing-education requirement that needed to be satisfied every few years. The longer she was away, the more difficult it seemed to go back. She periodically thought about work, imagining a new warren of offices and seeing herself wandering past cubicles and kitchenette or standing motionless before a bank of elevators. Once, early on, Amy had gone for an interview for a job at a huge firm, and at first it seemed to go well, but at one point the head of personnel began to ask her a series of questions that involved material she hadn't thought of for years. She took a long time to answer; she became quiet and increasingly inarticulate, so that he finally asked her, gently, "Everything okay?"

"Yes, fine."

"You seem a little uncomfortable with these questions."

"Oh, no, not at all."

"Great, just checking." He looked at his notes, then said, "I assume you're familiar with Juxtapose BriefScan, right? So I should begin with—"

"Excuse me?"

"Juxtapose BriefScan."

It was worse when he repeated it; the syllables still didn't form into words that made any sense. "I'm afraid I don't know what that is," Amy said. Then, desperately, laughing a little, "It sounds like a tongue twister."

"Oh," he said, surprised. "Does it? I never thought of that. Well, it's the name of the legal software we use now."

"I'm sorry, I'm not familiar with it. I've been sort of removed from everything."

The rest of the interview remained awkward, flat, and she left with her face baked and pink. She couldn't tell Leo about her shame; she didn't want to address it directly, and when she picked up Mason at Jill's apartment, where she'd dropped him off for the interview, she took him home and sat in his bedroom for a very long time, reading a marathon of picture books aloud to him, as if in a children's version of Bloomsday. Mason was warm and heavy in her arms, smelling of watermelon shampoo. Being there in that little circle with him was as gratifying as it would ever get, and fuck anyone who said otherwise. Fuck the law job she no longer had; it wasn't intellectually rich or all that much fun. It wasn't debate team. Fuck T&E. Fuck the office rituals and the arcana of legal language and saying "Good morning" to dozens of people each day and having to do Secret Santa each year. Fuck Juxtapose BriefScan.

Not working, she and her friends sometimes reminded one another, did not mean that you did nothing. There was always some complex skein of projects to do, but lately Amy had been restless and had been thinking of getting a steady volunteer job. Maybe she would work for a literacy program; she thought she'd probably enjoy teaching adults to read. She'd have to ask her friend Roberta Sokolov about this, for Roberta was the one among their circle who was propelled by activism. Roberta lived in a walk-up building with her husband and kids, and her son was on financial aid at the school. Essentially, she was lower on the food chain than Amy, and the two of them joked about their descending status, and how their other friends had far more money than they did. Yet Roberta made time each week to go to meetings about reproductive rights or work a phone bank for progressive causes, and she "did what she could," a phrase that no one could really question, because only you knew how much you were able to do.

It seemed, finally, that they all needed to stay in motion. A few years earlier, during a family visit to Canada, Amy's social-worker sister, Jennifer, had talked about how she sometimes asked a new client, "So, what kinds of plans do you have for yourself?" Often the clients were old or depressed, or both, but sometimes their eyes went from dead to sharp upon being asked that question, and they came out with startling soliloquies having to do with their own desires and sense of mortality. Everyone wanted forward motion; everyone wanted to be part of something that moved.

Today, though, Amy Lamb was only involved in the small and persistent tasks that awaited her. *Buy asparagus,* she remembered, picturing the erotized shoots bundled together in red rubber bands, embedded in crushed ice at the gourmet market Camarata & Bello, where she would soon be heading. *Get Pap smear.* And, as the subject-heading of the e-mail from the school had just reminded her, *Show up for safety walk.*

Safety walk at the Auburn Day School was a task that Amy did once a year, but today the idea of it made her surprisingly anxious. Her safety partner was to be Penny Ramsey, a woman whom Amy and her friends in the grade had been half glum about since all their sons were in the pre-K program at the school. The mothers had rarely spoken to Penny Ramsey, except in the most basic ways at parent get-togethers. But what Amy had gathered about this mother was enough to depress her a little. She was so accomplished and serene. Every part of Penny Ramsey's life managed to function in coopera-tion with every other part. She was tiny, golden-headed, pretty, intel-lectually rigorous; wife to an aggressive young hedge-fund manager and mother to an extroverted, confident son and two sylphlike teen-aged daughters.

Most impressively, Penny Ramsey worked in a full-time, real and powerful way, not in one of those vague "consulting" jobs some women held, where the hours were flexible to the point of non-existence. There were a few other intellectual mothers in the grade who worked in interesting fields, but you could usually see evidence of the strain of their complicated lives and feel the breath of time upon them. They had folders clutched in one hand and a child's sci-ence project involving a potato and a battery in the other; they rarely lingered; and they never sat in a booth at the Golden Horn before going off to work.

The entire world, of course, was studded with competent, bright women who held difficult and responsible jobs: physicians, human rights advocates, presidents of universities. They were referred to casually in the news every day, and Amy sometimes wished that there were an asterisk beside their names and that at the bottom of the page you could read the backstory: how this woman had come to make this all happen. Whether she had been struck by a thunderbolt of purpose. Where motherhood had appeared in the sequence, if it

had appeared at all. Where ambivalence lay. Whether her husband—
if he existed—was uncommonly wifely, staying on top of the small
and domestic and social and emotional and aesthetic details of the
life they shared, so that the powerful, Hydra-headed wife would not
have to manage them alone.

One of the mothers in the grade, Isabelle Gordon, was a theoretical physicist with a particular interest in string theory, and she
looked not tormented and overcome but happy. Amy had seen her
recently balancing a tray of sliding, homemade cupcakes for her son
Ty's birthday. It was true that the cupcakes bore smears of oddly
gray frosting that seemed like the outcome of a radical FDA experiment in food coloring, but so what? There was Ty, dancing around
his mother excitedly as she carried the tray into the building. "Cheer
up, Ty," Isabelle had joked with him. "You seem a little down. It's
your *birthday*. Have you totally forgotten?" Isabelle Gordon had a
weird, thick braid down her back but also a surprising propensity
toward good and stylish Italian shoes. She wasn't any one thing. She
couldn't be turned into a cliché about the absentminded scientist or
the nerd-mother. She was nice and an original; she knew the other
mothers' names, and she had agreed to come into Mr. Bregman's science class this year to talk to the boys about string theory.

Amy and her friends were impressed as well as puzzled by Isabelle Gordon. They had no idea of how she managed her life, and
they could not apply her techniques to themselves. All of them had
started off with similarly good educations and linear desires. Their
minds were fast, but Isabelle Gordon's mind roared through the
heavens. No one had any idea of who she really was. They knew that
she loved her son and that she loved string theory. The two sides of
her life did not have to do battle like fiery forces. She lay in bed with
multiple dimensions heaving before her, and maybe her son floated
past in one of them, contentedly eating a cupcake with frosting the
color of newsprint.

But Penny Ramsey, Amy's safety partner, was in a different category. Even with her petite feminine style and overlay of maternal
patina, she possessed power in the hard-shelled, armed male world.

She had never relinquished this for a single second but had held tight over the years. She was interesting but not odd; she was an advertisement for work and motherhood and glamour and a refusal to compromise. All of which made Amy think, this morning, how much she didn't look forward to the afternoon's safety walk, when she would have to spend two hours patrolling the streets with her.

"Honey, you'd better get cracking," Amy told her son, who lingered, drowsing and swaying, in the bathroom. So Mason came in and began to dress, and she left the room to give him privacy, meeting him in the kitchen moments later, where he sat on a chair in a heap.

"Did you hand in that form I signed about the recycling plant?" she asked.

"Why do we have to go to a recycling plant?"

"It should be interesting."

"You don't really think that."

"No," she conceded. "I guess not." They sat quietly for a moment. "Anything happening at school today?" she asked.

"No."

"Nothing?"

"No."

He was an intelligent and focused and sometimes thoughtful boy, but he rarely told her much that went on at school, unless it was something that had particularly upset or excited him. For all she knew, the boys wore Mardi Gras masks and fornicated with the teachers. But while nothing momentous usually happened to Amy during the course of a day, she could have spoken a monologue about all the quotidian details that filled her hours, if anyone wanted her to.

"Mason, do you ever wonder about what *I* do when you're in school?" she suddenly asked him as he bent over his waffle.

He looked at her, confused. "Is this a trick?"

"No. No trick."

He shrugged. "I don't know. Stuff, I guess. Different things."

He looked decidedly uninterested in the question, and she knew, from his answer, that she was a mystery to her child and perhaps to her husband—an unmysterious mystery—as perhaps many women were, everywhere.

B IP. BOOP. BEEP, went the alarms around the city and in the disparate suburbs and towns across the breadth of the entire country. COO COO COO COOOOO. AND LET'S CHECK ON THE WEATHER— They continued to rouse the sleeping women into a sometimes stinging memory of who they were and what, in the middle of their lives, they'd become.

"You've got your Vocab Ventures workbook, bud?" Amy asked Mason now as they walked toward the door of the apartment. More than once each week they turned back at this juncture, searching for some forgotten item of his. Amy was aggravated by Mason's forgetfulness, but he was a boy, and some of her friends said that their sons were exactly like this.

"Thank God we're here," Karen Yip, the mother of twin sons, had said recently when they were all discussing the inefficiency of boys over breakfast at the Golden Horn. "If we weren't, they'd be found dead in an alley."

"Yes, without their homework," another mother had added.

Today Mason had the Vocab Ventures workbook but had left his clarinet behind. He went and searched, and came up empty-handed. "Can't find it," he said. "So Mr. Livio will mark me unprepared. It's not a big deal, Mom."

"What kind of an attitude is that? Find it, please. Now." Her own words struck her as hateful. She was irritable lately, as though it were his fault that she felt a little aimless. "Go on, honey," she added.

Mason poked around, then suddenly he remembered something, and he dug into his backpack and retrieved the electronic object-finder that had been programmed for moments such as this one. He punched in a few numbers, and then they waited. A small voice began to speak elsewhere in the apartment, and Mason and Amy followed the muffled sound until they were standing in the doorway of his bedroom, where an android voice was repeatedly intoning

Your-cla-ri-net-is-o-ver-here from the dark cavern beneath the bed. Technology had rescued him yet again, as it always would.

While her son gathered his things together, Amy walked to the window and hauled up the shade, so that the dim morning light became yellow, white, optimistic, spreading. She and Mason headed into the hall and rang for the elevator. When it arrived, the doors opened to reveal two women dressed for work, both in suits. "Morning," one said.

"Morning," said Amy.

They smelled of shampoo and a light creeping of scent, and they both seemed highly alert. Stepping into the elevator with Mason, Amy felt as though she must seem to them like a rumpled bed, or a sweet old farm animal. She endured the ride with her eyes closed. Down in the large lobby there was a small crowd standing around the doorman's counter. On duty was Hector, a slender young man whose peaked hat was too big for his head, giving him the appearance of a child playing policeman. Today he was almost febrilely excited as he spoke to the various female residents who stood by him. The working women from the elevator glanced over only briefly but kept walking.

". . . and by the time the paramedics got here he had already passed," Hector was saying.

"It's so shocking," said a young mother whom Amy had frequently seen in the elevator, her young daughters twining around her legs. "He was what, late thirties?"

"Thirty-eight. Worked in equities," said a mother from the ninth floor.

Amy was drawn to the counter too, wanting to feed herself with the awful information she already understood. A young husband on the fourteenth floor in the H line had died of a heart attack in the night. Amy heard in detail about the paramedics and the gurney, the oxygen mask, the repeated, violent attempts at CPR, the wife and children who in the end could do nothing for the dying man except cry "Daddy, Daddy, take my good-luck owl-pellet key chain!" the five-year-old son had shouted, hysterical.

But it seemed that there was a postscript to the story. One of the women was saying something about the new widow in 14H and how she wouldn't be able to afford to stay in the apartment now. "She hasn't held a job in years," the woman said. "There's no way she could carry this rent herself. I predict that pretty soon they'll have to move out."

"Poor thing," said one of the other women. "And those little kids too."

"I was right there when it happened," said Hector, wiping his eyes with the back of his hand. "I saw it all. *His lips,*" he whispered, as if revealing inside information, *"were the color of blueberries."*

Amy had only an indistinct idea of the identity of the dead young husband in 14H. She thought she could envision a round late-thirties face with thin, fair hair, and a slight slope of paunch beneath a white banker's shirt, but families came and went in this building, revolving through the door. Here, in this monolith, you usually got to see other tenants' apartments only on Halloween, when you stood hovering behind your child, peering with prurient interest through an open door into dim rooms with unfamiliar smells and the dancing light of a too-big plasma-screen TV, trying to formulate a sense of how other people lived.

Now the husband in his white shirt and loosened tie, who had maybe stood in his doorway last Halloween and held out a ceramic bowl, letting Yoda-masked Mason grab Kit Kats in both fists, was dead. His wife and two young children would have to move soon, and their life would change its shape and shade as if it were another ephemeral image on a plasma screen. The apartment would be repainted and given a new dishwasher and a new obsidian slab for a kitchen counter, then rented to some other young family who thought they could probably afford it, and whose life would begin here, and continue here at least for a while.

"We'll be late," Mason said now, lightly pulling Amy from the brace of doomy women around the doorman's station, where she was poised, her eyes suddenly sprung with tears. She thought of that husband, whom she didn't know, and then she thought, self-indulgently, of Leo and herself, and she imagined everything ruined, lost.

"Sorry," Amy said. "I'm coming."

Mason looked at her with curiosity. "Mom. Are you okay?"

"I'm fine."

"So what happened?" he asked as they pushed through the revolving door.

"Oh, someone died, honey."

They stood on the sidewalk and Mason grew serious. "Did you know that someone always dies? Every second? *There.* Somewhere in the world, someone else just died."

"Yes, but this was right here," said Amy. "Last night, a man died on the fourteenth floor. It's very sad."

"What was wrong with him?"

Amy paused. "He was old," she finally said.

Outside now, the morning was startling in its clarity and temperament, a relief from the lobby, with its news of sudden death in the night. A handyman hosed down the sidewalk, the water running into the gutter and into the patches of earth by the curb with their rawboned urban trees. The air around the entrance of The Rivermere had a root-cellar funk about it. Every perfect fall day always forced you to think of that other perfect day when the city had been struck. But today Amy also thought about how this was a time in life when she was meant to be content. Her body remained slender, and her day was not yet spoken for. She had a close little family and a best friend whom she loved. The war in Iraq kept on going while really going nowhere, infusing everyone with helplessness, and there was still the real possibility of an act of terrorism, but people always said you couldn't stay cowering inside your apartment. Instead, they insisted, you had to "live your life," because it was all that any of us could do.

The other women streamed through the revolving door. In various parts of the city and in surrounding towns off the highways came the rest of them. Soon they would be depositing their children at the mouths of schools and kissing their heads and watching them disappear inside, and then the women would be free. They could have all the covered malls and plazas and fields of the suburbs, and all the buildings and shops and museums of the city if they wanted, and all the open air as well. The day waited for them with its bounty and its freedom, which their husbands almost never had anymore and swore they didn't even want. How it had ended up like this, no one really knew. This wasn't supposed to have happened.

But on a day as beautiful as this one, the sensations of despair and regret were mostly obscured by pleasure. All around the country, the women opened their front doors and stepped outside to take what was theirs.

S OMEONE BETTER CLOSE the shades," one of the women said
with a big, loony laugh, and then everyone else laughed too,
their voices rowdier than usual, because they had been drinking gin
and tonics for the better part of an hour, and there were no children
underfoot or husbands looming in doorways, casting long shadows
as they asked when dinner was or where we keep the scissors. Even
Henry Lamb had been banished for the evening, and he was one
of the best ones, a mild and introverted man with wings of fair hair
that floated up in static on either side of his baldish head, and who
had never devoted too much thought to the idea that women had
been given a raw deal in society. He was an academic, and he could
have found blatant bias right there in the small pie of the Economics
Department at McGill, if he had looked.

Right now his wife Antonia had forcibly barricaded him upstairs
in the Lamb house with their three small daughters, as she sometimes

did, and the girls made him play a board game with them called Race to the Province! that had myriad shifting rules that even he, with his Ph.D., could not follow. These three smart little girls certainly could, though. One flight below in the plant-heavy living room, the members of the consciousness-raising group spoke with individually tended flames of intensity about the role of women in the world today. Their voices rose up in columns and flumes and spirals.

A few straggler women rang the doorbell, and Antonia let them in. They stamped their feet on the rough mat, breathed their cold-night curlicue breaths, and then entered the house. They dropped frosted coats on the bench in the front hall, then went in to join the warm, bright, crowded female forest that had formed in the living room. By half past eight, Antonia Lamb tapped on a glass.

"I'd like to suggest," she said when the partly soused women were quiet, "that everybody take a quick slug of what's left of their drinks, because the drinking portion of our evening is about to end, and the enlightenment portion is about to begin."

"Uh oh," put in a woman named Carol Bredloe, who lived down the street. "You know what that means."

There was light snickering, and someone else said, "Abandon all hope, ye who enter here."

Final guzzles were taken of the G&Ts, and the glasses were placed on available surfaces, resting on copies of coffee-table photography books, volumes on economic theory, paperback novels, and the coffee table itself. Antonia looked around in slight dismay, picturing all the overlapping wet rings that would sully the wood and wondering what kind of cleaning fluid she should buy tomorrow at Loblaw's.

Stop, she told herself. Don't think about cleaning fluid now, of all times. Get outside yourself and try to be more than a housewife; this is 1972, for God's sake, and women are changing before everyone's eyes. Think about that change right now. Think about the evolution of women. Think about what is taking place here and in the States and across the ocean in Europe and all over the world. Think about what is going to happen in this very room tonight.

Antonia had invited a woman named Marsha Knowles to come

up from Toronto to give a demonstration to the consciousness-raising group. Every month for the past year, one of the women in the group cooked a casserole in a Pyrex dish, usually something with a lid of scorched cheese and some kind of ground meat underneath, and then baked a fruit crumble and brought out bottles of gin and tonic water and a bowl of ice and several bottles of Zinfandel, and banished her husband and children for the evening, opening her home to the other women. Since they had been assembling, the group had covered a great deal of ground, talking about subjects ranging from "Does It Matter If I Achieve Climax?" to "Nurturing a Political Awareness" to "How to Raise Confident Daughters and Soulful Sons." After the first few shy, tentative meetings, the talk became bolder. Often tears flowed in these living rooms, and once in a while a bolus of anger suddenly shot from someone as if from a blowgun.

"I am just so unhappy," a woman might say with quiet fury, and she would go on to talk about her husband, who simply did not understand why he had a moral imperative to empty the dishwasher once in a while. "Would it kill Martin to do some chores around the house? He thinks it's all meant for me to do. I mean, is there some logical connection between handling silverware and possessing ovaries?" the woman would ask, and the others would dutifully tell her no, there was no logical connection, and that she, and all of them for that matter, had a right to demand change. "When we got married, did I sign up for this?" the woman would continue. "Did it say in the ceremony that I shall be the person in this relationship who empties the dishwasher for all eternity?"

"Um, I don't think there were dishwashers when you and Martin got married," someone else put in, trying to be helpful.

Henry, Antonia knew, was not overtly sexist, like some of the husbands. Still, she had never entirely gotten over a moment that had taken place in 1969, when, at the Economics Department Christmas party, she had walked past his office and come upon him kissing his department secretary. Ginny Foley was a homely, pale little thing, all red hair and anemic milk-skin, in elephant bell bottoms, and it wasn't that Antonia felt threatened by her, but she did feel a tremendous rush of betrayal and a secondary wash of personal inadequacy. How was it that tall and graceful and articulate Antonia was not enough for her husband, who had to seek succor in little Ginny Foley, whose hands smelled of mimeograph sheets and who kept a jar of sour candy always filled on her desk? Economists would wander by and absently plunge a hand into the jar whenever they liked.

In the car going home from the Christmas party that night, Henry had been in good spirits, unaware of Antonia's angry, hurt simmer beside him. "I saw you," she said simply.

"You saw me?"

"With your stupid stupid department secretary."

He put a hand over his eyes, the way a child does, thinking it might render him invisible to everyone else. "Henry, you're *driving*," she reminded him. He told her how sorry he was. He'd been drinking, he said, and Milt Berkman had passed around a joint. The Doors had been playing on the stereo that had been set up in the hall, and everyone at the party had felt festive and had let loose a little, "especially the Keynesians," he added. He told her he had never done anything like that before.

So what could Antonia do? She forgave him, for it had only been a kiss, and a kiss with *Ginny Foley*, and Henry was so hangdog and apologetic.

But although they recovered, the pieces of the marriage resettled; she knew she could never love her sheepish, academic, distracted husband in exactly the same way. By the time feminism appeared in her life two years later, Antonia was ready to receive it. The women's movement would give her an imperative. It would also be her big distraction; it would be her Ginny Foley. The novelty of the meetings, the solidarity, the big-hearted conversations with other women, gradually absorbed and transformed her. Soon she was speaking in ardent ways about real and important matters.

She told her consciousness-raising group that she had always wanted to be an historical novelist and that she had an idea for a book, and they said, "Good for you," and "We know you can do it." The morning after the group met at her house, Antonia Lamb would wake up and start writing the opening of a novel called *Turning Around and Going Home*, about a schoolteacher in nineteenth-century Ontario who begins an erotic relationship with a local farmer. She imagined the farmer as being the temperamental opposite of her husband: visceral instead of intellectual, hard-muscled instead of wiry and academic-thin.

Lately, a few of the women in the group had complained that their sexual lives were disappointing and that their husbands were eager to screw and then happy to dive headfirst into snorey sleep. The men needed to be educated in the various components of female body parts, someone said, and in order to do that, the women needed to be educated too.

Enter Marsha Knowles. Yes, *enter* Marsha Knowles, Antonia Lamb thought in her living room. For on this evening Marsha Knowles, a middle-school guidance counselor in the greater Toronto school district, who had been invited here as a special guest, produced the black leather bag she had brought with her, a bag that had once belonged to her dead father, a doctor who would have been appalled by its current usage. Marsha Knowles was in her thirties, with dark hair shorn close to her head. She was a good-natured woman who seemed embarrassed at nothing, a trait that soon became clear to everyone in the living room.

In the voice of someone starting to make a toast, Marsha Knowles said, "I want to thank all of you womenfolk for being so brave and so curious." She was often on the road, going to houses like this one all over Ontario, speaking to the consciousness-raising groups that had sprung up in the past several years like newly planted little maple saplings. Just a week earlier she'd flown up to Moosonee to talk to a dozen housewives.

Now Antonia Lamb sat forward on her chair and watched as Marsha Knowles, who looked a little bit like a performing seal, inched out of her velour pants and her faded, slightly depressing cotton briefs with elastic that left pale pink teethmarks impressed upon her white skin, then scooted up onto the Lambs' couch, where a sheet had been laid for the occasion. It was one of Amy, Naomi, or

Jennifer's bedsheets, and a tiny pattern of strawberries ringed the edges. Briefly, Antonia wanted to take it back and give her an old picnic blanket or a frayed beach towel. Marsha Knowles took something metallic and glinting from her leather bag, and as the speculum caught the light, Antonia inhaled hard, as though she herself was about to be violated. But the speculum would be used only on and by Marsha Knowles; this had all been planned in advance.

Everyone adopted a studied pose of nonchalance; all these women went for internal checkups every year, paid for in full by the National Health. But away from the small cubicles and nurses, the speculum seemed like a medieval weapon. Without saying a word, Marsha did some quick preparation, lay back on the strawberry-edged sheet, and then, smiling smartly, she waited as the women lined up in order to get a look.

They might as well have been on line at a buffet, so calm and polite and orderly were they. Antonia went first; after all, someone said, it was her house. So she approached the supine figure of Marsha Knowles, who was like a baby awaiting a diaper or a chicken awaiting basting—domestic images both—but, however you described it, certainly it was evident that she was vulnerable, splayed, totally still, a tableau vivant for the new world order. Antonia peered hesitantly in, the reading lamp angled just so, the light thrown across this woman, illuminating this entrance to her body. Antonia Lamb looked in through the parted, vivid space and saw the dark and the light, the walls and the ceilings. She almost thought she saw stalactites and stalagmites; there were no clear channels there, but instead everything in the female anatomy was apparently dense and complicated, just like life itself. No path was ever easy or smooth.

Antonia gamely continued to peer into the gleaming time tunnel. She would be a novelist; she would inspire others like her. Her husband and children would accept this change in her and would embrace it. One of the women in the group would soon realize her own lesbianism. Another woman would die of cancer within a few years. Life was difficult and strange; this was obvious to anyone who really paid attention. But mostly, as Antonia Lamb, age forty, looked into the opening between the sturdy legs of a school guidance counselor from Toronto—a woman she now hoped never to see again—she visualized the future as something vast and gleaming, not blunt and knowable.

Her daughters Naomi, Amy, and Jennifer wouldn't need to be tough and complaining and groundbreaking, as Antonia and her friends now were. For these girls there would be no Popsicle-cold speculums slid with excruciating self-consciousness into oneself in the bright light of someone else's living room, G&Ts and crackers and cheddar-cheese balls rolled with nuts on a nearby sideboard and the snow whirling outside the dark windows.

Instead, all the women's daughters would become a generation of postspeculum feminists. They would grow up to be women who would live with men and children in a kind of harmony previously unseen in the world. Their marriages would be far better than Antonia and Henry's was; there would be no department secretary on the side, with her sad jar of candy. There would be only love and equality. As sinks filled with dishes, a woman might grab a sponge or else a man might; there would be no difference between the sexes, and no one would ever be surprised by men in aprons, women slung with tool belts, or men shouldering babies and women running board meetings. Everyone would work, everyone would have power, everyone would help out at home. The daughters would recognize the enormous changes their mothers had set in motion, the *no* turned irrevocably and historically into *yes*, and they would be grateful. Antonia would start her historical novel in the morning; she would do something new with her life now, expanding its dimensions.

"Well, goodness, what's so fascinating in there? Haven't you seen enough already?" asked one of the other women in a nervous and jocular voice, poking Antonia lightly, for apparently she had been standing in the lamplight transfixed, unable to turn away.

"Sorry," said Antonia Lamb, quickly stepping aside so that the next woman could have a look at all that lay ahead.

Chapter

THREE

S O HERE IT WAS, what lay ahead. When school let out every afternoon, the landscape was a mosaic of women and children. It
didn't matter where you lived—whether you led a vertical life in the
city or a spread-out, horizontal one anywhere else across the broad
surface of the country—at three o'clock, the outdoor world was at its
highest pitch of manlessness. As the double doors of schools swung
wide, the children were released back to you, and just for a second
it felt as though the separation had been extended and arduous,
instead of having been just seven hours long and involving the loose
and easy peregrinations of mothers.

Amy Lamb, waiting for Mason to appear, would have liked nothing more than to grab him hard, roughly hug him, then buy him
some ice cream or roasted nuts on the street and walk home side by
side. Often, when they walked together, he would first speak nearly
in monosyllables, but then the snack would open him up as if it contained truth serum, and he would tell her pieces of information from
his day.

"Mr. Bregman showed us a nebula."

"Was it nebulous?" she asked.

"What?"

"Nothing. A joke."

She felt peaceful on these walks home from school. Back in the apartment, Mason would noodle around with his homework, then he would IM his friends, and finally he would wander into the kitchen, where Amy might be doing something at the counter, and invite her to play cards. Always she accepted, and they sat at the table with the cards making little licking sounds on the surface as they were slapped down, and he might give her more details about the awesomeness of Mr. Bregman, who had told the boys that until recently, mankind in its hubris had thought it knew everything about the universe, but it turned out that what could be seen and understood of the universe made up only four percent. "The rest they call dark matter and dark energy but they don't even know what it is. It's unknown. They only know about *four percent*. It makes you think," Mason had said, turning over his top card.

But today they could not walk home together and could not sit at the table playing cards and talking about school and about the mysterious deep, partly open bag that was the universe. Today, like some women all around the city and the country, Amy would perform safety duty at the school, a responsibility that fell to her once a year; she had unknowingly signed on for it the moment she had given birth. No, she thought, she had signed on for it the moment when the bliss of full-bore unprotected sex had created a tumbleweed of cells that had rolled along, gathering volume and requiring, so many years later, that she shed her vanity and put on a bright orange woven plastic vest, drape a whistle around her neck, and grab hold of a walkie-talkie. Then she and her safety partner would set off into the world.

The bright chaos of the afternoon could be felt everywhere now. Children, giddy at being released for the day, jabbered and howled and did karate moves in the cool air. Amy Lamb, stepping out onto the sidewalk, felt that she might just as well have been wearing a clown nose and big floppy shoes, so touchingly absurd did she feel as she walked the beat. The school asked that two parents from different families show up each day to patrol the local streets. Then they would march side by side, knowing, in their hearts that beat beneath the weave, that ultimately they could not protect their children.

"Dear parent of MASON LAMB-BUCKNER," a letter from the Auburn Day School had read, "you and your safety partner, parent of HOLDEN RAMSEY, should meet in front of the school at 3 PM on MONDAY." The letter always used the word "parent," as opposed to "mother," and once in a while a father did come, and the other mothers tended to fuss over him, as though he needed special treatment for actually leaving the floor of the stock market before the end of the day. Or else the one father in the grade who didn't work might show up. His name was Len Goodling, and he could sometimes be seen standing thoughtfully for a moment during the day in front of the window at Camarata & Bello, looking in at the prepared salads as if they were porn. His wife worked in advertising, and she almost never came to the school; she was as invisible as many of the fathers.

"If we were a decade younger," Roberta Sokolov had said recently, "we'd have husbands who did safety walk."

It was true that their husbands, while mostly decent sweetheart-men who had changed many diapers, were not equal partners in child-raising or homemaking. It wasn't just that they held down full-time jobs; they had given so little thought to this world that they would be stumped. They could not "buy curtain rings," Karen Yip had once said. They could also not, someone else had also insisted, purchase a class present for their child's teacher. If given that task, they would only bring her something inadequate: a Whitman's sampler from a drugstore, with all the different types of chocolate delineated on the inside of the cover of the box. When they were left in charge of a child for the day, they invariably did something wrong. How many times, someone remarked, had you seen a man pushing a stroller, and then you looked down and noticed that the baby was wearing only one sock. "Wait up! Wait up!" a female passerby would call from farther back down the street, running toward the man and child with the teeny rogue sock in hand.

But such characterizations weren't accurate, someone else said. And even if they were, the deficits weren't fatal. It wasn't as if these men would take their children out naked in winter and drop them in the woods. It wasn't as if they would *starve* them. But the husbands they lived with were part past, part future. They were not the future itself. They were not, apparently, the fruits of feminism, offered up to the daughters of its founders as a perfect gift.

Change always required slightly longer than a generation. Amy and her friends took note of the occasional younger men, the ones around age thirty, who stayed home while their wives worked. God, they looked so different from the forty-year-old husbands. Those younger men had more youthful, narrow bodies, or was it just that, by virtue of not working, they had been freed of the monkey-wear that corporations required? The younger husbands wore T-shirts advertising the rock bands and lobster shacks of their youth. They had goatees and stylish geometric spectacles. They held their babies against themselves in fabric slings. Their wives, slightly shaky but calm, eased back to work, knowing that the babies would be at home with someone who loved them as much as they did.

Men and women were still both evolving; the younger men proved it because they could handle all of this, and the younger women proved it because they were comfortable letting the men handle it. Once in a while you would find a forty-year-old husband like Len Goodling, but his appearance at the school in the afternoon was confusing; it threw off theories about how the world worked. You were initially pleased by him, but then after a short while you felt slightly annoyed. He seemed like a loiterer here in the world that the women had formed for themselves.

Today Amy had made arrangements for Mason to go home with Karen Yip's twins, Caleb and Jonno, and so here she was now in the orange vest. Penny Ramsey, who had arrived at the school a few minutes late, appeared beside her, looking flushed. Snapping shut the clasps of her own vest, she said, "Sorry. Back-to-back meetings."

"No problem," Amy replied benignly.

Together, now, the two women walked in synchrony, observing a kind of silence that had less to do with a seriousness of purpose than a low-level social awkwardness. Penny Ramsey, the director of the Museum of Urban Vision, was likely still thinking about her back-to-back meetings, Amy thought. The museum, which occupied a townhouse down in Chelsea, was small and underfunded, and while most of the mothers in the grade agreed it was a very worthy place, whenever they went to a museum it was usually the Met or the Modern or the chalk-white helix of the Guggenheim instead of the small Museum of Urban Vision, with its modest, tender reminders of lost New York.

Sometimes the museum displayed photographs, other times artifacts from the tenements of the Lower East Side or even menus from turn-of-the-century restaurants that featured prices that seemed to have been made up by children. Ninety-five cents for a steak dinner! Twenty cents for a side of parsley potatoes! What world *was* that? Vanished, snuffed out, gone. The boys from Auburn Day had been invited to the museum last spring in order to trudge through the galleries, shepherded by Penny Ramsey herself. During their visit, they had looked at old, preserved photos of poor children playing stickball on the streets of the city, circa 1900. *Dead, all dead,* thought Amy, who had been a class parent that day, as she peered at images of those hungry, scuffed little mortal boys banging their sticks together. The Auburn Day boys, well-fed and clean and forced to gorge on undiluted history, had let their eyes roll up into their heads as they clomped along the groaning floorboards, but the director hadn't seemed to mind their indifference. She was gracious and good-natured and unflagging, both in her own museum and out in the world. Her picture and her husband's appeared on the social-events pages of the newspaper once in a while: Penny Ramsey shining with emollient and sequin, Greg Ramsey thick and bland in tuxedo.

Now, on safety walk, Penny, perfectly formed and small, wore her golden hair upswept and pulled into a vortex in the back; it was as though, Amy thought, all her secrets could be located somewhere deep inside that vortex, including what it was that allowed her to run a museum and be a patient, hands-on mother to three children and a wife to her demanding, entitled husband and yet still show up here nearly on time for safety walk. She was lovely without being a narcissist. She held an important job that she valued and that she hadn't traded in for full-time motherhood or even for a less-challenging, diminished version of itself. She hadn't been entirely swayed either by domesticity or by ambition but had managed to calibrate and temper both desires.

Where most of the mothers in the grade felt they had had to give up so much, Penny Ramsey seemed to have given up nothing. As the story went, she had briefly gone on leave from her job when her children were young, but had always held fast to her place in the world. She was said to be an exceptionally loving mother too, appearing at her children's concerts and soccer games and throwing her arms around them afterward, crying "Yay!" Penny hadn't gradually let go of the museum or, like the other women, the law firm or the film production company or the statistical analysis job or the puppet theater or even, in the case of Laurie Livers, a mother in the grade whom they knew slightly, the major publishing house where she had once been editor in chief.

How did you manage to figure everything out? Amy wanted to ask Penny as they walked along the street. This was the first time over all these years that they had ever been alone together. Now was the chance to say: I think you are some kind of unusual creature; I think you are magic. *Something* was supposed to give, Amy thought. It almost always did.

The fall afternoon was beautiful and chilled like a bottle that had been put in the freezer briefly, then removed. With this day as a surface, they might even have enjoyed safety walk, but Amy was too self-conscious. She cast sidelong looks at Penny, whose face was delicate, indisputably intelligent, and, Amy thought, subtly stoic. In the nineteenth century she would have been a homesteader, standing on her property with her hair in a loose bun and her rifle cocked.

"How are things going for you this year?" Penny asked. "Off to a decent start?"

"Not bad. You?"

"Fine. Work's good. Holden's happy, I guess. I rarely see any of my kids these days."

So that was what gave. Amy uncurled slightly to think that Penny's life was not thoroughly in balance. "I see a lot of mine. Maybe you're better off." This was disingenuous, but it was the kind of thing people said.

"Everyone thinks that boys have an idyllic relationship with their mothers," Penny said.

"I know. It's supposed to be the fathers who tangle with the sons, while the mothers get off easy."

"I think that used to be true for us. When Holden was little, I once wore a faded old nightgown, and he said, 'Ooh, Mommy, I like your ball gown.'" Amy laughed at this. "But lately, he seems tough to me, as if he's trying to be like his father, making deals."

"I know what you mean. Mason does little things—little *man* things. Though I do know it's age-appropriate."

"But it's depressing too, don't you think?" said Penny with sudden intensity. "Losing them to manhood. To being sort of removed."

Perhaps Penny wasn't judging her at all, wasn't trying to calculate how Amy possibly filled her nonworking days. Almost no one came out and directly criticized other women for choosing not to go back to work, but Amy knew how it appeared. She no longer had the excuse of having a young child at home to use as a human shield against all questions about what she "did," which was the first thing anyone ever asked when they met you at a dinner party.

Apparently in Europe, according to an Italian mother at the school, it was rude to ask someone a question like that within seconds of meeting. Instead, dinner parties in Paris or Rome were spent arguing about politics or films or chatting about trivialities, and no one's feelings got hurt by anything that was said, and no one discreetly tried to change any subject that came up. At the end of a long, fragrant, loose-limbed evening, everyone often disappeared separately into the night without ever having learned what the other people at the party "did." There had been no feverish networking, and nobody had tried to hump the leg of someone who had slightly more power. But here in New York City, and all across the spread of anxious, professional America, it was different. Here, you were often defined by how you spent your day.

Amy understood that if she didn't have a job, then at least she was meant to load her life up with elements of meaning. Some women had date books scribbled densely with entries like "Work on triptych" or "Visit the lost boys of the Sudan." She did stuff envelopes sometimes for a reproductive rights organization that Roberta Sokolov had gotten all of them involved in; she shelved books in her son's school library every week, standing in the placid blonde-wood room with its satisfying fish-tank low-hum of near silence; and she went to parent meetings. But somehow, over time, she realized that she had chosen for her life to be loosely filled, not packed in tight with hard stuffing.

She and Penny Ramsey were nothing alike, Amy knew, and yet today, dressed in identical orange safety vests, the uniform equalized them, as if they were prisoners in matching jumpsuits. One of them could have been doing time for shoplifting, the other one for running a child sex ring, but it didn't matter now; the uniform rendered them both anonymous and interchangeable. Together Penny and Amy walked past shop windows and the green canopies of apartment buildings where idling doormen stood, and past trees that were just starting to drop their leaves into gutters and onto the windshields of parked cars.

"I wonder if the boys learn a particular kind of maleness at the school," Penny finally said. "A *Lord of the Flies* kind of thing. I know their aggression is held in check, but I feel like it's still there, like I can almost see it."

Between moments of holding slides and transparencies of vanished New York in her fingers and between her back-to-back meetings, Penny Ramsey apparently obsessed in the same ways that Amy did. The school, both of them agreed now, could feel unrelentingly male and competitive, and also, conversely, somewhat precious. They were both made uncomfortable with the implicit elitism. Memorizing poetry was an integral part of the curriculum, and once, when Amy went in for a parent meeting, she had spied a second-grader walking in the hall alone, a finger moving dreamily between nostril and mouth, muttering to himself, "'In the room the women come and go / Talking of Michelangelo.'"

Before each holiday break the school observed All-School Day, when boys raised glasses of grape juice and recited the Auburn Day Pledge. There was also the upcoming Father-Son Weekend in the late fall, when the men and the boys took those same coach buses upstate to a nature center and stayed in cabins on an overnight. And the school celebrated Hand-in-Hand Day, when the boys were paired with underprivileged ones from neighborhoods to the north. On that day, visiting boys flowed into Auburn Day beneath the cerulean flag. They played the home team in an exhibition of basketball and wrestling, and received a baked-ziti meal. At the end of the afternoon they were each given an electric pencil sharpener and a pack of fresh, blunt pencils, and then all the boys in the building, black, white, Hispanic, poured back out into the world unchanged, and the world itself remained unchanged, and Amy always felt a brief unease and sadness that was carried off on the swell of noise.

"Do you think," Amy asked Penny, "we've gotten everything all wrong? The school. The life here. All the things we need to keep it going."

Penny looked at her. "Are you my long-lost twin?" she asked. "Sometimes I think about moving far away from the city. But then I remember my job, and that's the thing at the center of it all for me. I love it. I am never bored there. But right, this whole *life*... I know I agreed to it, and I know the school is amazing in a lot of ways. My daughters' school is too. But it's a big effort to keep all the plates spinning. I try to talk to Greg about the way we live, but oh, that's pointless."

They were quiet for a moment. "I obsess a lot about all of this too," Amy said, "and it becomes an exercise in self-flagellation." Then she added, "In case you were wondering, that's what I do with myself all day."

"Excuse me?"

"Self-flagellation." When Penny just looked at her, still not understanding, Amy mumbled, "Just a joke. About what women like me do all day. You know, the ones who don't work."

"Ah."

Conclusively now, she knew that Penny Ramsey didn't wonder about what women like Amy did all day without a job to go to. Maybe the idea of the supposed tension between working and nonworking mothers had been put out in the world just to cause divisiveness. Happiness didn't seem to be determined primarily by whether or not you worked; one of the most ebullient mothers in the grade, Ronnie Prager, hadn't held a job since she'd left Wall Street years earlier. Ronnie liked to say she had been around for every milestone in her children's lives instead of having to get a call at work from a baby-sitter at the same moment that Tokyo was on the other line: "Mrs. Prager, Anderson has something he would like to tell you." "Hello, Mommy, it's me, Anderson. I sat on the toilet with the musical seat, and I did my business *into* it." Either Tokyo or Anderson would have had to give, Ronnie said. They would have had to vie for her attention in that crucial moment. "Hanging up on one of them wouldn't have been fatal," she had admitted. But what made it easy to choose was the fact that she hadn't loved her job enough to miss it hugely after she gave it up. "I made money for rich people," she'd explained to the women. "I knew they would do just fine without me."

Another mother, Hannah Lowry, was high up at an advertising agency and said she would never quit, no matter what. The salary was essential, she said, and she was stimulated by the work and the tension and the wild pace of the agency; she liked the fact that you had to fight for accounts, proving yourself over and over, as if you had never proved yourself before. "I thrive in that whole environment," she had said. "The competitiveness makes me feel great. Makes me feel young. I knock myself out running around, staying in that room with my creative team until someone figures out exactly what was missing from a campaign, and everyone just *gets* it, and we all scream in relief. I just love it."

There were occasional slightly odd moments between the working and the nonworking women, inevitably; Amy recalled that a year earlier, as class mother, she'd e-mailed the other mothers in the class, asking them if they would please bring a thematically appropriate dish to the boys' Roman Banquet. Various women who worked or didn't work wrote back that they would bring "gemelli pasta with puttanesca sauce," or "baked Giudea artichokes," or "chicken Fra Diavolo," but one mother, a financial planner named Jane Stark, had quickly written back, "Great! We'll bring apple juice," which had caused Amy to forward the e-mail to Jill without a note of explanation.

Amy and Penny walked a little farther now, their conversation moving faster, easier. Penny began to talk about the stresses of running a museum, and Amy felt herself settle in to the good feeling of being the recipient of this kind of talk. "You're probably really overextended," Amy said.

"I am, yes. It's hard when you have virtually no endowment."

"Will you get a break soon?"

"Christmas. We're going to St. Doe's." Amy remembered hearing that St. Doe's was the kind of place where very wealthy families went for vacation; the island was privately owned by a billionaire from Melbourne whose company made those wholemeal biscuits called Bing-Bongs, which apparently everyone in Australia and New Zealand ate, either plain or smeared with Marmite. "The whole island is still unspoiled," Penny said. "Like almost nothing else is anymore."

Together the two women thought of the spoilage of the world. In the middle of a green ocean, singled out and exempt, was this place called St. Doe's, where Amy and Leo, in the pressure and dance of their monthly expenses and anxieties, could not afford to go, but where in a few months Penny would be lying down lightly on a beach. The women were quiet as they rounded the corner onto Ninety-first Street. Amy saw a brief slash of color that looked like Mason's windbreaker, and she turned toward it instinctually. Mason walked among several boys and a tall black babysitter, and stationed in the middle of the group was Penny's son, Holden. The boys were eating icies, those little fluted paper cups of rainbow-colored Italian ices that turned their tongues and lips and the skin around their mouths an uneasy, drowning-victim blue. Amy was suddenly reminded of the dead husband in the building, with his own blue lips. His image floated for a moment, then rippled and disappeared.

"Holden!" called Penny, and her son, a popular, dominating, masculine boy with a big head of dark blonde hair, turned in her direction. "How was school?"

"Good."

"I'll be home for dinner. Tell your sisters to wait for me, and we can all eat together."

"Mason!" Amy called too, as if she herself were drowning. She had always felt perplexingly anxious on the rare occasions when she saw her son from afar, under someone else's watch.

"Hey," Mason said.

"Did you have a good day?"

"Yeah."

"Great!" Amy said, too invested in this conversation.

He indicated goodbye with a vague movement of his wrist. He would not express his connection to her now or even act like it really existed. Holden Ramsey held a gaming device in his hand, and Mason wanted to be absorbed in it. The electronic music hummed, and the device bleeped as all the boys struggled to have a look. So Mason turned away from his mother, willing her to please let him go back to the handheld device, and to the icies, and to Holden and the other boys, and to whatever he could salvage of the dwindling day.

"Clementine," Amy heard Penny say to her sitter, "did you take enough money for the groceries?"

"Yes," said Clementine. "And if the broccoli looks no good to me, Penny, I shall get cauliflower. They are both cruciferous vegetables, and quite nutritious."

"Perfect."

The babysitter and the mass of boys turned the corner, while the mothers watched them go. "*Cruciferous,*" said Penny. "Wow. I really would be lost without her. She is on top of everything. When you have a full-time job you just have to cross your fingers and hope that everything goes fine without you there. So far I've been really lucky."

"Lucky" was a word that came up frequently when any of them discussed the kind of lives they led here. They all knew that most women in the world had a far narrower band of choices, if they had any choices at all; they knew that only a tiny percentage were able to stay home and that most simply *had* to work, no question about it, and that the survival of their families depended upon it. They knew that most women were not, in these particular and unusual ways, *lucky*. But among the lucky ones, there were sometimes unlucky stories about working mothers and child care, involving a babysitter who was found to have published a cheerful but sadomasochistic sex and drug blog, or who had gone on a weeklong trip to visit her family in Trinidad and was never heard from again. At first, fearing that she had been abducted or murdered, the mother called everyone she could think of, finally locating the sitter's cousin, who coolly said, "Inez? Oh, she's good. She has a new job taking care of a famous movie star's kids, though I am not at liberty to say who."

Then there was a story that had achieved the status of urban legend within this insular world. All the mothers seemed to know it, but none of them actually knew the person it had supposedly happened to. It involved a woman who was about to go back to work in public policy and so had hired a babysitter for her three-year-old daughter. The job was rigorous, and everything was fine until one day, after the mother went to the office, she realized she'd left some documents at home, so she took a taxi back to her apartment. While riding up Broadway, the taxi stopped at a light, and she noticed huddled on the sidewalk a beggar woman with a beggar child, wrapped in a blanket and holding a sign that read PLEASE HELP US WE HAVE NO MONEY OR SHELTER.

It was the blanket she recognized first. Her mother-in-law had crocheted it for her. Confused, the woman thought, *What are those homeless people doing with my blanket?* But then she realized that those homeless people were her babysitter and her three-year-old daughter. Every morning while the woman went to the office, the sitter had been taking the little girl out to beg on the streets.

If the story were true, it was awful; if it were untrue, it had been invented as a misogynistic, cautionary tale for any mother who might think about leaving her child to return to work. Could you ever trust someone else to watch your baby? Could you ever find a way to reconcile the dissonant spheres of motherhood and work? Articles in women's magazines continually posed these same questions, though the answers seemed to change from month to month: *Yes you could! No you couldn't!* Amy had heard the urban legend and had been scandalized like everyone else, but in truth she was also relieved that she had never had to leave Mason all day when he was small and that these particular worries had never been her own.

The women now walked on. They passed a couple of Amy's friends and said their hellos; Penny seemed to watch with sociological interest, for she really didn't have a sense of the climate around the vicinity of the school at three in the afternoon. Then they passed Geralynn Freund, the mother in the grade with the obvious eating disorder. She was so little and dog-scrawny that you always had to look away from her for a moment. She had gone through a harsh divorce several years earlier, it was said, and so, in her misery, had ended up falling back on her adolescent anorexic ways. For a while she had spent a good deal of time at the Flexon Gym, poised on a stationary bicycle in spinning class; Karen Yip had once sat beside her there and had said that Geralynn was frightening in her rapaciousness for exercise.

Another time Amy had seen Geralynn in the locker room at the gym, casually undressing, revealing her naked body to all the women, facing away from her open locker in such a way that everyone could see each individuated tendon and bone and ball-socket while she ran a roll-on deodorant into the deep concavity below her twigged arm. Geralynn was like one of the corpse-models in that exhibit that toured the civic centers of the world, showing dead people with their skin removed, participating in the sorts of activities they supposedly would have enjoyed when they were alive. Corpses golfed, or tossed a Frisbee, as though to distract themselves from the terrible realization that they were dead.

Geralynn Freund, divorced, fragile, a single mother without any apparent emotional support system, had stood naked, and the other women at the gym that day had stared, then stared at one another in appalled, tacit conversation. Not a word was said aloud about her in that locker room with the roaring showers all around and with the sound of hair being relentlessly blown into submission. But it was likely that she had been embarrassed about her appearance; no one had seen her at the gym since then.

Now Geralynn Freund walked along the street with her son Joshua beside her. He was a thickset boy who ate the last remnants of an icie, squeezing the blue and red slush from the flattened little cup. Amy said hello in perhaps an overly friendly voice, unable to modulate, and Geralynn said hello back.

After they turned the corner, Penny said, "It's really sad. Are there any other treatments?"

"Oh, she doesn't have cancer. Is that what you thought? She's anorexic."

"Oh. Of course, right. It's still sad," Penny said. "She looks like she'll blow away. She's such a tragic figure."

Amy had the impulse to tell her about the father from 14H who had died in the night. Penny would see that it didn't really matter that Amy hadn't known him, that still she was shaken, and that any of the terrible little family tragedies you routinely heard about could affect you. But Penny was distracted. She had stopped on the street and was looking ahead at something, so Amy looked too, watching as a man walked rapidly toward them. "A friend," Penny said in a nervous whisper.

He was in his early thirties, with the kind of appearance Amy would have found attractive at an earlier age but one she'd now almost forgotten about. The men she knew tended to be financially absorbed husbands with carefully combed hair, dressed in business suits or stretchy weekend sports clothes. This man was small, boyish, good-looking, in a pale, pretty shirt and no tie, and with a ruffled head of brown hair and fair, freckly skin. For some reason she pictured his bare shoulders as probably freckled too.

"You're here," he said to Penny as he approached them. "I timed it right." He was English, and that was a surprise. The English walk among us, Amy thought, and whenever they reveal themselves, Americans experience a moment of unaccountable delight.

"Amy Lamb, Ian Janeway," said Penny.

He shook her hand and said, "Great outfits."

"Don't mock us," Penny said.

"Sorry. You do look amusing. They should put you on *Style Bobbies.*"

"What's that?" Amy asked.

"British television. Women dressed as police officers go round giving out fashion summonses. It's the lowest thing in the culture."

"Oh, tell Amy your family's role in the downfall of British culture," Penny said.

"We don't have a role."

"Your aunt's role, I mean," she said.

Then, to Amy, he explained, "Penny loves this fact, weirdly. My aunt Lesley worked as Margaret Thatcher's personal assistant."

"His *auntie,*" said Penny. "The great Mrs. Thatcher. The most powerful woman in the world during the Reagan years. The only way a woman could be taken seriously then was to be ultraconservative. Antifeminist. Basically, she never promoted another woman to her cabinet."

"My aunt worshipped her," said Ian. Then, to Amy, "In my family, we all worship powerful women." He smiled slyly, and Penny laughed. She had turned slightly pink, Amy saw; even the round little tips of her ears had taken on color. Ian Janeway, it was established, was a curator at the National Gallery in London but was currently spending six months in New York working at the Met as a visiting consultant in the framing department. He also did freelance consulting to other museums.

"I looked at those prints of yours," he said to Penny. "If you want to talk, call me later."

"I will. When I'm done with safety walk."

The two of them were looking directly at each other, and Amy felt the distorting sensation of watching the scene through a keyhole. Her view widened all around to include the details she had missed before. Penny and Ian were gazing at each other's splendid self, each swelling slightly under the other's gaze, blood probably flooding the appropriate parts. As they looked, they talked about "the prints." Were there even any actual prints to be looked at, she wondered, or was this all some sort of code? Their conversation became increasingly exclusive and dull. Something was said about whether a person at the museum named Donna Belknap would need to take a look at the prints too.

They were letting the talk stall, and the boredom was meant to drum all but the devoted away, which would mean that Amy, after being drawn in, was now being encouraged to leave them to each other. But still she listened, because her middle-aged life was often barren of sex now. The ground had been partly stripped and strafed, and you didn't even realize it until you found yourself standing on the street with an excited, secret couple, around whom entire luxuriant fields flowered. They continued to talk about the prints and about Donna Belknap, their voices soft and vague, each sentence ending with a suggestive rise. In the background, faintly, Amy heard some sort of commotion. It was an annoyance. *Go away*, she thought, *I want to hear this.*

"What time will you be finished?" Ian asked.

"I think we have another hour."

"You work all day, and then you have to trudge around. That's not fair."

"Life's not fair," Penny said.

"No, it isn't."

Amy watched them smile at each other and shake their heads at the joke that didn't even have a point. In the distance, those other voices kept calling out, and as Amy stood watching Penny and Ian Janeway, she became aware that one voice was meant for them. "Help!" it cried now. "I'm being mugged!"

Finally, as if lifting herself out of a stupor, Amy snapped her head away from the couple, turning to see a small crowd on the corner, with the bobbing form of a boy in the middle, dressed in an Auburn Day uniform.

"What the fuck is that?" said Ian, and he sprinted toward the commotion, Penny and Amy following. The crowd split apart, and it was revealed to be comprised entirely of boys, none older than around fifteen, all of them black, wearing big, unseasonal jackets. On the ground sprawled the Auburn Day boy, a sixth-grader named Dustin Kavanaugh, unhurt but crying. Ian tried to grab at one or two of the boys, but they were too fast, their ripstop nylon jackets swooshing past.

"Ian, don't," Penny said. She put a hand on his arm—the first public touch between them. "Just go."

"I should chase those shits," he said, breathless.

"No, it's too late. Go."

And so, dismissed, Ian left, while Amy frantically pressed the button on her walkie-talkie to summon the school. Through tears, Dustin Kavanaugh explained that he had been walking along with his earbuds in his ears, eating a bag of little fried corn curls and listening to music.

"Oh, honey, are you hurt?" Amy asked the boy, crouching down and giving him some tissues from her pocketbook.

"No," he said shakily, blowing his nose. "But they got my iPod." Then he added, "And I met them before."

"You did?" Penny asked. "Where?"

"On Hand-in-Hand Day."

Whoosh, thought Amy, picturing the well-meaning but still troubling Hand-in-Hand Day struck from the calendar of the Auburn Day School. The white boys would stay forever with the white, the black with the black, the Hispanic with the Hispanic, and even that single designated day of unity would be shut down. Who knew if these were really the same boys as the ones who had come in to play sports and eat baked ziti? The school might never even try to find out.

The security guard from the school arrived along with a policeman, and after the women gave him all the information they could, the guard coolly asked for their safety vests and walkie-talkie, as if they were being stripped of military rank. There were no excuses; an Auburn Day boy had been mugged right on the block they were patrolling. They should have been able to break it up as it started, or stop it before it happened, but instead they'd been standing in a dreamy cluster with an Englishman, briefly forgetting the real reason they were here on the street in these orange vests.

Only now, as the guard and the policeman tended to Dustin Kavanaugh, did Amy see how upset Penny had become. She seemed stunned, nearly unable to speak, so Amy thought to take her to the Golden Horn. In the coffee shop, leaning against the aqua booth, Penny said, "I just feel so bad. It's my fault that this happened." She began to cry softly, and a couple of people looked up in curiosity. Penny pulled napkins from the dispenser and wiped her eyes.

"No it's not," said Amy, though she thought, it's *our* fault. "Even if we'd been paying attention, they probably would've followed him around the corner. Don't you think?" she added, wanting reassurance herself.

"Maybe." The two women sat glumly in the muted din.

"Thank God he's not hurt." Amy added, "We could send him something."

"A new iPod," Penny tried, blowing her nose. Her skin was so pale that the brief release of tears had inflamed her whole face. "I heard he likes show tunes."

"Yes, show tunes, he loves them." All the mothers had heard this about Dustin Kavanaugh, and it was always mentioned with a certain knowing inflection.

"Those kids, those muggers, they're going to listen to his iPod and get a big surprise," said Penny. "'The Circle of Life' from *The Lion King*." Both women, despite the somberness, began to laugh a little.

"And you know, we're going to hear from Dustin Kavanaugh's mother, and I don't blame her."

"Oh, right, Helen. She will be very upset. Anyone would."

Helen Kavanaugh dressed as though she were the chairwoman of a bank, though she hadn't held a paying job since right after college. Her stockbroker husband had made particularly good investments for them. As a result she was allowed to be motivated by something entirely unrelated to money, which distinguished her from almost everyone they knew. She was head of an antipoverty charity, and she was relentless in her involvement. Always, she was soliciting money; always, she was speaking at another banquet. Her altruism was entire and *wowing*. There was no hidden narcissism embedded in it. It was a force that awakened her in the morning and put her into the stiff shell of a suit and took her out the door. Mostly, the demands of the city didn't allow for the purity of altruism; usually, altruism got mixed into other things, so that everyone ended up "doing what they could" and leaving it at that. Amy had always admired Helen Kavanaugh but now felt personally afraid of her too. She could hear Helen's meeting-ready voice on the phone tonight, saying, "Amy? Hi there, Helen Kavanaugh. Listen, we ought to talk about the incident."

Everybody would be talking about the incident, Amy realized now. "We'd better get out of town on a rail," she said to Penny.

"With little hobo sticks."

Amy pictured the two of them walking side by side along train tracks. She saw herself playing a harmonica, and the scene was oddly peaceful. What if they could both escape their lives just like that, riding boxcars, ambling forward forever, unscheduled and untraceable?

"Everything I do leads to something like this," Penny said.

"What does that mean? You're responsible for a whole string of muggings?" But Amy knew that her role was to be passive and listen, perhaps in a way that no one ever listened to Penny Ramsey, a woman who had few free moments in which to sit over a plate of eggs or the spokes of a grapefruit half or an iced coffee riddled with chemical sweetener, the little ripped packets scattered all over the table, and just talk.

Penny stirred her seltzer with a straw, sending the ice chiming.

"No," she said, and then her eyes filled again. "God, I'm sorry," she said. "I'm a mess."

"It's okay," Amy said.

"I'm in such a strange place. You think that your marriage and your whole life are going to be one way, and then suddenly, guess what, they're not. You know?"

Amy just kept looking at her. "Yes," she finally said.

Then Penny said, "I know you figured it out before, on the street. I could tell."

Amy paused. "Ian," she said carefully.

Penny nodded. "I've never done anything like that. But Greg is so totally corporate now. And he has zero misgivings about what his investors do."

"Which is what?"

"Call it 'munitions,' among other things. Getting rich off funding this war, and war in general. I shouldn't be saying any of this; I know it's disloyal. Greg would tell you that his investors also build children's hospitals. But he was different once. He tells me I don't understand. That I should stick to the Triangle Factory fire and photomontages of . . . Hart Crane and the creation of the Brooklyn Bridge. Like he even knows who that is."

Amy thought of Greg Ramsey with his good shirts and nugget-sized cuff links and his hands-free cell-phone headset. He was a small, thick, vain man of forty-one, a scrapper, a success, and she suddenly remembered him at the Dads' Pancake Breakfast last spring, standing front and center at the griddle, lofting his browned discs into the air while a few other fathers struggled over the uneven heat with their own spreading, unflippable islands of pale batter.

Amy was here in this booth now in order to say to Penny Ramsey, "You can talk to me." This was her line, and she didn't even mind it. She suddenly wanted Penny to like her and be comforted by her; she wanted to appear like a soothing person who didn't judge others. Amy said her line easily. At which point Penny said, "I'm glad it was you here today."

Had you been sitting across the room at the Golden Horn at the time of this conversation, you would have noticed the way the two women inched their asses closer across the booth and leaned their heads forward, as if they themselves were having a love affair. *Oh, female intimacy!* Amy thought with longing. She had missed it so much since Jill had left the city. She recalled lying across Jill and Donald's bed on a weekday afternoon last year, before it was time for school pick-up, trying on clothes that Jill was thinking of giving away to a thrift shop. They'd talked about how their bodies had changed over time and how you had to accept this and not dwell upon it; each of them insisted to the other that she looked as good as she had looked back in college, and it wasn't really untrue. "The thing about clothes," Amy remembered Jill saying, "is that you never know which one will end up being your favorite and which one you'll never wear—and will be just like throwing your money down the toilet."

"Yeah. You should be able to say to your new clothes," said Amy, "'One of you shall betray me.'" They had laughed and lain back together on the wide bed as though they were in college again. Amy had let her head drop down over the side, seeing the room upside-down, feeling a disorienting, teenaged blood rush.

But their time together seemed stolen, pitched against the grain of family life. Marriage and children sometimes divided friends; the one or two women Amy knew well who had remained single and child-less seemed almost unaware of the astonishing differences between their life and hers. They would call her on a weeknight, when anyone with kids would be in the prime of high-homework and arguments and general noise and distraction and preparation for tomorrow.

"Hey there, Amy girl," Lisa Silvestri would say on the telephone at eight o'clock on a Tuesday. "What's going on? Is this a good time to talk?"

Amy had once crammed with Lisa Silvestri in law school, sitting together on the chunky, modular furniture of the library lounge, and then later on, by coincidence, they'd had offices down the hall from each other at Kenley Shuber, where Lisa still worked along with Leo;

she had been made partner, while he was forever to be a salaried associate. But Lisa Silvestri seemed to have little awareness of the rhythms of family life that often carried you away from your friends.

Some mothers felt secretly *pious* about motherhood; they were sure their childless friends could never reach anything approximating the gorgeousness of family bedlam: the intensity of teaching a child to read, the drama contained in a tantrum, the on-call mother love that was more concentrated and ecstatic even than sexual love. Life with children was bigger than life without them, these mothers were convinced, and so the childless women could seem austere and prissy, though this could never, ever be said aloud, for it was judgmental and certainly unfair.

When Lisa Silvestri called in the middle of the chaos of an evening, Amy had to casually say, "Listen, Lisa, I've got to call you back, okay? It won't be tonight, I'm afraid." In the background of Amy's apartment, there might be a crash and shouting and the roar of bathwater running unchecked from a tap. Over at Lisa's loft, the sound of light jazz noodled along softly.

But even when you made time for your friends, Amy thought, and they made time for you, at intervals the center of your attention reflexively moved back to your family. You sat with the other women in the morning here at the Golden Horn, but you thought, *Pick up shin guards for Mason.* Or else, you even used your precious time with your friends to ask them, "Do you know where I could get shin guards?" One of the other women might name a new sporting-goods store called Outdoorland, and you would pull out your BlackBerry, which, unlike your husband's—which was stocked with notes on depositions and meetings with clients—was stocked with names of shops and doctors and pediatric orthodontists and other mothers, and dates for meetings at the school about how to talk to your sons so they will listen. According to the school psychologist, Dr. Linda Kreps, mothers should never address their boys directly when they have something important to say to them. "Instead," Amy seemed to remember that the psychologist had actually said, "you should go outdoors and engage with them in an activity in which you can't stare into their eyes and intimidate them." You should fish, she'd said, or drive, or walk along a city street or a country lane as you tell them that you and their father are breaking up, or that you are dying.

Now Amy listened as Penny Ramsey told her the story of how she had become Ian Janeway's lover. Ian, Penny said, had come downtown to her museum six weeks earlier for a meeting with a curator and had sat in the anteroom outside the executive offices upstairs, waiting. Penny had been at her desk eating a quick lunch, "something sad, like beef cup-a-ramen," she told Amy, and Ian had poked his head around the doorway and said, "That smells good." By which he might have meant, *You smell good.*

Penny Ramsey, a harried woman in a good pale yellow suit with little flecks in the weave like vanilla beans, invited him into her office while he waited. He sat across the glass plane of her desk, inhaling her beefy, salty soup fumes and flirting so boldly that they both began to laugh.

"You want some of my ramen?" she finally asked. "Is that it?"

The sexual part started a week later, after he had called her on her cell phone half a dozen times. "Do you need a lunch date today?" he'd asked once. And, another time: "I call with urgent news from the world of framing."

On the day they first slept together, Penny had been coming back from a lunch meeting with a donor and was walking along the edge of the park talking on the phone to her assistant, Mark, when Ian text-messaged her. "Come see me," he wrote. "I'm home in bed."

She called him right away. "Are you sick?" she asked.

"No," he said slowly. Then, "I have to touch you." He lowered the conversation to a teenaged level, making them both laugh in a dumb, drugged way. Penny hurried into the subway. There was still a little time before she had to return to the museum, so she headed uptown on the express train to meet Ian Janeway, a thirty-three-year-old British man who waited for her in his bed.

Penny walked up the stairs to his apartment, a narrow one-bedroom in a tenement building in the upper Nineties off Fifth Avenue. Amy imagined the small bedroom, the slew of unframed prints angled at the foot of the bed, and the framer himself with his tentative scrape of a voice and pale narrow body lying against the golden complement of Penny, whose pretty clothes draped the chair. Amy saw Ian lowering himself down onto her, talking and cajoling in his wonderful accent, his mouth on her little breast, his body establishing itself against her, a finger going against and inside her until she was helpless and babbling, and then everything moving more quickly. The images were exciting, not because either one of the people in them excited Amy sexually but because she felt privileged enough to get a glimpse of the scene, at least secondhand. Now, unhappily, Amy tried to picture herself and Leo in bed, but she could only see her husband toiling away above her with the same diligence with which he toiled at Kenley Shuber.

"Please say something," Penny said to Amy. "I guess you disapprove."

"I have no opinion. I'm not your mother."

"My mother would die if she knew. She's so impressed by Greg's whole corporate thing. His money thing." Penny paused. "I want you to know that I don't go around talking about Ian. I have told no one else. You're it."

"I'm *it*? Can I ask why?"

"I don't know. The mugging; I had to talk. I'm sorry to burden you."

"It's not a burden," Amy said, although maybe, suddenly, it was.

"Well, thank you," said Penny.

She told Amy more facts about Ian: how he had studied at the Ruskin School of Drawing and Fine Art at Oxford and had hoped to be a painter, but had had a kind of minor nervous breakdown during his first term and was briefly hospitalized, then sent home. "The doctors decided he was just in over his head," Penny said, "and that he needed more exercise and 'fresh air'—they were always big on fresh air—and he basically agreed with them. He told me that he had far too many ideas for his artwork and that the visuals would keep him up all night. He was completely overstimulated, and he crashed. So he switched to art history, with an emphasis on Italian engraving, and finally he found his way into framing and then became a very good curator. But he's still kind of emotional; it never went away. He's also sort of boyish and romantic, which is part of what I like about him. He leaves me these long, nutty messages on my cell, these soliloquies. I guess I worry about him a little too; he's so intense."

Amy thought of the few men she had been involved with long ago, before Leo; their images were still individually preserved for her. She thought of those young men in their twenties whose arms were lined with light hair and whose stomachs hadn't yet been tenderized by a continual influx of breakfast-meeting pastries and nighttime cookies, or by the long spiral freefall of middle-aged resignation. She remembered how, when you are so young, you rarely think about the direction or purpose of love. Instead, you just follow it wherever it goes. That was what she used to do all the time, and it was what Penny was now doing with Ian. Amy watched it all from a distance, like the crippled girl in a wheelchair in an old storybook, looking on as Heidi and Peter frolic and fuck on the side of a mountain.

"And listen, one thing. I really have to ask you not to tell anyone," Penny said. "Not your husband, okay? And not any of those other mothers. Please promise. It's important."

"*Duh*," Amy said—a word Mason used—smiling and pleased.

T HAT NIGHT, when her son asked if one of his parents would read to him, Amy volunteered. She wanted the warmth of such an encounter, with Mason close beside her on his trundle bed, which was decorated with the remnants of old stickers glued and then half-peeled from the headboard. He was fast growing out of the desire to be read to, and soon the activity of reading aloud to him would stop forever.

"So which book tonight?" she asked, and to her mild disappointment he handed her *Blindman and the Moorchaser* by the Scottish writer Rachel Millar, which all the boys in his grade were reading this year. Blindman was the actual name of a character who had been born without eye sockets (was that even possible?) and who wandered a moor in a fully reconfigured and oddly futuristic nineteenth-century countryside, trying to avenge his brother Azajian's death. The book was enormous, as all books were for children lately.

Amy was resistant to fantasy; whenever Mason asked her to read to him she said yes, but in recent years she had felt betrayed by the books. All those questing characters and that dire, apocalyptic imagery were exhausting and so depressing, not unlike watching the news out of the Middle East. Everything was bathed in waves of blood described by Rachel Millar as being "the exact colour of King Moloral the Second's garnet ring." When Mason was younger, she'd read *The Secret Garden* with him, because it was her favorite book when she was a girl, and she had wanted her child to love it too, regardless of his gender. He'd liked it enough to finish it—there was an outbreak of cholera in the plot, killing the protagonist Mary Lennox's parents, and mysterious noise in the night—but Amy knew that Mason had never thought of it again and that it hadn't held him the way these darker, bloodier, fantastical novels did.

"Okay," Amy said, picking up his book now, "so where were we?" Her wrist ached slightly as she lifted it. The thick spine was crenellated and immodestly faux-filigreed.

"There's a bookmark, Mom," Mason said.

"Ah yes. Indeed there is a bookmark." She read aloud: "'Chapter the Eleventh: In Which the Moorchaser Learns an Invaluable Lesson.'"

"Why is it invaluable?" Mason asked. "Why don't they just say 'valuable'?"

"Please, just let me read," she said, and she started the chapter:

At the exact moment that the old clock in the Stillson Abbey tower began to chime, the Moorchaser was far from the village of Haddensdown-on-Clef. He had managed to slip past one of the Defenders and enter the Zone of Sorrow, from which no man has ever returned. But the Moorchaser, of course, was not a man; he was a Frailkin, and none of this species had ever entered the Zone before. As soon as he walked through the greenish copper gates with their twisted, strangulant vines, he felt something stir inside him. *I am home*, thought the Moorchaser, though surely this was not his home, nor had it ever been, except in a dream.

Mason's eyes were already half closed. He was tired, but if she were to ask whether he was bored by the book he would say no, no, it was thrilling. What the hell is a "Frailkin"? she wanted to ask him. How can you expect me to say that word aloud with a straight face? She wondered how he could find this book thrilling; something was inside his brain, as small as a legume, giving him a fascination with the promise of worlds that did not exist.

Maybe it was just that the actual world of adulthood, with its long meetings and requirements that you sit still, was too disappointing for most boys to face head-on. Or maybe it was that boys were in need of a belief that something more intoxicating than this world lay ahead, as though to buffer them against reality after they stopped believing in the existence of Santa Claus. You could lose Santa Claus and the Easter Bunny and the Tooth Fairy all at once in a terrible massacre with severed limbs and fur and blood and veined wings and fluffy material everywhere yet still hold on to Frodo and the rest of Middle-earth at least until high school. At which point, in order to weather the pain of losing that last fantasy foothold, you discovered the sexual wonders of girls, with their outsized breasts, nimble tongues, and the geometrical welcome of their open legs. You replaced one type of fantasy with another, and then you never, ever had to lose that one.

"The thing you have to understand about boys," an older, more experienced mother in the park had advised Amy long ago, "is that sometimes they're very simple. Sometimes all they need is to be run like dogs."

This had offended Amy a little; she'd felt she ought to be offended on behalf of all boys, everywhere, who could not defend themselves. But of course there was some truth to that remark. Amy remembered how once, when Mason was two, she had taken him to a mother-child swimming class at the Y and how afterward in the

locker room, when she had dressed him and still stood naked herself, about to change back into her street clothes, he had suddenly
pushed open the heavy door that led to the lobby, where dozens of
old men and women sat. Through the pneumatic exhalation of the
slowly closing door, she saw Mason make a break for the outside
world, and in that second she understood that he might easily slip
away from her forever.

"MASON, COME BACK!" she cried, and in a sense she had
been crying it ever since. Frantic, naked, damp, Amy had reached
for one of the towels that the Y provided. It was a small, niggling
square, big enough either to cover her breasts or her pubic hair, but
not both. In that moment, she had to choose: Which was worse for
the world to see? Her *breasts,* she decided, and she ran skidding out
into the lobby, frantically calling her son's name and displaying her
pubic hair to the elderly. A few people looked up from their drowsy
conversations. One old man with pickety teeth smiled and waved
when he saw her. She grabbed Mason by the arm; he was unperturbed as she yanked him back, but Amy was suddenly sobbing in
relief and unable to stop.

"Why Mommy crying?" he had asked over and over on the bus
going home. "Why Mommy crying?" Which had only made her cry
a little more.

Years later, stripped of all its fear and desperation, the scene
would become a funny anecdote at the Golden Horn. The women
went around the table and each of them declared which body part,
in that same situation, she would have chosen to cover with the
towel. Roberta had shrugged, coming up with the only good answer:
"I would have covered my face."

So boys, in their wildness, were simple, and girls, static and con-
templative, were complex. Boys ran and ran, and then, when they
were eventually tired, they sat and took things apart and put other
things together, while girls quietly braided friendship bracelets out
of little snippets of colored thread and gave each other the chills and
promised lifelong fidelity.

Amy, who had grown up among girls, had wanted a daughter

and had been shocked when she had given birth to a boy. Her parents had sent a baby gift of a handmade doll, a definitively male blob with its own tiny penis, the whole doll stuffed with all-natural-fiber filler and encased in a stocking over its flesh-colored cloth, giving it a disturbingly realistic, soft-sculpture quality. The doll had never been a favorite of Mason's, and once, when Amy was cleaning his room, she had screamed when she saw a line of ants crawling out of one of the doll's nostrils. The filler, it seemed, was infested. She had flung the doll down the chute in the incinerator room, and Mason had never missed it, and had never wanted another doll in his life.

He craved things that moved, though, and in the early years he ran cars and trucks along the floor, although once in a while, if a friend were over, he might lift one and casually smash it down on the other boy's head. Amy would force him to apologize, the way other children had been forced to apologize to Mason at other moments. "Sorry," intoned the insincere apologist. "Sorry for taking your Burning Engine Monster Truck. Sorry for breaking your skull." Sorry, sorry, sorry, for everything I have done and will likely do over my lifetime.

Amy and Leo had tried to instill in Mason some kind of spiritual consciousness from an early age. Leo, who presided over an informal, condensed seder for them and his parents every year, with the Jews skipping fast across the parted sea as if on a moving sidewalk at an airport, had casually dropped God's name now and then when Mason was small. But Mason had shown so little interest that it was as if his father were talking about some distant, elderly relative who was a pharmacist in Indiana. Mason was a literalist, interested not in God but in nebulas. He was scientific, list-oriented, not at all spiritual, yet just when Amy decided he was one thing and not another, he invariably said something that changed her perception of him.

When he was seven, he had confided in her before bed one night, "Mom, I am frightened of the escalator. Also, the yellow part in eggs. They look up at you like *eyes.*" The fears had been so strange but also human and understandable. The following day, walking home after a birthday party that had featured an overstimulating magician, they stayed silent for a while, slowly separating themselves from the images of flapping scarves and squealing, spontaneously exploding balloon dachshunds. The sky was a beautiful pale color, and she had suddenly asked him, "Mason, does time pass slowly for you, or fast?"

She had been thinking of his vulnerability, and of herself as a vulnerable girl growing up in Montreal during the long lead time before adolescence. Life had been so slow back then. Summers were spent in a hammock with a succession of realistic teen novels from the library, eating the crumbling crust of an ice cream bar and standing in the driveway with the garden hose, washing her father's car. Her sisters, Naomi and Jennifer, could be found inside at the kitchen table, pushing new subject labels into the slots of the dividers in their notebooks. Their mother was often locked in her study writing or off at a women's meeting, and their father was teaching summer classes.

Mostly, as Amy recalled, back then she thought that she would be a girl forever, breastless and unencumbered, and that she could loll around and read books as long as she liked. She thought that adulthood, when it came, would naturally pass as slowly as childhood had. The insult had been that none of that was true and that now, at age forty, Amy felt she barely had time to read books, even though she had no job. Girlhood had evaporated, with only a few photographs and report cards and friendship bracelets as primary-source evidence that it had ever existed.

But Mason, when she asked him that question on the street, simply looked at her and said gently, "Mom, that question is really queer." He meant it in the way that boys meant it: *Mom, no offense, but please don't ever ask me about this kind of thing. It will do neither of us any good.* So back and forth she went over time, giving him distance, then pressing in close.

When Amy turned and looked at Mason now in the bed, she saw that he was asleep. His hair had that slightly smoky, rotting smell to it, but his face was almost transparently innocent in this first stage of sleep. Mason was so *big*; his head smelled, and his feet did too,

sweaty inside his ribbed athletic socks and those heelie shoes with
the wheels embedded in the soles, as though boys needed extra propulsion, when in fact they could run and run on their own steam
for long distances. He was sometimes so ardent and tender, but
increasingly she glimpsed bits of what she considered a kind of male
remove, as Penny had mentioned. Maybe this was the thing that
would make it possible for him to go out into the world eventually.
For months now he had been in the process of building an elaborate
catapult, and he was independently developing a studious interest in
warplanes. Once, in his sleep, she had heard Mason fitfully mutter,
"Heinkel He51B . . ." and "Vought Corsair F4U . . ."

Amy left her son's small bed and went off into the other, big bed,
where she belonged. Leo was already there, with a glass of milk and
a plate of big, commercially soft-baked cookies and with pages of
legal briefs spread all around him. Though he was a solid, tall, somewhat homely man with slightly crushed features, she had always
loved the way he looked.

"Hi," she said, climbing onto the bed and then moving across the
papers and sitting down lightly on his chest. "Need a break?"

"Whoa, nelly," Leo said, holding up his hands, and at first she
thought he was being playful too, but when she kissed him, his
breath scented with generic cookie ingredients, she could tell from
how tentatively he formed his mouth to hers that nothing was going
to happen.

"I can't now," he said. "There's the Pittsburgh thing."

"Which one is that?"

"The lunch meat people. The salmonella defense."

"Well, maybe if you actually were Vishnu," she said, "that would
be better."

"What?"

"The joke you made last night. What you said to Stutzman at
work, and then he didn't know who Vishnu was? He thought he was
a new associate?"

Leo seemed to marvel that Amy had retained this slight and
trivial anecdote, for of course there was no parallel; when she told

him stories about her day, he often did not remember them. He was not interested enough to remember them and refer to them again, and they both knew that, but at least he could be interested in her now sexually. A husband was supposed to want sex more frequently than a wife; word had it that a wife was the one who was allowed to be grudging about it. And sometimes Amy was grudging, for by the end of the day she was so tired, which Leo could never understand. "What are *you* so tired about?" he'd ask.

Women who worked were exhausted; women who didn't work were exhausted. There was no cure for the oceanic exhaustion that overwhelmed them. If you were a working mother you would always lose in some way, and if you were a full-time mother you would lose too. Everyone wanted something from you; you were hit up the minute you rose from your bed. Everyone hung on you, asking for something, reminding you of what you owed them, and though the middle of each school day or workday seemed to be open and available, this wasn't the way it felt. Meanwhile, husbands often crashed ahead as if they, like their sons, had wheels in their shoes. Husbands sometimes wanted sex, and always wanted money, and stock tips, and wines, and good components for their audio systems. They seemed to want everything they could get their hands on.

But now, in bed at night, Leo didn't really want her.

In recent years he and Amy had taken turns being equally uninterested. The death of the married libido had been widely reported; it had happened to them too, as it had happened to many others. Now you were supposed to make an effort about such matters. Sex was meant to be a project, just like an assignment at work or a child's diorama. In order to keep yourselves from falling into indifference, you were meant to go on a "date" once a week. Shelly Harbison, a woman Amy knew from the school, said that she and her husband Alan got dressed up and went to dinner and a movie every Thursday. "And," Shelly had said, "we have a rule that we're *not allowed* to talk about the kids."

"That must be hard," one of the other women remarked.

"Yes," Shelly admitted. "It is. It's actually harder than you think." She paused, considering this. "You run out of things to say when you take the kids out of the picture," she said forlornly. "You start to realize just how much they dominate your thoughts and all your conversation. There are these *silences*." She paused again. "Once, I looked around the restaurant, and the whole place was silent. They had all forbidden each other to talk about their kids. You could hear everyone's silverware and glasses."

But Amy and Leo did not go out on date night, did not force themselves upon each other in a formal way, and still there was silence between them. He looked so unhappy now. "Sorry, Amy," he said, extricating himself from beneath her.

"The old reverse *Lysistrata* trick," she said softly, embarrassed, and he smiled and apologized again. She was wearing the undershirt he supposedly liked to see her in, and she smelled nearly edible from her pomegranate body wash, yet it didn't matter. She wondered if he sensed that she had climbed on him because she was anxious and overwhelmed and couldn't stop thinking about all that had happened today.

"I'm just too crazed," said Leo. "It wouldn't be fun." He grabbed another cookie and put it into his mouth, then picked up a file. He ate to calm himself, she knew, and to entertain himself. The cookies were a tiny treat, a coda at the end of something long and strenuous.

"It's okay," Amy said lightly, and she turned over on her side, with a book opened before her like a prop. "No big deal." She and Leo lay there like pieces of dry kindling in a tinderbox.

Penny Ramsey, she thought, had found a solution to the waning of love. Penny climbed the stairs of the kind of building that she would otherwise never enter, and undressed in a strange room. The British framer palmed and rubbed her breasts and held her to him, length to length, and his penis rose against her in happiness. How could someone like Greg Ramsey expect his wife *not* to take a lover? How could he ignore her longings for gentleness and empathy and aestheticism and humility, and instead strut around with his little Hong Kong–tailored suits and his squash racquet and the dull sheen of his unsavory money, and actually think it would be acceptable to her? Really, what was he thinking?

The story of anyone's love affair was exciting and easy to listen to; it cost you nothing to hear about, or think about. You weren't at risk of exposure yourself but could luxuriate in the simple, distant idea of it, which Amy did now as she lay on her side, facing away from her uninterested husband. She was soothed and engaged by the image of Penny and Ian. Still, she wished that Leo, good Leo— so much better than the apparently piggish Greg Ramsey—would put a hand on her shoulder and pull her back as if rescuing her, but he couldn't know that this was being asked of him.

Without turning and looking now, she knew that Leo bore the expression of a faraway husband. But even so, she willed him to reach around her—not Vishnu but just a two-armed, desiring man—and neatly peel away the thin skin of her undershirt and do one of the things to her that he had been doing for so long that the pattern had been thoroughly established. He did nothing; his hands didn't try to touch her, and she stayed facing away from him.

Deep into the soup of their long marriage it seemed to her that she was entitled to use Leo sexually once in a while. Married sex was strangely shape-shifting, and they gratified each other as circumstances required. At times it was the equivalent of parallel play. There were sudden, unexpected bursts of excitement punctuating long, fallow weeks during which she and Leo were like chaste roommates at a Benedictine college. Amy could pepper her face with benzoyl peroxide during sudden hailstorms of middle-aged, hormone-triggered acne, and Leo could feast on Thai take-out noodle dishes in a slick of hot red oil that fired and furred his breath, and neither of them cared all that much. Any moment together just represented one small and possibly poignant or ordinary moment in the long and varied story line of their marriage.

Leo kissed her shoulder, and the audible *pock* of his lips on her skin became his closing word of the night. It did not occur to him to think that sex might provide her with reassurance. He'd been sympathetic that day when she'd called him at work, first in the morning to tell him, shakily, about the young husband in the building dropping dead and then, later in the day, in near-tears, to tell him about what had happened to Dustin Kavanaugh and how it had partly been her fault because she'd been obliviously chatting with Penny at the time.

She had not told him about Ian Janeway; she'd promised Penny she wouldn't. It used to be that Amy and Leo told each other all things, but now, in her awareness that he didn't listen attentively to much of what she said about herself—and that he would probably need Ritalin to do it—she felt uneasily within her rights. The idea that her day could contain small mysteries was fine with him, for these tended to be limited to the home and the school and the coffee shop, none of which were places he usually wanted to know too much about. That was her territory; he knew she'd do what had to be done there.

"Good night," she said in a small voice to her husband in the dark.

So he stayed in his territory and she in hers. His was filled with corridors, and invoices, and phone lines that sprang to life, and the wet slurp of the copy machine, and a continual cycle of meetings with other lawyers in a room where the lighting was the color of grain, falling in circles on a table that was the color of grain too, so you soon felt as if you'd dropped into a field of wheat where you would lie immobilized for years. Her territory was populated by thoughts of the husband in 14H, whose time on earth was up, and a sexually appealing English framer, and a few idling, good-hearted, occasionally self-doubting mothers, as well as an accomplished, ambitious one who apparently knew the secrets of the world, and was about to reveal them.

R ISE, SORROW, *'neath the saffron sister tree,"* the girl sang in a strange, minor key. Deep inside the house, with its various levels and echoing surfaces that gave off the forlorn quality that was often a side effect of newness, she examined the constellations lining her ceiling and sang to herself a song that was both melancholy and beautiful. Where she had learned it, her mother had no idea. Her daughter was a mystery to her and always had been.

The mother, Jill Hamlin, walking up the wide carpeted stairs toward her own bedroom, heard the singing and stopped in the hallway to listen. No one was really used to the house yet, and the little girl in particular seemed agitated at night—not that she'd been a solid sleeper back in the city, either. Jill paused at the top, then walked into her daughter's bedroom and sat on the side of the bed, under the shaped spray of luminescent stars that Donald had glued there. "I heard you singing," she said. "What's going on in here, honey? You shouldn't still be up."

"I can't sleep, Mom."

"Anything on your mind?"

"No."

She always said no when asked this question, and it was a slightly unsettling answer, making Jill worry that nothing much was on her mind as she lay on her back in this ideal suburban-girl's bedroom, singing oddly and looking up at the constellations. In all likelihood she had no idea they were constellations but just saw them as green points of light that her father had affixed there to entertain her. The question that Jill frequently asked herself was: What *did* her daughter know?

The only sure answers seemed to be: The alphabet, in fits and starts. The names of colors, at least the main ones. Right hand versus left, from time to time.

The little girl's knowledge was spotty and intermittent, which distinguished her from all the other children who cried out, "I'm brachiosaurus! My name means 'arm lizard'!" as they galloped past their parents on the playground, or even the younger ones who pointed to stop signs while pinioned into car seats or strollers, observing drolly, "Octagon."

Each time these children made another pronouncement, some delicate part of Jill was crushed a little bit more. She had understood early on that she was only at the very beginning of what might prove to be a long sequence of slights and insults. She would bravely fend off each one over time, her hands held up to her face against the battering. Her daughter, though, was oblivious of her own failings, but on the day when other people began to point them out to her, Jill's heartbreak would be complete.

"Well, you should go to bed now," Jill said needlessly, because her daughter was already in bed and what more was there for her to do, knock herself unconscious with one of the heavy china dolls that sat on her window seat? Apparently she had inherited Jill's own insomnia. Maybe not inherited it, exactly, but absorbed it through the shared, circulating air. Jill stood up in the dim room and moved to the door.

"Good night, Mom."

"Good night now. Love you lots." And then that was *it*; Jill Hamlin left her little girl alone and awake, then walked silently across the pale carpet that covered so much surface area of this house, the way sand covers desert, or *is* desert. Suburban houses were inextricable from their carpeting; part of the point of living here seemed to have to do with the softness beneath your feet, both inside and out on your lawn, all of it replacing unforgiving wood and pavement and jackhammered asphalt. She wondered how frequently her daughter thought about their life back in the city. Many experiences seemed to pour through her without her reflecting on them.

They had been living in the house in Holly Hills for only a few months, but it had been over four years now since they had brought her home at age twenty-three months from the Tuva Infant Custodial Centre, an orphanage situated in southern Siberia. You were supposed to want to "inhale" your baby all the time; in those first few months, Jill did not. She could not tell anyone her feelings, not even Amy Lamb. She told Amy everything else, including, recently, how much she and Donald had made on the sale of their apartment, and about her long-ago grief over her mother's suicide, and now about the current of loneliness that ran through this big, modern house, but she had never told Amy about the heart fashioned of ice that pounded inside her. It was mostly shame that kept her from saying anything, but lately, too, the move had changed the pace and flow of the friendship. Jill and Amy couldn't just pop out and see each other, meeting for a quick coffee, or join up to go to a movie at noon, sitting among the other women and the old people. Even in their conversations on the phone recently, it seemed that all Amy wanted to talk about was Penny Ramsey.

"You'd like her a lot, actually," Amy had said.

"Great," Jill said mildly, not having any idea whether this was true, for Penny Ramsey wasn't really a person to her but remained simply an idea that had been mentioned over the years by the other women: the mother at their sons' school who slid past you in her perfection and achievement, making you look at yourself in dismay and say, *Oh well.* She had been pointed out to Jill once or twice; Amy or

Roberta would say, "That's the one we told you about." But she didn't want this phantom mother to be colored in and wholly realized, preferring to leave her at the conceptual if well-dressed level. She wanted Amy to talk about her only occasionally and not actually to become good friends with her. She wanted to be Amy's only intimate friend, even though, ironically, she was unable to tell Amy the most intimate thing right now, which was her rising fear about Nadia not being quick, not being exactly right.

So many women who adopted older babies from Eastern Europe found that the children had attachment disorders; it was more common than most people knew. But Jill had never heard about the *mother* of an adopted baby having an attachment disorder; there were no references to this in the literature. The baby's original name was Manya, which had immediately brought to mind a stocky, grinning woman in a field, with a scythe. Jill had met some mothers online through the vast adoption network who gave their foreign-born daughters clever, contemporary American names such as Jenna or Harper or even eccentric names like Pandora. Jill was determined not to do that, and so she chose a new name that seemed cultur- ally appropriate and also had had meaning to her personally long ago when she was a girl.

Nadia Comaneci had been the fourteen-year-old Romanian gymnast who, with her talent and slight, bendable tulip body and Eastern European discipline and unknowability, was the gold-medal star and international crush of the 1976 Olympics. Jill, nine years old at the time, had lain on her bed in Philadelphia watching Nadia Comaneci on TV and, later, had listened repeatedly to the piece of seafoam piano music called "Nadia's Theme," imagining what it might mean to whirl through space like that, to be mosquito-light, to land exactly where you wanted.

Decades later, Jill thought that if she could coax the same elegance and grace from her rashy, unhappy, and earthbound baby, then her future would be secured. As it would turn out, Nadia Comaneci's future was not so perfect; it was said she had become part of Ceauşescu's circle as a teenager, wearing garish eye makeup and hanging out in bars with the dictator's son. Eventually, a few weeks before the revolution, Nadia Comaneci defected to the United States. Now apparently she was making a good life for herself somewhere in this huge country, an American citizen just like the little girl who had been named after her.

Jill and Donald had tried so hard to have their own baby! Even now, Jill could recall the ordeal of continual and conscripted sex. He would come home from the accounting firm, and Jill would be waiting for him. Donald would slip off his tie and shirt and trousers, and together they would try to forget anything that had happened to them that day and to focus only on themselves and their shared mission.

They would have sex on the bed or sometimes on the couch in the living room until her back became embossed with the twill of the cushions, and both her insides and Donald's outsides pulsated in synchrony. Though there was no joy in the act by then, at least there was humor. "That was *beautiful*," or "That was so *moving*," they would say afterward, laughing a little. But no matter what they did, the egg and the sperm would not join together like the two halves of a necklace clasp.

Her life bore no resemblance to the way she once had imagined it. Over the years she had changed and changed again. By the time she started to try to get pregnant, she barely understood her own "goals"—that word used by guidance counselors and career planners. Jill had always been a wonderful student, handing her papers in by the deadline and receiving praise. Physically, she knew she gave off the superficial appearance of success: pretty, fair-haired, athletic, well-mannered, and very tall, though she was the kind of female tall that tends to slouch, rounding her shoulders against the assault of appearing different. She did not want to stand out; she wanted to succeed, yes, to become someone who was admired, but she wanted to do it in a quiet and modest way.

Jill's work history hadn't been what was expected of her. After college she'd entered a new graduate program at NYU called Studies in American Cultural Modes. This was during the late 1980s, a time when AIDS had begun to terrify everyone, everywhere, and the dreamy gauze of Reagan wealth and self-satisfaction had started to lift, and all things seemed in transition, even academia. In that moment, various indescribable and wafting departments flourished at universities, and Jill had been seduced. The description of her program seemed to suggest that she wouldn't have to narrow herself too much, that she could remain a generalist with various pockets of knowledge.

At first the experience actually was expansive. Jill eagerly attended seminars for three years, but after the course work ended—a thick paste of history, political science, and popular culture that moved swiftly and madly through gender, race, and consequence, jumping from the Civil War to the civil rights movement; nodding briefly at the invention of music videos and the rise on campus of queer theory, black studies, and women's studies; and incorporating the mobilization of AIDS activism, all of it part of the questing American experience—she had found herself left thunderously alone to write her dissertation.

Ever since prep school Jill had found herself in the swimmy light of academic fluorescence, wandering serenely up to the reserve room at the library to spend a few hours with the handout that the instructor had left for the students. She liked to sit and study with absolute stillness, like a dog listening for its master. Every part of her body would be attentive, even her wrists, she thought, her spleen. What always made her do well was the presence of a mentor. Since she was very young, she had been the kind of girl who latched on to a teacher and stayed there. She took page upon page of neatly written notes; she also allied herself with the brightest teacher she could find who was also very kind and seemed interested in mentorship. That way, school was never frightening, and she never felt particularly alone.

This had happened in graduate school too; like almost all the other students in the fledgling department, Jill had become enamored of Dr. Michael Dearborn, one of the younger lights there. When he spoke during seminars, the graduate students felt a mixture of awe and jealousy, for he was not that much older than they were, and yet he possessed a fluency that they couldn't imagine ever possessing themselves. He was a handsome, black-bearded man who wore jeans and a tiny hoop earring and was said to be bisexual, the lover of a male semiotics graduate student at Brown. Jill was often among the group of acolytes who sometimes had beers with Dearborn at any number of bars along Bleecker Street. When the weather got warm they would all sit outside at night after their seminar, and he would stretch out his long legs and put his feet up on an empty metal chair, dominating conversation and talking in a ranging and free-associative way.

"When I was a precocious young thug at Yale, no more than nineteen, I went to hear Susan Sontag give a lecture about French theater," he said one night. "And afterward, at the little reception, I went up to her and said, 'Excuse me, Ms. Sontag,' or, no, worse, I think I said, 'Excuse me, *Susan*,' though I'd never met her before in my life. And then I said I thought that maybe there was a link between her remarks on Sartre and a certain feeling of dread and emptiness that I had noticed in 1970s popular culture, particularly television, which I'd grown up watching plenty of. I explained to her about the flatness of set on certain TV shows, the ugly burnt-orange color scheme, the use of the 'intrusive neighbor' to provide camaraderie—but really, inadvertently, to highlight the notion of the nuclear family's aloneness—and the generic and nightmarish dullness of the family construct that was always insisted upon in American television sitcoms of that period, like *Count Me In*, or *Back to Back*. And how the whole aesthetic seemed, in its own way, to reference the ugly entrapment that Sartre had depicted in *No Exit* and elsewhere."

The students around him sat in anticipation, excited, waiting to see where this would go. "So what did she say?" Jill had asked.

"Sontag? She said, 'Oh.' And then she said, 'Excuse me, I'm going to get some more cheese,' and she walked away."

"Did she actually get some more cheese?" another student thought to ask.

"No," said Dr. Dearborn after a moment, perplexed, as if just realizing this for the first time, though he'd told the story numerous times already. "She didn't, actually. She just started talking to some-one else."

They shook their heads sympathetically, and they put their beers to their lips in the half-dark outside the bar. He, like Susan Sontag, was both high and low, serious and frivolous, dark and beautiful and intelligent, and just beyond their reach.

"Should I be jealous of this Dearborn?" Donald asked that night when Jill came home to the apartment they were now able to live in on West Eleventh Street, primarily because of Jill's trust fund. Her family had founded the successful company Benecraft, which manu-factured shellac. "You are a *shellac heiress*," Amy had once marveled. Donald Hamlin was on the way toward double degrees: an MBA as well as a Ph.D. in accounting, "which is not the way it looks," he had assured her at the very beginning, when they had met at another graduate student's potluck dinner. Jill had convinced herself dur-ing that evening, before they'd had a chance to really speak, that Donald was a student either of history or philosophy; she had been a little disappointed when she learned the truth about his two fields of study. Donald was serious, observant, prematurely bald, slender in a pale blue Brooks Brothers shirt and pressed pants, his napkin opened on his lap. He resembled a polite greyhound as he sat on the floor by the coffee table, eating. He went on to prove to her that though he was cultivating "a somewhat wonkish persona," he would not become dull. "I am still going to be sarcastic and dry. I won't be like Dr. Michael Dearborn, of course," he said, "but I will try to be very piquant."

Jill saw that Donald didn't really understand exactly what she was studying; that the high-low, smorgasbord quality of her class work made no organic sense to him. Donald imagined that her doc-toral program was beyond him intellectually, and he seemed to like to think this, so she let him. But it wasn't really true, for he was extremely bright, and even she wasn't exactly sure of all the connections behind what she was studying, either, though she was generically excited by ideas—by the *idea* of ideas. Her powerful transference toward Michael Dearborn wasn't sexual. He had a seraphic face that was set into relief by his thick black beard, but she didn't want him to touch her. She wanted Donald, whom she now loved, to touch her; she wanted Michael Dearborn to love her academic work.

As long as Dearborn approved of her short papers and encouraged the direction of her thinking about the doctoral dissertation that lay ahead, she didn't falter. "Sometimes," Jill would tell Amy, who was then in law school in Michigan, "I have an uneasy sensation about staying in school so long."

"Oh, you mean because it's like never growing up?" said Amy.

"No. It's just that, as you know, I'm someone who always did well in school, and that's my primary strength, and one day it's going to catch up with me."

"I don't think so. You have to keep moving forward, that's all. School will end eventually, and then you're going to have to do something with all of it."

So on Jill went through the course work and the office hours with her advisor and mentor Michael Dearborn, and then she began the development of her thesis. After much embattled thinking and many long conversations in Dearborn's little office, she had chosen to write about "Women's Unheard Voices in Antebellum America," which would allow her to combine a particular Civil War interest with a twist of femaleness, "thus marrying history and politics," as she wrote in her proposal. The component of popular culture— always Dearborn's favorite part—would have no place here; there was no way she could sensibly draw it into her topic, though he was clearly a little disappointed. He wanted the students in the department to cast as wide a cultural net as possible in everything they studied, and he wanted them to trawl at the bottom of the culture for meaning too.

Then the actual writing began. She barely saw Dearborn anymore. He had sent her off with kind words and a distant glance toward the next student waiting outside in the hallway during office hours. Yes, he was her mentor, but he insisted that she would do just fine on her own during this protracted period. Jill, who was used to completing short papers and receiving compliments for them, now found herself stalling when she had to write something long all by herself. She sat in her apartment at times when she was meant to be working, and actually watched a string of the crummy old American television shows that Dearborn was so interested in.

Amy and Donald both told her that she should try to focus and "just get through it." She ought to write her thesis in one long burst, they said, and then go defend it and be done with it. Then she could start the search for an academic position somewhere in America. So she did what she was told, and artlessly she wrote her dissertation, feeling the loss of her mentor, picturing him in the classroom lecturing to a group of prethesis graduate students who lapped up the sweet wine of his intelligence. Lucky them; they weren't on their own yet.

"I should make an effigy of him," Donald said one afternoon upon coming home from work to find Jill slumped sadly at the desk she had set up in their bedroom. "Or I should pretend to be him. 'Look at me, I'm Dr. Dearborn. I once met Susan Sontag, and she gave me the brush-off. I like to groom my handsome beard.'" Jill stopped crying and began to laugh. "'Would *you* like to groom my handsome beard?'" Donald asked, and she moved into her husband's arms, telling him that he was the best, that he was as piquant as he'd said he would be, and that he was wonderful. She was fortunate, she knew, to have a husband who amused her and worked double-time to keep her buoyant. But regardless of her strong marriage, she still couldn't write her thesis well outside of the big shadow of a person more powerful than she was.

Eventually the writing got finished; she did her footnotes and she went through the motions of all that had to be accomplished: the acknowledgments page, the attention that had to be paid to the binding. But even as she did this, she knew, oh she knew. Dearborn had spoken to her in recent weeks about his worries about her dissertation, and when she walked into the seminar room late on a Friday afternoon in order to defend her thesis, the first face she saw was his. He sat at the far end of the table, looked up only briefly, then looked back down at the hard black-grained cover of her dissertation.

He squeaked his fingers along the table and seemed to be trying to let her know that she had let him down. Of course she had. A mentor, she knew, took pleasure from the achievements of the mentored. In their absence the mentor was personally insulted. Truly, Michael Dearborn looked angry. He barely spoke at all.

"Your writing seems diffuse to me," one of the others said in an irritated voice. "You don't seem sure enough of yourself. You've got the facts under your belt, but we get the sense that you don't trust your own instincts enough. You *suggest* very well, but then nothing is entirely brought to fruition. Did you and Dr. Dearborn discuss your central argument in depth? It doesn't seem as if you did."

The rejection left her gasping on the shallow front steps of the building afterward; a woman locking up a bicycle finally came over to her and asked if she needed help, because apparently Jill had been doubled over, her eyes shut against the pain of her own failure. She hadn't been able to tell the committee that in order for her thesis to have come out well she would have needed a mentor to sit beside her every single day while she formulated her ideas and then wrote them out.

"Maybe when you're feeling better, you could try to rewrite it, and publish it for a general audience. It's got a lot of interesting material," Donald said kindly that night. His own dissertation had been successful. It was larded with graphs and charts, and he'd gained mastery of all the necessary accounting and business concepts. The writing itself hadn't been an agony for him; he didn't still need a mentor at that point, he said. What Jill didn't understand, Donald explained when she questioned him, was that men eventually must *kill* their mentors. But Jill told him he just didn't understand what it meant to have been so promising your whole life and now to be so disappointing in the end.

But of course it wasn't the end; it couldn't possibly be. Jill was still young, and there were all those decades ahead to fill. This was the point at which her passion for her work dimmed into a new desire just for movement of some kind. She wouldn't be a graduate student anymore or eventually a college professor, and at the moment she couldn't imagine trying to rewrite her dissertation. She never wanted to look at it again; she was done.

"So what do you think you'll do?" Donald asked. Back then everybody did something.

Soon it had gotten around her group of friends that Jill, the perennial best student among them, had left graduate school. The news came to the attention of a college acquaintance, Claire Madding, who had been successful in film development, first at a major studio in L.A. and now, in recent days, in the New York office of a production company. Tilt-a-Whirl Productions had gotten attention for its small, prestigious films; when Claire first called to discuss the possibility of a job, Jill was surprised and pleased and didn't know what to do.

At lunch, Claire Madding said, "It's actually a good thing that you're getting out of academia. It's such a surreal place; it has no real relevance to the outside world." The two of them ate seared tuna salad in a minimalist SoHo restaurant near the Tilt-a-Whirl offices. Everyone at the tables in the room seemed as if they too worked in film or its less glamorous stepsister, book publishing. The young women were leggy and intense, and the men sweetly good-looking, in their soft baggy shirts and scatter of stubble. "There are quite a few refugees from academia in Hollywood; you'd be surprised," Claire said. "All of them were stopped in their tracks at one point or another in their academic careers. They were *relieved* to get into film. The guy who wrote the screenplay to *The Healing House*? Until recently he was in the doctoral program in linguistics at Harvard. Now he gets high six figures. I considered grad school too," she went on, "but these days you end up having to fight for a tenure-track job at some second-rate Mennonite college. Not that I even know of any first-rate Mennonite college," she added with a chirping laugh. "And then you spend the rest of your life living somewhere you would never have chosen to live."

"I don't know anything about film," Jill said. "I only know about school. I've been in school forever."

"Then you would be so great in film, Jill. You're smart and serious.

And of course it doesn't hurt that you're this tall, blonde person. Tilt-a-Whirl is in an exciting place right now. But we're still in our infancy, and we're trying to bring in a select group of smarty-pants types. And I know Selby will really get you."

"I don't think I've ever been called a smarty-pants type before," Jill said. But she was flattered, flushed. This was the temporary antidote to having had her dissertation rejected. She wanted to telephone Amy immediately in Michigan and ask her whether she was absolutely sure it was all right for Jill to exchange all that graduate school for *this*. Was education meaningless if you didn't do something with it, or was it justifiable in and of itself, bolstering you for the world that lay ahead, whatever it turned out to be?

At first, being part of the development group at Tilt-a-Whirl felt like being on the ride itself; Jill was off-balance, disoriented. The staff slouched on low couches and free-associated aloud about the films that they wanted the company to produce. Everyone had high-flown, dreamy ideas, which were encouraged. They agreed that they hoped to develop a really beautiful biopic; the name Willa Cather was mentioned longingly more than once. The head of Tilt-a-Whirl was Selby Rothberg, forty-three, based in L.A., tall and thin, her shock-white hair gelled and chaotic. She used lip balm obsessively, swiping it from its little pot while she was thinking, and during meetings. She was known to have no real personal life—no friends, no lovers, no children—to be only about work, to be difficult, people in the office said with a tinge of admiration, for they knew how rough it was for a woman trying to gain credibility and traction in Hollywood—or, really, anywhere.

Mostly, Selby Rothberg was difficult to PAs during movie shoots and to office assistants bearing floppy cardboard carriers of lattes. She yelled at them freely. Still, young women looked up to her, for she was someone who had survived the ritualistic antifemale hazing that all women in the industry had to endure if they wanted to get anywhere. Jill looked up to her too, without really knowing her at all. She was primed for the mentor-protégé relationship, although in this case she knew that Selby Rothberg might not even be aware that the potential for such a relationship existed.

Of course Selby needed to vent, they all said; of course she needed catharsis. They could understand this. Men still dominated the industry even then, decades after feminism had been established, though women were coming up through the ranks with a kind of stealth now, as if not wanting anyone to notice how much power they were gathering, until one day it would be too late, and women would have *taken over* Hollywood, producing and directing an entire slate of sensitive films about strong, interesting female characters like Willa Cather. Until that day in the utopian middle distance, stealth was the main tactic.

Jill, early into her job, had the idea to try to option Amy's mother's first and still her most well-known historical novel, *Turning Around and Going Home*. All the characters, except for the farmer lover, were women. Amy had told Jill that Canadian writers tended to have a hard time finding many American readers because their books were often "about the land," and, of course, that land was Canadian; much time, in these novels, might be spent describing the view from Bathurst Inlet. But Antonia Lamb's work, while being geographically detailed, also focused on character, and her first, exquisite novel from the 1970s seemed to Jill as though it could pleasingly be reimagined for film.

Selby Rothberg read the book, or at least read Jill's synopsis, and gave her the go-ahead to option it for a small sum. Antonia Lamb was so excited and sent Jill flowers on the day the contracts arrived in the mail in Montreal. Jill began to take meetings with a young screenwriter to talk about the adaptation; she wrote up elaborate progress reports that were then faxed to Selby in L.A. She returned home late at night to find Donald often already asleep.

One afternoon, it got around the office that her colleague Claire Madding had just received word that a film project she had been quietly nurturing had gotten the green light from the studio. It was about a professional assassin sent for reeducation to an assassins' academy after a botched job, and it was going to be a big, violent, expensive film with male stars and, said Claire, "a beautiful demographic." Jill had not recalled hearing the word "demographic" used in casual conversation until that moment, but once she heard Claire use it, she began to hear it spoken everywhere. She and the two other people in development talked anxiously: Why hadn't Claire told them about this project? Why were the rest of them made to think their mandate was solely to make quiet, meaningful, literary films?

Soon, faxes chugged in from Selby in the L.A. office, asking them "to think more about who would actually go see your film once it got made." You could not just bring in sensitive women viewers, she said; no one really wanted them anymore. Or else everyone wanted them, as long as they came to the film with their boyfriends and their younger brothers. "THE YOUNG MALE DEMOGRAPHIC IS ESSENTIAL," Selby wrote in a fax. "IF WE DON'T HAVE THAT, PEOPLE, WE ARE FUCKED."

Three months later, *Turning Around and Going Home* was dropped. Jill could not explain to Amy's mother that just because a film production company was run by a strong woman did not mean, in the end, that its product would be progressive or sophisticated or, of course, about women.

"This is not going to be good," Jill said to Amy on the phone. "I can see the way it's all heading." Selby Rothberg, who had been described with such admiration by the staff, finally turned her anger on the New York office, and none of them should have been caught off guard, yet they all were. They were not bringing in enough projects of the sort she now wanted to foster, she said. (Except, it was understood, for Claire Madding, who had been promoted, and moved to the L.A. office.) They did not understand her MISSION, and they had BETTER PULL IT TOGETHER, ASAP.

The three remaining development people, Jill, Harold, and Peter, convened secretly at a coffee shop around the corner from the office one morning to discuss what to do. They decided that one of them would call Selby in L.A. and say to her, on speakerphone, "Selby, we really respect you as our employer, and of course you're an incredible mentor, and we think you're brilliant, and please don't take this the wrong way, but we don't think you've been treating us fairly." They drew straws and shy, slight Peter Chen was designated the imparter of these words. He almost hyperventilated when he was chosen. The phone call was to be made at lunchtime.

But by eleven A.M. EST, Selby Rothberg had sent a fax to say that she was shutting down the New York office—or at least the studio was—and so as a result none of them ever had a chance to tell her the way they felt. Jill, suddenly without a job, was frantic and humiliated.

"I have failed at two things," she said to Donald the night she lost her job. "It is not what I do."

"You didn't entirely fail at the first thing. You just haven't reimagined it," he said. "And the second thing has nothing to do with you."

"Those are semantic distinctions," she said, but again she was relieved by his belief in her. He was optimistic, she realized. His parents were living; he did not have a mother who had killed herself. A parent who commits suicide, people said, leaves a door open for the child to do the same thing someday too, as if following the parent into oblivion. Donald, though, knew nothing of this door. He was both an optimist and a pragmatist, and she was grateful for this paradox. Jill clung to him. They were young then and married and living in New York City, and love drew a circle around them both. They would have a baby, they decided one night shortly after, in the agitation of lovemaking. This seemed like a good time, didn't it? Jill was "between things" and would not have to put off a career. She could think about reworking her dissertation later on, after the baby was born. She could rewrite the whole thing over a series of nap times.

But no matter what they tried, they could not conceive. They spent a year and a half trying, and then they started arranging for Jill to have injections, and for Donald's sperm to be spun and washed. It was a full-time job for her, and it replaced actual work. In bed at night Jill thought only about hormone levels and ovulation schedules.

Eventually, their story ended like many couples' did: After years of this, bowed and spent, ravaged and dry, debased from procedures that had had no effect, they found their way to an adoption agency called The House of Hope, which dealt exclusively with Eastern European babies—"trafficked in them," Donald said darkly.

After all that sex and loss they were now open to anything. Suddenly, the idea of someone else's newborn baby delivered into the world and handed over to them while still damp from its uterine bath became an unrealistic image. Now they could actually begin to consider adopting a dried-off, much older baby.

Manya was whom they were finally offered, and her photograph was solemnly passed around the caseworker's small office. What they saw in that Polaroid snapshot was a wide, round face revealing an expression not of actual happiness but perhaps a wish for happiness. They were told that Manya resided in a large room in the orphanage among many other babies and possessed very little language. They were warned that her skin was prone to rashes and that she had been diagnosed with "a nervous constitution," which could mean anything or nothing, because the Russian pediatric academy used terminology that had no English-language equivalents.

They had also been warned about one of the orphanage's policies: In order for a non-Russian couple to adopt a baby, the child had to have been previously rejected by three Russian couples. What was so wrong with Manya that none of her kinsmen had wanted her? Was it her rashiness, her silence? Mrs. Feld, the caseworker, whispered that while the orphanage *claimed* the three-Russian-couples rule, there was rarely any documentation to prove that anyone else had previously refused the child.

"Show me the Refuseniks," Donald had said.

"Pardon?" Mrs. Feld said.

"Donald, shut up," said Jill. Then, to Mrs. Feld, "Ha ha, he's just trying to be funny."

"Yes, I'm a jokester," said Donald blithely.

Jill disliked her husband turning deadpan funny in front of people who didn't know him. No one could ever tell when he was joking, because they saw him as a thin, bald, well-dressed accountant, which in their minds meant that he could not also be wry and deadpan; the two images seemed to have no business being in the same frame.

But Mrs. Feld at The House of Hope hadn't minded or even paid much attention to Donald's mild jokes, and so the slush of paperwork continued, along with the FBI fingerprinting and the home study, and eventually they made the long, multilegged trip to Tuva. The orphanage, to Jill's surprise, was a bright, sanitary place, and though the large, barracks-style bedroom was congested with babies, the attendants who worked there proudly fretted over them.

When Donald and Jill walked through the room, a musclebound woman was tickling the plump baby girl who occupied the crib beside Manya's, and another woman was making goo-goo faces as she changed a baby boy's loaded diaper. The problem was that there weren't nearly enough of these women to go around, and most of the babies had to wait their turn to receive something as basic as a hand scrabbling to tickle a chin.

"Look, look, here is your Manya, waiting to meet Mama and Papa," another woman said proudly, bringing the wide-eyed, serious-looking baby to them.

"Oh, Manya!" cried Donald, and he flung out his arms and began to cry.

"Manya!" Jill echoed, but her throat constricted. A real baby, she saw, not just a photograph, made you think about possibilities, and also about death. Specifically, about the unbearableness of death—the end of possibilities. She thought of how her dead mother would never see this baby or be a grandmother. Her father, who had died of pancreatic cancer years earlier, would never see the baby, either, of course, but it was to thoughts about her mother, Susan Benedict, that Jill cleaved. She shielded herself against the flying sparks of sensation, the way she had once imagined she would have to do during childbirth. When Manya was zipped into a pink snowsuit and handed over to these American strangers, Jill could still not cry, though Manya and her new father were both crying in hearty bleats.

Jill busied herself with paperwork, and she also took as many photographs as she could with the little camera she had brought along, relieved to be hidden behind it even briefly.

We don't *belong together,* she thought later as they rode in the beaten, boxy Lada to the airport. Their baby, as in the Polaroid picture, had a perfectly round face, black hair, pale, eczematous skin, and eyes spread far apart. Jill was very pretty and blonde, and Donald was bald and physically vaguely insectlike. They sat together in the springless backseat, and the baby, imprisoned between them, wept for all she was leaving and all she was about to get.

"Hold on, little girl, it's going to be okay," Donald said through his own giddy tears. "Mommy and Daddy have you now." It was startling to hear him speak this way, his voice cracking like a romantic's.

I am so sorry, stoic Jill silently told her. My own need for a baby got so strong that eventually you felt it all the way on another continent, and got sucked out of your surprisingly pleasant orphanage, and away from the highly perfumed women who cared for you and spoke to you in your language, and dabbed Vaseline on your rashy cheeks, and fed you little sips of beef-tongue soup, and did the best they could under difficult circumstances.

So now Jill would have to do the best she could too. In New York City, Manya became Nadia, and she and Jill were alone together during the long days while Donald was at work. Sometimes in desperation Jill would plant Nadia in her high chair in front of the television for a couple of hours, hoping that the mix of voices and pictures and commercials would entertain or teach her. Jill enrolled her in Maestro 'n' Mommy, an interactive class that Amy had taken Mason to, in order to grip bacterially overrun maracas while listening to original songs that whipped everyone into revival-tent ecstasy. The name of the class sounded uncomfortably suggestive, as though Mommy was having an affair during the day with the maestro while the baby watched somberly. It depressed Jill to see the way that mothers were bossed around. "Remember, moms," said the young instructor, "always make sure your little ones are no more than *one maestro's baton length* away from you."

The mothers obeyed; they guarded their children, and they gamely sang the prescribed songs that came on the CD you had to buy when you signed up for the class. *"Rum tum tum and a ho ho ho,"* sang the willing and tired mothers. *"Everybody on your trikes, and go go go."* Nadia became just one baby among many in that class and among the volume of stroller traffic on the city's sidewalks, and no one seemed to recognize how different she was, except for Jill, who was forever appraising Nadia's face and trying to imagine her becoming a schoolgirl and then a woman. Jill found herself unable to picture a direct and gratifying route taking Nadia from toddlerhood to adolescence to adulthood.

Once, early on, when Jill and Amy were together at the Golden Horn and Nadia lay asleep in her stroller, Jill said to Amy, "I have to ask you something. Do you like Nadia?"

"What? No, Jill, I actively dislike your two-year-old daughter. She is such a bitch."

Jill tried to laugh at the little joke. "But come on, do you really like her? Please just think about it."

"Look at her sleeping there. She is beautiful, and she is your baby. That means I automatically like her. I automatically love her. Why? Do you not like Mason?"

"Of course I like Mason. I love him too. I don't even know why I asked you this. Ignore me."

But Amy had looked concerned. "I think," she'd said, "you just have to be patient and see how things unroll. That's what parenthood is, basically."

"What do you mean?" Jill asked.

"All these long waiting periods. And then things happen all of a sudden—these developmental growth spurts—and you end up saying, 'I can't believe it went by so fast.' Even though everybody always warned you it would."

In bed at night now, looking up at the constellations on the ceiling of her new room and thinking thoughts that her mother could not imagine, six-year-old Nadia Hamlin sang to herself that strange song of uncertain origin. Her voice was interesting but parched-sounding, the words smashed together. To the extent that Jill could figure, it was some kind of folk song that Nadia had probably learned back at the orphanage and had retained in the peculiar way that certain small details in life might be retained forever.

Nadia lay on her back in the dark, and over and over she sang that single line: *"Rise, sorrow, 'neath the saffron sister tree."* The words were elusive and beautiful. Why would the children have been singing in English back in that orphanage in Russia? Maybe as a way to prepare them for the American families they would likely be joining? It didn't exactly make sense. The first time that Jill had heard the plaintive song, she was shocked and moved, picturing Nadia standing alone in her crib in Tuva, bouncing lightly on a mattress and singing.

Rise, sorrow, 'neath the saffron sister tree—what words for a baby to know! American toddlers were usually taught some of the more anodyne Beatles songs, the house music of Maestro 'n' Mommy, and all the songs from that somewhat manic children's TV show *Ahoy, Mateys.* Jill sometimes tried to ask Nadia about her song and to tell her that folk songs were an essential part of a country's tradition. For a brief moment she had imagined her daughter developing a folkloric fascination. ("Yes, Nadia is a professional *folklorist,*" she would tell her friends years from now, enjoying the yeasty syllables of the word.) But the song remained simply the song, and it had not yet led to an interest or a passion for anything in particular. Nadia sang other, identifiable songs too; quite often she could be found humming or singing, but music seemed to be some sort of private experience for her, not the joyful and communal one that it was for many children.

Was Nadia mentally retarded? You could put off the truth for a surprisingly long time, even in this sophisticated time in the culture. She had known a couple back in the city named the Devlins whose autistic son Teddy had gone undiagnosed for years. His problems were obvious: He disliked eye contact, and he loved thermostats. Once, on a visit to another family's apartment, he broke off the tiny red metal needle of their thermostat, and making sure everyone saw him, he put it slyly into his mouth, as though he thought this was witty. But you weren't meant to mention any concerns to Teddy's parents, for if the suspicions were not true, then it would be an enormous insult, from which your friendship would not recover. Besides, his own pediatrician was not worried yet. "We can't have an entire world of extroverts," the pediatrician had said more than once when the mother expressed her fears.

No one would dare tell Jill that Nadia was a little slow. None of Jill's friends in the city had said a word to this effect, and she had no real friends here in Holly Hills. A few of the mothers in this suburb appeared friendly or articulate or both, but they also struck Jill as being as opaque and smooth as their houses. It wasn't lost on her that Nadia, so far, had no friends here yet, either.

"I'm just not interested in the women here," Jill said simply over the phone to Amy during the first week that school started this fall.

"They can't all be one way. There's got to be one person you'd like. Even just one."

"I'm sure there is." Probably Amy was right, and there were all kinds of women pocketed away in their houses, including smart ones who read demanding books and were invested in what happened in the world around them and were also kind of a kick to be around. But Jill wasn't looking for new friends. "I'm too old," she said. Then she felt the need to add, sullenly, "You're not, though."

"What?"

"Penny Ramsey. She's your new friend."

"Oh. Well yes, true," said Amy.

But Jill couldn't imagine finding a new person to be close to. She had Amy and several others in the city, and they knew her and accepted her. They also accepted Nadia, treating her as if she were just like their own children, which she wasn't. Amy's son Mason tended to be sullen and entitled but was also clearly snapping smart. He knew everything about aeronautics and the cosmos and American history. When he was younger he read books with titles like *Look at Me, I'm Benjamin Franklin!* and for years had eaten breakfast on a plastic place mat with the presidents' disembodied heads floating on

a field of red, white, and blue, so that he had long ago internalized all
their names and relevant dates.

A few years earlier, Jill had been at Amy's apartment when Mason
began talking about how William Howard Taft's obese corpse had
had to be lowered from his window in a piano box and how George
Washington "was not the actual first president," but instead someone named John Hanson was, having been elected in 1781 by the
Continental Congress. Even Mason's use of the word "actual" was
somewhat depressing to Jill. Nadia would never have used that word;
it wasn't in her vocabulary, nor was "continental," or "congress." What
Nadia knew about the American presidents could fit inside the tini-
est of all the Russian nesting matryoshka dolls.

But it wasn't just a lack of knowledge that distinguished Nadia
from other children. Several times a week in the morning, she
appeared in her parents' bedroom and stood waiting for the alarm
clock to ring, so that she could shut it off before her mother had a
chance to. Jill did not know how this practice had started, and no
matter how many times she asked Nadia to stay in bed, to please
sleep in, the little girl always woke up first and walked silently into
the master bedroom, standing there in anticipation of the tinny *BIP
BIP BIP* clarion call.

"Wake up, Mom," Nadia would say with great seriousness as she
stood there.

In her guilt at her own ambivalence, Jill would reach out her long
arms from the bed and sweep the solid and stoic Nadia against her.
Their bodies in pale fairylike nightgowns collided awkwardly. "Good
morning, sweet pea," she'd say. "Let's get the day started."

But now, at eleven P.M. on a cold night in October, when Jill
heard Nadia singing her strange folk song, she went into the room
only briefly and then went back out. Nadia exhausted her, or at least
her worries about Nadia exhausted her, and all she wanted now was
to lie in bed and read the new book she had bought about the Civil
War; always, every season, there was another new book about some
underexplored facet of the Civil War. If Jill had become an historian,

she might have written one of them, and she found herself sometimes critical of their content or style, as though she thought that
she herself could have done better, which she knew was absurd.

And then she wanted sleep.

Unlike Nadia, Jill wouldn't have trouble falling asleep tonight,
because she had five milligrams of Noctrem to guide her down into
the depths. She had taken it almost every night since moving here;
it made life tolerable. Before she started taking Noctrem she'd suf-
fered chronic insomnia. It had begun after her mother's death, and
over the years she had refused to take the sleeping pills she'd been
offered. The drugs all had sedative effects, and she wanted to stay
animated and alert the next day; she didn't want to change her basic
self, despite her grief and the way it would not let her rest. But in
the past year, everyone had been speaking about the non-sedating
power of Noctrem; they talked about it at dinner parties in the same
animated way that, in earlier decades, they had once talked about
important novels or plays.

Recently, though, there had been some reports of problems with
Noctrem that had received attention in the science section of the
newspaper. Very occasionally, someone on the drug did something
bizarre in the middle of the night: A man in Pennsylvania walked
out into the garden behind his house in the pitch dark and began
planting sunflower seeds. A woman in California phoned the police
and confessed that she had shoplifted a tube of Kiss Me Twice lip-
stick thirty years earlier. A woman on a transatlantic flight took the
pill when she got on the plane, hoping to sleep the whole way, but
found that the drug wasn't working, and so she spent the trip sitting in her bulkhead seat filling in a very difficult cryptic crossword
puzzle in the British newspaper, one of those tough ones that everyone in the UK seems constitutionally able to solve, with clues such
as "Hounds who eat jam before Boxing Day? I'll say that's a bit of a
muddle! (8)." When the plane landed at Heathrow, she awakened to
find the puzzle on her lap, completely untouched. Instead of filling
in the squares, the woman had apparently spent the flight happily

drawing enormous circles over her breasts on the front of her white blouse with her pen while everyone walking up and down the aisle had watched her.

But most people tolerated Noctrem fine, Jill included. Without it, she did not know how she would ever shut down her anxieties about Nadia. Donald had gotten into bed at nine, as he did five nights a week. Jill felt widowed late at night, because he was rarely there to talk to her or rub her feet or listen to her worries about Nadia's intellectual inadequacies or her descriptions of her own loneliness.

Her desire to leave the city had been as intermittently fierce as Donald's; in spasms she had felt an ache for safety and lawns, as though somehow lawns themselves could provide safety, and shrubbery and fences could create a fortification against nuclear holocaust. Forty-eight miles away, the entire city might one day tilt and slide into the river, but the residents of Holly Hills would survive. At first, after September 11, the exodus from the city had been slow and deliberate, not immediate and hysterical, the way the real estate agents roaming the suburbs in their cars had probably secretly hoped but would never say. Instead, throughout that fall and into the start of the new year, city people occasionally left, trading in footage for acreage.

Some left with candid sadness, suspecting that this meant that being young was over. Soon the men, who had once gone clubbing, began to worry that they would be wearing thick, feminizing sweaters on weekends and operating garden tools that quaked in their unsure hands. The women, for their part, pictured themselves chopping scallions forever at an island in the center of an enviably big and futuristic kitchen. Jill and Donald had taken several years after the attack to consider the idea of selling the apartment and leaving, before they finally got up the nerve or the resignation and acted swiftly. Having done so and then having settled into the house on Jacob's Path, Jill had immediately begun longing for what she'd voluntarily given up.

Holly Hills had seemed, at the buildup to the move, like a seductive and reasonable alternative to the city; it gave its residents ample ammunition against the question Why would you ever live there? Because, you could respond, it was less than an hour away from the city, and it had an enormous slate-and-glass public library as well as a Pacific Rim fusion restaurant that featured a bar where you could order wasabi oyster shooters. The schools were equipped for the twenty-first century and were tuition-free. The town had an arts center that, the winter before, had performed the entire cycle of Wagner's *Der Ring des Nibelungen* over four nights, with strudel warming on a hot plate and *Kaffee mit Schlag* available in the lobby during intermission. Afterward, all the couples who had attended left the parking lot in a long line of cars, their high beams flipped on in the darkness of such an unusually late night for this neck of the world. Vapor swirled in the headlights. They sat in their cold cars, yawning but happy; everyone felt that they had received something unusual that evening, that they had been nourished by it, that their lives here were not entirely mall-dominated or at all empty, as some people in the city assumed.

What more could you want from a place? Wasn't it enough that there was a palpable attempt to create an alternate, tolerable world? Wasn't it enough that everyone out here had apparently said, "The city does not have to have a claim on us forever. We can go far and wide, into green lawns and broad, quiet streets, away from the possibility of terror, and no matter what happens, we will still be who we are."

But sometimes in the darkening afternoon, when the new house was spectacularly quiet, Jill knew that she had partly used the attack on the towers as an excuse to leave. It had simply accelerated, not precipitated, their departure from a city that increasingly seemed hard and ruthless. Besides, she remembered how much she herself had liked growing up surrounded by greenery, first as a young girl outside Philadelphia and then later on at boarding school. Nadia craved the outdoors too; it seemed selfish to keep her under constant watch in the city. She was not a child who needed culture and sophistication in order to be complete. Actually, did any child ever really need those things, or was this just what parents told themselves? The move had been inevitable; something had been bound to make them jump, and this, they told everyone, was it. She always had the sense that someone she loved was about to leave, that there would be an imminent experience of loss. It was better to be the one who leaves, Jill thought, than the one who is left.

"I don't know," Donald had said of the name Holly Hills when they had first been driven around to look at the older, well-tended houses on the market and the newer, starker ones. "It sounds to me like a porn star."

"Well, then that's a *plus*," the realtor had replied cheerfully at the wheel.

Now, each morning, Donald made the four-minute drive to the train station and stood on the dew-damp platform with his briefcase and newspaper, like a throwback to an earlier era. There were always several women there, but it was primarily men on that platform, while at home many of their wives slept on for a little while longer, waiting to be awakened by their own alarms.

Jill was always among the population of the sleeping, and when Donald left the house and drove away, she stayed behind with Nadia, the child she could not understand: flesh of her flesh who wasn't really of her flesh at all, though if she said this aloud, she would have seemed cold. So she said nothing, and her silence was interpreted as the silence of any mother who loved her child so hard and so fiercely that she never had to say a word.

D o you know anybody yet?" Roberta Sokolov asked right away as they positioned themselves on their rubber mats on the living room floor. "Not that I'm rushing you."

"I know a few people," said Jill.

"Name names."

"Leave her alone," Amy said. "She'll come around."

It was the morning of Columbus Day, and Amy, Karen, and Roberta had taken the train out to Holly Hills. The purpose of the visit was the casual yoga class that the four of them had been running for the past couple of years in rotating homes. Today was Jill's turn, and so the group had dutifully convened here at 11 Jacob's Path. Nadia, who was home from school today, had followed her mother from room to room all morning, asking if she could help straighten up. Jill gave her a little bowl of potpourri to put in the guest bathroom, and she thought how strange it was that she had become someone who had potpourri on hand. Back in the city, no one she knew had potpourri.

"I actually did meet some people recently," Jill said. "They were fine. But I don't think we're going to be friends."

"Why not?" asked Roberta.

Jill began to tell them about how, a few weeks earlier, she had received an invitation from one of the mothers in Nadia's first-grade class at the local public school. Her name was Sharon Gregorius, and Jill had seen her at drop-off in the line of vans and SUVs and the occasional hybrid electric car. Back doors were flung wide, one by one, and the chauffeur-mothers called out, "Bye! Have a good day! Bye! Bye!" and then continued on along the mazy wooded roads and commercial turnpikes.

One day, a large silver family van had pulled up parallel to Jill's car, and the window lowered, revealing a redheaded woman. "I'm Juliana's mom," said Sharon Gregorius, leaning across the seat as far as her seat belt would allow. "I saw you at the class breakfast. I wanted to say hi and invite you to something. A kind of scheme of mine. Can you come? Forty-six Daniel's Lane."

So Jill, if only because she could not imagine what this meant—a *scheme?*—decided to go. In the Gregoriuses' dining room, she went and sat at the maple table of the pale gray colonial along with several other mothers, eating those rolled-up turkey pinwheel sandwiches that were delicious but had long ago become a cliché: "the sundried tomato of our time," Amy had said. The women themselves were not all one *type*, as she had condemned them in her mind. One of them was amusing and arch, and reminded Jill of a girl at boarding school who had once climbed onto the slate roof of the Westaway Refectory and planted a dildo on the weathervane. Another woman, a former therapist, had an empathic if slightly moony manner. Jill could imagine lying down on the couch in this woman's living room and telling her about her mother and about her fears about Nadia. But, sternly, she did not allow herself to become socially involved with these new women. Jill had listened as Sharon Gregorius spoke. This was a business proposition, Sharon said. She was going to present to them the prospectus for the creation of a greeting card company called Wuv Cards, whose name had been derived from the bastardized phrase "I wuv you."

"What differentiates this line of cards from every other," said Sharon, "is that these are for kids."

"I'm playing devil's advocate here, but lots of greeting cards are for kids," said the former therapist, whose name was Denise.

"True, but what will make Wuv Cards distinctive is the fact that they will be the only ones designed to be from kids to their parents. Look, I know that it's extremely hard to break in any new product. I worked in the wall-coverings industry for ten years. It was always a lot easier to handle the tried-and-true, but whenever our sales team had to deal with something new, there was a certain enthusiasm about it. I haven't worked since the kids were born, but I'm sure it's still the same way. Or I hope it is," she added with a laugh. "Now, these are just mock-ups; my kids helped me with the desktop publishing aspect. Once we get them printed for real, they'll look much more professional."

Sharon passed the mock-ups around, and the women wiped their turkey-hands on napkins and peered at the desktop-published cards, laughing a little or nodding, or politely saying they were quirky. One read: **"Mom and Dad, I messed up BIG TIME."** And inside, it read: **"And I'm really sorry."** On the cover of another: **"Mom and Dad, I have something I need to tell you."** When you opened the card, you saw the words **"YOU WERE ADOPTED."**

"Sharon, this one's funny," said one of the women.

"I'm glad."

"I'm sorry, I don't really get it," Jill found herself saying. She had barely meant for anyone to hear her, but now it was too late.

"Oh no?" said Sharon. "That's not good. We'll tweak it."

"Sorry, maybe it's me."

"Well, I should explain what we were going for," said Sharon. "In real life, parents would tell the *child* that he's adopted, but in this case the child gets to pretend that his parents, who of course seem nothing like him—"

"No, I understand the concept. It's fine. But I mean the whole thing…I guess I have to ask why would children actually spend their own money on these cards?"

Sharon looked so unhappy, and all the others grew quiet and unsmiling at Jill's candor. She was already the interloper, and she was being subtly tested here at this lunch, and look how she'd behaved. The joke about adoption bothered her, but also both the idea and the name of the line of cards were clearly dumb. Couldn't everyone see that? But the others had been sitting there looking at the mock-ups and thinking of putting money into this venture, and one of them was even taking notes on her BlackBerry. Jill began to feel sickish; the taste of the turkey pinwheel was suddenly gamey in her mouth. Was it venison? she thought, disgusted and a little panicky at the whole scene. Was it rabbit? Was it a *monkey* pinwheel? She could not bear being here in this house.

"It's good to hear criticism," said Sharon Gregorius evenly. "We really need that at this stage. So thanks for that, Jill." Then, to the table, she added cryptically, "Jill worked in film."

"So there you have it," Jill said now at yoga. "They made an overture of friendship. They tried to include me. And they were nice, and at least one of them seems like she might even be interesting. But there are two words for why I am not becoming friends with these women: 'Wuv Cards.'"

They laughed, for it was easy to laugh and all hold the very same views; they had always done it, and it was like breathing. But Amy, unrolling her yoga mat in Jill's sunny living room by the potted fig tree, said, "I don't know. Maybe you're being hard on them."

"How so?" Jill said.

"I know you have a lot of regrets about moving here. Maybe you didn't give them a fair shake. But at least they're trying to do something with themselves now that their kids are in school. I mean, *I* haven't figured it all out for myself yet, and Mason's in fourth grade."

"I don't know," said Karen. "Why do you say 'at least' they're trying? Does everyone always have to 'do' something? Can't they just enjoy their lives? I do."

"But they've got no innate sense of imperative," said Jill. "They have to make it up, and you can almost see the effort. All of them worked before, and all of them stopped."

"Right," said Amy. "Partly because corporate America didn't love them."

"How do you know that, Amy? Just because you wanted out forever?"

Amy paused for a moment. "I don't know that it's 'forever,'" she said. "I think about working all the time. I am slowly heading toward some formal volunteer position; I don't know why it's taking me so long, but it just is. And I know that a group of women whose kids have started school and who are a little bored and want to put their former business knowledge to use and create some kind of start-up are supposed to be encouraged, right? That's what my mother would say."

"Not every idea should be encouraged," said Jill. "Isn't there something better that people can do with their time?"

"But I guess I don't understand why you're so concerned about what other people do with their time. Would you want them to judge the way you spend *your* time?"

The other women stayed upright on their mats, their spines straight, frozen in attention. They had never heard Amy and Jill, such close friends for so many years, speak fiercely to each other. They were slightly shocked and uneasily excited, listening to this.

"Back in the city," Jill said after a moment, "you and Karen and Roberta all live in the center of commerce of the entire world, and yet you've chosen to drop out. Out here, everyone's sort of agreed to drop out in a way, whether they work or not. I mean, they're all staying away from the geographical epicenter, like it's this hot stove."

"I wouldn't say I've dropped out," Karen said, but no one replied.

"Who says the city equals life?" asked Amy. "Why are we assuming that? People live in all kinds of places all over America. Aren't cities just these fake constructs? Didn't you used to tell me something like that back in graduate school, when you were studying urbanism or something?"

"Yes, but I'm much older, and I see it differently now," Jill said. "Donald and I left because of Nadia."

"I just think your attitude could hurt you," Amy said, more gently now. "You sound like you have contempt for the place where you chose to live."

"'Contempt' is a very harsh word," said Jill.

"I just feel protective of you. And my God, I miss you. You're my closest friend. Don't forget that I'm the one who got left behind."

"I gather you're adapting," Jill said dryly.

"You mean Penny?"

"Yes."

"I've told you, she is a really good person," said Amy. "She's interesting and smart, and she's involved in all aspects of the arts. She said it's really disturbing the way funding for the arts has been dismantled."

"I don't need Penny Ramsey to tell me that," Roberta said. "It was that way when I left art school."

"But it got ten times worse under the Republicans," said Amy.

"Isn't her husband a big Republican donor? Greg Ramsey?"

"He is, but it's complicated."

"Well, I hope you'll both be very happy together," Jill suddenly put in, laughing unpleasantly. The single syllable of her laughter came out like a gong in the echoing room.

"She's not what you think, you know," said Amy.

"I don't think anything," said Jill. "Why shouldn't you be friends with her? It's no more or less surprising than you becoming friends with anyone else."

"Well, it would be less surprising than, I don't know, Geralynn Freund," offered Karen.

"Oh, poor Geralynn," Roberta said. "It's awful."

"Let's get started," Jill said suddenly. She didn't want to hear any more bulletins from her abandoned city life. And, she suddenly realized with an unexpectedly pleasurable feeling, she now hated Penny Ramsey.

So they turned on the DVD and began their makeshift yoga class. For once Jill was relieved not to talk but just to stay in one place and move her long body swiftly, fluidly. "Class" was an inexact word, because all they really did was sit in a row in front of someone's plasma TV and assume an unbroken flow of *vinyasa* poses to an instructional DVD. But it didn't matter; the class had been created, Jill knew, in order to provide some partial shape to their day, to give them purpose.

Once, long before Jill was a graduate student or a film development person, back when she was young and just beginning at the Pouncey School in New Hampshire, she didn't have to worry about what she would do with all her learning; that wasn't meant to concern her. Learning and preparing were enough, and that had carried her through school. She had loved the all-girl residential environment; it was a relief not to hear the voices of boys everywhere, or even anywhere. Later on, as graduation approached, the boylessness caused all the girls to become a little agitated and skittish. But for a long time everyone felt that adolescent boys were as dominating and dangerous as rutting elk and that it was better to be kept apart from them during this vulnerable time, when girls' intellects were first being formed.

Jill was also relieved to be out of her home, though she hadn't known she would feel this way. Susan Benedict had often looked to her young daughter to make certain decisions, even ones that seemed trivial. When Jill was eight, the meter man had rung the doorbell of the house, and her mother had come into the living room, asking her, "What do you think I should do?"

"Well, I guess you should let him in."

"But I can't tell for certain that he's really the meter man," said Susan Benedict, and Jill recalled that she had looked as anxious as a child. The meter man was eventually let in, and Jill watched as her mother nervously followed him downstairs to the basement, making sure that he actually was who he said he was.

Jill knew, in such slightly disconcerting moments, that her mother was more frightened and tentative than other mothers, but Jill almost admired these qualities. They had a beauty to them, as though her mother were a flower, and all the other mothers were logs. During the times when Susan Benedict became excessively sad and said she needed to stay quiet for a few hours, Jill would come sit on the side of the bed in the dim master bedroom and talk to her mother about school and her brothers and a book she was reading. Jill's mother would ask her questions and sometimes would tell her stories from when she had been an actress, and had appeared in a single Broadway musical, *A Funny Thing Happened on the Way to the Forum*, before giving up her career.

Jill never understood exactly what was wrong with her mother, only that she felt compelled to retreat from the family every once in a while. Jill would help her do this; her older brothers—scrambling, wild, independent—certainly never did, and her father was off in his office at the Benecraft shellac factory all the time. "It must have been really hard for you," Jill's friends said in adulthood, when she described those early days. But a sad mother isn't so difficult to manage, at least not at first, when you don't even realize she's sad, exactly. Jill had actually enjoyed sitting on the bed beside her mother, hearing about her theatrical days.

"Don't go into theater," Susan had advised from the half-darkened room. "The life is very unstable. It was wonderful to be in Tennessee Williams plays, though; he was so brilliant, but the characters were ultimately always so heartbreaking. But just try to do something other than theater."

"Okay, I will," Jill promised. She had no interest in performing and could barely imagine her vulnerable mother standing onstage in front of an audience. Though, of course, the reality was that if such a person did get up onstage, her whispering voice and nearly translucent presence might well hold everyone in place, forcing them to look only at her. Susan Benedict sank back into her bed like an

aging Tennessee Williams character, and she was the compassion-
ate, female presence whom the other people in the family loved but
who needed them to make decisions such as whether or not to let
the meter man inside.

Jill often sat with her mother in the bedroom, but she only
revealed what she thought her mother could handle. When another
girl at school accused Jill of being "too smart, and boys hate girls
who are too smart," she had kept the sting of the remark to herself; it
would have upset her mother so much to tell her about it. This was
how she had gotten through childhood. When it came time to go
away to the Pouncey School in Weyburn, New Hampshire, Jill worried about leaving, but her mother made it easy for her.

"Go," her mother said, to Jill's surprise. "Write me letters. Have
a wonderful time."

Pouncey, as it turned out, encouraged the girls to succeed.
"Please, Ms. Babcock," Jill remembered saying to her teacher in her
American Civil War seminar, her hand waving in the air, "I really
have something to contribute."

"I'm sure that's true, Jill," said the young and ironic Ms. Babcock,
who was Jill's first mentor ever. Ms. Babcock probably wasn't more
than twenty-five at the time but had seemed so powerful. She was
amused and awed by the girls, and had had them reenact the Battle
of Gettysburg on the playing fields of the school. They had tramped
around in boots and in improvised blue and gray uniforms; they had
fallen to their deaths, crying in their last moments, "Ah'm a-dyin',
brother of mah'n." Then they had gone back to their dormitories in
a pack, arms thrown over one another's shoulders, and had written
bold if overreaching papers with confident titles such as "General
Lee in the Shenandoah: A Close Analysis" and "The Battle of Pea
Ridge: A Turning Point in a Nation's War with Itself."

"Where are all you meek types? All the ones I've been reading
about in that book *Setting Free Rapunzel*. The ones who have 'com-
plexes' and can't speak up?" Ms. Babcock asked. There was laughter
among the girls who sprawled out around the big classroom table.

"What? You haven't heard that girls are supposed to be shy and inarticulate?"

The education at Pouncey had always been classical and rigorous, although generations earlier, back in the 1940s and 1950s, it was said that the girls there were mostly headed for their MRS degrees. Still, the students in those eras had rarely thought about the discrepancy between what they learned and what they were planning to do with that learning. Knowledge didn't just evaporate and get released into the atmosphere like a gas. It stayed within you, filling you up and changing your cellular structure, so that by the time you graduated from Pouncey and went on to college or secretarial school or, during World War II, perhaps an aviation-parts factory or even an early marriage, you were different from the person you had once been. When Jill arrived at the school in the early 1980s, she imagined that her education would lead her to more education, which somehow would lead her and everyone she knew to a formidable life.

There in their New Hampshire cloister for four years, the loud girls were predictably loud, the quiet ones quiet, but despite their dispositions, they were now all in possession of facts and the ability to analyze a passage from just about any kind of book that existed. Everything they were taught was slowly absorbed by them on that green-gold campus. Over time, as Ms. Babcock and other teachers told them, many people would gravitate toward what they had. Men would be attracted to their intelligence and their capability, as would future employers, and the world would await the moment of their intellectual ripeness.

Upon graduation, Jill won the Vivian Swope Prize, given annually to "A Graduating Senior Who Demonstrates the Most Promise." The prize had been endowed by the family of a brilliant Pouncey girl who had been accidentally killed long ago in the spring of 1931, during a senior hiking expedition, when she lost her footing and hit her head on a rock. Jill had seen only one photograph of her: Vivian Swope had worn her wavy hair with a big silk bow and had had an appealing overbite, but the photograph revealed nothing more, and she became a stock symbol of excellence unfulfilled. All the Swope winners, at the time of their win, had occupied a certain glancing, golden place at Pouncey. They were the ones who swanned and glittered, the ones with their hands perennially up in class.

Promise, it seemed, was everywhere at that school, but it was best embodied by someone superior whom you secretly tried to dislike but just couldn't. Promise, for one, came in the form of Jill—back then still known as Jill Benedict—a member of the class of '85. At Pouncey, Jill was tall, strong, naturally blonde, a field-hockey player who charged toward the goalposts. The Benedicts came from "good stock," everyone said, which always made Jill imagine them all aswim in some kind of thick, nutritionally enhanced broth. She was brought up to be kind and intelligent but modest in a big, meandering, slightly unkempt house outside Philadelphia, with two laughing older brothers who had bedrooms that smelled of body odor and something indefinably male. ("Oh, poor innocent you, look, I'll spell it out for you: S-E-M-E-N," another girl had said one night at Pouncey after Jill mentioned her brothers' mysterious room-smell.)

Jill wasn't necessarily destined to be a Swope winner, but in the end, death clinched the prize for her. In Jill's junior year at Pouncey, her mother became noticeably more withdrawn and sadder than she'd ever been. No one understood; everyone just let her sleep late and tried to be understanding, and gave her time to herself when she was in a particularly unresponsive mood. Then, one morning in spring, Susan Benedict walked into the family's garage, which stood separate from the house, stuffed the tailpipe of the Cadillac with her husband's balled-up dress socks, and sat in the idling car in her nightgown and coat until she lost consciousness and finally died.

One of Jill's brothers had called her at school with the news and said, "Jill, listen to me. I have to tell you something really, really terrible." He made a sound like a croak, then a belch. "Mom committed suicide."

To which Jill responded, dumbly, "Will she be okay?"

"What? No, listen to me. She died."

"Mom *died?*"

Panicking, Jill had run across the playing fields, slipped into the woods, and sat in a patch of dirt, crying in a howl until she was ready to return to the world. The next day she somehow got down to Philadelphia for her mother's funeral, and it was arranged that she would take her final exams at home over the summer. Her room was packed up and sent on after her.

Her mother's suicide note had said that she loved her family more than she could ever say, but that, as they all knew, she had always been "emotional," and lately she had been unable to feel any happiness at all. "I don't understand why she couldn't talk to us," Jill's father had said to anyone he could corner in those early days after the death. Bob Benedict knew his wife was troubled. Now it was as though he would be made to inhabit the pain he'd never understood. "Why didn't she say she was suffering so badly?" he said to his children in tears. "Why didn't she tell us the extent of it?" Susan Benedict had always seemed to Jill both sensitive and special. Her melancholy nature was simply a part of her that other people had known about and had always accepted with alternating irritation and patience.

When Jill returned to New Hampshire in the fall, having spent a long trance of a summer in the house with her shattered father and helpless, sobbing brothers, she had changed in ways that everyone could see. When she spoke in history class, she was quieter, less desperate to be heard, but more eloquent. At meals in the faculty dining room, teachers passed her paper on the Industrial Revolution from hand to hand. On the grass, playing field hockey, she knocked a battered puck around as if it were Death itself.

Sentiment rushed toward Jill Benedict like something flowing downhill. Everyone knew now that she was better than the rest of them. They suddenly saw what they hadn't quite been able to see before: that she was uncommonly intelligent and would likely do big things with her life. Jill, it was decided, was the member of the class of '85 most deserving of the Swope Prize. Even her classmates who had held aspirations in this direction now conceded the point over a late-night secret Kahlúa session in the dormitory. They drank right from the stash of miniature bottles stowed inside the hanging shoe-bag in someone's closet. "Jill Benedict will so totally get it," they told one another philosophically. "There's no point in pretending she won't."

And so Jill received it, on a wooden platform at graduation, on a bright spring morning. Vivian Swope's surviving younger sister, by 1985 a handsome copper-haired woman in her sixties, handed her the scroll bound in lavender ribbon. Jill remembered that the woman wore a large gold oval Pouncey ring on her finger, engraved with the Latin *"Ad omnia parata,"* the school's motto. "Prepared for everything." The ring caught the light as the woman read from her written remarks.

"This is for promise," she said. "My sister Vivian never had a chance to fulfill her own promise. By giving you this award today, Jill, we acknowledge and honor your past achievements and those that are yet to come."

I N THE LIVING ROOM in the middle of yoga, Nadia Hamlin appeared, standing over the women the same way she stood over her mother in the morning. Gradually they became aware of her, and someone pressed the remote control. Nadia had an *Ahoy, Mateys* towel with her that she now spread out on the floor to use as a mat. "Nadia," the other women said. "How are you? Are you enjoying your big new house?"

"I like it a lot," said Nadia softly.

"Come join us," said Karen Yip, patting the floor, and Jill watched as her daughter sat down and tried to form her legs into the lotus position. But she wasn't flexible or poised; she was nothing at all like little Nadia Comaneci had once been. She fiddled around on the floor for a while, yanking on her left leg, and finally Jill bent over her and said quietly, "Do you want to do something else? Maybe go get a book and sit in the corner and read a little?"

"Okay, Mom."

Jill followed behind her, telling her friends that she would be right back and not to continue without her. Mother and daughter walked down the corridor toward the playroom, and Jill watched as Nadia stood at her bookshelf, pulling out one book after another, examining the covers with squinted eyes. Jill knew that Nadia couldn't read the names of the titles yet. At age six and in first grade, she was still not a real reader, although at the end of last year, her pretty, neophyte kindergarten teacher back in the city had assured Jill and Donald that this would come with time. Nadia frowned over the lineup of picture books on her shelf, selecting one based on its cover illustration. She tucked the book under her arm; she did look good, as though she was a very young student skipping off to her morning class in Bioethics and the American Dream.

But Nadia wouldn't be able to survive in a world where she would need, if not raw intellect, then at least a certain kind of pack-oriented female dynamism. Now Jill watched her daughter walk back out into the living room, holding a book in her hands that she could not read. Over the rest of the hour, to the gentle instructional voice of the yoga DVD, the four women repeatedly rose up on their haunches on their little blue rubber rectangles and sank back down. They folded and unfolded their arms and legs, and lifted their heads like animals at a drinking pool in the Serengeti. They did the downward dog, the dragonfly pose, and countless salutations to heavenly bodies. They metamorphosed into animals, and trees with roots that spread like long fingers through the ground, holding themselves steady, and they became grateful to the sun for warming them and the moon for simply providing nighttime beauty. The DVD ended, and there was silence. But from the corner of the room, where Nadia sat with her book now, they heard her distinctive singing voice. The women opened their eyes.

"Nadia," said Karen. "That's so pretty. What is it, honey?"

Nadia shrugged shyly. "Just a song," she said.

"*Rise, sorrow . . .*" repeated Karen. "And what's the rest?"

"*'Neath the saffron sister tree,*" Jill quickly put in. "It's some Russian folk song, we think, but we don't know what it is."

"I've heard her sing it before. The words are beautiful," Karen said. "So sad and haunting. I always like hearing you sing, Nadia. You have a really nice voice." She turned to Jill and said, "You should get her singing lessons out here. I think she's very good."

"Oh, thanks," said Jill, but she was sure that Karen was simply being kind. Nadia did have a sweet if unusual voice, but Jill had mostly been struck by the fact that Nadia's voice stood out from the other children's. "Okay," she said, "we should probably end. Want to do an *om?*"

They all tried one now, sitting quietly and closing their eyes again and chanting the single syllable. Jill opened an eye and saw that Karen was looking at her. They both smiled and laughed slightly, and then the others broke their concentration too.

"Sorry," said Karen. "I can never do this with a straight face. You know," she said, "maybe we should end with Nadia's little song instead. With actual words that are pretty. That seems more fitting. Would it be okay if we did that, Nadia?"

The little girl nodded, and Jill knew that Nadia had no idea of what Karen was talking about. They all said they liked the idea, and so they closed their eyes, Nadia too, and in unison they chanted *"Rise, sorrow, 'neath the saffron sister tree."*

They repeated the melancholy line a few times, and various thoughts of female friendship and loss and anything else that occurred to them were given entry into their brains. *"Rise, sorrow, 'neath the saffron sister tree,"* they said over and over.

Roberta Sokolov thought: How can Jill live here? It feels so empty. And why am I here now? My friends can be kind of monotonous. How did I end up with them?

Karen Yip, a former pure mathematics major and superior manipulator of numbers, thought: $[\sigma_i^m, \sigma_j^{m-1}] = 0$ if σ_j^{m-1} is not a face of σ_i^m. $[\sigma_i^m, \sigma_j^{m-1}] = \pm 1$ if σ_j^{m-1} is a face of $\sigma^m \ldots$

Amy Lamb thought: I wonder what Penny is thinking about. The New York seaport at the turn of the century? Or her lover Ian Janeway? I should call her and say hi. Would anyone notice if I slipped into the bathroom and called her on my cell phone when yoga is over? I definitely feel like calling her.

Jill Hamlin thought: *Rise, sorrow?* What do those words really mean? Is Nadia depressed? Is she lost and alone and confused? What if they had given us the plump, laughing little girl in the next crib? Everything would have been different. But if they had given us that other little girl instead, then maybe Nadia would still be living in that orphanage, in a room full of girls, all of them ignored, unloved forever. And it's just unbearable to think of her going unloved. Oh, I have to talk about it all with Amy. But look at Amy over there, sitting on her mat and probably focused only on Penny Ramsey. Just look at her; she's lost to me.

Rise, sorrow, the women all chanted, and their sorrows obediently rose, and kept rising.

Chapter

FIVE

Philadelphia, 1962

"I WOULD LOVE to see you in *The Glass Menagerie*," Bob Benedict said to the young woman who sat in front of a smeared mirror in the open space backstage. The place was unheated, but all the actors wore shirtsleeves, for the play tonight had been *Summer and Smoke*, and the setting was moistly southern. This was the first Tennessee Williams production that Greasepaint Amateur Theatricals had attempted, and there had been some difficulty coaxing these long-held Philadelphia accents into patient southern drawls, but in the end the entire cast felt pleased with its progress and infused by a moody sexuality that floated over into the audience as well, bringing the serious young businessman Bob Benedict backstage and into the sightline in the mirror of Susan McCrory, resident ingénue. She turned around.

"I don't think I could carry that yet," she said softly, but she was pleased at the attention. The businessman came to see all the Greasepaint productions, attending by himself and then, after the curtain calls, appearing backstage with a bouquet of lilies for her in damp paper. He wasn't a bad-looking man, only sort of plain in his dark suits and horn-rims, yet after a while, seeing him show after show bobbing and grinning in the mirror, Susan began to appreciate his thorough lack of artifice, especially when compared to the men of the theatrical troupe, a mix of the narcissistic, the frankly homo-sexual, and the "character-actor" peculiar. All the performers were deeply aware of themselves in relation to the world; everything they did seemed somehow as if it were being done onstage. Their laughter during table reads had a patent falseness about it, as though they imagined they were secretly being observed by a Broadway producer who would step out from the wings and say, "I have been quietly watching all of you, and there's one of you whose mannerisms I have been most impressed by—not only when in character but also when simply sitting at the table, responding to the performances of oth-ers." And then he would name a name and take that person with him to New York, where he or she would be deposited in short order upon a Broadway stage.

During the day Susan McCrory worked at her low-paying job as a nursery school teacher in downtown Philadelphia, but every eve-ning she went to rehearsals, and for the past two nights she had been onstage in the auditorium of a church in front of a small, though not humiliatingly small, audience. She had become accustomed to praise, and knew that as long as she stayed in amateur theater, she would always do well. She was an unusual combination of shyness and self-display, a very pretty if slightly too broad-shouldered and tall, vividly blonde girl of nineteen who knew she wanted to act pro-fessionally. She didn't have enough money yet to try to become an actress in New York City, though she planned on doing so in the next few months. Her roommate, who owned a Brownie camera, had agreed to take head shots. And then, in March, during the nurs-ery school's vacation, the plan was that Susan would go to New York, sleep on her aunt's sofa, and answer ads for casting calls that she had circled in the pages of *Backstage*. If she had any luck, she would give up her life in Philadelphia, move in with her aunt, and have a go of it; if she had no luck, she would return home and try again the following season.

But until vacation, Susan McCrory would continue to perform with Greasepaint, this friendly if slightly sad-sack collection of housewives, office workers, and professionals. Community theater was always a mixed lot. Dr. Carlson, who was given most of the male leads and whom Susan was usually asked to kiss at some point during a production, was the only one in the troupe not referred to by his first name, out of respect for his medical degree. He was a married obstetrician of thirty, weak-chinned but vain. Susan had played opposite him last spring in *The Man Who Came to Dinner*, and when it came time for them to kiss, his lips had been pinched and prissy as he turned his whole body at an angle that would give the audience the most generous view of his face.

But Bob Benedict, businessman—Susan liked the alliteration—seemed, compared with this crowd, pleasingly manly and lacking in self-congratulation. He appeared unaware of the way his body moved in space as it parted the curtains and came toward her, holding out a cone of flowers. Apparently no one had ever taught him to be coy or boastful.

They began dating, and he took her out in his big green finned Cadillac to steakhouses with tasseled menus, and then they started making love every weekend in his bachelor apartment. Susan had herself fitted for a diaphragm and was moved into an adult world that, while not exactly as she'd imagined it to be, seemed at least like a decent facsimile. Bob loved her desire to be an actress, and he escorted her home each night during the brief run of a production. The other cast members all murmured, "Hi, Bob," or "What did you think, Bob?" as he strode backstage.

But then she changed it, she shifted the rhythms, she almost *ruined everything*, as her mother had feared she would. Susan insisted on going to New York, as she'd planned to do, and it was there, at an open call for a black-box production of something forgettable, that she was discovered. Her lines at the audition included "I am Mary, the mistress of the loom. I sit and weave and weep and keen. I am Mary, the mistress of the loom." Though she was not cast, one of the producers said he had a friend who was currently casting the chorus for the new Broadway play A *Funny Thing Happened on the Way to the Forum*, and he told Susan to give the friend a call. She sang and pranced for that man, and when he asked her if she'd ever worn a toga—technically a *stola*, he told her, for that was the female version of the toga, though most people didn't call it that—she'd said, "In an earlier life," and he'd seemed amused by this and gave her a part.

"GOOD LUCK ON THE GREAT WHITE WAY," the other members of Greasepaint Amateur Theatricals had written on a banner they taped across the doorway of the rehearsal room in the basement of the church in Philadelphia. Dr. Carlson gave her a kiss as dry and obscure as a piece of scrimshaw and shook her hand and told her to stay in touch, but really this was it. She wouldn't return to these southern sets where she was always being stage-directed to fan herself or "drink a sweating cold glass of lemonade," or wipe the back of her hand across her brow. She wouldn't return even to see their productions, because then she would be made to observe herself from the outside: how much like high school plays these plays had been and how embarrassing, in retrospect. She didn't want to see herself accurately; she couldn't bear the idea of such clarity.

In the beginning, after she moved to New York, Bob Benedict telephoned her every day, and at the end of the conversation he told her he loved her. But soon, when Susan was off singing around someone's scuffed, upright piano in a walk-up apartment in Greenwich Village and drinking in a bar with all the other chorus kids after a rehearsal, it became clear that Bob might soon lose her to this new life, and so he became anxious, calling frequently, laughing too much, nervously asking her if she loved him.

Her mother Margaret said to her, "You know that Bob Benedict is a very good man and that the Benedicts have lots of money—Benecraft Shellac—and we don't, and I don't know how you will survive unless you have someone like him to provide for you." Margaret McCrory had always worried intensely about money, so much so that she sometimes wore herself out from her despair, and had to lie down in bed for a couple of days in order to recover. All the women on Susan's mother's side of the family had always been a little sensitive this way. Once, Susan's father, who had come to New York to visit his daughter, sat with her in the kitchen of her aunt's apartment and showed her what kind of a budget she would need to keep if she continued working as a chorus girl. "There won't be any leeway for extravagance," he said to her, as if she'd ever known extravagance before.

The Broadway play opened, and was of course a hit, and every night Susan sang and danced, and changed back into her street clothes in a room with a half-dozen other overheated girls, and then stayed out very late. After two months of this she was wound down and underslept, and caught viral pneumonia. She lay on the daybed in her aunt's apartment, where Bob, who had driven up from Philadelphia, sat beside her all afternoon in the slatted light from the Venetian blinds. Susan was weak and sick, and for reasons she never really understood, Bob took that opportunity to propose to her. "You can't go on like this forever, can you?" he asked gently. "You've had the experience of being on Broadway, and it was what you said you always wanted. Now you've done it; it'll be in your scrapbook. But you want other things too, don't you?"

"Yes," she said. "I definitely do."

He enumerated them. "Marriage," he said. "Taking care of a home. Motherhood, certainly. We both said we want a family on the soon side."

She conceded, through the codeine, that she did want these other things and that she didn't want to lose him.

The night before the wedding, Susan briefly thought about killing herself. There was no reason for this thought, but still she imagined jumping off the roof of their hotel and landing in an alley with her long white legs scrambled and her pretty blonde head caved in. It would be the last moment of attention she ever received, she thought with some dark, vicious satisfaction.

But she couldn't do it. She married him, and the wedding went well, even if none of her friends from the chorus could attend, because it was a Saturday afternoon and they all had to be in the matinee. That night, after vigorous sex in the suite at the hotel with her very pleased husband, the newly minted Susan Benedict slept for twenty hours straight. When she woke up, Bob promised her that she would love her life with him, and that she would "want for nothing." He actually spoke those words, as though he were reading them from the script of a bad play.

"Thank you," she said, speaking her own awkward line.

Once in a while, in their Tudor house down a private road outside Philadelphia in the middle of the day, with the air smelling of rain and the maid vacuuming discreetly in the living room, she would think about how the joke she had made to that casting director had turned out to be true: In a previous life, she had worn a toga.

Chapter

SIX

THERE HAD BEEN a time in the world when art was art and craft was craft, and everyone knew the difference. Art could be spotted right away, because the real thing was rare and gave off a particular sheen—and also because the artist could usually be found lurking nearby, anxious to know what you thought about "the work." But craft was all over the place, splayed out on folding tables at country fairs, or on drop-sheeted floors of houses and apartments where children were in residence. With art, you might be said to have a good eye; with craft, mostly what you needed were *hands.*

Roberta Sokolov had both. She'd long known about the art part; had known it when she was a standard-issue, politically active, bohemian girl in a magnet high school in the Chicago suburb of Naperville; and had still known it throughout art school and even afterward, when she was trying to make it as a painter in New York City during the early 1990s—the era of the white male painter, her friend Cindy Skye called it. "Every era is the era of the white male painter," Roberta had said. Back in the '90s, art dealers went trolling for young men who rubbed steel wool and glued doll heads onto their huge canvases and then stood belligerently in front of them with folded arms. The dealers were often seduced, if only by the physical magnitude of the work.

But when Roberta tried her version of this, the dealers weren't drawn to her the same way they were drawn to the men with their huge, frenetic canvases. Sometimes she was invited to participate in group shows, or in women's group shows, which inevitably took place in a gallery no one had heard of—Ovum, or the Marilyn Heinberg Artspace. She tried to show off her good, capable, figurative paintings, but few people paid attention. It was better, Roberta eventually thought, to paint quietly, discreetly, expecting nothing and asking for nothing. Maybe, if you were lucky, something good would happen to your career; for the first few years after art school, Roberta Sokolov had believed this. But still almost no one came to the quiet corners where she painted.

For a long time, whenever people asked her about what she did for a living, she always said, "Artist," though that implied that she was compensated on a regular basis, which wasn't true. Then, during the period when she began to support herself by becoming a puppeteer, she would tell them, "Puppeteer and artist." In recent years, she'd say, "I used to be an artist and a puppeteer, but then I had kids. I still try to do some art when I can." But her voice was stiff, for she knew that the financial necessity of puppetry had eclipsed art, and then, finally, motherhood had eclipsed both, bringing with it the thing called craft, which was ubiquitous in both childhood and motherhood.

Now, no one in her daily life had even known Roberta back when she had been an artist; they just had to take her word for it that she had been one and that she was good. Because of Nathaniel, though, people still thought about her in terms of puppetry. Just yesterday morning, the annual call had come from the woman in the special-programs office at Auburn Day, hitting Roberta up for a one-day puppetry workshop. Each fall this same woman phoned with the same request, and each fall Roberta said yes, as they both knew she would. Because her son, Harry, was on financial aid there, she felt slightly guilty and grateful, besides which she genuinely liked doing things for the school. It really wasn't a big deal to come in and perform her little puppet demo. So this time, when the woman from Auburn Day telephoned, Roberta said to her, "You know, you could probably just save yourself the call each year by putting me down as a permanent yes."

There was a pause, and then the woman said in an uncomfortable, formal voice, "Actually, we're never sure what our plans are year to year." As though Roberta shouldn't feel *too cocksure* that she'd be invited. She was the one volunteering her time and her expertise, and the school "wasn't sure" what its plans would be next year!

Now, over breakfast at the Golden Horn, she told her friends about the call. "So call them back and tell them you realized you can't do it this year after all," Amy Lamb said. "Tell them you're too busy."

"That's the thing. They know I'm basically available. I am at their mercy. We all are."

It was morning, and the women were sitting in the back of the Golden Horn in the booth by the swinging doors through which the agile flamencan waiters pushed in and out in a continuous swiveling dance of eggs and coffee, eggs and coffee. The room was crowded, as it often was, and the friendly, ubiquitous owner brought them their water glasses and took their orders. Today, below a lit-up niche in the wall that featured a vase of acrylic flowers salted with dust and a small painting of Greek fishermen hauling in their catch, there were five of them. In addition to Roberta, Amy, and Karen Yip, there was Joanne Klinger, whose seven-month-old baby, Zachary, drowsed in a huge, fully loaded Magnetti Supremo stroller, its handlebar dangling with its own nets. The waiters had to dart around the stroller each time the doors swung wide, but they never complained. Also in the booth was Shelly Harbison, whom no one liked very much, but it was all right, because Shelly wasn't around a great deal. She had her own infant at home at the moment with a babysitter, and she could often be seen heading off to various motherhood lectures and all-day workshops.

"The school never asks me to do anything except give money," Karen said.

"You were a statistical analyst," said Amy. "They can't bring you in and have you demonstrate that for the boys. It's not visual."

"They could give her an abacus," said Joanne Klinger.

"That's a wee bit racist, isn't it?" Roberta said.

"I've actually used an abacus," said Karen, unfazed. "They're amazing." Then she added, "Actually, I'm thinking of going back to work. That headhunter called me again."

"The headhunter always calls you," said Amy.

Karen Yip seemed to go for a job interview every few weeks, dressing up beautifully in the kind of suit with little buttons like lozenges that she used to wear when she worked. Though she never accepted any of the jobs she was offered, she liked to talk about her interviews, as though they themselves were the point.

"The school never asks the fathers to come in," Amy said. "To take a day off and do a workshop. It would never occur to them to ask."

"And the thing is," said Roberta, "most of the fathers would like it." She paused, thinking about this. "*I* actually like it," she said with a little surprise. "Talking to the boys about puppetry, even though it's not the way I identify myself anymore. So really," she added, "I can't complain when the school calls. They know that I'll do it and that I would be sorry not to. Just so long as I don't actually have to become a puppeteer again."

"I would have liked to know you then," said Amy. "Hearing you use those little voices."

"You didn't know me as an artist, either," Roberta said.

"We sort of do now," said Karen. "All the projects you do with your kids. I love how creative you are."

Roberta's apartment had long been loaded up with plastic boxes of beads and sequins and containers labeled MARKERS and COLORED

PENCILS. Her friends didn't make the distinction between craft and art, the way Roberta did. It wasn't that she didn't love craft; actually she did, and some of her happiest times had been spent with her children, Harry and Grace, making a project that would engage them for a long while, until eventually it was relegated to a closet, where it would quietly decompose.

But craft also made Roberta think of the shadow of art in which it inevitably sat, and the loss that remained. In her other life, as she often thought of it, back before motherhood and puppetry, Roberta had been a figurative painter who lived downtown, where she had gradually become involved with the "puppet-making community," a phrase that even now embarrassed her slightly to say aloud.

The puppeteers tended to all find one another eventually, and so it was not surprising that she had met her husband, Nathaniel Greenacre, twelve years earlier at a puppet show. It was one of those Saturday morning multiact shows that cater to children's temperaments and attention spans; you would get a compressed and accelerated *Hansel and Gretel*, followed by a wordless wrestling match between two hands in white gloves, and then an incomprehensible Hungarian folktale with painted wooden marionettes that were long and menacing and lax-jawed. Roberta was part of the fourth act of the morning, a three-woman show with a barnyard theme.

She was pacing backstage with a pig puppet on her hand when she saw Nathaniel Greenacre rooting through a trunk for an errant puppet. "He can't have run out on me," he said.

"You never know. They have their ways."

He smiled approvingly, and one half of his mouth lifted in a way that was sexually suggestive. Roberta was not someone to whom men were often instantaneously attracted. It usually took them an extra beat to warm to her, and she would have to make sure they saw her personality right away—her independence and nerve—and then they would become interested, if they were going to be interested at all. But Nathaniel Greenacre did not know how men usually perceived Roberta; he was much older than she was, and the pool of women he'd been drawing from in recent years tended to be in his own age range and wary from more than a few relationships—and in many cases a marriage or two—that had come undone.

"You in the next act?" he asked her, and she told him about the barnyard routine.

"We're not great," she said. "It's just a way to pick up a little cash. Please don't listen."

"I wasn't going to," he said. "Not to worry."

Many puppeteers spoke in a dismissive, arch manner about their own and one another's acts, preferring to think of themselves as performance artists who had been forced by necessity to work before child audiences but who were really meant to be wearing ectoplasmic structures on their hands made of neoprene and bubble wrap as they performed for other performance artists in somebody's loft.

Yet here were Roberta and Nathaniel backstage at the cheerless auditorium of an urban YMCA. Several homeless Paul Bunyan types drowsed in the rows, waiting for the soup kitchen to open upstairs. Percussive children's coughing emanated from the audience along with waves of audible restlessness. During the Hungarian act, after the strange marionettes teetered on tiptoe and clacked their jaws, and one of them cried out to another, "Count Szilagyi, I demand you pay me back my ten gold pieces!" a small boy in the second row shouted, "OH MOMMY, WHEN WILL THIS BE OVER?"

Several parents tittered in solidarity, and one even clapped. They were all held hostage to children's demands and limited interests—parents and puppeteers alike. Sometimes now, over a decade later, whenever a movie or a play or even just a quarrel between Roberta and Nathaniel felt particularly unbearable, one of them would turn to the other and say, "OH MOMMY, WHEN WILL THIS BE OVER?"

When they first met backstage on that snowy day, she, at twenty-eight, was decidedly still young and he, at thirty-nine, was not. Roberta's body was slightly squat, and her nose clearly too bluntly large for her face, though more than one sympathetic female friend had told her that she possessed a sort of soulful, Semitic look. One had even said she looked like Anne Frank, and then reassuringly added, "but in a really good way." Roberta wore her wavy black hair with a few odd ceramic clips in it, as she'd done since college, and she had about her a certain recognizable artistic look that you either responded to or did not.

Nathaniel was older than anyone else Roberta knew and possessed a slightly bitter manner that was appealing to her, because she did not yet know many older people and did not understand that this was a fairly common feature of them. Nathaniel Greenacre's face was tired even then, at thirty-nine, and he kept his already gray hair swept off his face, long in back. He was a handsome and quiet pothead who had a trunkful of complex, ingenious felt puppets in his apartment in Brooklyn, which he shared with another puppeteer named Wolf Purdy.

When Nathaniel and Roberta first went to bed together a week later, he showed her every one of his puppets, trying them on for her in the swirled bed after sex, a gesture that seemed at the time like a pleasurably perverse, nearly sexual act in itself. His best puppets were a duo named Nuzzle and Peeps.

"You know, these could be a big hit," Roberta recalled saying to him in that bed. "You should really do something with them."

"I try," said Nathaniel. "But you know how corrupt the puppetry world is."

She didn't, though. It was only a job to her, not a life, and she had thought of it as somewhat incestuous and low-level mean-spirited, in the way that any small and self-contained world often is. The smaller the world, the more territorial people behaved around it. But Roberta, a former figurative-painting student who had entered this field almost accidentally, thought that Nathaniel Greenacre understood hierarchies and social systems in a way that she did not. She gave him credit because of his age and the years he had clocked in puppetry and his demonstrable devotion to it. His puppet Nuzzle was a glossy-furred, golden brown creature that seemed part bear, part newborn baby, part wise guy, while the sidekick, Peeps, was a dazed and self-important chick, newly hatched.

Roberta thought right away that Nathaniel Greenacre had brilliance, though it was clearly underexploited and undersung. Sometime soon, she knew, he would become famous, a sardonic, fringy hero to the children who constituted what people were now calling "the juice-box generation." It wasn't as though Nathaniel's puppets were matted with blood or saying obscenities, but they were a little *off,* in some original and essential way.

At first, after they married, Roberta and Nathaniel became a professional team, performing Nuzzle and Peeps shows at preschools and in the basement rooms of libraries around the city and in nearby suburbs. She was Peeps, giving the puppet a stringy little voice and the barest of stammers. They needed no one else, which was just as well, because no one else seemed to need them, either. Children's puppet theater was not a very gratifying milieu. Once, as they set up their small stage in an all-purpose room, they were warned by a librarian, "Please don't disturb the arrangement of chairs. As soon as you're done, Narcotics Anonymous is coming in."

The income they brought in back then was modest, but so were their financial needs. Roberta's parents, Norma and Al Sokolov, the original crafts-centered people—both small, round-bodied, deeply connected to each other, and industrious—worked as a husband-wife team themselves and loved it. They ran a small company in Chicago that created centerpieces for banquets: accordion-tailed turkeys, bicolored maize, and oversized wooden acorns for Thanksgiving; miniature crèches for Christmas; and so forth. They had made a single, excellent investment with their earnings: one year, back in the late 1960s, on a business trip to a party-supplies convention in New York City, they had met a woman who also sold real estate and who knew of a "steal," a walk-up apartment on the Upper East Side that she said would one day be valuable.

Norma and Al believed her and bought it, renting it out right away. And though they were difficult parents over the years, more impressed by each other than they were by their daughter or her artwork ("I *realize,*" Roberta had said to them once during a terrible argument in her twenties, "that my paintings do not display the creativity and brilliance of, oh, an Easter centerpiece made of shredded-plastic grass and cheap dyed eggs"), they were shockingly generous upon her marriage to Nathaniel and gave the newlyweds the New York apartment.

If only the place were better. The rooms were shot through with light but breathtakingly small: two little square bedrooms and one old, corroded black-and-white bathroom on the fourth floor of a walk-up building in the East Seventies, near the river. Roberta and Nathaniel would never have chosen to live in this neighborhood, which seemed more static and dull than they had ever imagined for themselves. They should have been living in Brooklyn, or even up in Harlem, which despite its dangers was becoming popular—anywhere but here. Theirs was the kind of building where the mostly elderly neighbors left items they no longer wanted on the windowsills of the stairwell, so that as you descended like Alice down the rabbit hole, you might come upon a pair of singed but usable oven mitts and a softly rotting paperback copy of *All Quiet on the Western Front*. Yet the apartment was theirs free and clear, and they had no money to move somewhere more exciting and diverse, and they were in love, and so they would figure it out. Later, after the two children were born, the close quarters became more oppressive, and Roberta was reminded of the feeling she got from crouching behind a puppet theater with other puppeteers, everyone elbow to elbow.

For a long time the Sokolov-Greenacre family managed. Now, though, Grace and Harry were eight and ten, and a couple of the mothers at the Golden Horn occasionally warned Roberta that eventually the children would reach an age when their bodies would begin to develop ("Grace will *get boobs*, Roberta") and that it would no longer be appropriate for them to share a room. For the time being, though, the children had bunk beds and remained inseparable.

Roberta pretended to her friends that she agreed that someday soon the children would need their own rooms, but she knew that from a practical standpoint it could never, ever happen. Harry and Grace would share this room long into the years when he grew constant boners and she did indeed develop breasts, and both of them staggered in and out of adolescent storms with no warning or reason. The free apartment in this age of impossible real estate would belong to Roberta and Nathaniel forever, and they would remain in it along with their children, regardless of the fact that they belonged elsewhere.

After Grace was born, Roberta had stopped doing puppetry completely, and though the enclosure of the apartment had depressed her at times, she'd also seen it as a refuge from the long, damp mornings of children's theater. Nathaniel still valiantly dragged himself around to libraries and schools with his friend Wolf, performing Nuzzle and Peeps, but Roberta didn't miss the work at all. When Grace started kindergarten, Roberta thought hard about rejoining Nathaniel on weekends, but when she figured out the calculus of such an arrangement she saw that it would never make sense. She would be paying a babysitter almost the same amount of money she would be earning herself. There was no reason for her to leave the children, except some indistinct one that had to do more with the generic idea of *working*—of wanting to "do something"—than with logic.

So she stayed home and tried to paint, but nothing happened at the easel. It was excruciating. She helped Harry and Grace with their crafts projects, using the same care and attention she'd given to painting. Her children loved doing crafts with their mother. They weren't self-critical yet; instead, they just kept creating more and more *things*.

How wonderful to be free of self-criticism, Roberta often thought. This lack of self-consciousness and condemnation was probably a fleeting state. Back when Grace was in preschool, and it had been her turn to select a body part during the Hokey Pokey, she had sung, "You put your nipples in, you put your nipples out, you put your nipples in, and you shake them all about. . . ." The young teachers, poker-faced, had gone along with it but couldn't resist telling Roberta about it at pick-up. "She was just completely comfortable with herself," one of the teachers had said with admiration. "It was so lovely to see."

Roberta wanted Grace to be free enough to say and do and create what she wished and not care about other people's opinions. Unlike her mother, she would be a real artist, and she would be ambitious; she would rise.

Artistic talent, Roberta Sokolov thought, was like the soul; in the absence of an actual product, you couldn't prove its existence. Nathaniel had no question that Roberta's talent was slumbering but still present. He imagined it as a kind of positive entity, able to exist underground for decades, and was sure that one day, when the circumstances were right, it would emerge, intact.

In art school in Providence, she had been a serious figurative painter. How was it, she had asked Cindy Skye during portraiture class, that almost no one in the world looked exactly like anyone else? That the slightest flare of nostril or convexity of forehead could make one person entirely different in *character* from someone else? And how too did children become what they did over time?

When her own children were small, Roberta had had the idea to do a series of paintings based on famous people who had died young, showing what they would have looked like had they been given the chance to grow old. In addition to the obvious inclusion of Anne Frank, she would paint Princess Diana as an elderly, beakish dowager, and the murdered and violated child beauty queen JonBenét Ramsey looking old and ridiculous and vain. The series was going to be called Old Children.

She'd tried to begin work on it during Grace and Harry's afternoon naps. The first of the paintings, Anne Frank, came out timid and unformed, suggesting very little about the nature of innocence or loss, or the banality of evil. It suggested nothing. The woman in the portrait looked like no one who had ever lived. One eye was slightly larger than the other. Roberta's skill for portraiture had apparently disappeared, just like brilliant, vivid Anne Frank. *Poof.*

She didn't know what had made her lose it, but she was relieved that motherhood, with all its projects, absorbed her the way it had. She needed something to concentrate on, and there were times when she admitted to herself that it was a relief not to have to try to make it as an artist anymore. It was also a relief not to have to work at a nine-to-five job that wasn't creative and couldn't make her happy. She felt sorry for her workhorse husband Nathaniel, who still performed in the same old puppet shows on weekends and who, several years earlier, had uncomplainingly taken a day job as a news cameraman at CBS.

They had sat down together and figured out exactly what it would take to raise their kids in the city; with ambivalence they'd applied to private schools for both kids after someone had suggested that they would have a decent shot at receiving financial aid. This was exactly what happened. Because of Nathaniel's salary and the free apartment and the slashed-price schools, Roberta was able to stay home and continue to try to paint. They were among the least financially flush families in the grade, but their needs were far more modest than those of most families. It felt almost petty to sit here in the Golden Horn on this fall morning, complaining about the woman from Auburn Day who had called to hit Roberta up for a puppetry workshop and yet did not value her enough. It seemed, finally, spoiled.

She didn't want to be spoiled. She wanted to be someone who had a political consciousness and who didn't simply live without thinking in an all-white patch of land in the most privileged city in the world. The field of whiteness bothered her tremendously. "How did we get so white?" she once asked Nathaniel.

Roberta made a point of taking the kids all around Brooklyn to visit old friends who had moved there and also up to Harlem, where her friend Cindy Skye now lived in a renovated floor-through. There was a new charter school there, Cindy said, which was supposed to be decent. "You guys should move here," said Cindy. "It takes some adjusting—the supermarkets are bad, and you have to go really far to get anything decent—but I love the neighborhood." Roberta wanted her children to feel comfortable among nonwhite people and in an environment where money did not flow. She wanted them to learn that the world did not revolve around them—even though, quite often, it did.

But mostly she wanted to be reassured that she herself had not closed up and changed and lost the vigor of her own political drive—along with her art. It was perfectly okay to be a stay-at-home mom (though she loathed that expression) with a real political consciousness that extended beyond the act of packing organic sunflower cookies and pesticide-free-juice boxes into her children's lunch bags. It was perfectly okay to be one of the passionate, caring mothers who thought about the horrors of the larger world, and did what she could, in her small way, then picked up her kids at the end of the day and brought them home. There would be scales of laughter there, shouting, crafts projects—until one day, when the children grew up and left, there wouldn't.

And then what will you do? she often asked herself. *How will you bear the rest of life?*

On Sunday morning, as if in answer to her own unhappy questions, Roberta would be flying to Sioux Falls, South Dakota, as a volunteer with her reproductive-rights group. She would spend most of the next week driving a few South Dakotan women to and from the one clinic in the state where you could still get an abortion.

Briefly, she and her friends had all gone through a short "political" phase, but then each of them had fallen out of it except Roberta. It had started after 9/11. On that day, all the parents—mothers and fathers, working or nonworking—had run to pull their children out of class. One of the few children who remained for a couple of extra hours at Auburn Day was a little dimpled boy who was in third grade at the time, Jackson Pershing, and whose similarly dimpled bond-trader father worked on the 102nd floor of the North Tower. Jackson's mother had spent the day searching downtown for any signs of her lost husband. By breakfast two days later, with the ruins still smoking, the women sat in their usual booth and talked starkly about the end of the world and cried a little with their heads in their hands and wondered aloud what they could do and how they could manage to be "involved," that floating and noncommittal word.

Later, when the war in Iraq had begun, several of the parents supported it. Roberta had been appalled. Karen said at the time that Wilson thought the invasion was "horrible but necessary," though he changed his position soon enough. Nathaniel and Roberta had watched the early war coverage on their small TV after the children were asleep. "Those dicks in Washington," Nathaniel had kept saying. At one point during that newscast, he had gone into his dresser drawer and brought out his little drawstring bag of pot, as if to say that there was nothing to do about the problems of a bullying administration and a frightened country except, somehow, to forget them. Eventually the war was often no more than background din, not unlike the sound of plates and silver that could be heard all around the Golden Horn shortly after the start of the breakfast rush.

Here the women sat now on this late fall morning in their usual booth, no longer marching or really political or consistently involved, except for Roberta. Being political wasn't like being an artist; everyone was "welcome." No one told you to stay away. No one said that you weren't male enough or phallic enough and that your canvases weren't big enough or didn't have enough broken doll heads attached to them. Her involvement in the reproductive-rights outreach group was participatory and immediate.

But Roberta was not yet willing to give her news over to the maw of breakfast conversation, where it would join all the other percolating remarks. "Oh," Joanne Klinger might say, "that's really admirable, Roberta. I think it's so great that you're doing this. You're both creative and political." They would reflect upon the slippery and melancholy nature of time and what kind of debt an individual owed the world. The environment might be mentioned next, for they could all imagine their children wandering lost through a poisoned planet, in which fish lay with flapping gills on the shores of half-gelatinous rivers, and the polar ice caps had been reduced to a broth, and there was no such thing as winter, and *this* was their children's inheritance, and yes, it had been the parents' fault, for they hadn't done enough to stop it in time. The group of women at the table might soon become depressed and quiet.

Finally, in the haziest of transitions, someone might ask, "Did you read the op-ed piece about that aid worker who was killed in

Darfur? I knew her sister at Wesleyan." Or else, "Have you seen Geralynn Freund lately? She looks worse." Or, "Is everybody getting excited about the father-son weekend?"

Today at breakfast, conversation meandered from Roberta's creativity to the children's art curriculum, to Amy Lamb's friendship with Penny Ramsey, that sleek mother in the grade who ran a museum. Roberta had noticed that Amy talked about Penny Ramsey a lot lately, invoking her name with a certain private satisfaction, as though Penny were a celebrity. "I'm going downtown to meet her for lunch later," Amy said now. "She's giving me a private tour of her museum's permanent collection."

"Oh, that should be interesting," said Shelly Harbison. "Getting a behind-the-scenes look. Let me know what it's like."

"I will."

"Have you been to her apartment?" Shelly asked. "I heard it's beautiful: all white. Where would your children be able to sit in an all-white apartment? You'd have to give them orders all the time about what they could or couldn't do. No homework done in ink. No grape juice."

Just then, Joanne Klinger's cell phone rang and she turned slightly away from the others to take the call. In a second she got off the phone and explained that her mother-in-law's friend had been planning to give her some hand-me-downs for the baby to wear and that the clothes needed to be picked up now. "Could I leave the baby with you?" she asked. Everyone said it was fine, so off she went. The other women kept talking and almost forgot the baby was in their midst until a few minutes later, when one of the waiters dropped and shattered a dish and Joanne's baby, Zachary, was startled awake in his stroller and began to cry.

"Mommy will be right back," Roberta said to the uncomprehending infant, and they all leaned their heads in so close that they must have looked like asteroids about to crash into him.

But Joanne did not return, and Zachary's cries grew more insistent. Amy tried to call Joanne's cell phone, but it went immediately to voice mail. "Hey, Joanne?" she said. "Are you on your way?"

Without saying anything, Shelly Harbison reached over and unstrapped the baby from the stroller. Shelly was someone for whom motherhood was everything; the other women all knew this about her, though until now they had understood it only abstractly. At breakfast sometimes she spoke ardently about her three children, and she was often carrying around a hot-button nonfiction sociological book with a motherhood theme. Years earlier, she had made them all reread that classic *Setting Free Rapunzel*, and in recent days she had urged them to buy *The Call of the Mild: Why Women Have Trouble with Aggression, and How It Holds Them Back*. The women at the table had periodically listened to Shelly's pronouncements on subjects such as the friction between motherhood and work in the half-distracted fashion with which they listened to many of the stories that came their way across the booth at breakfast.

The baby arched and flailed now in Shelly's arms and seemed in increased desperation. People at other tables began to take notice; across the way, a table of third-grade mothers from the school looked up from their own breakfast and whispered. Roberta knew one of them a little; she was the blandest mother in the whole school, perhaps the whole world, her face as round and closed as a pie.

The crying obliterated everyone's words as well as all the ambient noise in the coffee shop. "Oh, what the hell," Shelly said, and before anyone could understand what she was doing, Shelly had lifted her own blouse, exposing the enormous peach-colored cups of her nursing bra. She deftly snapped open a flap, revealing her right breast with its startlingly big, rough nipple and its reticulation of pale veins. Joanne Klinger's baby, that fool, that bigamist, gamely and indiscriminately latched on.

Horror and silence descended upon the table. "Shelly," Karen finally said, during the clicks and swallows of Zachary's quiet feasting. "That is not your baby."

"He doesn't know the difference. Look at him."

It was true that the baby looked peaceful; one hand played with the curve of this strange mother's breast while the other reached up and gently twined her hair around his fingers. "I don't know about this, Shelly. It seems weird to me too," Roberta said. Then, nervously joking, she said to everyone, "I guess Joanne could nurse *Shelly's* baby next. It could be like *Strangers on a Train*, with breastfeeding." But no one laughed; they all looked down at their plates in dread and excited anticipation of the moment when Joanne would return.

Seconds later she did appear, her arms loaded with shopping bags. She saw the empty stroller and then the nursing baby, and she must have thought, *Wrong, wrong, wrong,* as her brain pooled with some dark, maternal chemical. She said, "What the hell are you doing, Shelly?" Then she dropped the bags and swept her baby back up, making him unlatch so quickly and unexpectedly that there was a hollow *pop*, like the breaking of a vacuum seal on a bottle of Snapple. The unloved nipple was left exposed, a wet point that punctuated the morning. All eyes in the room saw it. It radiated light and heat.

"He was getting hysterical," Shelly said defensively, tucking it back inside. "We called your cell. What was I supposed to do, let him keep crying?"

Shelly and Joanne argued in a petulant, tearful way; both were highly upset and neither knew exactly why. All the women at the table were aware that there had been an obscure violation, with sexual overtones and suggestions of domination. Do we *own* our babies? someone later mused. Are they objects, no more than little radio-controlled vehicles that aren't allowed to be separate from us? And, someone else had ventured, isn't the act of nursing itself obliquely sexual? Men put their mouths on our breasts during sex, and we love it! We squash their heads down against us and hold them there. Roberta knew of an outrageous case in which a mother had actually had her baby briefly taken away from her by Child Protective Services because she had admitted to a friend that, whenever she breast-fed, she felt slightly aroused.

Life with a baby was as primitive and powerful as life with a lover. You could never really tell where one body ended and another began; the lines were drawn as crudely as if they had been rendered by a child. When Shelly had nursed Joanne's baby, they'd all entered some strange territory of thought. They didn't understand it, exactly, but they knew it was as bad as if Joanne had returned to the table and found another woman giving a blowjob to Joanne's husband.

Now Joanne stuffed her bewildered baby back into the stroller and hurried out of the Golden Horn, with Karen following after her. Shelly turned to the women who remained in the booth, miserably asking, "Was it so terrible, what I did? I wasn't trying to overstep my bounds. I was only acting on instinct."

But the rest of them hardly knew what instinct really meant anymore; it had been a long time since they'd nursed their own babies. Almost nothing in their lives seemed biological or pure; everything had to be considered and reconsidered.

The incident would be talked about briefly among some of the mothers in the grade, and it would even be talked about among a scattering of mothers from other schools, who gathered in other coffee shops: the Copper Skillet, the Sizzling Pan, and, in a suburb not too far away, The Parthenon, which was located on the side of a busy turnpike.

But sitting in this booth now, on the day it happened, Roberta was already tired of it as an anecdote; in fact, there was far too much anecdote in all their lives. All she could think was, OH MOMMY, WHEN WILL THIS BE OVER?

S o ON SUNDAY MORNING Roberta Sokolov was in South Dakota, driving at dawn to a small town called Lorton that was, according to the GPS that glowed on the dashboard of her rental car, exactly 192 miles away from her present location. She and the other volunteers had flown in from New York City the night before. Lying in bed in the motel, Roberta remained awake and sensitive to every smell and sound that thrived around her. The room was infused with ambient smoke, which reminded her of her husband, with his thin joints held between thin fingers. In the room next door, someone watched a police procedural on television, and Roberta could hear the dialogue: "Did you check under her fingernails?" "I checked." "And?" "Nothing."

But finally, somehow, she slept, and then the wake-up call came, and she now stood peppered by light hail in the parking lot behind the motel. One of the other volunteers handed around mini-muffins and cups of coffee from the bleak breakfast buffet, and then they all nodded to one another and somberly got into their cars to head off all over the big, roughly cut rectangle of the state. With the South Dakota sky dark and huge, Roberta steered the Chevrolet Cobalt out of the parking lot and went to pick up a sixteen-year-old girl named Brandy Gillop who lived with her mother in Lorton. Brandy's parents were divorced, Roberta had been informed, and Brandy's mother had told the intake people that she felt terrible that she couldn't drive her daughter to Sioux Falls, but there was no way she could get off work at the casino where she was a cashier, and, besides, her car was in the shop.

Twice during the drive, with her coffee cup in its holder and public radio softly playing, Roberta had called Nathaniel at the TV station, because she could sense the increasing presence of her own apprehension.

"Hey, baby," Nathaniel said. "You okay? You in the car?"

"I am not only in the car; I am in the heartland of America."

"I thought I heard the sound of an eagle flapping."

"Yes, you did. Very perceptive."

"I miss you," he said. "Boring day here. Just entertaining the crew with a little puppet action."

"I miss you too."

Nathaniel had encouraged Roberta when she'd first brought up the possibility of this volunteer job. Recently she'd taken tentative steps, hosting an envelope-stuffing session for reproductive rights in their cramped apartment, and dragooning her friends to sit around her little living room and write notes that they would stick into the invitations to something called, inanely, Roberta thought, A Very Special Evening for Choice.

"Hi," her friends had inscribed. "This charity means a lot to all women. Hope you can make it."

She had asked them to come, and they came. They were good

that way; if you asked them to do something, they did it, though of course she was always the one who organized anything political in nature. Mostly they struck her as only mildly political at best; if pressed, they would reveal politics that were sound and empathetic, but they didn't get riled up the way she did. "Why am I the only one who obsesses like this?" she had recently asked Amy. "We share the same views. Why am I the one going out there?"

"It just takes the rest of us a long time to move," Amy said. "I guess it's a kind of procrastination. I have it and you don't."

"Ha," said Roberta, remembering her languishing canvases.

But it was true that there were differences between her and them. A few of them had changed their names when they got married. "I want to have the same last name as my kids," one of the women had explained when Roberta inquired. "It helps when I go to the pediatrician. And I love my husband, so who cares?" Most of them didn't seem to think this was at all retro; they were much more accepting of one another than Roberta was. Even the powerful and enlightened Penny Ramsey had changed her name.

"Do you realize," Roberta had said in the living room that day, "that most of us in this room are probably too old to ever need an abortion again?"

"And we're way too old even to be egg donors," Karen had added. "I always see those ads: 'Women, are you 35 or younger? Earn $7,000.' How did they decide that that was how much our eggs are worth? Doesn't it seem arbitrary? I'm sure there's an economic model, but I have no idea of what it is."

"*Our* eggs aren't worth $7,000," said Amy. "We're all too old. They wouldn't even do the ultrasound. They'd use the ejector seat in the waiting room."

"Oh, they would always have rejected me on the spot," Jill said lightly, and a couple of the others looked up, startled, suddenly remembering the infertility anguish that she had gone through.

"Sorry, Jill, sorry," they intoned, but Jill just waved their apologies away and kept on working.

"I always feel a little insulted," said Karen. "Are our eggs so terrible? So defective that there's really no one who would want them? They're better than nothing."

"You know," Amy said, "if it makes you feel any better, I'll buy your eggs. And I'll give you cash. Twenty-eight dollars and fifty cents."

All the women laughed, and they returned to the quiet shuffling of envelopes, but the subject of aging and failing and losing fertility and sexual vibrancy had been raised and couldn't be dropped now. Over time their bodies had changed, the parts loosened, unscrewed a little, and once every so often, a crazy, mixed-up hair poked out from chin or nipple, and fertility was rapidly on its way to a complete fade-out in the imaginable future—if it hadn't faded out already.

"But the thing is," Karen said suddenly, "that's partly why we have kids. In addition to perpetuating the human race, and the fulfillment factor, and all that. Because even if you can't be young, you can be attached to someone who is."

The other women murmured that this was true. Someone said, "The children are everything," and there was a moment of quiet emotion, as each of them thought of their offspring, those idealized, miniaturized versions of themselves. Roberta, too, was made silent with reverence when she thought of Harry and Grace, the last of her really ambitious productions before her actual art had been stopped by some invisible force.

She thought of the children again now, while she was on the road in South Dakota. Nathaniel had said that he would take care of everything in her absence; the kids could go home with friends in the afternoon, and he would pick them up when he left work. She knew, of course, that he would forget to send Grace with money to buy chips from the vending machine at school and that he would neglect to help Harry study for his vocabulary test of words pertaining to the text of *Charlotte's Web* ("arachnid," "boastful," "porcine," "mortal"). She knew these lapses, but she already forgave him for them.

Nathaniel, at fifty-two, a full decade older than the other husbands, was lost inside his long days of work and his persistent, almost defiant love of the puppets he had created himself back when he was a much younger man. He had mastered their voices and mannerisms in front of a mirror, and then, many years later, had employed his own children as tough-nut critics. The presence of the puppets had diminished for him, but still he stayed with them. Sometimes Roberta knew that she had pulled Nathaniel into a big and complicated life he had not asked for; left alone, he would probably still be living with Wolf Purdy either in their old shared Cobble Hill apartment or else upstate, where Wolf lived now, the two men smoking pot and tinkering in an unheated puppet-making studio all day, with snips of felt and caramelized glue guns on all surfaces, and plastic googly eyes crunching underfoot.

But the love of a woman had transfigured Nathaniel into a responsible family man and a grindstone husband. True, he remained an intermittent marijuana smoker, though never when the children were awake or around. There used to be a time when Roberta and Nathaniel would frequently smoke together and fall into bed. A couple of times, early on, they had taken Ecstasy, which had created a crisping and glorifying of everything that Roberta saw and touched, so that she had gasped in appreciation for hours and thought that the world itself was like an art exhibit with interconnected galleries that you could walk through forever. But that sensation had ended after they had children.

"We can't *do* Ecstasy now," she had said to Nathaniel recently, when he had suggested it. "Poor us," he'd said with a shrug. But it had seemed, she thought, to be the truth: They couldn't do any sort of ecstasy now, or perhaps ever again.

Nathaniel had taken it upon himself to find a day job that actually brought in a salary and benefits. He never complained about it, except in the same cursing, low-level way he complained about everything. But he was getting too old for this job; most of the cameramen at the station were young, strapping guys. More to the point, she knew that it must be difficult for him that puppetry had not worked out in a substantive way and that during the week he was left in the netherworld of work he didn't care for. Yet his mournful, doglike decency was always endearing, and there remained a strange symmetry in the dull and plodding ways they spent their weekdays. By which she meant that both of them were mostly unfulfilled. Both of them, she thought when she was really feeling sorry for herself, were *losers*. She would never insult Nathaniel by saying this to him; but she could already see far ahead into the rest of their life together, as though their loserhood provided them with a spectacularly clear view of the downward slope.

Now, after a phone call to Nathaniel and reassurance that life at home would continue on just fine without her, Roberta started to enjoy the nervous drive across South Dakota, along the broad highways with the expressive, blunt tableaus in the distance. She was relieved to be away from the ordinary routine of her daily life: the spackling of peanut butter onto bread; the low roar of conversation in the Golden Horn—the disquisitions upon their children's homework load, and the banter about politics, and Amy Lamb's monologues about Penny Ramsey.

Goodbye to all that, Roberta thought as she drove. She reached Lorton in about three and a half hours, the GPS urging her gently in the right direction, and she found herself leaving the wide highway and going down a service road that narrowed into nothingness. The apartment complex where Brandy Gillop and her mother lived revealed itself from an outcropping of sparse, scorched trees. The two-story stucco building of connected units was so dispiriting that there was no way to imagine framing it vividly and concisely for the other women in a couple of days at the Golden Horn.

As the car approached, Brandy Gillop came outside, and Roberta saw that she was a very pretty teenager, her hair cut in a birdlike, feathered way that could be found almost everywhere in the country except in New York City. Though she was wearing a down jacket, she was visibly thin, self-conscious, unhappy. Her mother, Jo, a starker, ropy version of her daughter, came out of the apartment door behind her.

"Hello," said the mother when Roberta got out of the car. "You came a long way. I guess you want to use the ladies' before you get going."

"Pardon?" said Roberta. "Oh, right." She laughed at her own incomprehension, the sound trilling out foolishly, and then she went inside to use the bathroom, trying not to look at the rooms and see the despair that she thought would surely be in evidence. Of course, despair was probably in evidence in Roberta's small apartment too. But this was different.

When she came out, Jo Gillop offered her a glass of diet soda, which Roberta thanked her for profusely, embarrassed by the heightened and false sentiments of the eager New York liberal Jewish woman but knowing no other way to speak. Was it better to stay home and never to have come here but just to send money in various directions, as some of her friends did? Karen and Jill wrote jumbo checks every year to the hungry and the disadvantaged and the homebound with AIDS, and sometimes they sat on benefit committees that made life better somewhere far from the benefit's banquet rooms and gilded bamboo chairs. But Roberta had no extra money to send to anyone, and she had been eager to come to South Dakota. Yet now, in this small kitchen, her throat caught, and she thought she seemed embarrassing, that she *was* embarrassing.

But maybe it was in her head. The girl's mother was friendly, tired, thankful, and the daughter was shy to the point of strangeness, but neither of them mocked her. There was no irony to this moment, and in its absence Roberta felt confused. How should she behave? Which part of her personality was she meant to show?

"Well," she said brightly, "I guess we ought to head off now."

"You're not too tired?" Jo Gillop asked, and Roberta was touched by her show of concern, but then thought, Oh, of course, she doesn't want me falling asleep at the wheel and killing her daughter. She tried to imagine letting little Grace drive partway across a state with a stranger, and of course it was not something she could envision at all. As though her own child were more valuable than this one.

"I'm wide awake," Roberta told Jo. "And completely ready." She was wound up and caffeinated from motel coffee and could have driven straight through to Minnesota and even on into Wisconsin without showing signs of exhaustion. Jo and her daughter Brandy hugged goodbye and whispered words to each other that Roberta could not hear, and then Roberta got back into the car. Oddly, she had not imagined that the girl she would be driving would sit beside her. For some reason, she had seen herself as the abortion chauffeur, with her passenger sitting mutely behind her in the car. The idea of conversation had not really occurred to Roberta, but now, as Brandy slid into the passenger seat, Roberta felt panicked about what they would possibly talk about for so long.

"So off we go," she said, turning the key. The mother still stood by the front door, as if making sure that Roberta actually knew how to drive. In anxiety about this, Roberta put the car in neutral by mistake and stepped on the gas. "Oh, fuck," she said. Then, "Excuse me."

To which Brandy responded, softly, "I'm taking driver's ed next year."

"Apparently I could use a refresher course," Roberta said. "Maybe I could come to your school and take a class."

Brandy looked at her, considering, then said, "I think you're out of the age range."

"I think you're right." Roberta swung the car around. In the rear-view mirror, the girl's mother stood with her arms wrapped around herself, and then she went back inside. Roberta got the car back onto the road. There was silence for a moment, and then she said, "I know this is a difficult day."

"It's all right."

"I'm sure you wish your mom could have taken you."

"She signed the consent form."

"Yes. But this has got to be hard."

"Yeah. You're nice to do this," said Brandy. "To fly out here and drive all this way. My mom wanted me to be sure and say that."

"Thank you." Then, impulsively, Roberta said, "I had an abortion too. When I was in art school."

"Oh."

"It was a long time ago. If it means anything to you, I hardly remember it anymore."

What she did still remember was that there had been no consent form, no drive across an enormous state. The boy who had gotten her pregnant was a tall, angular art student from Miami named Seth Brennan who made wall-sized paintings that resembled antique maps. He had become quite successful later on. There had been a diaphragm involved, she recalled, but when Roberta thought about it afterward, she realized that she had sometimes forgotten to apply the spermicidal jelly.

Roberta had had her abortion at a clinic in downtown Providence, accompanied by Cindy Skye, and that night she'd lain in bed in her off-campus apartment drifting a little on Percocet while her friends drank beer and played "Would You Rather?" in the living room. Once in a while someone poked in a head to check on her. By the next morning she was back in her classes drawing, painting, and wearing goggles as she held a soldering iron. The abortion did not become the subject of any of her work. It did not transform into art but instead stayed a slightly difficult experience that became less difficult as she moved farther away from it in time.

Only after Grace and Harry were born did Roberta ever sometimes feel disturbed by it, thinking, Who would that blastula have become, if it had been left to grow and run its course? What child would it have been, a girl or a boy? What color hair? What favorite book to be read to at night? How much would I have loved that baby, if I had let the pregnancy continue? Oh, so much. And then she had stopped herself from such circular, obsessive thoughts, because they got you nowhere and only forced you into an untenable posture of sadness and regret.

She did not want Brandy to be besieged by regret, either, nor did she want her to be cavalier. She realized that, actually, she wanted to control the girl's response in every way, to make her feel grateful for her help but also not suffer. In Roberta's mind, she imagined that Brandy ought to seem slightly frightened but brave, yet really she seemed neither. She was ordinary, quiet, alert, prim, sitting in the passenger seat with her seat belt across her chest.

"What was it like?" Brandy suddenly asked.

"What was it like? Well, they give you Percocet. It's not so bad. And I think the feelings that you'll have...they're complicated. Of course there's a little sadness. A kind of mourning. It's—"

"*Art school.*"

"Oh! What was art school like?" Roberta was surprised. "I loved it," she said.

"You did? I want to be an artist too," said Brandy. "I do abstracts."

What were the chances of this? It was as though the reproductive rights agency had matched her with Brandy Gillop the way college housing matched roommates. "That's wonderful," Roberta said, and now quiet little Brandy was off and running, talking about art class and how Lorton High School was being overrun by a pervasive crystal meth problem and how she couldn't wait to get out of there and eventually out of South Dakota too.

"And also, what's it like to live in New York City?" Brandy asked.

"That's a good question. It never really shuts down. That's the city's most distinguishing characteristic, I think." Although, of course, at Roberta's age, and with two kids, she hardly went anywhere late at night anymore like she used to do every weekend when she was single—she didn't even want to—but she didn't feel like telling this to Brandy.

The girl wanted to hear more about the city that never slept. Was it true that there were clubs that were like caves, into which you could descend and not have to leave until dawn? Was it true you could walk around in the middle of the night without being murdered? Was it wonderful? Was it beautiful? Was it everything she had read about?

So Roberta became a New York tour guide as she drove across the state of South Dakota. Brandy was easier to please than anyone Roberta had ever met. She had become guileless and open. When they stopped at an aggressively fragrant Cinnabon to use the bathroom, she said to Roberta, "Can I ask you something? "

"Sure."

"Are you Jewish?"

It bothered Roberta slightly whenever this subject came up, because, really, the person who mentioned it was always at least indirectly referring to Roberta's nose, which was too big for the dimensions of her face. But when Brandy asked the question now Roberta was touched and didn't feel self-conscious or offended.

"Yep," she said. "A hundred percent."

Later, she would tell Nathaniel that she had been Brandy's "first Jew," and she decided that she liked this role. The girl knew nothing and had seen nothing. Her life was small and its edges well-defined, and then, suddenly, becoming pregnant had made it turn both more finite and less certain, and now she was relying on a stranger to drive her across the state so she could be an ordinary teenaged girl, so she could be returned to herself. Roberta was doing the returning, and this realization braced and awed her, as though it was the first selfless gesture she had ever made in her life.

THE GYNECOLOGIST at the clinic—young, overworked, female, in need of sleep—did not want to let Brandy be driven all the way back home that afternoon. She had seen plenty of women being ferried here from all over the state. "It would be good if she could stay somewhere local," she told Roberta when Brandy was resting in a small back room. "She's bleeding, and she vomited a little, and I'm not thrilled with letting her get into a car."

Which was how the forty-year-old from New York City and the sixteen-year-old from Lorton ended up in Roberta's motel room for the night, Brandy lying on the bed while Roberta sat in the vinyl desk chair watching her sleep. She thought of all the times she had watched Harry or Grace sleep, sitting anxiously on the floor of their tiny room while one or the other of them was sick with a fever in the night.

Brandy napped now from all the IV Valium she'd been given. Her hair was run through with sharp blonde highlights, and her skin was veined at the temples. She slept with an open mouth all through the run of crime shows in the next room, accompanied by the sound of cars and trucks on the interstate and the shuffle of people walking up the shuddering wooden outdoor stairs to the second floor of the motel. Roberta wanted to bang on the door of the next room and go up the wooden stairs and even run out onto the shoulder of the interstate, telling everyone to be quiet, because a girl was trying to sleep.

Roberta remembered the kitchen in Lorton and the taste of the soda in her mouth and the overburdened mother going to her job at the Kubla Khan Casino. She imagined the abstract paintings of Brandy Gillop stacked up in her room, all the canvases signed neatly in her girlish hand in the lower right corner: *Brandy G.* Maybe they were actually terrific. Maybe Brandy Gillop *had* it—not only the talent but also the drive. Art appeared in the strangest places, just popping up out of nowhere, growing like an experiment with lima beans and damp cotton kept in a dark closet and suddenly, *whoa,* the cotton was overrun with curling sci-fi bean flora. Roberta felt herself excited at the idea of this girl's art, which she imagined to be original, unschooled, authentic.

She would help Brandy; she would give her a significant leg up. The girl slept now as the motel room darkened behind its pale green curtains, and when she finally woke up in the evening, Roberta darted across the service road to fetch some food from a burger place, and they sat in the motel room eating supper together. The room was filled with a meaty fragrance and soft light, and there was no lack of conversation. Brandy wanted to hear more about art and galleries and the whole scene in New York City, and Roberta told her whatever she could, letting her own voice grow more instructive and sure.

"If you want to be a painter," Roberta was saying, "then you just have to keep working. You just have to work and work and get better at what you do. Then once that happens, you start to show it to people. Bit by bit, you might get attention. You can come to New York and sort of push it a little further."

"I would really like to go there," Brandy said. "That's actually kind of my dream."

"It's a pretty good one."

"I just think it would be awesome."

"Why don't you send me some slides of your work? Maybe I could pass them along to someone in the art world."

"Wow. Slides?" Brandy said uncertainly.

"Do you know anyone with a decent camera?"

"Yeah, I think so. My friend Chrissy. Thanks a lot, Roberta." Then, suddenly, she said, "The boy's name was Tyler."

"What?"

"Tyler Parvell. He's in my fifth-period art class. He thinks he's good at drawing, but in my opinion he's basically a show-off."

So they had that in common too: the two male art students with their vibrant, questing sperm. Roberta's eyes became bright with tears. What could she do for this girl? She wanted to figure it out. The remark about "people in the art world" was boastful; Roberta had talent, but not enough ambition to give her talent an engine, and as a result she had bombed out of that unfair world a long time ago, when the male artists commanded all the attention, and she'd had to show her work in those makeshift galleries with other women, all of them made to feel a little bit defensive and second class. She knew hardly anyone in "the art world" anymore, and the use of the expression revealed her as the art-world outsider she was. The loser she was, along with Nathaniel. Yet, of course, she could actually get Brandy's slides to an appropriate person, because she lived in New York and was connected to people who were connected to other people in the way that a teenaged girl who lived in Lorton, South Dakota, with a mother who worked at a cashier's window at the Kubla Khan Casino was not. In the way that most people in the world were not.

She thought about how Amy Lamb had become close with someone who ran an entire museum. When you lived a certain kind of life, pushed along by good colleges and internships and jobs and a shared, tranquil neighborhood and a world of privilege in which your children overlapped, you were inevitably part of a long chain of connections. All of them could help one another; the possibilities were there if they wanted them, though many of them didn't seem to want them anymore, or maybe they had somehow forgotten they had once wanted them.

But here in this motel room off the interstate, Roberta was once again struck for the first time in years by unmistakable ambition—not for herself now, for that wasn't happening—but for this girl sitting on the bed whose fingertips glittered from the fries she ate, and who talked about art in a tentative but excited voice, as if it was an actual place she could visit, and as if Roberta Sokolov could take her there.

Chapter

SEVEN

Naperville, Illinois, 1969

R UNNING A BUSINESS together had been Al's idea, not Norma's, though as the years passed they would tell anyone that they had "no clue" whose idea it had been in the first place, for it had become a partnership in every sense, and why try to unbalance it? But Al Sokolov was the ideas man and his wife, Norma, the execution gal, and together they managed to turn what they had once envisioned as a modest little enterprise into something big. They were now serving the entire metro and suburban Chicago area with their party decorations. Just this week, they had had to do a Woodstock theme. Norma had come up with the idea for the centerpieces: baskets that included an electric guitar, a naked man and woman clasped in an embrace, and sugar cubes nestled in a container marked "LSD." That last bit had caused a stir, though they had had to insist to the customers that it was only a joke and that everyone at the anniversary party would surely know that.

"We are the last people in the world to hand out LSD to people," Al had said that day when they had finished the whole order of centerpieces and were driving back to Naperville.

"I wonder what it would be like?" Norma asked. "Taking LSD. Seeing things that aren't really there."

Though they had lived through the '60s, they had done so as suburban parents, and neither of them was experimental or sophisticated. "I don't think we would like it," her husband had said. "Apparently you feel very dizzy. Last year, you had that vertigo for a week, and you hated it," he pointed out.

"True," she said. "I did. But it would be interesting to see things. To have actual hallucinations. Maybe it would give us ideas for new centerpieces."

"Oh, we got a request for Butch Cassidy and the Sundance Kid today," said Al.

They were driving home from downtown Chicago on a cold winter afternoon. At home, their only child, Roberta, little Bertie, was right now being fed fish sticks and canned corn by her grandma Ruth, who babysat for her every day and was a godsend. Norma Sokolov had not ever planned to go to work. She'd assumed that she would stay home with the baby, the way all mothers did. But then Al kept coming home from the company he worked for with these adorable little baskets for different holidays, and Norma couldn't stop herself from saying, "Why don't you add a few more silk flowers here and give it a whole-field-of-poppies effect? That was my favorite scene in *The Wizard of Oz*."

Lately, they had joked that, between the poppies and the LSD, their business would be shut down by the FBI. They joked in such a manner all the time now, sitting across from each other at the big two-sided desk in their office in downtown Chicago. Norma had become a smart and competent businesswoman without having had any training. Al had worked for years in the field, laboring on the phone all the time with customers and distributors, his sleeves rolled up, inquiring as to the location of a stray order, peeling antacids out of their little foil containers because there was now so much to keep track of, and he could not handle it all without feeling anxious and sick. When it became clear that Norma was packed with original ideas, he brought her in, and they ventured out on their own, persuading his mother to babysit for little Bertie every day, and everything simply worked well from there on in.

Husband and wife were never apart. They sat across from each other in the dusty office, and at night they lay against the padded headboard of their bed, looking at the ledger together and discussing business. It was a twenty-four-hour-a-day deal, and some of Norma's friends said they couldn't imagine such closeness with a husband, but after a while Norma wondered how a marriage survived when you didn't know many details of the other person's day. What did you talk about? The weather? Vietnam? What was for dinner tonight: Oh, chicken again. Didn't we have chicken last night? No, we had chicken Tuesday. Together, through their centerpieces and themed decorations, they talked about the world. They imagined what it would have been like if they'd gone to Woodstock. "I can just see you in the mud, Norm, with your blouse off and a string of flowers in your hair," Al had said to her, laughing, and it was a ridiculous image, for they were similarly built, made for wear and tear, sturdy as tops.

Their little daughter, Bertie, sensing their unusual closeness, would sometimes clamber onto the bed at night, saying, "Me too, me too!" and they would draw her in and hug and kiss and reassure her. But she was on to something, surely, for she understood that her parents' marriage, which had always been strong, was made even stronger by silk flowers and tiny elves and green or gold or orange leaves, always leaves, which were scattered everywhere, providing adornment for weddings and graduations and retirements and even, in their case, the simple passage of time.

Chapter

EIGHT

I N THE NIGHT, just before husbands called out to wives during
sleep and children called out to mothers, the women were often
already awake. They lay suspended in bed, and so when the moment
came, they didn't even have to judder to attention before dropping
a light female hand onto a trembling male back, or skittering down
the hall toward a dreaming child. But the women, who were still
conscious then because of hormones or the delayed kick of a cap-
puccino that had been drunk too late in the day or a continual churn
of anxiety that had become indistinguishable from normal metabolic
rhythms, weren't thinking about their families.

Late at night in New York City in November, with the street
outside opaque and frozen, in the brief period before Leo Buckner
grunted and shivered and called out in his sleep, Amy Lamb lay
awake thinking about the couple. That was how she had come to
think of Penny Ramsey and Ian Janeway all fall: "the couple." Earlier
that day, she had met them for lunch at the Metropolitan Museum
of Art, where Ian consulted in the framing department. Penny had

wanted to visit him there and then walk through the galleries, so she had called Amy in the morning and said, "Can I drag you out to lunch too?" surely confident of what the answer would be.

Intermittently throughout the morning, Amy had thought about the couple. They preoccupied her as she sat in the meeting at the school about the new parent newsletter. Amy often dreaded such meetings, yet felt it was her responsibility to attend them. Even before she arrived at the school she could already picture the usual suspects assembling in the room and the fruit platter that would be laid out on a table in front of them, as though they needed to be rewarded for showing up. She saw the large, hard strawberries staining the pineapple slices beside them; the translucent starburst jade of the sliced kiwifruit; the flesh-toned flesh of the out-of-season melon. Meetings at the law firm, Amy distantly remembered, had had only a fraction of the sense of pomp and urgency that these meetings did. The school meetings were somber and reflective, and tended to go on and on. The rest of life seemed as if it had been atomized, and somehow time itself appeared to have been bribed to stand still for these women alone.

The atmosphere in the music room at the Auburn Day School on this morning was clotted with smells of moisturizer and undereye-circle concealer and something indefinably, pheromonally female. The mothers smelled different from one another, but most of them smelled vaguely of nectar or gummi bears—fruity and girlish—and together in this big, bulky knot of mothers taking their seats among the stacked xylophones and zithers and cymbals and wood blocks, they all smelled good.

Often, in the middle of a meeting at the school, a mother would ask a free-associative question that wasn't really a question at all. "My son takes soccer on Mondays and Wednesdays, and I sometimes find that he's really exhausted the next morning. Do you think I should arrange for him to switch out of Tuesday-morning Latin, because basically he can't even think until lunchtime? Also, I'm wondering whether the student-teacher ratio at the school is really where we want it to be?"

At which point, Amy would find herself doodling frantically on her napkin. Once, back when Mason was in kindergarten, she had gone to her first school meeting ever and had written "KILL ME NOW" over and over on the napkin. The short, dark-haired, slightly funny-looking, sympathetic woman sitting beside her had noticed it and been amused, and that was how Amy and Roberta Sokolov had become friends.

Today, at the meeting about the parent newsletter, Amy didn't doodle. Her thoughts were mostly off with Penny and Ian, whom she would see when this ended. She was the token nonworking mother in their life, the ironic one who could dip in and out of these experiences and bring back a full report. Ian always listened to her in a good-natured but slightly confused way, whereas Penny seemed truly interested.

The discussion at the school was well attended. The usual collection of mothers had come, plus a couple of the ones who worked part-time. Dustin Kavanaugh's mother, Helen, who ran a charity that helped to transmit enormous sums of money to the poorest people in the world, had graciously taken off an hour to help out. Even Isabelle Gordon the string theorist—everyone always referred to her this way—had taken it upon herself to show up, briefly postponing her study of the universe in favor of a school newsletter. She sat in the back of the room with her braid and fantastic shoes. She was poised at attention between Geralynn Freund, the anorexic mother, and the one full-time father in the grade, Len Goodling, who prompted a new wave of thought across the room about whether or not he had *ever* worked and whether he was rich or depressed or simply enlightened, the way some younger fathers on the horizon seemed to be.

The discussion today was unofficially led by Laurie Livers, who had once been editor in chief at a major publishing house. Earlier in her career, Laurie had been the person responsible for plucking the manuscript of *Bigfoot Was Here: A Father's Letters to His Newborn Son from Iraq* out of the so-called slush pile, and as a result her fortunes had been tied irrevocably to those of the slender, emotional, epistolary memoir. The book had remained on the best-seller list for over a year, and Laurie had followed up the success by publishing that financial expert's self-help book on gaining personal wealth, *Beggars Can Be Choosers,* but despite her swift elevation, she left publishing to have a baby, and then eventually another one, and had never returned to work. She was the mother who habitually stood in place in the lobby selling Auburn Day paraphernalia, while the boys and their mothers whirled all around the nucleus that was her unmoving form. She was as familiar and imperturbable a fixture as a guard outside Buckingham Palace. Everyone said Laurie was invaluable to the school, but what they meant was, they were glad that she enjoyed selling that crap, for they didn't.

The way she now talked about the school newsletter was likely the same way she had pitched *Bigfoot Was Here* to her colleagues. "This book is about bravery and loss," Laurie Livers had probably said. In the classroom at the school, she leaned forward in her chair and said, "*Auburn Days,* our parent newsletter, will make you aware of the community around you. It will be the vital link between you and your sons."

"Aye aye," said Len Goodling.

A mother sitting in a nearby seat squinted slightly and waved a small white hand. "I have to say, I'm a little concerned about finding a good font for the newsletter," she said. "I think it's important that the look be right. And so I'd like to suggest Courier 12."

"Courier 12 looks exactly like it was written on the Smith-Corona typewriter I used in high school," said Laurie.

"Well, that's the point, isn't it?" said the other mother, Sari Handler, who everyone knew to be a bit of a dunce. She was the same person who had once, during a discussion of the upcoming woodwind concert, somehow referred earnestly to "*Taco Bell*'s Canon in D." (She had also, apparently, when the boys were studying dictators, insisted that "Baby Doc" Duvalier was a pediatrician, though Amy thought this anecdote had to be apocryphal.) "My feeling is that Courier 12 gives it a homier quality," Sari Handler said now. "Like something from the past."

"Then maybe we ought to use Butter Churn 12," Amy put in. There was a light spurt of laughter, and several of the women looked up to see who had said that, and one of them was Geralynn Freund. Her smile appeared almost concave, giving her expression a rictus-like, death's-head aspect. The conversation among the women in the room ground on, and several other women were drawn in, drafting their own powers of logic and reason and knowledge into service now. Someone groaned and complained, and someone else said, "Can we move along here?" Isabelle Gordon was looking at her watch—one that had no hands or numbers, just inexplicable overlapping translucent circles that moved in a pattern, suggesting a specific time only to her—and smiling apologetically; she needed to get back to her office at the research institute. Palatino 12 was eventually mentioned as a compromise font, and after a show of hands, it won. All this for a newsletter, Amy thought, with content about upcoming field trips that would prove to be as thin as a haiku:

Please send ten dollars
To the planetarium
Their gift shop is neat

The women continued to talk, their conversation moving in widening, overlapping circles that were rhythmic and hypnotic. A couple of the mothers inched or ambled toward the door. Amy willed herself out of the gabble and trance. It was almost time for lunch at the museum, she realized, looking at the clock, and so she slipped quietly from the music room, relieved to be going past the rows of hard knees and the bags swelling with children's soccer jerseys and rolled yoga mats and beautifully wrapped birthday presents. Some of the mothers had lacrosse sticks casually leaning against their chairs, as though they were part of a team of female athletes on a break, instead of mere stick-carriers for their sons. Also leaving the room at that moment was Geralynn Freund. Out in the hallway, the two women converged.

"I'm not very good in groups," Geralynn Freund explained.

"This could have gone on forever. And the conversation was ridiculous."

"Yes," said Geralynn. "It was."

"Sometimes the meetings are a lot better," said Amy.

"True."

"But when they're like this, you just feel life passing you by."

Geralynn agreed. She shrugged her small body into a black shearling winter coat that made her look like someone rolled up in a rug, although it also seemed to Amy that there wasn't a coat in the world that would be thick enough or warm enough to protect her. The women pushed through the double doors. Cold sunlight flowed in, and Geralynn Freund stood in it for a moment, blinking rapidly, then smiled and hurried off.

Where did she have to *go*? Amy wondered. What was her day like? What did she do with herself, her hair spiky and damp, her body like a rope knotted here and there to make elbows, knees, a head? Amy could see Geralynn walking for hours and hours, calculating in her head how long it would take to burn off the calories of the kiwifruit and pineapple slices she'd eaten, until it was time to return and pick up her son.

Amy imagined this woman perpetually in motion, all wound up and then slowly winding down. But then it occurred to her that some people might in fact ask the same question about Amy: What did she do with herself all day?

T HE COUPLE was already waiting in the cafeteria of the Met when Amy Lamb arrived. Penny's hair was falling loosely from its knot, and Ian Janeway wore a tie only half knotted and no jacket. Seeing them from the entrance of the huge, bright room, Amy thought how vivid they always appeared, whether separately or together.

Over the fall, from her fixed place in Holly Hills, Jill Hamlin had become increasingly and transparently annoyed at Amy's friendship with Penny. "Just observing the whole situation objectively, I would say you have a little bit of a crush on her," Jill had said recently, when she'd come into the city for the day. "One of those girl crushes. I'm thinking back to that party at Penn."

"The girl I kissed?"

"Yes, James Dean. The androgyne."

"You just like saying 'androgyne.' Penny is not androgynous like that. She's completely female-seeming."

"So maybe you have ecumenical tastes when it comes to women."

"I have no tastes. It's not a crush. Is it really so shocking that she would want to be friends with *me*? Are the women who work supposed to be completely separate from the ones who don't? Do we need separate drinking fountains?"

But she couldn't tell Jill that while she didn't love Penny, she did love Penny and Ian together—the idea of them, the couple they were, the way they softly inflated her days. She wished she could tell Jill about Penny and Ian's affair, and then Jill would understand why Amy was somewhat evasive and protective whenever the topic of Penny Ramsey came up. But she couldn't tell her. She had promised she wouldn't, and so there were occasional moments like this one, in which Jill revealed a jealousy that was childish yet almost touching, and Amy could do nothing to lessen it.

Penny often called Amy to relay the latest piece of affair non-news: "Ian sent me a big piece of truffle cheese at work. My assistant Mark carried it in, and it smelled very strong. Mark kept *looking* at me." Amy, hearing one of Penny's anecdotes, would laugh or exclaim or do whatever was called for, but always she would be on Penny's side; that was what she was meant to do. Once in a while, Ian himself called Amy's cell phone. In his accent he would say, "Hullo, Ian Janeway here. Have you spoken to her today? She's not picking up her mobile."

To which Amy would say that she thought Penny was at a meeting of the museum board or at a parent conference, and Ian would say, "Right, brilliant, I totally forgot."

Amy sometimes served as a go-between, but usually she was a

simple witness. At lunch this afternoon at the Met, she sat across the table and watched their faces with a kind of slow, appreciative interest. They were lively, connected, sexual. They liked to talk about themselves in the way that adolescents do, lazily unaware of how much space and time they are taking up, and how no one on earth is really entitled to this much of it. But in the same way that the world indulged adolescents, Amy did too.

"So Penny here is actually letting me see her the weekend after next," Ian was saying. "At her apartment."

"Really?" Amy said. "On the weekend? Oh right, it's the father-son thing."

On that weekend all the boys from the fourth grade and their fathers would be traveling on coach buses upstate to the Nature Exploratorium, where they would sit in the cold around a campfire and then spend the night inside warm cabins before being returned to their families. Amy would be alone overnight for the first time in a long while. She couldn't remember the last time that this had been the case. Leo traveled a lot to see his clients, but Mason was usually home.

"Yes, and my girls are both going to go on sleepovers," Penny said. "I promised Ian that he and I could have an extended playdate, so to speak."

"A sleepover," said Ian. He grazed on his salad thoughtfully for a moment. "If you're married and you have an affair with someone," he said, "there's a word for it. And there's also a word for you if your wife has an affair. But why is there no word for what *you* are if you get involved with someone who's married?"

Around them in the enormous room the sounds were relentless but acoustically pleasing. There was no doubt that their conversation would go unheard by anyone else; the cafeteria was too big, and no one would even think it would be worth it listening to. This wasn't a place to stoke or even vigorously disguise love. It was a place for schoolchildren in groups of thirty, blowing the wrappers of straws aloft, and for old people in groups of two, shattering crackers into china bowls of minestrone, and, at least at this back table beneath the skylight, for a pair of animated middle-aged women and a slightly younger man, talking with great familiarity about the topic of surreptitious love.

It had become a common topic for the trio. Any conversation that dipped into other topics—the resurgence of museum culture, or the way that warlike America was now hated by much of the world, or really anything at all—might slowly turn itself toward this subject. "That was around the time when Penny and I started our thing," Ian might say in the middle of something else, or Penny might say, "Yes, and ever since, I've been sleeping with him," or Amy would begin a sentence, "As the keeper of your secret . . ." and the couple would settle into the enjoyment of all this attention.

For who else received attention like this in adulthood? By the time childhood ended, all the benevolence that had been directed toward you just because you were young and your hair was silky and you hadn't yet been spoiled by the grit and hailstorms of life unfairly changed into a kind of indifference. Suddenly you, who had once been youthful and golden and special, were now treated as just another customer waiting in line for something. The world was suspicious of you; you weren't so special after all.

Unless, of course, you were in love. Briefly, two people in love received the attention of everyone. Weddings were celebrated and wept over; the couple was always seen as temporarily beautiful and perfect and in no need of anyone else. Amy remembered how special she and Leo had felt early on, walking along the street to work in the morning after a night that had included the kind of sex that was every young person's divine right. Leo had appeared brooding and reflective as they walked, and she supposed that she had too; perhaps the people who passed them perceived that they were sealed inside the contemplation of their own love. With Penny and Ian, Amy was still the only one in the city—"the only one on earth, if you want to be exact," Penny had said—who knew about the affair. "I haven't told anyone else. Greg can never find out. So I'm just shutting up." Without Amy's knowledge, it almost seemed as though the thing itself wouldn't exist. For who would be there to say it did?

Since that afternoon in September when Dustin Kavanaugh was mugged on safety walk and the friendship with Penny was set into motion, Amy had folded the couple into her pliable routine. Beforehand, she'd been thinking about getting some kind of full-time volunteer job, but that idea had somehow gotten lost after the mugging. For now, Penny and Ian seemed to fit neatly inside her brain, clasped in an embrace like twins in utero.

At lunch at the Met, sitting across the table from them, Amy said to Ian, "It's just as well that there's no name for you. This way, it almost seems as if you're just a bystander."

"He is not a bystander," said Penny. "He's an instigator."

"So there is a name for me after all. Why, because I told you I liked the way your ramen noodle soup smelled that day in your office?"

"No, because of what happened later."

And with that, he did something to her under the table, some quick feel or pinch or squeeze, and Penny drew back and said, "Ow, Ian, stop!" in the tone of a teenaged girl having her arm twisted by a boy. "You're such a baby." Then she lifted her foot onto the free chair and rubbed at her ankle. Amy glimpsed her little bootlet made of fine-grained brown leather fringed in some kind of fur that made her look like a cantering Shetland pony.

Penny and Ian would sometimes rise up from the swell of their own self-interest and draw Amy in too, and she was gratified to be asked questions and to have their eyes upon her. "So, what about you?" asked Ian now. "Do you think marriage is inviolable?"

"Apparently not," Amy said.

"We're a very bad influence," Ian said. "Penny says you're happily married. That's a nice thing to hear. Have you been married long?"

"Thirteen years," said Amy, and for some reason she thought of Leo on their wedding day. She remembered how the white flower in the buttonhole of his jacket had reminded her of a miniature version of his face, poking out bravely, openly, waiting for her.

"That's an impressive amount of time," Ian said. "I can't even imagine it."

But now Leo, off in his own environment, was so separate from her. He didn't want to sleep with her anymore, and he no longer needed her to be his comrade. He had his colleague Corinna Berry, with whom he commiserated about the workload and much else. Sometimes he and Corinna talked on the phone at night too. It had been a long time since Amy had stepped into Leo's law office, and yes, she could picture his walls with their textured wallpaper and diplomas and photographs. And surely there was a picture of her and Mason there from a few years earlier; she seemed to recall her son's corrugated, empty front gum, awaiting the shingle of a tooth. But what did she really know anymore of life in a law firm—the use of Juxtapose BriefScan, the way it all worked?

Leo's daytime universe was now as foreign to her as the enclosure of anyone else's world. As a little girl, Amy had loved gaining even brief entry into any small and previously unexplored place: the clothy sepia darkness below the kitchen table; or the provisional tent made from her bedsheet with its strawberry pattern on the edges, draped across two chairs; or the space beneath the desk in her father's study, while he sat at his desk chair, grading economics papers. She could see her father's trouser legs and his long feet in black socks, and she would grasp one of his legs as if it were a safety bar on a ride at an amusement park. It was her father's space she was in; she could feel the sense of him there, just as Leo's office was suffused with Leo, and just as her own office had once held the sense of her, until she had abandoned it.

Leo, in his work life, traveled every month or so, going to see corporate clients out of town for one or two nights, staying in those business-traveler hotels where the robes were thick but the grain of the terry cloth was flattened from continual business-traveler wear, as person after person, tired and alone, slipped into the garment and sat on the bed with the remote in hand, sending the channels streaming by.

Amy and Leo had become separated from each other over time; she knew that she could have used Penny and Ian as a way back to him. She could have ignored Penny's explicit request for secrecy and instead told Leo everything, and then he would have been drawn into the story too, and there would now have been two couples in the mix, not just one. She could have told Leo all the details about the love affair, and maybe they would have been restored to each other.

"I think you should use this information against her," Leo might say after Amy told him. "Threaten to tell the hedge-fund husband. Extort big money out of her. Hey, tuition time is coming up."

"Or at least I could extort her for a family membership at her museum."

"Yes! But wait until they have a really good show there. Like . . . an exhibit of photos of immigrants in babushkas walking down the gangplank into the New World. Do you think they'll ever have an exhibit like that?"

"Oh, Leo, the question is, will they ever *not* have an exhibit like that?" And they would both laugh unfairly and embrace each other in the marital bed, secure in their love and their openness and in the fact that they had far more than Penny Ramsey and Ian Janeway would ever have together.

But Amy didn't tell Leo about the couple. She didn't tell Jill either but let everything languish, unsaid, and she didn't tell any of her other friends at the Golden Horn over the stirring scents of coffee and butter, which theoretically could make anyone confess something of an erotic nature. She kept the secret close to herself, as she'd been asked to do.

It was slightly unsettling to see Penny regarding Ian with such a crooked, besotted expression; it was not unlike looking at Penny's tiny foot encased in leather and fur. Ian, with his hair that never seemed quite combed, and the spray of freckles upon his face and neck and the back of his hands, had no real power at all except what he had over Penny. He was charming, but mostly he seemed to be one of the obscure and transient floaters who passed through the city so easily each year, absorbed into its undulating crowds, barely noticed by anyone.

"How will I manage over Christmas?" Ian asked. "Amy and I will have to see a lot of each other. You're going to be here, Amy, right?"

"Oh yes."

She and Leo probably couldn't afford to go anywhere, she knew, which was disappointing but not unexpected. Winter break was still in the distance, and the Ramseys would be on the island of St. Doe's, while Amy and Leo and Mason would be at home. They had made no plans, though at the tail end of Mason's school vacation, Amy's mother, Antonia, was coming to visit for several days when she traveled down to New York for her women's conference. She would move into the tiny study in the apartment and sleep on the inflatable mattress on the floor.

"You know, Amy, you could come to St. Doe's too," Penny said now.

"No we couldn't," Amy said, but it was pathetically wonderful to imagine lying side by side with Penny on a white beach, while their sons played in the waves. Penny and Amy would coax the last of the sunblock from the snouts of bottles, would talk in discreet voices about Ian Janeway: where the relationship was going, whether Ian was "too much" in love with her. "It's out of reach for us," Amy went on. "I can already hear Leo's response."

Penny paused. "Are you positive? Don't you have any mileage you could use? That would take away at least a little of the cost."

"We do have mileage," Amy said, suddenly too loud, the way Jill's daughter Nadia sometimes spoke when she became excited. For maybe it could work, she thought, maybe it was doable. She would ask Leo tonight.

"I have mileage," Ian put in, pointlessly.

After lunch the three of them walked through the galleries, stopping before a cluster of paintings by Magritte. The man with the green apple wasn't there now, but still Amy recalled that day with Mason so long ago. She read a placard about Magritte's relationship with his wife. Georgette had posed for him early on in their life together, and he considered her his muse. "I guess they were very domestic," Penny said to Ian. "Not wild at all. She posed and he painted, and then he got famous and they traveled a lot and were very close."

"Live with me," Ian said quietly.

"*Shh,*" said Penny.

There on the walls were the floating objects of dreams, but set among them, almost scattered discreetly, were occasional female nudes, and Amy thought that maybe these were all based on Georgette Magritte, who populated her husband's thoughts and gave him big ideas. Could that ever be enough for a full life? Karen Yip liked to please Wilson and make him feel good, and enjoy their life together. It would never be enough for Amy, though. She didn't know what would be enough in the long run. For now, she was content to stand here, watching. Ian said something softly to Penny, then glanced all around the gallery before coming close to her and putting his lips to her forehead. They were both small, well-designed people—as compact as sexualized children. She felt oddly proud of them for their love, as though she were their generous chaperone. She thought again about the trip to St. Doe's and wondered if it was possible to go. The couple stayed for a moment like that in the dim gray light of the gallery, and it seemed, from where she stood, that they shone, if only for each other.

Mason had recently told Amy yet another fact in his store of endless knowledge: in satellite maps of the earth, he said, you could always tell where the people were, even from great distances. Their faces, upturned slightly, gave off a shine that was like nothing else on earth—useful in love and a liability in warfare. Humans, no matter what they did, could not hide their incandescence.

N OW, IN THE NIGHT, when Leo began to groan and quiver slightly through his nightmare, Amy laid her hand on his broad bare back, and he turned toward her.

"Why did you wake me?" he said.

"You were having a nightmare. You were making those noises."

"No I wasn't."

"You always deny it, Leo. But you were like a rabid dog."

"Oh. Sorry." He rubbed his eyes. "I shouldn't eat before I go to sleep," he said, nodding toward the plate on his night table that held crumbs from pecan shortbread cookies. "But right, I did have a bad dream. I was very upset," he said, slowly remembering. "Something terrible was about to happen, and I saw you and Mason walking toward the woods—I don't even know where we were; it didn't look familiar—but it was dark in there, and I didn't want you to go, because I had a feeling that you'd never come out. It was sort of apocalyptic. Although I guess with apocalyptic you can't have 'sort of.'"

He lay back down in the darkness, Amy close against him. "I think it's because you're already thinking about the father-son weekend," she said.

"The weekend. Shit."

"It'll be okay, Leo."

"It'll be okay for you," he said. "You get to stay home. But I'm dreading it."

"It might not be so bad."

"It's not even as though we have to sleep in tents," Leo went on. "We've got cabins with electricity. But think about it: all those fathers and their sons in one place. And Mason and I are supposed to take a hike together. I don't hike. I'm not one of those dads who climb up the rock face of K2, or wherever they go for fun. Dads who hire Sherpas. I'm not like them. I don't have their money; I'm not aggressive the way they are."

"Well, I'm glad you're not, obviously. Just be with him. I think that's the point: ultrabusy fathers spending time with their sons."

"I don't know what's fun for Mason anymore," Leo said plaintively. "I don't really have time to know whether he's happy or not."

Happiness had become an elusive state in them and in most of the people they knew, but still made frequent appearances in children. Even if you yourself were unhappy and anxious, whenever you glimpsed happiness in your child, you suddenly became happy too. It was like unexpectedly spying a fawn paused on its stilty, trembling legs in a meadow. Without any self-consciousness you cried out, "Look!"

"I think he's happy," Amy decided. Then she added, "Once, an old woman in a museum said that Mason and I looked really happy. But it was a long time ago."

She and Leo were quiet together in a moment of uncertainty about their son. They both felt the distinct strain of melancholy that accompanies the ritual relinquishing of a child to the world. But if it was their own happiness they were pondering at that moment, neither of them wanted to mention it. Leo closed his eyes and squished the pillow against the side of his face. Amy closed her eyes too and thought about Penny and Ian. Then she snapped her eyes open.

"About the Ramseys," she said.

"Yes?" Leo opened his eyes again, looking right at her. Their noses were close, the points almost touching.

"I think I told you that they're going to St. Doe's over winter break," Amy said softly. "She wanted to know if we could come. I told her we couldn't."

"That's good," said Leo.

"I know it's totally out of reach."

"Yes. It is." He yawned. "In another life we can go," he said. "In a parallel universe. For now, I can barely deal with the father-son weekend."

"It'll be fine," she said.

There was a pause. "The guy who owns St. Doe's," said Leo. "He manufactures those biscuits, those Bing-Bongs. I wonder if they're any good."

"No idea."

They lay in silence, and Amy listened for Leo's breathing to shift, as it often quickly did, moving into a semi–sleep apnea that was troubling. Because he had gotten a little heavier in recent months, she worried that he would one day drop dead like that father in 14H. Sleep apnea happened in overweight men; you could hear the thin vibratory reed that was their air passage, and you lay awake beside them, knowing that all was not right. You were frightened, listening to your husband, the way a mother whom Amy had met in her Lamaze class a decade earlier had been frightened of her baby dying of crib death. As a result she had stayed awake all night in those early months, listening to the baby's inrush and outrush of air, until finally the mother herself collapsed from exhaustion. But Leo's breathing didn't change at all now, for he wasn't falling asleep. Both of them were awake; the conversation about St. Doe's and, in a sidelong way, about money, had agitated them equally.

"You still up over there?" she asked.

"Yeah. I keep thinking about that island."

"Sorry," she said. "Forget it."

"You know," he said after a moment, "we do have mileage."

Mileage! It was as though she controlled him like one of Mason's electronic devices. Delicately, Amy said, "I wondered about that. Penny mentioned it, in fact. And what about those credit card points we have? But I didn't want to bring it up with you. I know we can't afford it at all. It's an insanely expensive place. It's not for us."

"What reason did you give her that we couldn't come?"

"I said I didn't think we could manage it."

"You said that? 'Manage it'?"

"Well, it's true."

Leo shifted in the bed. "It makes me look failed," he said. "Like I can't take my family on a nice vacation."

"Not to St. Doe's, at least," said Amy.

"So what did she say?"

"That was when she asked if we could use our mileage," Amy said. "And then I thought about how we have a lot of credit card points too. Between all of that, maybe it would cover a substantial amount of the trip, wouldn't it?" Leo didn't reply. "We are always getting statements in the mail telling us that we've accumulated this huge number of points and this huge number of miles, and we always say we should do something about it," Amy went on, "but basically it's all theoretical. Can't we go somewhere big, finally?"

Leo sat up in bed, dazed, his shoulders slumped, and she remembered the day on the street, after they had gone to look at the public school for Mason, when Leo had stood and done calculations on his BlackBerry in the rain. She could see that he was going into calculation mode again. "I didn't mean that you should run the numbers now," she said. "Obviously."

Still, her husband rose from the bed in his boxers and with his thick bare chest, then plodded down the hall, which was vaguely lit by the pale green night-light that glowed from the guest bathroom. She followed him, saying, "Leo, don't," but he kept walking. The light made him look as if he were in the underground passage of a hospital, going on some ghastly, middle-of-the-night surgical mission or even some morgue mission. "Come back to bed," she said.

But he was troubled, threatened, interested, and he sat down in the tiny study, that room that was even too small for a child to live in. Leo did not seem to fit into this room at all, and he adjusted himself in the creaky, too-low office chair and began pulling various papers from the little pigeonholes of the Sven desk. "Leo, stop," she said. "Why are you doing this now? Are you just trying to make some kind of point? We can look at it tomorrow. You have to sleep."

"Too late. I'm up now," he said.

As he shuffled through papers, she saw the invoices and receipts from various business trips he had taken, and the interchangeable names of hotels in other cities: *Omega Park Centre. Woodbridge Suites. The Inn on Dover Green.* She watched as Leo continued to burrow through the piles.

"What are you trying to find?" she asked him.

"A mileage statement."

He found one a few moments later. Usually the freebies that were offered in daily life were of a very low caliber, but always the act of receiving something for free was itself uncomfortably satisfying. For dinner they would sometimes order take-out from Szechuan Treasure, and if they spent twenty dollars there—which was easy to do—they would receive a free plastic container of cold sesame noodles, nestling vermiculate in a soy and peanut bath. *O, free noodles!* Amy would think, pathetically.

Still, even in this urban setting at a time during which everything was slightly beyond their means, something free was like a little miracle. It did not even really matter exactly what the free thing itself was: noodles, a certificate for a .05-ounce container of antioxidant face cream to be redeemed at a department store cosmetics counter after you filled out a "Facial Type" form handed to you by a distracted and facially perfect young woman. Amy would eat those free noodles and she would ask for her thimble of anti-oxidant just the same way that, if Leo finally said they had the mileage to get them all to St. Doe's and then maybe enough crazily racked-up credit card points to grant them a big discount on a few nights in a beautiful room on that precious island, she would take it, she would grab it, she would do it.

"We'd probably have to leave at some terrible hour to get a decent fare," Leo said. "And sit in the cargo hold."

"I wouldn't care," Amy said.

"I'm just curious. What is it about Penny Ramsey that suddenly got you so interested?"

"She's got a big life," Amy said helplessly. "I like hearing about it, I guess."

Leo nodded. His small desk was suffocated with papers and invoices and monthly statements. They were everywhere around him. He folded his arms and put his head down on top of it all. Amy recalled, distantly, that back in the beginning, when they had first met at Kenley Shuber, Leo had worried that being a commercial litigator would "stunt" him; that was the word he had used. It was over this question of self-doubt that they had first fallen in love. They had gone to drink beers together one evening at Taggart's, a bar frequented by all the young associates at the firm. It was the first time they'd ever been alone, except for brief moments in the elevator. During the conversation at the bar he had told her how much he'd loved college, how he'd gotten excited reading Tolstoy and Kafka and Thomas Mann. They'd both been literature majors—she in English at Penn, he in comp lit at Rutgers—but he couldn't imagine doing anything bookish professionally. His term papers tended to be awkward and formal, yet he knew he would be a big reader his whole life; he was the kind of person, he said, for whom books were built. He told her that when he was younger, he'd imagined that the work of being a lawyer—the attention to language and phrasing and specificity—would allow him to retain some of his intellectual sheen, which would deepen over time into a burnish.

Mostly, though, Leo had been relieved by the idea that you could make a steady living from being a lawyer. His family had always been on the verge of being poor. His father would come home from the magazine stand he ran, bearing a new copy of *Ladies' Home Journal* for Leo's mother and *Mad* magazine for Leo. He and Leo would do the *Mad* fold-in on the back page and read that month's movie parody, and then both of Leo's parents would go into the master bedroom and argue about money for an hour. "We are being killed!" he had once heard his father cry. "We are getting it from all sides!" And his mother had shouted, "Calm down, you'll have an aneurysm!" Leo prayed to God, "Please don't let my dad have an aneurysm," though he did not even know what that was. Becoming a lawyer himself would protect Leo against such strife. He would take care of his own family; he would valiantly save them from aneurysms, from being killed, from getting it from all sides.

But the dream of hard work and a steady salary didn't take into account the idea that, in college, Leo would fall in love with literature and would then put it aside, the way many of the literature majors did. "The truth," he had said to Amy at that bar, "is that college is like this beautiful forest. And then if you leave the forest to go to law school or business school or something, everything changes." They sat side by side on bar stools, and as he spoke Amy imagined their two bodies rolling together in wet leaves inside the gates of that beautiful forest. "By the time you get safely ensconced in some corporate job," Leo went on, a little drunk, "you realize that the way you're going to spend the rest of your life has nothing to do with Tolstoy and Kafka and Thomas Mann."

Why, she had thought, lightly drunk herself, do people always say "Thomas Mann," instead of just "Mann"? Tolstoy and Kafka were one-namers, but not him. "Right. I *know*," she'd agreed urgently, and she wanted to leave the dark bar and head into a bookstore and buy Leo a beautifully bound edition of a Thomas Mann novel to keep on his night table and read a little bit of before he went to sleep at night. And then she just wanted him to kiss her; she would have done anything to get him to kiss her.

She pictured herself and Leo Buckner running back to that beautiful forest, but somehow it wouldn't be there anymore. Then Leo would look down at himself and see that he was dressed like an upgraded version of his potbellied, embattled magazine-seller father, Murray Buckner; and she would look down at herself and see that she was wearing a little skirt and panty hose, which she would have to take off and wash after work each evening in her single-girl sink and then wring into a tiny piece of seaweed and throw over the shower handle.

That night at Taggart's, Leo and Amy discussed whether he ought to leave the firm and become a public defender. She imagined him working in a government office with posters pinned to the walls and poor single mothers lined up on folding chairs in the hall with their paperwork in their hands, patiently waiting to see him. The floor would be covered with the worst burgundy carpeting in the world; his cheap desk chair would screech in protest whenever he leaned back.

But both of them knew that such a job would make the rest of life difficult and in many ways unmanageable. For slowly they were getting used to the not-bad salary that Kenley Shuber gave its young lawyers and the little extras that this life casually offered. Neither of them was very acquisitive, and neither was willing to sell out completely. ("I won't be representing Big Tabacky," Leo had said. Later, they would joke that he represented Little Baloney, and Little Honey-Smoked Turkey.)

By the time Leo paid for the beers, his fantasy of working as a public defender had already been roundly rejected, as had the more briefly sketched fantasy of becoming a specialist in constitutional law and teaching at a law school, like a highly intellectual friend of his had done. Amy and Leo had stood up, wobbly from drink, and headed back for another late night at Kenley Shuber, where the desk chairs cushioned the sacroiliac like a loving mother's hand, and a town car rolled the young lawyers gently home after hours. Leo stayed on at the firm, and his desire to be a public defender never again overtook him with ferocity. Recalling his parents' anguish about money, and his own need for comfort, he subtly shifted his desires, becoming more skilled and sure-handed at litigation. Amy was a pretty good lawyer too, competent at what she thought of as the safe and reliable art of trusts and estates. Then, like so many other women, she left the job she had never loved the way she had hoped she would.

Now, in the middle of the night, Amy thought she heard Leo sigh at his little desk in the study, where he sat unmoving with his head on his folded arms on top of all those papers, though the sound might have just been the heat, crackling and clapping through the vents.

"So do you think we can actually go?" she asked him, and she waited for the answer. At first, there was nothing.

"What?" Leo finally said, lifting his head. He had momentarily fallen back asleep under the desk lamp at three in the morning, with his wife standing right beside him, watching. "Where?" he asked. "Can we go where?"

"Over winter break. To St. Doe's."

"Oh," said Leo. Then, finally, "Yes," he said. "We can go."

Chapter

NINE

"S O WHEN DOES your vacation with the Ramseys begin?" Karen Yip wanted to know. It was early evening, the road was dark, and they were traveling in the Yip family's SUV, heading north. Karen sat up front with Amy beside her; in the back were Roberta and Jill; and in the very back was Jill's daughter, Nadia, who sat with her face almost pushed against the glass, singing quietly as she watched the black road and the other cars pulse by. Even while she was talking, Karen was able to convert miles into kilometers for entertainment, each mile of course being 1.609344 k, and the numbers bowed to her touch as the total distance increased accordingly.

"We'll leave on the Saturday after break starts," said Amy.

"Will you travel with them?" asked Karen.

"No, no. We'll meet them there. I don't even know Greg Ramsey. And what I do know, I don't love."

"Which of course explains why you're going on vacation with them," said Jill quietly, and Karen listened to see whether this criticism of Amy would flourish into something bigger, as it had lately done between the two friends around the topic of Penny Ramsey. But Amy didn't say anything. The others talked about their own upcoming Christmas vacations: where they would go, what they would do. Roberta said she and Nathaniel and the kids were staying home, as they usually did, but that this year she would be very busy, because she was actively involved in helping Brandy Gillop, that teenaged girl she'd taken for an abortion in South Dakota.

"We e-mail each other almost every day," Roberta said. "She's in the process of making slides of her artwork. I've seen a few. She's got a lot of potential, actually." Roberta leaned forward as far as her lap belt would allow and said, "Amy, I was thinking maybe you could pass along Brandy's slides to Penny Ramsey."

"Oh. Well, I guess so," said Amy. "But I don't know what Penny could do for her. It's not that kind of museum."

"Yes, but Penny obviously knows people in the art world. One thing leads to another. Brandy is off in South Dakota, and she's completely out of the loop."

"Sure, okay. Not a problem. Karen," Amy said, "this is so great; it's like the Golden Horn on wheels. Can't we just drive all night?"

"Fine with me," said Karen. "I love to drive."

They were comfortable and chatty and relaxed; the three other women were mildly talking about Brandy, and about Penny Ramsey's small and earnest museum, and whether people had a responsibility to help other, less connected people. Yes, they agreed, they did. The others didn't know it, but Karen was processing numbers in her mind during the drive, counting to herself and trying to guess exactly how much mileage came between exits, then checking the dashboard to see if she was right. She always came very close, with her innate feel for the way numbers unrolled and revealed themselves. Throughout her life, whenever there was a "guess the number of beads or nuts or candies in the jar" contest, she would always win, though the prizes had never been very interesting; once she had actually just won all the beads in the jar.

The women were on a mission. It was a Saturday evening, and the four of them and the little girl were heading for the Nature

Exploratorium upstate. The men and the boys had all left that morning for the father-son weekend; two coach buses had arrived at the school at seven A.M., and it was a safe bet that within a little while they had all begun to sing "Ninety-nine Bottles of Beer on the Wall," a droning, repetitive song that adults were supposed to hate but that secretly comforted Karen—not that she'd ever sung it or even heard it as a child.

Among the women in the car, Karen was the only one who had never been to summer camp or had even had a weekend camp experience as a girl. Back then, summers were meant for sitting in a hot room and studying ahead in her textbook, *Mathematical Concepts for Nimble Minds*, or, when she got a little older, for working the cash register at the Ideal Dumpling Palace on Stockton Street in San Francisco, where her parents had cooked and hosed down dishes. Summers were not for singing or for living in a cabin tossing jacks and braiding lanyards.

In the very back seat now, sitting alone and apparently content, Nadia had no memories or fantasies of camp either. She was simply a shy, uncommunicative little girl along for the ride, forced to accompany her mother on this trip. Jill and Nadia had taken the train into the city this morning and would be spending the night at Amy's apartment. In all likelihood, Nadia Hamlin thought only about today and the day before. At any rate, she was still singing lightly to herself, as she often did, and Karen had no idea if she was particularly aware of the women's conversation around her.

They were not supposed to be going up to the campgrounds this weekend; instead, while the husbands and sons were upstate, they were supposed to be staying behind in the city. It had been an agreeable plan until a moment late this afternoon when Karen Yip, busy straightening up her duplex apartment on East Sixty-third Street, saw that her husband, Wilson, had forgotten to pack the night-vision goggles for the twins, Caleb and Jonno. She could not believe it; the goggles were still lying on the front hall table, where they had been all week. She had placed them there days ago so that Wilson would be sure to pack them.

Wilson was a conscientious husband, and she had realized this was his future shortly after the two of them first met in the dining hall at MIT, side by side at the vegan steam table. Both, as it would turn out, were only temporarily vegan. All around them, students filled their plates with crumbling cakes of tofu, and lasagna prepared with soy or nut cheese. Easily forty percent of the students at the vegan table, she noted, were Asian, and not just from the subcontinent. And so there they were, Karen Tang from San Francisco's Chinatown and Wilson Yip from New York City's Chinatown, both freshmen, skinny, and slight. It was 1984, and Wilson, a nervous, hyperventilating type who played bass in a punk band on campus called Fermat, looked worried as he regarded the foods on Karen's plate, and finally, though they were strangers, he spoke. "Sprouts have a fairly high incidence of *E. coli* 0157," he blurted out.

"You're saying I should skip them?" Karen asked.

This was years before *E. coli* was to become a notorious poisoner of salad bars and bagged, prewashed greens. He shrugged and said, "I just thought you should have that information before you eat." Then he spooned some pinto beans and caking brown rice onto his own plate and went to sit with the other members of his band. She stood there, conflicted, then scraped the contents of her entire plate into the trash. Wilson Yip struck her as someone both worried and thoughtful. He had been looking like that ever since that first encounter. In many ways, they found that their lives were parallel. In addition to the two-Chinatowns coincidence, they had each attended a public science-and-technology high school in their respective cities and had then wound up at MIT on nearly full scholarship. At age eighteen, both of them were still virgins, though periodically beset by silent, unbearable longings for other people, which they never summoned up the nerve to vocalize or act upon. And, like everyone else on campus, both of them were calisthenically limber in mathematics.

When Wilson confessed to her that before he went to sleep at night he lay in bed reciting a litany of prime numbers to himself— Lucas prime, or maybe Mersenne, whatever the night seemed to call for ("For me, it's like choosing a wine," he had explained)—she was shocked, feeling that she'd located her other half. To this day, reciting sequences of prime numbers aloud at night was a ritual they both still enjoyed.

Wilson remembered everything. Nothing escaped his nervous, fact-trapping brain, and so it made no sense now that he had left their twin sons' goggles behind. The two sets of authentic, spy-grade night-vision goggles had been a present from Wilson's boss at the bank, who was a bit of an armchair espionage enthusiast. For an entire month the twins had been patiently waiting to use them on the father-son weekend. Caleb and Jonno, two hemmed-in city boys, had longed for the moment when they could wear the goggles in the cold sylvan darkness of the campgrounds.

As a rule, the twins did not take frustration well. Karen could picture their faces screwing up in disappointment when they realized the goggles weren't in the duffel bag. It wasn't an emergency, Karen knew. It wasn't Jake Giffen's EpiPen that Wilson had forgotten to pack, but still she was agitated by his lapse in the way she sometimes became agitated when certain details did not fall into place: when people were late, or when numbers did not agree. And so she had called Amy, sensing that her friend would convince her that, if it mattered so much to her, Karen could drive up to the campgrounds and personally deliver the night-vision goggles to her sons. Which was exactly what had happened. Even better, Amy suggested they could turn it into a group outing, and so she had convinced Roberta to come along too (her daughter, Grace, could go to a friend's apartment for a sleepover), and also Jill, because Donald would be flooded with work all weekend anyway.

So there they all were now, on the parkway heading northward eighty-five miles to a place where the natural beauty was abundant, even at this time of year, and the men and the boys had thought they would be alone for a weekend. "Is this a mistake, do you think?" Karen asked at the wheel. "Invading their privacy like this? The twins were really looking forward to using those goggles, but maybe they'll be annoyed to see me."

"Enough with the goggles," Roberta Sokolov said. "We are half-way there, Karen. I'm sure they'll be glad to have them."

"Anyway," Jill put in, "what do you think they're doing that's so private?"

"I have no idea," said Roberta. "Nathaniel probably feels so out of place." This, Karen thought, was true; Roberta's puppeteer/cameraman husband was like someone from the '60s, and while he had always been nice to Karen, she never knew what to say to him.

"Leo was dreading it too," Amy said.

"At least Leo fits in," said Roberta. "He's part of that whole corporate world. Nathaniel hasn't worn a tie in decades."

"Leo doesn't fit in," Amy said defensively.

"Well, Wilson was looking forward to the weekend," Karen said.

"I can just picture them all," said Amy, "dancing around a campfire half naked."

Karen dutifully envisioned the men dancing around a campfire, getting themselves all worked up, beating the skins of drums. She rarely came up with vivid imaginary scenarios on her own but was an astonishingly literal person, and her friends often teased her about this, telling her that although she had no imagination, they loved her anyway. They were right, of course; she had almost no imagination at all but tended to visualize the world as a series of orderly channels and corridors inlaid on a gigantic grid. Wilson visualized it this way too, and so, probably, did Caleb and Jonno, who both enjoyed math puzzles and Rubik's Cubes but demonstrated no interest in the capriciousness of nature or in storybooks or generally in narrative of any kind. They came by it honestly; the entire Yip family was literal, focused, concerned mostly with the quantifiable.

Yet when someone else came up with a starter image—men dancing in the woods, for instance—lately Karen had found herself gently nudged toward a desire to shade in the rest of the details. So now she dutifully tried to visualize Wilson sitting between Caleb and Jonno, and Leo beside Mason, and Roberta's lanky husband, Nathaniel, and their son, Harry, and the collection of highly imposing husbands in the grade, including Penny Ramsey's short, thick,

bantam husband, Greg, and their son, Holden, and all the other
men and boys. She carefully placed them in this setting; the smell of
pine would mingle easily with the smell of wild boar being roasted
over a fire, and then suddenly, through a clearing in the trees, four
women and a little girl would appear, feminine and flushed, bearing
goggles.

THEY ARRIVED at almost nine at night, and Karen steered the
big car into the makeshift parking lot at the entrance to the
campgrounds. The coach buses were gone and would return tomorrow afternoon to take the boys and their fathers home. The Yip car
seemed out of place here, a remnant of the paranoid city. It was a
jumbo SUV, and Wilson had begun leasing a series of them since
right before the twins had been born, ten years earlier, at only thirty-
two weeks' gestation. Karen's water had broken one morning when
she was shopping at Camarata & Bello. She had been standing by the
sloping glass of the meats counter in the rear of the store while
the butcher sliced mortadella for her with a knife like a scimitar.
As the blade buried into the meat, she suddenly felt a sharp pull, as
though she herself were being cut, and she said, "Oh my God."

Then there came a slap sound like wet laundry being dropped,
and she understood it had come from *her*, though she felt no connection to the sound at all. But there was some sensation then too,
and Karen looked downward with dread and saw that the white tiled
floor below her had been splashed with water. The woman next in
line took Karen's arm and said, "Honey, your water broke. You have
to get to the hospital."

"It's too early," Karen cried.

"Oh, they're open," the woman said with a laugh, then abruptly
stopped, realizing.

In the hospital the doctors said that the babies would have to
be delivered within twenty-four hours. When it became clear that
Karen's cervix was not going to open, she was taken into a deliv-

ery room and her stomach was swabbed bright rust with antiseptic. The obstetrician, a stylish woman who looked, as Roberta had said later upon seeing her, like a buyer for designer sportswear, seemed almost irritated that Karen had not found the discipline to keep her water from breaking, to keep those babies in place until near their due date. Karen felt like a negligent mother who has forgotten to strap her infants into their car seats and has instead let them hurl freely through space. Everyone told her it wasn't her fault, she had done nothing wrong, but she still felt furious with herself and forcefully ashamed. A month later, when Caleb and Jonno were released from the NICU, their lungs finally mature, Karen was obsessed with conveying them in perfect safety, as if to make up for her earlier, inexcusable lapse.

On the morning the twins came home, the first of the cars that Wilson would lease sat high up on its haunches at the curb on Fifth Avenue in front of the hospital. Wilson slid Jonno and Caleb into their car seats in the same order in which they had been delivered into the world. Karen's mother, Chu Hua Tang, had flown in from San Francisco and had been there in the car that morning too, helping to transport the babies, braying at her son-in-law in rapid Chinese, saying, "Do it this way! No, not like that. Too tight around the neck. Do you want your sons to end up stupid?"

Karen was often made breathless by her mother's insults to Wilson, but he just received them indifferently; because Chu Hua was not *his* mother, he said, the words could not disturb him. That day outside the hospital, Wilson and his mother-in-law even seemed to be co-conspirators, and Karen felt like a visitor who'd had nothing to do with the creation of these tender fraternal twin boys. The babies still seemed alien to her, and the car itself did too. Cars like this, Karen had thought at the time, were for large American families with children who sprawled out playing with Game Boys and decks of Uno, who littered every available surface with their garbage, who sucked juice boxes into convexity as if on life support. The Yips would not transform into such a family for years, if ever.

But they needed the car, Wilson had insisted before the babies' birth, and she understood that he had been waiting for much of his life to own a car like this. SUVs hadn't existed when he was growing up, but there had been boatlike Lincoln Continentals and station wagons, neither of which his family had owned, of course. No one they knew growing up had even owned a *bad* car. So the wet dream of those two types of automobiles had fused into one and created a car that looked like this one: big and fat as a pregnant wife, but as powerful as her husband.

The SUV, in Chu Hua's eyes, was a golden coach, and she behaved as if it were a present for *her*. Of course, for every noise Chu Hua made that indicated how excited she was by Wilson and Karen's money, she made another one to indicate her displeasure with some detail of their lives. The car was beautiful, she had declared, but the upholstery was "cold and leathery." *That's because it's made of leather, Ma,* Karen had wanted to cry, but she'd said nothing.

That morning had taken place a full decade ago, and now Karen rarely drove their car anywhere outside the city, except in the summer, when she took the boys upstate to their summer house. And here were Karen and her friends in the parking lot of the campgrounds, sitting in the stilled car. "What do you think they're doing right now?" Jill asked as they sat there. "What do men do when women aren't around?"

"I don't want to know," said Roberta.

"Maybe they form a little consciousness-raising group, like my mother and her friends used to," said Amy. "My sisters and my father and I had to stay upstairs. My mother told me that one night, back in the early seventies, they looked into another woman's cervix."

"Imagine if you'd come downstairs," said Jill, shaking her head.

"Did they eat their own placentas too?" Roberta asked. "They used to do that back then."

"No one really did that," said Amy. "It's sort of a myth. Or maybe a few women did, forever giving feminists a bad name."

"I really don't think feminists have a bad name," Karen said. "I just don't think it's a necessary name. It's part of the past. It's some angry, old-style image."

"Don't tell my mother that," Amy said. "She hates when women our age don't call ourselves feminists. I think she thinks we ought to do it almost in honor of her and her friends." Uncertainly, she added, "I call myself a feminist. You don't?"

"Theoretically I do," said Roberta. "It's not like it usually comes up. You don't have to put it down on medical forms or anything. But of course I'm a feminist. They accomplished a lot."

"Yes, and look how equal we are."

"Don't blame *them*," said Roberta. "It's not their fault. People blame mothers all the time, and it's deeply unfair."

"You're always blaming your mother for something," said Amy.

"*My* mother? Well, that's different," Roberta said, and they laughed.

"It's so quiet in there," said Jill after a moment. "I can't believe even the *boys* aren't making any noise."

"I think," said Amy, "the boys are playing video games, and the men are on conference calls."

"No," said Karen. "They wouldn't do that. It's not allowed. 'Leave your work behind,' the note from the school said."

"I was kidding," said Amy.

Karen was reflexively protective of Wilson; even a joking kind of criticism that included him as part of a group made her uncomfortable. He was the most ethical and elegant husband of all of them, with his hairless face and body and shining black hair and long hands, and she would be reminded of this fact as soon as she saw him at the campgrounds. Her eye would go directly to him, as if only he were illuminated, separated from all the others by some kind of special goggles she would be wearing that showed the world in Wilson-vision. Everyone else would fade away until all she could see was him.

"We're going camping, and camping's fun," Jill's daughter Nadia said.

"Not really camping, honey," said Jill. "Just a quick visit into the woods to give the twins the goggles that they left behind. It's freezing outside." They all got out of the car, and Karen popped the trunk, her breath rolling through the cold air as she scrabbled inside for a few flashlights that she'd thought to bring and the two sets of goggles. "So let's see these amazing objects," Jill said, and then, on an impulse, Karen took one of the pairs of goggles out of its box and attempted to strap it to her own head. But the rubber strap was meant for the much smaller head circumference of a child. She loosened it, flicked a switch, and the night became a sickly yellow.

"It's like looking at the world through a urine sample," Amy said, when she tried them on. Every bush and tree had become individuated.

"Can I try?" Nadia asked tentatively, holding out her hands, and Karen strapped the second pair of goggles to the little girl's head. "Oh!" Nadia cried as the yellow light was turned on and the world lit up just for her. "Wow!"

There seemed to be two different entrances into the campgrounds, and the women arbitrarily chose one. They walked and walked, but after about five minutes the trail ended and they found themselves wading into the cold woods. They shuffled through drifts of leaves and twigs, using the flashlights and the goggles to guide the way. Instinct drew them in a particular direction, and they went from tree to tree and bush to bush, finding another trail and then choosing which fork in the path to take next, all of this done in a darkness that was punctuated by flashlights and urine-vision and lights from the cabins in the distance.

"If we were all to be eaten by a bear in a moment of ursine barbarism," said Roberta, "nobody would ever know what we had been doing here. It would be this huge mystery: why we were all in the woods at the father-son weekend. It would become a legend, and every year our husbands would tell the kids another version of what they thought had happened to us."

"They'd tell it to their second wives too," said Jill.

"What second wives?" Karen asked, confused.

"Karen. It's a *joke*," said Roberta.

"Oh."

"And then our husbands would say, 'Well, son, I've begun to

believe that the reason that your *original* mom and her friends drove all the way up to the campgrounds was to say "I love you."'"

"'But unfortunately, son,'" Jill said, "'one of Mommy's friends had her menses at the time, and that attracted a bear.'"

"I actually do have my period," said Karen. "Fairly heavy too."

"Oh Karen," Amy said, "your idea of fairly heavy is probably a thimbleful of blood, am I right? Like a pinprick on a sewing hoop in a fairy tale."

"No, as a matter of fact, it's not," Karen said, but the others seemed to suspect, accurately, that her neat little body was rarely overcome by torrents, the way their bodies apparently were.

"I see a light up ahead," Jill said.

"'I see a ring,'" said Amy.

"A ring? Where?" Karen asked.

"It's the opening of *The Waves*," explained Amy. "Virginia Woolf. My senior thesis at Penn. I still know exactly how the novel begins." She began to recite:

"I see a ring," said Bernard, "hanging above me. It quivers and hangs in a loop of light."

"I see a slab of pale yellow," said Susan, "spreading away until it meets a purple stripe."

"I hear a sound," said Rhoda, "cheep, chirp; cheep, chirp; going up and down."

When she finished, the women were silent for a moment. "That's interesting writing," said Karen. "Kind of strange." She was thinking: *Too strange. Much too strange for me.* Words, to Karen, were what numbers were to almost everyone else; they confounded her and always seemed as elusive as a quivering ring hanging in the distance just past fingertip reach.

"It's not my favorite of her novels," said Amy, "but it's mesmerizing. I once read the entire thing out loud to Leo."

"And he let you?" Karen asked.

"Oh, he loved it."

"I can't imagine Wilson letting anyone read to him that much, even when he was a baby, unless it was the NASDAQ."

As the women drew nearer to the center of the camp, a bonfire scented the air, and the sky became slightly lighter from the flames. The smell reached them first, then the light, and soon they heard the singing. It was this that stopped them, finally—the surprising sound of a hundred male voices, all joining together in some kind of idealized, testosterone-drunk vocal perfection. It was a world without women, Amy said later, as though they had stumbled upon an encampment of Civil War soldiers stopping for the night.

"Whoa, listen to that," said Karen.

The men's voices were lifting up in a song that Wilson would never have sung on his own, so dismissive would he have been of its sentimentality. He still liked the '80s punk music he'd listened to in college and had played when he was in the band Fermat. Over time, though, that punk streak had made fewer appearances in him. He rarely played the expensive electric bass he'd treated himself to on his thirtieth birthday, after he'd received his first big bonus from the bank. Karen knew enough to realize that here, out among the logs and stones, and the bits of cinder that flew into the eye, and the marshmallows pierced dully by crooked twigs, it was very unusual for Wilson and all the others to be singing that old Joan Baez folk song "Donna Donna." But that was what they were doing, and they sang with improbable beauty:

> *On a wagon, bound for market,*
> *there's a calf with a mournful eye.*
> *High above him, there's a swallow,*
> *winging swiftly through the sky.*
> *How the winds are laughing,*
> *they laugh with all their might,*
> *laugh and laugh the whole day through and*
> *half the summer's night . . .*

"They sound *great*," said Jill. "I'm floored."

The men were singing angelically, and without obvious irony inflecting their often-ironic voices. The women closed in on the campfire, and through the night-vision goggles and with their flashlights, they watched the scene. One or two fathers stalked the periphery on illegal cell phones, whispering into them with agitation. But they were a small minority; the other men had agreeably left their business behind overnight. There were Wilson and the twins, all three of them wearing parkas with reflector strips on the side. There, a few feet away, was Leo Buckner with Mason beside him, the big uncomfortable man and his intelligent son, their eyes glittering in the night. They were all singing openly, willingly, without rolling their eyes or demonstrating any overt sarcasm.

How, Karen wondered, did Wilson even know the lyrics to this song? The men and boys sang all the verses, and then, when the singing ended, the women watched from their place behind the trees as Alec Giffen, the father of Jake, the boy with the peanut allergy, suddenly stood up in the center of the circle. He was dressed, like all the fathers, in lumberjack clothes. It was established that he had been a designated "team leader" during the games today, and so tonight he had been given the task of addressing the group at large. "Guys," Alec Giffen said. "Listen up!" He raised a hand, and the talking soon subsided. "You all sang great," he said. "Give yourselves a big hand."

There was a round of clapping and fist-pumping. It had been a long day in the woods, Alec Giffen said. They had hiked and climbed, and had had a "most excellent" cold-weather color war, and even if the red team had crushed the heart and soul of the blue team, it had been all in fun, and everyone had performed admirably. There was more applause, and then he said, "And now I'd like to invite one father-son team up here to recite the Auburn Day School Pledge. One team in particular, whose spirit of cooperation and skill today has been outstanding."

He looked around the group, going one by one, as though he was mulling this choice among the various firelit faces when instead the choice had likely been sealed from the beginning. Karen longed for Wilson and Caleb and Jonno to be the chosen team, but she knew this wouldn't happen; her sons' twinness served somehow to cancel them out and probably always would, in various ways. Yet the twins needed each other. They were so much smaller than the other children. Just the fact of their prematurity and how much they had endured back in the NICU, Karen thought now, should be reason enough for Alec Giffen to choose them.

You could have fit them in your hand back then, she wanted to remind Alec Giffen through the bushes. She and Wilson had sat there in the unit with the beeping monitors and the rows of sick babies night after night in chairs by the incubators, and they had put their gloved hands in through the holes and touched the twins with smooth, fingerprintless fingers, encouraging them toward life, when it seemed as though the twins might just as well have preferred not to exist, so clearly in pain were they, hooked up to tiny tubes, the heels of their feet as darkly translucent as jam. What more did Alec Giffen need to know?

Choose the twins, Karen Yip thought with powerful concentration, and she could picture both boys' faces overcome with excitement upon being selected. She had no idea of what it meant to be chosen for this particular honor: Would they also receive a trophy, a plaque, or be held aloft on a sea of crossed arms? Whatever it was, she wanted it for them. Alec Giffen's eyes looked all around, taking the measure of these eager boys and their anxious fathers. Well, Karen thought, it certainly wasn't going to be unemployed Len Goodling and his son Felix. It probably wouldn't be slouchy, commune-style Nathaniel and little Harry. Every one of the males made eye contact with Alec Giffen; it was impossible not to feel how desperate the boys were to be selected. Poor Caleb and Jonno, Karen saw, were both sitting up straighter, trying to appear like models of team spirit, but she was sure it would do no good.

Alec Giffen, the CFO of a company that made ink-jet cartridges, turned slowly in a circle, looking and looking. Finally, when he stopped, everyone could see where he had landed.

"Well," Amy whispered darkly beside Karen. "Who could have guessed?"

"*Shh,*" said Karen.

"Holden Ramsey and his dad Greg," intoned Alec, "would you both come up here?"

Greg Ramsey was not a tall man at all but was solid and strong, a starter of fights and a broker of significant deals. He and his son, Holden, both of them appearing entirely unsurprised, stood and walked into the center of the circle. Sounds of furious whispering came from among the boys, and Alec quickly told them to pipe down. Karen recalled all the times when the twins came home from school in the afternoon and sat at the table and spilled all their heartfelt secrets and aggravations to her about how Holden Ramsey always won everything.

"It just isn't fair," Caleb said once, near tears. "Basically, Mom, I don't even think he's better at anything than anybody else. I just think he cares more about winning."

If there was a contest of some kind or a physical or academic challenge, Holden would win it. And so, Karen understood, would his father. When Amy suddenly became such good friends with Penny this fall, she'd made it clear that Greg was not part of the friendship at all. "We don't have a 'couples' friendship," Amy had said defensively. "I've never really spoken to him, except to say hi over the years at curriculum night and at the pancake breakfast. He probably has no idea of who I am, actually."

But in a few weeks, when school let out for winter break, Amy and Leo would be going on vacation to St. Doe's with the Ramseys, and Amy would get to know him then. Karen watched now as Amy peered hard at Greg Ramsey; it seemed as though she couldn't stop looking. Greg stood in a tan sheepskin coat with his son by his side; both of them with their chins tilted slightly upward.

"You know, he willed the other fathers to choose them," Amy whispered.

"What do you mean?" said Karen. "He hypnotized them?"

"He gets what he wants. Penny says he's very entitled."

"Oh, we're all entitled," Jill said.

But Karen could barely listen; she was distracted by the obvious way all the other men and boys wanted to please the Ramseys. Really, there was nothing to do about it, she thought, and probably the Ramsey father and son had in fact summoned up every ounce of team spirit today that circulated in their bodies. Karen's own sons tended to be cautious, and Wilson was never particularly fixated on winning. Still he was extraordinarily successful, though a different type: the modest, results-oriented whiz-kid banker.

Greg and Holden Ramsey had been born to be chosen. This was the way the world worked, and even though this fact was usually hidden more skillfully, there was something startling and almost bracing about its openness now. After a moment of posing, Holden and his father acknowledged each other with crisp nods of the head, as if a business deal was being transacted, and then they high-fived each other, knocked their knuckles together, and finally Holden put his arms behind his back and looked heavenward, reciting the first stanza of the Auburn Day Pledge:

In excellence shall I find my home,
In honesty shall I seek my guide,
In innocence shall I place my trust,
In knowledge shall I reach my stride.

His father took over at this point for the final two stanzas. The other boys twitched and rustled, but no one spoke. They all seemed to hold some reverence for the school pledge and for the school itself, which despite its pretensions and too-frequent smugness was a place with many passionate teachers who often had students clustered around them. The boys were educated in ways that would alter and expand them. They would learn how to give a speech and how to look an adult in the eye during a conversation. They would learn how to conduct themselves in the world, how to be civil. Their own fathers had likely been clueless about all of this at their sons' age. Certainly,

Karen thought, Wilson at ten had spent a lot of time cringing and stammering and trying to disappear into himself.

Now, in the circle, the love that the boys and the men felt for the school overtook the resentment they felt for the Ramseys' irrevocable control, and soon the resentment lessened. By the time the ceremony broke up with an Indian chant, arms crossed and linked, everyone in that circle was content, and all was forgiven. No trophy or plaque was handed out; the reward, apparently, was simply being allowed to stand in the center of the circle, establishing quiet dominance and expressing tacit sentimentality about the school. The men and their sons dispersed, walking away from the now-dead campfire and down a hill toward the lights of their waiting cabins.

"Quick, go give them the goggles now," Amy said to Karen. "Here's your chance. We can't really follow them to the cabins."

Karen watched the back of her sons' heads, saw them bobbing around Wilson like fireflies. *Like fireflies!* A freestanding image had occurred to her for a change; something had overtaken her that was visual in nature. Was *everything* changing for her here in the woods tonight? Was this what her friends had felt when they were girls, spending the summer at camp? Whatever it was, it made her not want to approach Wilson and the twins, at least not yet. She didn't want to disturb them; it would be like bothering a raccoon family that was stopping to eat in the forest. *There.* Another image. Instead, she wanted to quietly follow behind and observe them in their habitat.

"Aren't you going to do it?" Amy asked.

"Not yet," Karen said.

So they followed from a distance, still staying in the outlying woods. The men were deep in talk, and the boys ran in front of them, zigzagging back and forth across the path. Karen observed a quick moment that she might easily have missed: The twins were in a crowd of boys, and when they went past the men, Wilson reached down and scooped both sons up briefly, swinging them in the air. They were shrimpy, small, only 60 pounds a boy—just 54.55 kilograms total   so it wasn't too hard for him to do.

"Dad!" Caleb cried, as in, *Dad, I'm too old for this,* but there came a hoot of laughter, and Karen saw that the boys were having such a good time right then, and that Wilson was too.

"You know what?" Karen said to the other women. "I don't want to bother them. I don't even want them to know we were here."

"Really?" said Jill, stopping and turning.

"It just feels too intrusive suddenly."

"I know what you mean," Jill said. "They were all so sweet, in a way. Singing 'Donna Donna.'"

"Except Greg Ramsey," said Amy. "He's not sweet."

"True," said Karen. But men like Greg Ramsey were everywhere, she knew. Wilson occasionally referred to these kinds of men with disdain. The corporate money world was by nature male and treacherous, of course, and it attracted some preternaturally competitive men like Greg Ramsey. There was nothing surprising about them or even all that pungently repellent. You didn't have to love them; you didn't have to marry them yourself, but you somehow had to find a way to share the earth with them.

Then, Amy suddenly said, "Penny can't stand him, you know."

"Who?" asked Roberta.

"Greg."

"She can't stand her own husband?" said Karen, who found this a shocking statement. How could anyone say such a thing? Wilson was her darling. Husbands and wives were meant to be each other's protectors; otherwise, what was the point of marriage?

"No, she can't. She says he's changed."

"Is he unfaithful to her or something?" asked Roberta. "That wouldn't surprise me at all."

Amy didn't reply, and so Jill said, "Amy?" There was a long look between the two close friends. They had known each other for so long—much longer than any of the others had known one another— that Karen realized an entire conversation was taking place between Amy and Jill right now, even though the rest of them could not hear it. Karen looked back and forth between their faces: Amy seemed uneasy, and Jill appeared mildly triumphant, if unhappy. Then, finally, the silent conversation was over. Jill nodded and said, "So that's it, right? It's not that Greg is unfaithful; it's Penny. It's *her*. Just tell me if I'm right."

"Jill, I really cannot talk about this," said Amy. "Please don't make me. I swore to Penny that I wouldn't."

"Well, there's my answer," said Jill. "End of story. Thank you." She was quiet for a second, and then she said, "I guess that's what you talk about with her. That's what the closeness is all about: her love affair! She talks, and you listen. You've always been a good listener, Amy."

"Just stop, Jill, okay?" Amy said. "Penny and I do have an actual friendship, despite what you think. And listen, I have to reiterate: None of you can discuss this with anyone, okay?"

"So who's the lover?" Jill asked.

"It doesn't matter," said Amy. "No one you know. A museum person."

"What I don't understand," Karen suddenly said, because she could not suppress it any longer, "is how she can be so disloyal."

"She needed someone to talk to," Amy explained. "We had an intense moment together, back when Dustin Kavanaugh got mugged. And she just basically blurted it out."

"No," said Karen, "I mean the affair." Whenever Karen Yip learned of someone's marital infidelity, she felt immediate distaste.

"And excuse me, but you're actually going on vacation with the Ramseys over winter break?" asked Jill.

Karen was lightly appalled, but she had no personal stake in this; Jill, however, sounded almost furious with Amy. Everyone knew that ever since Jill had moved away, Amy had sometimes ignored her in favor of this glamorous museum director, this newly revealed marital cheater.

"I barely know him," Amy said in a small voice.

"But you're going to sit around with them the whole time," Jill went on, "knowing what you know? And knowing that Greg doesn't know? Does Leo know too?"

"I told you, no one does except you."

"Mommy, I have to yuniate," Nadia suddenly said. Karen had nearly forgotten she was there.

"*Urinate*," Jill said. "Oh, honey, now?"

"Yes."

"Okay." Jill turned to the others and said, "Wait for me, okay?" She headed out into the woods behind her daughter, and Karen was grateful for the distraction from the awkwardness of Amy and Jill staring each other down. Karen had never had a friendship with another woman as close as theirs, and she'd never wanted one. She had all that she needed with Wilson; there was no reason to look anywhere else.

Within a moment they all heard Jill say, "*More* privacy? Well, where do you want me to go, Nadia?"

"Over there."

Then there were footsteps and the parting of branches, and Jill said, "Okay, Nadia, I'm over there. You've got more privacy now."

They heard a sizzle of urine falling onto a bed of leaves; it was such a personal moment, and it seemed strangely invasive to be listening like this, just as it had begun to seem invasive to be here at the campgrounds at all. The twins had been doing fine without their mother and without the goggles. Their faces, viewed briefly through the branches and the yellow light of the equipment they would not use this weekend, had evinced no sorrow. They had moved on from their great goggles-yearning; they had adapted. The women would drive back to New York City as quietly as they had come, and there they would wait for their men to return the next day.

Karen knew mothers at the school who said they had given up their jobs for their children. Sometimes they said they had done it for both their husbands and their children. "I just like to be there at the end of the school day," Amy had recently said at the Golden Horn. "I like the idea of being there for Mason, at least for now. It's not going to last much longer."

But Karen had not given up her job for her sons or for Wilson. She knew precisely whom she had given it up for, at least originally: her parents, her mother-in-law, and all her relatives who lived in either the New York or the San Francisco Chinatown, among streets strong with fish heads and star anise. Whenever Karen's parents came to visit—both now retired and living in a senior citizens' complex in the Bay Area, thanks to Wilson's continual generosity—they marveled in Chinese at the two-floor apartment, the built-in shelving in the twins' bedrooms, and the enormous SUV, perhaps bigger than the vessel on which the Tang relatives had long ago set sail from Jiangsu Province. Karen's parents, still seemingly tired from having worked for so long in a restaurant kitchen, her father limping slightly for obscure reasons, her mother waddling a little, walked up and down the stairs of the duplex with satisfaction. Karen's mother started to cry when she picked up a particularly ornate silver dish, saying, "This pretty as anything."

After the twins were born early and in such turmoil, and everyone worried that they might have intellectual deficits (*that* proved laughable, for they were mathematically brilliant boys), Karen knew she would not return to her statistical analysis job for a long time. Her parents had essentially told the relatives, "Karen stays home with the twins, but she does not need to go back to work, *ever*, even when they are older. Her husband Wilson the banker makes so much money that they live in a two-floor apartment in New York City, and she never has to work again in her life." The relatives were suitably impressed.

Karen knew she was supposed to dissuade them from thinking this way. But the enjoyment she felt when her mother and father flew across the country business class, paid for by Wilson, and then walked around the apartment fussing over the shining objects and commenting on the fact that Karen had a husband who could take care of everything, was profound.

Once, back when the twins started kindergarten and Karen mentioned during a telephone call to her parents that she was vaguely thinking of returning to work, her mother had said in an alarmed voice, "Wilson he lose his job?"

"What?" Karen said. "You're talking nonsense, Ma. Of course not."

"Then why do you want to go to work?" her mother asked. "Work made my hands look like cut-up pieces of gingerroot."

"I didn't work with my hands," Karen said, knowing her words were snotty, and she was ashamed. Perhaps her brain looked like gingerroot, gnarled from all the numbers she had pushed through it, distorting its shape. She didn't *need* to work, and this fact was a gift to her mother and father, former employees of the Ideal Dumpling Palace in San Francisco, who could not fathom the different components of their daughter's life but knew enough to be dazzled.

It was a gift to them as well as an excuse, but whatever it was, over the years Karen's vague desire to work rarely got specific. She didn't question her own feelings very often, except once in a while when she imagined herself accepting a position as a statistical analyst working for one of the most prestigious firms possible. But the fantasy halted there, because she didn't actually want another job yet, though still she accepted interviews. She was given tours of the facility and shown the view from corner offices and told all about the corporate trip to Maui taken by all the top-level analysts.

But really, Karen enjoyed her life as it was. She had a view already; she could go to Maui on her own. Her life had aesthetic and airy dimensions; it wasn't hectic or brutal, ugly or frantic, like her family life as a child. Now she kept freesia in a vase in the front hall, which Wilson liked, and commented on. Sometimes she attended a morning concert, sitting and listening to chamber music in a room full of retirees and other women. Soon she might learn to speak Italian at one of those language schools, because it was such a beautiful language. She shopped at Camarata & Bello a few times a week, even though she still had a strong memory of the time her water had broken there, and even though the prices were so ridiculous that everyone said it was criminal. But when she brought home the little containers of bright salads flecked with currants and Aztec grains, she thought about how extraordinary it was that she had reached a point in her life at which she could have comfort and serenity and luxury. Wilson liked seeing her happy; he told her this frequently. Her happiness, he said, inspired him; the nape of her neck inspired him; the way she mothered their sons inspired him; her mathematical intelligence inspired him too.

"Is it selfish of me?" she had asked him once in bed. "You work all the time." But Wilson reminded her that he loved working all the time; he was treated very well at the bank, and he couldn't imagine doing anything else with his life or retiring early on the money they'd made, the way some people did. He had no interest in golf or woodworking or taking cycling trips through British Columbia. He wanted to stay a banker forever, in the beautiful suits that his wife liked to help him choose, sitting behind the broad surface of his desk, on which the papers lay in geometrical and beguiling piles. And she wanted to create a home for him that was calm, exquisite.

Karen was genuinely grateful for what they had, and she and Wilson gave a lot of money to charity every year. Their names appeared on the donors page of the programs from various charity events, listed under the category "High Hurdlers," or "Foundation Builders," or "Director's Circle," alongside the names of other couples, and sometimes several corporations. "Giving back," people called it, strangely. Karen knew how privileged she was. After she had asked Wilson that question about whether she was selfish, she felt almost no residual ambivalence about her own desire to make her family life run beautifully, and to stay in one place, eating an expensive little salad from its container. All that she lacked was more direct contact with numbers and number theory.

In the distance now, Karen heard Jill's voice suddenly rising up. She was calling out something about Nadia, who apparently had wandered off a few yards into the woods for privacy, and Jill couldn't find her right away and was suddenly quietly hysterical. So they all hurried in the direction of Jill's voice, pushing through the trees and out into the clearing that the men and boys had so recently occupied. There was a little light from the moon now, and from the lit path to the cabins, but no sense of life anywhere around them.

"Nadia!" they called. "Nadia!" She'd been right *here*.

"We'll find her in two seconds, Jill," said Karen.

They moved their flashlights in widening circles around the trees and patches of dark sky. "Nadia! Nadia!" they called.

"Something is not quite right with her," Jill whispered to the others.

"She's just dreamy, Jill," Amy said. "Nadia! Nadia!"

"I feel as though she has no idea of where she is in the world," Jill went on, aching and frantic. "She sings that sad song: '*Rise, sorrow, 'neath the saffron sister tree.*'"

"Our yoga mantra," said Roberta, for they used Nadia's song at the end of every yoga session now.

"Maybe she's still in trauma," Jill said. "Nadia! Nadia! How can I know anything about her? Nadia!"

"I don't know anything about the twins either," Karen offered. "Your kids just *live* with you. When I brought the boys home from the NICU, I thought, Who *are* you?"

"I'm sure she's just past these trees," said Amy.

"Sometimes I actually think I should have left her there," Jill said in a whisper.

"Where?" asked Roberta, straining to hear.

"In Russia. She could have grown up and worked in a grocery store. Her name tag would have been written in Cyrillic. She would have been *Manya* instead of being forced into my stupid fantasies. As if," Jill whispered in an aching voice, "she was really going to be graceful and a self-starter like Nadia Comaneci."

The other women looked at her, shocked. "Who knows what she would have been like?" Amy finally said, because someone had to say something. "Is there one life we're supposed to be living? Look at us. You won that prize for being the most promising."

"Yes, the Vivian Swope," said Jill. "Thanks for reminding me."

"I'm sorry, Jill, I didn't mean it that way," Amy said. "I didn't mean, 'Oh, you won the prize, and now look at you.' I just meant, you know, life is never this straight path."

"I know that," said Jill after a moment. And at that instant they found Nadia sitting in the dirt and hugging herself tightly in the cold. When she saw them she leapt up and threw herself against her mother.

"Honey, thank God!" said Jill as her daughter clung to her waist. "How could you have gotten lost?"

"It wasn't my fault, Mom!"

"I didn't mean it was. I am so glad you're all right. But didn't you hear us calling? I was so worried. But you're fine now, you're fine."

Nadia kept sobbing, no matter how much her mother told her it was all right, it was fine, everything was okay. Wasn't there something that Jill could say to make her feel better? Even Karen, with her sequenced mind that missed nuance where others easily found it, could quickly comfort her children. Only a mother—not just *a* mother but *the* mother—could extinguish fear; yet Jill seemed unable to put aside her own fear and locate the one private little thing Nadia needed right then that would change everything.

Karen's friends often complained to one another that they had trouble with direction and that whenever they looked at a map while sitting in the passenger's seat with their husbands driving, they needed to turn it upside down in order to get a sense of where they were in relation to everything else. Karen never knew what they were talking about; why would you turn a map upside down? She let them all into the SUV now and drove them swiftly back down toward the city. This time they didn't stop at all, and she didn't bother to translate miles into kilometers in her mind, and they made it home in very good time.

T HE NEXT NIGHT, when the men and the boys returned from the weekend, Karen felt relieved. Wilson asked her what she had been doing in their absence, and she told him not much. It seemed easier right now not to say that she and her friends had driven up with the goggles in hand; one day, later on in the week, she would tell him. She didn't like keeping secrets from Wilson, no matter how innocent. She planned to tell him everything: about their adventure, about how Nadia had gotten lost in the woods, and about how Penny Ramsey was cheating on her husband. There would be no reason not to tell him all of this; he was the most discreet and trustworthy man she had ever known.

For now, though, she didn't say anything. She put the goggles back on the front hall table, and there they sat in their box, embedded in their casing.

"Dad forgot to pack these," one of the twins said with indignation when he saw them there.

"I know. But did you have fun anyway?" she asked, and both boys admitted that yes, they had had a lot of fun. They had built a campfire, they said, and had sung folk songs, and had taken a hike in the freezing woods, and had gotten up in the morning and cooked oatmeal in a big iron pot over logs.

In bed, Wilson told Karen that he was so tired from the overnight that his bones ached, and she rubbed the back and neck of her beautiful husband, then shut off the light. They would both be asleep soon—they were equally easy sleepers—but Karen said it anyway, because no night would have been complete if they didn't engage in this ritual.

"Lucas primes?" she asked.

"Sure. Jump in somewhere."

"2207."

"3571."

"9349," said Karen Yip.

And so on and so on, until they had gone as far as they could go.

Chapter

TEN

San Francisco, 1975

W HEN THE KITCHEN got so hot that the cook fainted, it was time to put in a fan. But the fan didn't work so well, and soon the line cooks started to weaken one by one. Everyone tilted a little, but no one tipped. Chu Hua Tang stood steady at the stove with the tongs, plucking dumplings out of the rolling water. When she left at the end of the night and walked outside onto Stockton Street, the chilly air smacked her face like cold water. It was too cold here in San Francisco; you could never get comfortable, either inside or outside. The temperature was wrong. But no one had ever said that life was going to be comfortable.

She had grown up seeing her two brothers die. They had a disease that had no name, or at least she could not remember the Chinese name for it. But here everyone had vitamins to keep them well. Chu Hua Tang believed in the power of vitamins, but she had to force them down her children's throats. "Take them!" she said, giving them to the boy, Kevin, and to the girl, Karen. Kevin swallowed them easy. Karen said, "Ma, I hate the smell. They smell like a wet dog. And I don't like the feeling of the big pill in my throat. I will choke."

"You will not choke," Chu Hua said. "Take them, take them!" The vitamins did always stink in their brown bottle, but the smell was a sign of their potency; they would keep her children strong. She had bought them at the big drugstore that stood kitty-corner from the Ideal Dumpling Palace. She had bought them on payday, and her hands had pulsed with pleasure at being able to make the purchase. So how could her daughter complain? She was selfish: a selfish little girl. It made Chu Hua furious.

She often came home from work furious. You were supposed to leave the hot kitchen and go out into the cold night, and then go home to your family, as if you would then be able to enjoy one another. "How was your day?" people asked in San Francisco. Or, worse, they called out, "Have a good day!"

But at home, her son, Kevin, was always waiting by the door, ready to leave, saying, "Ma, I have to meet Chris and Danny in five minutes to go play Pong." He spent all the money that he earned as a messenger playing this stupid game at the arcade nearby, where he stood in front of a machine with his friends and poked his head into it. Karen, though, was always in her room studying. Chu Hua was supposed to like this and be proud of her, but it often irritated her to see the girl lounging on her bed with a math book, yawning with her mouth open, revealing her tongue, the way Americans sometimes did, so immodestly.

"You could help set the table," Chu Hua said to Karen. "I have to come home and take care of everything here too? I have to work at *home*, like it is restaurant?"

Karen was eight. She was helpful only when you pushed her; she would finally put down the book and say, "Okay, Ma, okay." Then, still yawning, as though she had been working all day too, Karen would stagger into the kitchen and say, flatly, "What do you want me to do?"

But always her mother would shoo her away; the girl did not know how to do anything useful. Chu Hua did. She was the only one in the family who could work this hard. Even her husband, still at the restaurant for the cleaning-up, had a stubborn, ungiving way about him; the girl got this quality from him, certainly. But Chu Hua was not like them. She was hardworking and fast; her hands worked the pork into a big pink pellet, then crimped the dough around it and dropped the thing into the pot without any thought. Her hands "flew," someone had once observed in the restaurant kitchen. If my hands could fly, she had replied in Chinese, they would fly away.

It did not matter, though, that she hated it here in San Francisco. It did not matter that she did not like California or Stockton Street or the Ideal Dumpling Palace. Or that it was not a palace, only a restaurant with mirrors on the walls. For some reason, whenever there were mirrors in a restaurant, people said "palace." She did not like it, but she was working steadily, and she did not care that she did not like it. With her money she bought a big jug of vitamins and pulled out the cotton that clogged the top of the bottle, and then she forced the vitamins down her children's throats. "Leave me alone! I just want to do my math!" Karen said. "I am trying to memorize as many digits of pi as I can."

No, little girl, no, Chu Hua should have said. You cannot sit and dream for your whole life. You cannot memorize pi. You have to take your vitamins and get strong and go out and work. Unless, of course, you find a man who is rich. A rich American business guy—that would be okay. You could live in a real palace, not a restaurant. There will be mirrors on the walls of your living room, and I will come visit you there, and I will sit down and put up my feet. But that is probably not going to happen. So I will keep making dumplings, and you will set the table, and we will move around our little rooms doing our work, and our hands will fly.

Chapter

ELEVEN

T HE ISLAND of St. Doe's sat at the heel of the British Virgin
Islands; all the islands in this chain had a similar rough and
glorious topography, and all were steeped in the same warm wind
and breaded with the same blanched sand. But on those other bigger, louder, and more commercial islands, men and women and
their children felt simply lucky and happy to be there, able to spend
the money required to leave their urban or suburban backdrops
at the time of year when car exhaust and litter and ice scalloped the
streets.

On St. Doe's, almost everyone was more than lucky and more
than happy. They had a secret: Their whole island was unknown
to most people and unavailable to all but those who could manage
it. Amy Lamb had learned about it and edged her way in, though
her friends did not approve of this trip, and now, lying on a linen
lounge chair beneath an umbrella like the interloper she was, with
the sun and the trees and the occasional paraglider dotting the sky
above her, she wondered if she could possibly stop feeling overstimu-

lated and worried, and start having what she might recognize as a good time.

All around her were strewn the supine bodies of men and women from the States and from France and England, with a small minority from Scandinavia. A covey of nearly identically ethereal, albinic Danish women occupied the next block of chaises, reading novels like Danielle Steel's *Sikker Havn*. Some of the European women untied the tops of their bathing suits, exposing hide-colored nipples to the sun. A middle-aged Frenchwoman stroked lotion into her breasts, which moved slightly beneath her hand, as if animate. Mason and Holden had taken one look at her and run away, yelping. Now they were off on the beach up to their waists in the nearly transparent water, with snorkels pressed into their faces. Beside Amy was Penny, her eyes either closed or open behind her dark glasses. The women lay quietly, but once in a while someone would say something. If Penny spoke, it usually concerned Ian.

"I guess he's managing," she said.

"I would imagine."

"But he's very dependent," Penny said. "He said he's always been like that. He had a girlfriend in London for a few years named Jemima. He would walk past her flat just to look at her window, to see the way the shade fell or something, even if he knew she wasn't home."

"What will you do when he goes back to England?"

"We don't really talk about it yet."

The husbands were elsewhere, though not together. Since they had all arrived here two days earlier, Greg Ramsey had disappeared for most of the day, going off for solo aquatic activities or, mostly, just heading to the business center that had been set up in a centrally positioned hut or to the fitness center that occupied the hut right beside it. He appeared only in the evening for dinner at the thatch-covered outdoor dining room, with its long torches and bongos and boatloads of langoustines. At the dinner table he'd been in a pressed white cotton shirt, his hair freshly washed and still wet, but Amy thought he could not lose the essence of the office, the distant, dark perfume of the deal.

"Do not talk politics with him," Amy had warned Leo before the trip. "He will say things that will be upsetting. We're all on this tiny island together, and Penny was the one who invited us to join them, and I do not want it to be tense."

Leo agreed. "Sure. He's not my friend," he said. "What do I care?"

Greg Ramsey carried an air of impersonal courtesy about him; he looked beyond everyone he talked to as if poised in thought—as if he were a poet. He was not an overly hateful person, at least in terms of the things he said, Amy realized, though she had rarely seen a man as self-satisfied and impatient. At the table he scooped up a fresh mash of avocado and lime on a fried plantain, and stretched his mouth wide to receive it.

". . . then we got some new investors from Iceland, but I really didn't want anyone new," he was saying to Leo, who sat there looking like a *dope,* Amy thought, his face not even adopting the appropriately shifting expressions it was meant to when someone else told you a story. Instead, his head was tilted a little, his mouth puckered, his eyes squinted, as though he did not understand a word of this language. "My partners did, though," Greg went on, "and they convinced me. Have you ever been to Iceland?"

Leo blinked, then glanced at Amy briefly like a child who is not sure how to answer when an adult has spoken to him. "No," Leo said after too long a pause.

"Amazing place. Amazing vodka. Amazing bands. The best indie rock is coming out of there."

"Don't say 'indie rock,'" Penny said quietly.

"What?" He turned toward his wife.

"You sound like you're eighty years old, Greg, and trying to be young. Like you're out to dinner for the white-belt special." Everyone laughed politely at her meanish joke.

"Do you think I sound old?" Greg Ramsey asked the boys.

Mason and Holden, who until that moment had been engaged in a thumb wrestle, unwound their hands long enough to both tell Holden's dad that no, he did not sound old. Greg Ramsey seemed satisfied with the opinions of two ten-year-olds, and he regarded his wife as if he had won an obscure battle that they had been fighting for a very long time. "The boys don't think I sound old," he said, and then he took another curling plantain chip and pushed it into the bowl of avocado.

"But you look old," Holden said, and Greg made an expression of mock rage and pretended to swing a punch, which Holden ducked, laughing. Mason laughed too. Amy saw that for them it was *fun* when a father sparred with a son; for a moment, there was a faint metallic blood-taste of true aggression but no actual danger.

In the torchlight, a gamelan ensemble played. The water in the distance was black now; the entire night was black, though far away on the horizon the lights of a cruise ship moved slowly past. Inside it, unseen passengers were dancing to an unheard orchestra.

"We are nowhere," said Greg.

"What's that?" Amy asked.

He turned his big head toward her. He seemed, in that second, to become aware of her for the first time: Oh, right, the friend of my wife. He didn't know that she knew far more than he did about his own marriage. But because he didn't know this, he had no interest in her. She ran no hedge fund, she had no job; she was not a potential investor, she was not beautiful, she was not a husband; *who was she?*

"I said we're nowhere. Out in the middle of nowhere. And the connections are pretty iffy."

"The connections?" she asked.

"Cell phone. I had three calls get dropped in the middle today. It's only recently that you can even pick up service here, and of course you have to sit in that hut they call the business center to get Internet. But we're practically inside a volcano, so I shouldn't complain." He nodded in Penny's direction. "My wife collected all this information in advance and prepared me for the primitive conditions that lay ahead."

"Yes, Greg," said Penny mildly, looking over. "The thread count of the sheets here is so primitive."

"You know what I mean, Pen."

At that moment, Leo put an arm across the back of Amy's cane chair, and she was suddenly grateful for the tiny gesture, even though it might have been coincidental, not signifying intimacy so much as an establishment of teams. The Ramseys could be lightly hostile with each other, but Amy and Leo would not be. Watching another family up close was always alarming; their ways seemed tribal and unfamiliar and somehow wrong, as though if you looked even more closely you might detect hints of incest or some other aberrance. Greg Ramsey was a cuckold; that was the word that Ian Janeway had suggested over lunch at the Met. But he was also a shit, a *prick*, Roberta might have said, highly involved in himself and his fund and his investors. Amy compared all this with the image of Ian Janeway's sweet, freckled hand curved around a glass. She could hear Ian's British accent, and remembered that she'd never once even heard him talk about money. When you were married to Greg Ramsey, Ian Janeway must be a tonic, a dunk in clear water.

At the table now, Greg spoke to his wife in a shallowly attentive but distant manner about their evening plans and the arrangements for Holden and Mason's surfing lesson later in the week. In the moments when he addressed his son, he seemed to feel the need to reach across and rumple Holden's hair. It confused Amy a little that Greg was such a demonstrative father; it clouded the image. He seemed proud too of both of his teenaged daughters, with whom he talked in tender tones.

Amy and Leo were far out of their element here on St. Doe's. The whole island and the layout of its resort overwhelmed Amy. She had seen wealth and its consumption as she and her little family fought to stay buoyant in New York City, but this was different. The Europeans here spoke only to one another. The elegant women bared their breasts openly during the day and then turned their backs in the evening, revealing the bones at the base of a beautiful neck and the clasp of a good necklace. Families traveled here each winter from Big Sur and Malibu, their skin already a slightly baked color upon arrival. Their children jumped into the water without ceremony, as if stepping into a daily bath, hardly seeming to notice the extravagant drama of this rock formation that provided them with their annual vacation. Above everyone in the sky, the distant, bright figures of paragliders sometimes dangled from their parafoils, like children casually hanging on to the branch of a backyard tree.

The staff laid out fresh exotic fruits all day on long tables in the shade. You could just point to something, and within moments it would be hacked to bits, skinned with a blade, and then laid out on your plate. It was understood that there was nothing here that you couldn't have. If you wanted the furniture of your bungalow changed, it would be done. If you wanted a small tree uprooted and replanted a few feet away, so as not to hamper the view (according to Penny, this had been done for a telecommunications-titan guest in the recent past), it would happen. But the stories themselves were satisfying; like a child, you were meant to be shocked and titillated by other people's demands, usually so much worse than your own. The level of solicitude had been established right away, as soon as the airplane from Newark had landed in San Juan on the day after Christmas. Amy, Leo, and Mason had been still slightly weary from the holiday and from the trip as they switched to a tiny, jerking little flight to Tortola, where the three of them then waited briefly at the tiny airport in the haze and stink of fuselage and the marination of their own travelers' stink, until they were approached by three staff members from St. Doe's.

The staff members were dressed in white, giving them the appearance of admiralty. One of them was white, blonde, and Australian, and the other two were black and from the islands. All three were beautiful.

"I'm Hamish," said the Australian, "and this is Thomas and Pierre. You must be whacked from all your travels. From here on in, leave everything to us."

Bags were taken by strong arms, Mason was handed a packet of "chocko-flavoured" Bing-Bongs, and the family was ferried from airport to dock, where they were then loaded into a skiff. Off they went with their three caretakers. During the thirty-minute trip over pale green chop, Pierre spoke about the kind of weather they had been having on St. Doe's during the preceding days. "Not a cloud in the sky," he said in his French accent, "So beautiful it could make you cry."

In the mornings on St. Doe's, Pierre and Thomas could usually be seen setting up tables and covering them in tablecloths; always there was to be a barbecue in the afternoon, a pig roast, a cocktail hour with Cosmopolitans and fried conch accompanied by four dipping sauces. Drinks were continually handed round, along with plates of tiny, delicate crustaceans that had been tricked into entering puff pastry.

Certainly, Amy thought with increasing intensity each day, she and Leo and Mason shouldn't have taken themselves to this piece of volcanic rock, with its ambient gamelan music and ovoid fruits and outdoor tables laid with silver by beautiful black men. Instead, they should have stayed in the city over break, doing every cheap or free family-type activity that Amy could find in the newspaper listings under the wishful heading "Family Fun." That was what they had done in earlier years, going out in a big, ungainly herd along with Roberta and Nathaniel and their kids—"all the homebodies," Roberta had said one Christmas with a light laugh, though she never complained about their modest means. They'd gone to the winter wonderland at the Bronx zoo; to the tree-lighting in Rockefeller Center; to the caroling in the park—all of these outings providing ways to celebrate the city at the holidays and also to ease up the financial fear of one day not being able to cope anymore and having to pack up and leave, like many people did each year. When Mason was younger, they had gone to see Nathaniel's puppet shows on occasional weekends, but now, of course, Mason's interests had expanded exponentially, and he could not be contained inside an auditorium on a weekend morning.

Increasingly, Mason wanted an array of things that Amy could not give him, things that had to do with technology and freedom and the larger world. Really, she didn't know exactly what he wanted anymore, though he seemed so happy to be here on St. Doe's with the dominant, future world-beater Holden Ramsey. The boys, shirtless, ran together on the sand during the day, their little penises evident beneath the wrinkled wet sculpting of their trunks. Because you were a mother you weren't supposed to notice, but of course you did anyway, even though you hadn't really seen your son's penis in a long time. Once it had been your right to see it. You had diapered him and been squirted in the face more than once by him, and in these moments the penis had seemed somehow to be yours too. There was enough of it for everyone; it was a small, tender prop in the family constellation. Then, over time, Mason had become healthily modest in the bathtub, hiding it when she entered the bathroom to bring in a plastic action figure that he had requested, warning her, "No looking." She would drop Zapman or Deathrayman into the tub with a little resounding *plip*, turning away, but even as she did she saw something in her peripheral vision that floated upward to the surface like a tiny lily pad.

Now, years later, it might look like anything. It might have sprouted wings by now; she really had no idea. He was no longer hers.

O NE MORNING on St. Doe's, Penny accompanied her to the gift shop to look for a present for her mother, Antonia, who would be staying in the apartment this week, and would still be there when they returned from their trip. The gift shop was a little hut filled with expensive glass and beaded and silken things. A tall black woman in a batik blouse stood behind the rush surface of a counter as Amy and Penny browsed among the long rippling scarves, the bottles of lotion with tropical scents, and jewelry and items that would probably have been classified as "miscellany." "This is pretty," Penny said, pointing to a paperweight that contained branches of pale blue and green coral, along with a whirl of turquoise trapped inside. "Your mother could keep her manuscript pages under it."

"Well, it's not like she sits and writes in a windstorm," said Amy, but after the woman behind the counter unlocked the glass case and drew out the dome, she saw the way Penny held the object in her hand, turning it around to see it from all angles. Somehow the rotation of the piece of delicate glass made Amy able to appreciate it. She felt as though her mother would appreciate it as well. "It *is* nice," she conceded.

"*Two hundred tirty-tree,*" pronounced the woman, without seeming at all scandalized at the price.

But it *was* a scandalous price. Still, did Amy have to make every moment refer once again to money? Did that have to be her only theme, she thought, her little repeating aria? The scale was off here; you had to get used to it, just the way you had had to get used to the scale of life in New York City, and just the way you had to get used to the scale of modern life, if you hoped to survive in the world. She smiled and nodded to the woman, and the transaction was completed.

It was on day four of the six-day vacation that the boys took their surfing lesson with the handsome, masculine Pierre. She watched as he waded into the surf with a board under his arm, the boys following behind. Later on, Amy would remember the surfing lesson as if it were representative of the last moment of beauty and ease: the boys and the man roaming in the loose waves.

Leo was there too, lying on the chaise on Amy's other side with *Doctor Faustus* by Thomas Mann, but he was unable to stay still and read for very long. Every few minutes he would spring up to get a drink or fix the angle of the umbrella or stand by the shore and watch the surfing lesson. It was as though he, who had always been a great reader, had forgotten how to read. Like most people, he'd somehow recently lost patience for the slow unraveling that took place in novels, the need for the reader to wait in order to find out what happened in the end. Oddly, she realized, the boys were the ones who could still read long novels; this was the one trace of the previous world that they had inherited and that their parents were starting to shed.

"Are you okay over there?" Amy asked Leo.

"Fine. Why?"

"You keep getting up. It's like you have adult ADD."

"I'm just not used to the idea of rest anymore. It doesn't suit me very well," he said.

Penny drew herself up from her chaise on Amy's other side. "I'm going to take some pictures of the boys," she announced. "I brought my camera out with me today for the surfing lesson." Amy watched as Penny went down to the water's edge and began taking digital photos of Holden and Mason. Leo remained behind them, eating fried conch and trying to read but not really reading. A few yards away, by the bamboo counter where towels lay in warm, waiting stacks, a Frenchman and his female friend spoke quietly and, it seemed, ardently. The sound of gamelan was sprinkled like pollen through the quiet morning, and waiters brought drinks to the voluntarily helpless figures. Amy thought of the expression "This is the life." As though there were one life, as though you would really want to stay here like this for eternity, inert and being tended to, and passively regarding beauty.

A few minutes later Greg Ramsey wandered down from the bungalow. Sleep creases striped one side of his face. "Penny, I need batteries for my recorder," he said.

"I assumed you brought them."

"They ran out. You were the one who packed."

"I didn't think about your little tape recorder, Greg," said Penny. "It was the last thing I thought about when I was packing. You have an assistant, you should have asked her." She paused. "What size do you need?"

"Triple A. Can't you take the batteries out of something else?"

"I have nothing that runs on triple A. Sorry."

"What about your camera?"

"I'm taking pictures at the moment. The boys' surfing lesson."

"But I have to dictate."

As he reached for her camera, Penny drew her hand away from him, and they squabbled in a low-level, ugly, married way. Amy wondered how frequently batteries were the subject of American marital arguments.

"Look up there, Chloe," said one of the West Coast husbands, walking past with his adolescent daughter. He pointed far into the sky, where two figures hung suspended on harnesses from their parafoils.

Amy briefly watched the figures in the sky too, looking at them as everyone was meant to do. Their plumage was bright, one red, one yellow. There were endless possibilities here for the dangerous, the risky. The boys, out in the surf, likely possessed the gene for risk taking that supposedly you were either born with or not. They swam out farther, and Amy felt herself clench a little, wanting to pull Mason back as though he were attached to her by an invisible, electronic dog lead. But he was uncollared, in the water up to his neck. Again and again he and Holden rose up and pulled themselves onto their knees on the smooth planes of their little starter boards.

"The trick," Holden had explained this morning over breakfast, lecturing Mason at the table though he was a surfing neophyte too, "is in getting up and staying up. Lots of guys wipe out. But it's all about positive thinking. You have to think you can do it, and then you can." Mason listened to his friend as if Holden Ramsey were a motivational speaker, and one day, Amy thought, he would be. She pictured the boardroom and the way that grown-man Holden Ramsey would puncture the air with an index finger and how all the businessmen and businesswomen around him would take notes.

But now, in the water, Holden could barely get onto his knees on a surfboard. Everything was difficult, Amy thought, watching the lesson, though up above, the two paragliders seemed to move around effortlessly. "They're so pretty," the teenaged Chloe said to her father, and as she spoke the yellow paraglider jerked at an unnatural angle and swooped out over the water, heading rapidly down toward the beach on a steep diagonal, as if on a rope line.

Some of the people on the shore took notice, standing with open, helpless hands as he bore down in their direction. It happened quickly. Amy instinctively reached up and protected her head, as if he might crash on top of her. Down he came, this figure with the yellow canopy, strumming the sand at first, then decisively landing, snapping down harshly, smashing onto his back with the harness making a loud whipping sound. Immediately he began to scream. "Fuck!" he cried, holding the syllable.

There was no time for anyone to do anything, for the wind continued to pull him along. He was dragged forward, his parafoil sucking inward and outward in jellyfish locomotion. A line of people, everyone shouting, began to run after the paraglider as he banged and skidded on his back along the shore. When he did stop, several people formed a circle around him, and Amy could not see anything, though she could hear shouting in a few different languages. "Do not move him!" she heard. "Do not touch him!" And, "Is he alive?" And, "Sir, can you move your arms and legs?" The second paraglider made a neat and perfect landing nearby, frantically explaining in a French accent that he was the instructor, that he had been giving a lesson, and that the student had apparently lost control.

Amy was only vaguely aware that Penny had pushed into the circle of onlookers too, but suddenly she heard her cry out and back away. Greg came up to his wife and said, "You've seen accidents before." She just shook her head, her hand to her mouth, then turned and started running toward the bungalows, Greg following behind her.

So Amy had to go see what Penny had seen too. She joined the circle of people shouting instructions to one another and to the fallen man, and she looked down directly into the freckled white face of Ian Janeway. His eyes were closed. He wore a helmet, his curling hair pressed inside it, giving him the appearance of someone alien, perhaps an early cosmonaut who has touched down on the wrong side of the world. His mouth formed into an expression of primitive pain. Just as Amy had felt that she should not be here, he should not have been here, either; she could not believe that he had come. She wanted to cry out too, as Penny had automatically done.

But as astonishing to her as Ian's nervy and inexplicable presence here was the fact that Penny had turned and fled. She hadn't automatically screamed and knelt down beside him. Instead, she was already running down the path toward the bungalows with her husband beside her, the argument about batteries forever forgotten. Penny must have been shocked by the violent fall of this stranger, Greg Ramsey probably thought. She would continue to let him think this. She would go back to their bungalow, and Greg would tend to her. He knew his wife was highly sensitive and emotional sometimes. This, apparently, was one of those times. She was also strong and tough and good with acquisitions and at dealing with the demands of the trustees. But Greg Ramsey had probably always admired complexity. It might have attracted him to her when they were young and unencumbered and not yet rich, and not yet in possession of the knowledge about what their marriage would be like over time.

Amy and Leo stayed in the circle with the others as two of the staff members came racing up with a stretcher and a contraption that was meant to brace Ian Janeway's head and neck. The boys were there too now, having left the water, along with Pierre and various guests, all of them speaking words of upset and disturbance in their own languages.

In the middle of it all, Amy Lamb said to anyone who was listening, "I know him."

"You do?" said Leo. Then, presumptuously, "No, you don't."

"Yes, I do."

Because she did know him, at least a little, she was asked to come to the infirmary and answer questions, following the men who carried Ian in. There was much activity in the small medical building that abutted the main lodge: blurted, hysterical landline calls and cell-phone calls and walkie-talkie conversations in French and English, as though spoken by a simultaneous interpreter. Arrangements were made for the transport of the injured man from the island to the Hospital del Maestro in San Juan. The in-house doctor on the island and two guests who were also physicians stood around Ian behind a curtain, and a hurried, muted discussion was conducted about whether he had damaged his spinal cord, perhaps irrevocably, or had instead bruised or badly damaged the vertebrae.

One of the guests drew something on a piece of paper for Amy. "This is the spinal cord," he said in a strong French accent. "Imagine it as toothpaste packed in her tube." She remembered "her tube," but she couldn't remember much more of what he said. She understood that Ian urgently needed an MRI and might well have to have surgery, which could be performed in San Juan as soon as he was airlifted there. He might also need an injection of a steroidal drug called Medrol, but it would have to be within the next several hours, the doctor warned, or it would have no effect. Anyway, if his spinal cord had been completely severed, there would be no hope of recovery; the lower vertebrae controlled the legs, and he would never have use of them. Hearing all this, she chewed the inside of her mouth furiously, willing Penny here, as she should have been.

Amy was taken into the next room and asked to quickly fill out a form with all the information she knew about the injured man: name, age, occupation. She told everyone that she hardly knew him and that she didn't remember his address or his telephone number. Really, she didn't know Ian Janeway at all.

She could hear Ian's brief, stuttering cries as the doctors tried to assess him. A sedative was administered by needle; he would be unconscious soon, and one of the staff said that if "Mrs. Buckner" wanted to go see her friend, she ought to do it now. Perhaps it would be comforting to him. Amy knew that Ian had obviously come to St. Doe's on a lovesick prank for Penny's benefit. She thought of his lovesick nature and how because of it he had been seriously injured and would perhaps be in debt for years and maybe never able to walk again. Maybe he would even die. Maybe this would be one of those stupid, leisure-time deaths that occur because of parafoils or snowmobiles or the Plunge of Doom at an amusement park, entirely unnecessary and frivolous and leaving behind no residue of meaning.

She didn't want to go in and see him—she'd already been so

shocked when she first saw his pale, recognizable face after the accident—but the doctor asked her to, so Amy went behind the curtain to where Ian lay pinned to the stretcher, his neck braced, his entire body wrapped in some sort of laced canvas, his face white and frightened.

"Ian," she said. "It's Amy."

He rolled his eyes toward her. "Where's Penny?" he said.

"I don't know."

"Shit."

Ian's eyes closed, and his mouth opened slightly in a morphine hangdog expression. Someone put a hand on Amy's shoulder and told her she should go.

She circled the Ramseys' bungalow, but she could see nothing through the curtains. No one ever knocked on anyone's door on St. Doe's; everyone maintained a certain, agreed-upon distance. Maids slipped in and out during the day, and so did discreet masseurs with massage tables folded under their arms. There was no sign of movement from the bungalow now. It was very late in the afternoon, still hot outside, the time of day when everyone, lightly sun-sickened, usually returned from the beach and disappeared into their darkened rooms to recover. Today, almost everyone had gone inside early.

Amy climbed up onto the porch and knocked. Soon Gabrielle Ramsey came to the door. She was a beautiful fifteen-year-old girl, tiny like her mother, but with her father's wide mouth. A minuscule piece of silver pierced the flesh of her nose.

"Hi, Mrs. Buckner," she said. "My parents are both lying down."

"Oh."

Amy imagined a large bed, identical to hers and Leo's, draped with netting, on which a husband and wife lay together in the heat under a single cold white sheet. "Tell your mom I stopped by," she said, and she left the family to themselves.

Leo was waiting for Amy in their own bungalow. "I have to say that I'm a little hurt," he said when she had told him everything, "that you kept this to yourself."

"Would you have really wanted to hear about it?" Amy asked him.
She walked into the bedroom and he followed her there. She sat
down heavily on the bed, parting the netting and lying back. Above
her, the fan spun slowly, and she lay looking at it, not moving her
head at all, imagining what it would be like to be permanently fixed
in position like this.

"You always used to tell me things," Leo said, as though it were
proof, somehow, that he had been wronged. Amy rolled her eyes
toward him, but could only see the edges of his face. She sat up.

"I know," Amy said. "So did you."

"I tell you things," he insisted.

Their arguments were never protracted. Instead, in short bursts
they usually stated their case like lawyers who had been told by a
judge to wrap it up. Not *like* lawyers; they *were* lawyers. She still
had her degree and her license from the New York State Bar buried
somewhere in a drawer with all the other reminders of the past that
she had held on to. So the small argument began and then mostly
ended as the sun lowered over the Virgin Islands, and later on they
heard the stuttering of the helicopter landing, but neither of them
remarked on it. Amy knew that Leo was a little upset and even
baffled, but that he would get over these feelings by morning. They
were left with two more days here with the Ramseys, during which,
in public, they apparently could not discuss Ian Janeway in any other
way except as "the guy who had been in the paragliding accident."

Even Penny would barely discuss the subject that night before
dinner, when Amy approached her alone on the steps leading to the
outdoor dining room. Amy whispered, "I went to see him."

"Thank you." Penny looked around to make sure no one was listening and continued to walk up the steps with Amy beside her.

"He was in a lot of pain, but they gave him something. He was
going to have an MRI and maybe surgery in San Juan. I came by
your bungalow to tell you, but you were sleeping."

"I'm glad you saw him."

"A few minutes ago," Amy went on, "I asked at the infirmary if they could put through a call to the hospital. You know, find out his status? They said they would, but there's nothing yet."

"I appreciate it." Then Penny added, "But I can't talk about it anymore. Obviously."

"I know. I won't say anything else here. We can take a walk on the beach later."

"No. I mean I just can't. Not anymore."

"Ever?" Amy laughed, because it seemed comical in that moment. What would they do, forever keep silent about it? Maybe, she thought, the theme of "Ian and Penny" would shift to become "Injured Ian and Penny"; the two women would adapt their conversations accordingly. Except Penny was saying no even to this.

Penny shook her head. "I don't think so."

"How can we never discuss it?" Amy asked. "This thing happened, and he's alone in some hospital, and he might be paralyzed. I know it's an awful situation," Amy went on. "But shouldn't you see him again or call the hospital and have them tell him you called or *something*?"

"I have to figure it out. I'm in a fishbowl here. I'm very confused."

Another waiter approached them now to take their drink orders. Penny tilted her head up toward him with relief, and in a small voice she described the way she would like her margarita prepared.

At dinner a little later in the torchlight, Greg Ramsey brought up the subject of the accident they'd witnessed, while beside him Penny sat and ate a piece of some kind of broiled white fish. Amy could almost not bear sitting there like this, yet they would have to endure several more meals until the vacation was over. She'd inquired at the hotel desk whether it was possible to leave early—she would have made some excuse and just gotten them out of there—but she was told that all the flights out of St. Doe's were booked. So here they were. "I never thought of paragliding as dangerous," Greg said easily. "I tried it last spring when we were on Turks and Caicos, and it seemed pretty straightforward to me. You can get in trouble with the thermals and with wind shear, but you're supposed to have a hook knife ready. I don't think that guy knew what he was doing at all."

"When I'm twelve I'm going to be allowed to paraglide," Holden announced to the table.

"Can I do it when I'm twelve?" Mason asked his parents.

"No," said Amy.

"It scares the women," Greg said. "Penny's been keyed up about the accident all day. But I've seen much worse. I once saw a terrible water-skiing accident. It was really something."

A great deal of wine was drunk that night all around the outdoor dining room. The other families and couples from their various scattered points on the globe ordered more alcohol than usual. They had all seen something today that was disturbing to them, and the excitement of it had taken them by surprise too. Someone at another table could be heard talking about freak accidents: how an errant wind could send a vehicle tumbling, a parasail blowing, a body falling.

The next morning, Penny came out onto the beach and positioned herself on the chaise beside Amy. Amy waited, but Penny did not bring up the subject of Ian. She didn't say anything at all, and so Amy didn't either. Regardless of what now happened to poor Ian Janeway—whether he recovered, or died of an infection after his surgery, or became a paraplegic—this would be the way it was. The accident was the end, the message sent to Penny about how unstable Ian was: Imagine appearing like that on St. Doe's when her family was with her! She would let go of him swiftly, and she and Amy would talk of other things.

Maybe then it would finally be Amy's turn to talk and Penny's turn to listen. *Leo doesn't want to have sex with me,* she could have whispered as they lay on the beach. But really, Amy could barely look at Penny now, and they lay side by side quietly for much of the morning. The day was as beautiful as the last, though for most people the vacation was coming to a close, and a slight depression colored their movements. The Frenchwoman who massaged lotion into her bare breasts every morning now did so with slower motions, like a lonely masturbator, her hand seeming to convey sadness at the idea that she would soon have to leave.

That night, a message was slipped beneath the door of Amy and Leo's bungalow. "Your friend rests in San Juan at Hospital del Maestro," it read in handwriting that was old-fashioned and beautiful and not American. "Vertebral lumbar fractures, *very* severe, but no spinal-cord damage. Surgical procedure performed. Long recovery period to be expec." Amy relayed this message to Penny furtively the following morning on the beach, and it was accepted with a quick nod and, astonishingly, no questions about what would happen next: Would Ian be okay? Was there anyone to look after him? Would he ever be able to walk?

On their last day on St. Doe's, Mason and Holden disappeared for so long that Amy became concerned. "They're boys," Leo said. "Leave them."

But she needed to know where Mason was; it was a reflexive response, in such a moment, to want to gather everyone around you and take a head count. She'd tried to call Jill last night in Holly Hills in order to tell her what had happened here, hoping that Jill would somehow be sympathetic and horrified all at once, and say the right things. But the connection had been weak, and the call kept being dropped. She heard Nadia's peculiar little voice answer the phone two times, then slip away.

"Nadia! It's Amy! Is your mom there? Can you get her?" Amy had cried from her bungalow, as though her friend could save her. But then the little voice was gone, and the connection was lost. Amy's friends seemed to occupy a distant world: Jill with her suburb and her unhappiness; Roberta with her frustrations and her activism and the girl in South Dakota she was trying to help. Those stories, at least from this tropical island, seemed unreal, and yet Amy wanted them to be made real for her once again; more than anything, she wanted them back.

Now she set off in search of the boys, walking quickly along the shore past the place where she and Penny had walked each morning until the accident, going beyond the joggers and snorkelers and resort guests pushing off in their kayaks. She went very far, and the beach curved around so she could no longer see the lodge or the bungalows. The scenery changed, sharply, and even the beach shrubbery turned less beautiful and became thick, thorny, dark. A sign read ABSO-LUTELY NO GUESTS BEYOND THIS POINT, but Amy Lamb kept walking.

A crop of low buildings appeared, one after the other, like a shan-tytown, all of them constructed poorly out of big pieces of corrugated, unpainted tin, instead of woven bamboo and rush like almost every-thing else here. Shack after shack materialized, and black people looked out from the open doors that led into depressing rooms. She saw men sitting on old cots, smoking cigarettes. Briefly, Amy was startled and confused; there was a *slum* on St. Doe's, hidden away past all the beauty and excess?

She walked past another doorway and looked inside, and there she found herself looking directly at Pierre, the lovely, shy man who had been teaching the boys how to surf. Pierre was wearing white underpants now and no shirt, and he was smoking. Rap music played softly behind him. This wasn't a slum, she realized, it was merely employee housing, and he was taking a break. Pierre stepped quickly out of sight, and she didn't know which of them was meant to be the more embarrassed.

U PON THEIR RETURN to the city, they found that Antonia Lamb had forgotten to water the Christmas tree as they had asked her to do, and so its needles had poured down upon the wooden floor of the living room and all over the Persian rug. "It's a fire haz-ard now," Mason had said when he saw the parched tree. Lightly he touched one of the ornaments, a golden painted ball he had made in school years ago, and another flood of crisp needles fell. The tree would have to be taken away sooner than they had planned. "I'm so sorry," Antonia said to them. "I have been really involved with my women's conference, I guess. Forgive me, kids."

While they were on St. Doe's, Amy's mother had installed her-self in the tiny study, as planned: The air mattress had been inflated, and her toothbrush and tube of organic sunflower toothpaste lay coiled on the ledge of the small sink in the guest bathroom. Amy had not seen her mother in six months, and while Antonia looked well, she also looked measurably older. Her hair, always silvered, was now silver. She was a dramatic-looking woman, prone to capes when she went outside; on her book-jacket photo she appeared vaguely Wiccan. Now she was here in the apartment, and the visit would have been fine, even welcome, except for what had happened on St. Doe's, which Amy did not want to tell her about.

Penny had left a message on Amy's cell phone the day after their families had flown home separately. "Amy, it's me. Hope you had a good flight. Well, flights. Whatever. I'm just, you know, checking in. Give me a call, okay?"

Each time Amy thought about calling her back, she recalled Penny running away from Ian and not going back, and then easily lying on the beach the following morning. Amy just couldn't find the energy to make the call. Finally, after three days in New York, she did call Penny back, and the conversation took place in the new, forced style they had developed after the accident. "So, have you heard any updates about Ian's condition?" she asked Penny.

"No."

"But you've called the hospital?"

"I will; I just can't yet. I don't know what I'm going to do about this. It's such a mess. It's really hard for me." Penny suggested they could meet for coffee later in the week, but really, Amy knew, there was no point. There was no couple now, and so there was no friendship. It didn't exactly end during the cell-phone call, the way the love affair between Penny Ramsey and Ian Janeway had ended the moment he had come smacking down onto the sand. But the friendship had no subject now, and they were both lost.

A<small>T DINNER</small> in the apartment that night, Antonia said, "My darling, why are you so melancholy? I can see it in your eyes. Even when you were a little girl I could see this."

"Mom was melancholy?" Mason asked, interested. "We had that word in Vocab Ventures. Its synonyms are 'mournful' and 'woebegone.'"

"She wasn't generally melancholy. But she was very sensitive. All three girls were."

Antonia had cooked dinner for the family: vegetarian lasagna, which she prepared well. After the Christmas tree negligence, she was proving to be a surprisingly unobtrusive houseguest, though maybe it was only because Amy still felt so peculiar about Penny and Ian that she hardly noticed her mother moving around her in the rooms.

"I'm not melancholy," she said. "I'm just thinking about things."

"If you want to talk, I'm here," said Antonia. "Although not during the day tomorrow, because I'm at NAFITAS."

"That's an acronym, right?" asked Mason.

"Oh, my intelligent little grandson, yes it is. It stands for North American Feminists in the Arts and Sciences. Basically, it gives old friends a chance to get together. It used to be that all the women who liked one another had very specific reasons to hang around together. We were always having meetings, first against the terrible war in Vietnam, which is not unlike the terrible war in Iraq. But then, later on, when we had our consciousness-raising group, our cause became ourselves."

Amy saw that Mason looked confused by this and probably bored, but he kept his face arranged in a position of politeness toward his grandmother, whose feelings he would never want to hurt.

"Naomi and Jennifer and I always wondered," Amy suddenly said, looking at her mother, "what you and those other women did down there in the living room on those nights. Sometimes we thought you were hosting a séance."

"Yes, I guess we were raising the spirit of Susan B. Anthony," Antonia said, laughing.

"I have her coin," said Mason. "No one liked the shape or the size, Grandma, so it was taken out of circulation."

"I knew that, and I was not surprised," said Antonia, pouring herself more wine. "Oh, Amy, Leo, after my meeting tomorrow after-noon, I was wondering if I could bring a few of the women here for a get-together. Most of them are from out of town, staying at hotels."

"Of course," said Leo. "Not a problem."

"Thank you." Then, turning to Amy, Antonia said, "I wanted to ask, have you thought any more about the possibility of becoming a public defender?"

"Excuse me?"

"You know, the e-mails I've sent you. It's a decent life, a good thing to do with a law degree, I think."

"I'm not considering that, Mom," Amy said tightly, "but I have been thinking about some kind of real volunteer work. Maybe a job with a literacy program or something."

Leo looked up. "Oh yeah? Since when?"

"Since a long time," she said defensively. "I've mentioned it."

"Oh. Okay. Fine. Just asking."

"I just never took it further. I don't know why not, exactly. It's been part of my long and very slow odyssey toward work," she said.

"All that law school," Antonia said, swirling the wine in her glass. "I sometimes wonder why you went in the first place. You could have taken more time after college, figuring out what you wanted to do."

"Yes," said Amy, "I could have."

At the table, in the orange candlelight, Amy's mother's hair shone silver like a Susan B. Anthony dollar, and Mason's hair shone polished brown, still so springy with protein, the color of the beauti-ful floors of the corridors that someday he would walk along. Leo looked from his wife to his mother-in-law, and then he quickly returned to the safest place: his own plate, where he hastily began to eat his dinner double time, calming himself with food, his shoulders rounded, his concentration on his dinner complete, apparently not wanting any part of this moment that had nothing to do with him. The conversation at the meal now continued mostly as a dialogue between grandson and grandmother. Mason happily showed off for this woman who loved him in a singular way that no one could object to, not even a quietly angry grown daughter.

.   .   .

O N THE MORNING of the first day back to school after Christmas vacation, the first snow fell upon the city. From the windows of their financial and legal towers, men and women peered out upon the natural phenomenon. The men thought of sleds and of their children and of being a child. And from those same towers or their apartments or the warm light of the small shops that lined the avenues, more than a few of the women wondered if their children's boots from last year still fit. The men thought of freedom, and the women thought of necessity. With that first snow, everyone in the city looked up at once to admire its assertive but casual whirl. There was a shared sense of anticipation: Perhaps school would be canceled tomorrow. Perhaps work would be canceled too! But work was not one *thing*, and everyone knew that most offices would remain open and that life would go on as it usually did.

The first day back always had a kind of sad capitulation to it. At seven in the morning, Amy's alarm rang out. Without telling her, Mason had changed the setting, so that instead of a dove-coo, there emanated from her clock a gentle whinnying, growing louder and more impatient as it continued. *NEIGH NEIGH NEIGH NEIGHHHH*, the horses called, nosing her harshly from sleep.

Amy awakened and began to shout from her bed. "Mason!" she called, but heard nothing in reply. She took a breath. "MASON, IT'S THE FIRST DAY BACK TO SCHOOL!" she cried. "COME ON, BUDDY!" The entire apartment was still. Leo had long gone off to the gym and the office, and Amy's mother still slept deeply on her air mattress in the study—she wore earplugs, and slept through everything—and Mason slept deeply too. "I DON'T WANT TO HAVE TO TELL YOU AGAIN!" Amy cried out. "WE HAVE TO GET THERE EARLY FOR LICE CHECK!" She wondered whether Penny would show up for drop-off, and she imagined them standing together and making an unpleasant attempt at small talk.

The gym, when Amy and Mason arrived, was a force field of sound. The boys, who had been apart for two weeks, responded with puplike happiness to one another's company. The mothers and the handful of fathers stood talking while the boys whirled around them. Details of vacations were traded. One mother talked about a ski trip; someone else said she had lain in the sun, "not moving a muscle." A father said his family had stayed in the city and skated together every night at the rink in the park. Over by the wall stood Isabelle Gordon the string theorist, telling another mother how she and her husband and kids had traveled to CERN, the particle physics lab near Geneva, so that she could visit the Large Hadron Collider. "It filled me with inexpressible awe," she said. The other mother could only shake her head and smile.

The school conducted lice checks twice yearly, and always the mothers worried that their sons would be identified as the bringer of insects, the pariah. Today someone had released a few basketballs from the hanging net bags where they had been stored over vacation like coconuts, and now many of the boys were shooting hoops in their jackets and ties, while some of the others slumped on folding chairs to have their heads checked.

Mason plopped down on one of the chairs, and a heavy black woman in a medical coat that had the words "Nitz Away" stitched over the breast pocket stood above him with a long metal barber's comb and something that looked like a nail file, raking through his hair so that little patches of scalp suddenly appeared and then disappeared. How white his scalp was beneath that dark mass, Amy thought each time the woman lifted his hair. The whiteness of the scalp was like the whiteness of bones, revealing the self in a way that was always ghoulish when it was displayed. Karen's twins, Caleb and Jonno, sat side by side on the next bank of folding chairs, nearly napping, as two bored women sifted through the silky blades of their hair.

Amy kept looking toward the doorway, waiting for the moment when Penny and Holden might walk in. But when Holden Ramsey finally entered the gym, he was trailed only by his babysitter Clementine.

"Penny didn't bring Holden today?" Karen asked right away after she came up beside Amy.

"No."

On the telephone after vacation, Amy had told each of her friends about the accident, describing the fall and the shock of seeing Ian's face and the unresponsiveness of Penny. "I know you're upset with her," Karen said now as they talked. "And I think it's immoral to cheat on your husband, as you know. But it would have been pretty hard for her to just rush over to him in front of Greg." All around them came the sound of basketballs thudding and the occasional silverware sound of lice-scavenging tools. "What did you expect her to do, exactly?"

"I don't know," Amy said. "Ian was lying there. It was horrible. You should have seen it, Karen. So yes, I guess I really expected her to go to him. Even out of some kind of instinct."

Roberta, who had just deposited Harry on one of the chairs, said simply, "You idealized her. Please don't object; you know I'm right. We all had a fucking transference to Penny Ramsey. And anyway, it's been so long since we had someone to idealize. We're all so separate with our little scheduled lives and our kids."

"I know," said Amy, and she had a darting, sad image of Jill, who was probably right now behind the wheel of her car, in the slow morning traffic in front of the grade school in Holly Hills. "She was my big project. But I think I need something more worthy of my time."

"Hallelujah," said Roberta.

"But I still think," said Amy, "that she could have done the moral thing."

"And what, lose everything?" said Roberta. "Oh, Amy, think about it."

"I am thinking about it. It's what I've been thinking about."

"She had an affair," said Roberta. "It was very exciting. It made her feel not middle-aged. It's like the life force: knowing that someone wants you and that you want him and that you've created a secret world together."

"But she still needs her real life," said Karen. "Her married life. It provides the foundation for this other life. Greg Ramsey makes it all possible for her."

"Greg Ramsey is so *depressing*," said Amy. "You saw the way the other men chose him at the father-son weekend. The way he needs to be seen as so dominant. And you should hear the way he talked on vacation. The things he talked about. Indie rock. Money. Always, money."

"Greg Ramsey supports her and their kids," Karen persisted. "If their marriage broke up, she would lose her whole way of life."

"Penny Ramsey actually has her own big job," said Amy. "We're here hanging around at lice check, and she's probably already at her office running a meeting."

"*Amy*," said Roberta, exasperated, "so maybe Penny Ramsey has many impressive qualities, like a lot of the women we know. But she works for a nonprofit, and she probably couldn't support her family, at least not the way they live. What do you think she makes at that museum?"

"No idea."

"Whatever it is, it's not remotely enough to manage with three kids and private school and clothes and food and vacations and child care and the kind of life she got herself into. Greg is the one with the investors, the big corporate one. He and Penny have to keep the whole thing going all the time. I know it's like a horrible trap, but it's what they chose, and so now they're stuck."

Amy thought of the young husband in apartment 14H falling dead months earlier and how the women in the lobby had speculated that his widow wouldn't be able to stay on in the building for long. Suddenly Amy needed to know what had happened to that family. Were they gone already? Had they been forced out of The Rivermere? She imagined the mother and her two children sent whirling, coatless, into Isabelle Gordon's terrifying and mostly unknowable universe.

"I'm not sure you're right," Amy said to Roberta, but the basketballs in the gym suddenly sounded louder, and she began to feel sick. She thought she should be sitting in one of those folding chairs like the boys, her head dropped back, letting a woman from Nitz

Away softly stroke her hair. But she also imagined the women from Nitz Away coming to these schools at the start of a day and setting up their tables and chairs and digging into the thick heads of hair of privileged children. Whose idea of a perfect job was *this*? Who ever longed for such a life? But maybe the pay was not horrible and the benefits were half decent, and you made of it what you could, and somehow it let you live. She saw that she had no idea at all about the different ways in which people lived.

Mason approached her then and said, "Mom, I'm going to shoot hoops. You can go."

"I can *go*? Thank you, sir," Amy said with forced jokiness.

"What?"

"Nothing, nothing. Have a good day, okay?"

If he'd had any idea of how upset she felt, she might have let him console her for once, at least a little. But of course he was unaware of these feelings, and it would likely be another forty years before he would really take care of her. Now Mason's tie was aslant, slightly milk-dipped from his cereal bowl this morning, his hair raked through with fresh crop circles. His eyes looked past her to the other boys and their bouncing balls, and this was how it was supposed to be. This was the state you hoped to achieve. Her son would be all right on his own. He had things he needed to try without her.

"So, Golden Horn?" asked Roberta.

"Yes, please," said Amy.

"Look at you, you're so upset," said Karen gently. "It's like you didn't go to St. Doe's; you went to a gulag."

"Hey, that's very funny, Karen," said Roberta. "Surprisingly very funny, for you."

"Thank you."

As they all started to walk out of the gym, Shelly Harbison fell in beside them. "Oh, you're off to the Golden Horn," she said. "Mind if I invite myself?"

Sure, fine, join us, they told her in polite voices. But as they were about to leave, Shelly's son, Dylan, came clattering up to his mother and hissed, in tearful shame, *"I have lice,"* and so, miraculously, they were released from her.

L ATER, WHEN AMY brought Mason home at the end of the school day, she turned the key in the apartment door and heard varying notes of female laughter. Going down the hallway she followed the sounds until she came to the living room, where a group of women sat in a circle on the sofa and the chairs that had been dragged in from the dining room for the occasion. "Amy," Antonia called. "Come say hello."

The women of NAFITAS were in their sixties and seventies, a couple of them with dyed hair that fell on the mother-grandmother spectrum between apricot and snow, and others with hair that sprang out wild and gray. Some were slightly hunched over, their bodies curling slightly forward like jockeys in a race toward the end of time; others were tall, straight sitters, adherents of *vinyasa* and *ashtanga* and Bikram "hot room" yoga in the different towns and cities where they lived.

The women dutifully introduced themselves. "Do you remember Marsha Knowles?" Antonia asked her daughter, gesturing toward a small, spry woman with straight silver bangs and the body of an old pixie. "You may have met her at the house when you were little. She's a health educator in Toronto, and she came to my consciousness-raising group many moons ago to teach us not to be so apprehensive about our sexual selves."

Marsha Knowles laughed. "Oh yes, my motto in those days was 'Have speculum, will travel.' I still can't believe my nerve. But I was young. I've become very modest in my twilight years."

"Ah, you're still youthful, Marsha," Antonia admonished, and the other women mildly complimented one another in the way that women often know how to do as easily as anything. Generic kindnesses fell from their lips without hesitation.

Amy took a seat, feeling the strange formality of being a guest in her own living room and being outnumbered here. "We had a productive day today," said Theda, a pigeon-breasted woman in a pretty shawl. "I went to a great seminar on whether, at our age, you should lower or raise your expectations."

"The thing is," said a small, delicate woman named Lee, the only black woman in the room, her head shaved close (recent breast cancer treatment, Antonia confided to Amy later), "I don't think I have any more expectations. I have already done what I wanted to do. I knew that if I waited around forever, it wouldn't come to me."

"*Carpe diem*," said Marsha Knowles.

"So I went to law school," Lee continued, "and I worked in international trade law for twenty years. I loved it! My husband and I broke up amicably somewhere in the middle of that, and then I fell in love with my partner, Carol, who taught constitutional law for three decades before she retired."

"Someone should write up our stories," said a tall woman named Janet. "Antonia could do it. We've got so many marriages and late careers, and some of us have had lesbian experiences and grandchildren—"

"—with their own lesbian experiences," said another woman. There was more rolling, unreconstructed laughter.

"Sorry, I write historical novels," said Antonia. "With an emphasis on *novels*."

"What's your new one about?" asked Marsha. "Can you talk about it?"

"Of course. It's called *Mitigating Circumstances,* and it's about three women in the Netherlands during World War Two, working for the Resistance."

"That sounds interesting," said Theda. "My book group will buy it in bulk." She turned to Amy then and said, "You're very nice to let us take over your apartment."

"She's used to it," said Antonia. "She grew up with my CR group meeting downstairs once in a while and with the sound of female ranting."

"No one rants anymore," Janet said wistfully. "And there's still so much to rant about. There are no women running the world."

"There was Margaret Thatcher," someone thought to say. "She had tremendous power."

"That was an exception. A freak moment in history," said Janet, "and she was so conservative. Besides, it was a million years ago." To Amy, she added, "Your generation was supposed to take over. Both the ranting and the running of the world."

"It's not their obligation," said someone else with a wave.

"If it's not going to happen naturally, then they have to be pushed."

"No one pushed *us*," said Lee.

Wine was poured in the middle of all this, and Antonia produced a burrata cheese she had bought that day at Camarata & Bello. It was tied up in some kind of leaf, which she unfolded now onto a plate that she passed around with crackers. The women ate the silky white spreading cheese hungrily and knocked back quantities of wine. They were older; they could do what they wanted. They weren't asking for the world anymore.

"I am willing to accept that the young generation is moving on in and dictating the way society will live," said Betty Jean, a woman in a corner of the room. "Mortality is not a cause I feel I can take on. Although, as a political progressive, I'm used to losing almost all my battles." The women nodded in sympathy. "I follow every single story about injustices toward women, and there are plenty," Betty Jean continued. "But what with fundamentalist Islam and the threat of terrorism, it's gotten even harder to get anyone to invest their energy in this. It's as though there's just so much political interest most people can sustain. It's like that game Scissors, Paper, Stone. Terrorism is 'Stone' now, and feminism—along with everything else—is 'Scissors.' Terrorism wins."

Everyone agreed that it was much harder to keep the light lit, the rage fresh, and to find adherents to the cause. So much else had come in and demanded attention. "It's not just terrorism," said Lee. "It's also *technology*; that's a huge preoccupation out there. My son in Tampa, Florida, keeps trying to send me digital photos of my grandchildren, but I have no idea how to download them. I've basically stopped trying. Technology is one thing that's beyond me."

"I know what you mean," said Theda. "I am just not interested in mastering the Internet. I have enough in my head by now; I can't learn this too. It's like a whole new language. Didn't we do enough already over the years?"

"We did. One thing that bothers me in particular," said Marsha Knowles, "is the way my grandchildren and their friends talk to people on the Internet. Or so-called talk, anyway. They have conversations with virtual strangers, and they pretend there's a kind of intimacy there, with all that shallow language and all that shorthand. It's so generic, and it's all unearned! They don't know each other; they don't love each other. They don't speak to each other the way we used to do when we were their age. The way we still do."

The moment became quiet, interior, sliding into the regretful, and Amy, somehow feeling it all too, remembered that she was the host, and was somewhat responsible for the mood here. "You know," she thought to say, "it would be nice if you could at least download your grandchildren's photographs. I use a computer and a BlackBerry. But I know nothing compared with my son. He knows it all." Then she called out, "Mason!" There was no answer, of course; he was in his room with the door closed. "MASON, CAN YOU COME HERE?" she called. "AND BRING YOUR LAPTOP!"

Soon her son brought his laptop into the living room and sat cross-legged on the floor by the coffee table. He gave the women a brisk but gentle tutorial on all the points that had scared off a few of them previously and that their brains had sometimes felt too crowded for until now. As they asked questions and listened, they saw that there was in fact still a little more room.

Then, as Mason was about to close the lid of the laptop, he said, "Can I show you something? There's a sound—like, a certain frequency—that only kids can hear, and it actually hurts our ears. But the weird thing is, nobody over thirty can hear it. Their ears aren't sensitive enough anymore." He located a website, clicked on it, and the women listened keenly.

There was no sound at all. There was absolute silence, and yet Mason put his hands to his ears and made a face. The women looked at one another and shrugged.

"Is this a prank, Mason?" asked Antonia. "None of us can hear a thing. Are you pulling our leg?"

"No, Grandma, it's real. I swear. See, like I said, it's a high-pitched frequency that my ears can hear but yours can't. No offense, but you're all too old." The women all laughed, though Theda pretended to put a gun to her head.

"Oh yes, that's true," said Marsha Knowles. "We're all too old for many things. We're packing up our tents now."

Amy too had heard nothing; the screech of technology and the heraldic trumpets of the future had eluded her as well. She was probably halfway through her life, bumping ahead. In the diminishing but clarifying light of late afternoon in her living room she could see the lines in the faces of her mother and her mother's friends, and the furring of pale hair that softened their profiles. She saw, briefly, the way the world rarely stopped to salute you or admonish you, regardless of what you had or had not accomplished.

THAT NIGHT, before bed, Antonia Lamb stood in the kitchen in her white nightgown like an apparition, talking on the phone. Amy came into the room and saw her there: Antonia had loaded up her face with night cream, which made it glisten in the dim kitchen as though marbled, like the counter at which she stood. Her hair was pulled back off her face, and through the nightgown Amy could see the intimation of her mother's small, low-slung breasts. She did look like someone who would not be able to hear a high-pitched whistle; she seemed slightly flummoxed, a senior citizen who has lost her way in a municipal building.

"Well," Antonia was saying into the phone, "did you defrost the pork loin yet? Really? I'm certain it's in there. Probably under a gallon of ice cream. Yes. Yes. I know, it's ancient, it's bound to have that awful freezer taste. Remember the ice cream we had that summer?

Butter brickle?" She laughed lightly, then said, "Do you want to go look for the pork loin while I'm on the phone? No? All right, then, Henry, I'm sure you'll find it. She's fine. She's just walked into the room, in fact. Say hello."

Antonia turned and said to Amy, "Your dad is on the phone," and handed her the receiver.

"Hi, Dad," said Amy, and there was her father's voice, asking her about life in New York.

"Next time your mother comes down, I'm going to come with her," he said.

She imagined her father lying beside her mother on the air mattress: her body more majestic with age and his a little smaller, like a terrier. He still taught economics at McGill, though he was thinking of retiring soon. "I send you my love," Henry Lamb told his daughter, and Amy sent hers back too, then handed her mother the phone. Talk returned to the subject of the pork in the freezer; Antonia seemed genuinely anxious that Henry should locate it. He did, over the remainder of the phone call, and then he placed it on the counter in their own kitchen up north, where it would unfreeze itself slowly over the passing hours and become a meal he could cook for his wife when she came home from her travels.

"Well," said Antonia to Amy after she was off the phone, "I guess I should say good night. And say thanks for letting the women of NAFITAS come for a visit today. And for letting me sleep on your floor and get to spend all this time with Mason. He's such a marvelous boy."

"My pleasure." Then Amy suddenly said, "You know, I never wanted to be a public defender. That was always your idea."

"Oh. Well, it was just a thought."

"I wouldn't be passionate enough," she tried to explain. "And you'd need to be passionate for that job. Otherwise your clients wouldn't even have a chance."

"That makes sense to me."

"You were always so passionate," Amy added. "Back when you started writing."

Her mother smiled slightly. "I didn't know you noticed. You three girls seemed very wrapped up in your lives. I needed something to do, and I always loved to write. Work changed everything. For me, work is anti-death."

"I think it was really a big deal to have a mother who suddenly wanted something," Amy said, "and was also really good at it."

"I tried to set an example."

"You did." She felt her throat constrict and was ashamed at herself for the petulance she could already feel. "Just because things become possible," Amy said, "it doesn't mean that everyone has something they're all that good at."

"Oh, come on, you're very smart," said her mother, "and very capable. You've always been that way."

"And I expected things of myself," Amy said. "But not everyone is that driven. And not everyone is really talented. And also," she said, "sometimes it's too difficult to make it happen."

Amy recalled herself and her sisters standing outside their mother's door, banging with their fists, telling themselves they were undermothered, when in fact for so long they had been so well and fully mothered by their intelligent and creative and adoring mother that surely her mothering would have a long half-life.

But all they knew, then, was that Antonia had said, "This is *my* time," and that she'd gently closed her door. The girls played *Jane Eyre* once in a while over the years; they imagined themselves orphaned by their wonderful mother and even, somehow, by *feminism* itself—that word that sounded to them so formal and unappealing. It sounded, Naomi had once said when they were girls, like the name of a brand of menstrual pads: *Feminism: for the days when you really need a little extra protection.*

"Oh, darling, I know it's complicated," said Antonia now. "Sometimes you have to cobble things together. But you could have found something to do in recent years, couldn't you?" she asked kindly. "Some sort of thing that would matter and would also make you feel good?"

"I feel good," Amy said, her voice stiff. "Good enough." Then she said, "I don't know why I haven't found it. I thought I was going to."

"Well, you'll keep figuring it out," said her mother. "We did, or at least we tried. We put it together and hoped that everybody got at least a little of what they needed. But back then it was the beginning of everything. We were the early ones. I know we got some things wrong, but we did try to do right by everyone. And now I guess it's out of our hands."

T HE NEXT DAY, after Antonia had taken a taxi to the airport to return to Montreal, Amy found the receipt. She was deflating the air mattress in the study, listening to the soft hiss of release, when she noticed some papers that must have been knocked out of place by her mother. The room was so small, and it would have been difficult not to have disturbed something in it. The papers lay scattered on the Sven desk, having apparently fallen from one of the pigeonholes. Amy glanced through them without much interest; here were some of Leo's hotel and restaurant and store receipts from his business trips that he was apparently planning to submit to his firm as expenses. And then here was another one, but it was peculiar; some typing at the top had been whited out by hand, ready to be Xeroxed, she supposed. Across the top Leo had written, in pen, "Client Gift."

The bill was for $233.00, and at first she didn't know what it was or why that number sounded familiar. Then she recalled the woman in the gift shop on St. Doe's: *"Two hundred tirty-tree,"* the woman had said, musically, as Amy admired the paperweight with the coral and turquoise inside. Then Amy had bought it for her mother, who had loved it and said she would use it for all her manuscripts, as Amy had suggested. Leo had never gone into that gift shop or any other one. He would have been magnetically repelled from a small room jammed with unnecessary decorative things. As a boy he'd had to accompany his own mother to gift shops and women's clothing stores and sewing shops with their strips of rickrack and rolls of muslin and denim. He hated entering fussy, decorative places like that, and Amy understood that he had certainly not gone into the gift shop on St. Doe's but was simply passing off the purchase of the paper-weight for her mother as a client gift, expecting to be reimbursed by his firm.

She knew then that if she were to look through the pigeonholes of the Sven desk—this place that had always been as boring to her as a gift shop was to Leo—she would find at least a couple more receipts like this one. "Client Dinner," one would say. Or, perhaps, "Drinks with Client." She knew it with alarm and dread, even as it also made her feel she had no idea of what drove Leo or of what he cared about now. She understood that the pigeonholes of the desks of other overstressed working people all over the city and dotting the surrounding towns contained similar receipts, and that the world was swollen with these piles of paper, and that wherever you looked, you could always find somebody asking somebody else to pay up.

Chapter

TWELVE

Montreal, 1973

THE GIRLS DIDN'T HEAR him come home from work, for he was a quiet man, discreet with his key in the door. They were in the living room deeply engaged in something—at first he didn't know what—and he stopped for a moment to listen. It wasn't like eavesdropping; it was more like getting some information about his daughters with whom he shared a house but who seemed bewildering to him, the way his wife did sometimes too.

"Jane, you and Helen Burns must walk around and around in the rain as punishment for your sins," Naomi was saying to Amy in an attempted deep voice that Henry Lamb supposed was meant to signify maleness.

"Please don't make us do that, Mr. Brocklehurst," said Amy. "I beg of you."

"Please don't," echoed Jennifer.

"I am afraid you have given me no choice. You are all terrible children, and you must learn humility."

"You don't even know what humility means, Naomi," said Amy.

"My name is not Naomi, it is Mr. Brocklehurst. And of course I do. Humility is the thing that the Christian martyrs had. It is . . . their thing. And you have to learn it as well." Then the youngest of his daughters reached out and lightly began to shove the oldest, and then the middle one joined in too, the three girls engaged in a mock fight that seemed to them to be deeply satisfying. Their father watched, still unnoticed, as they banged and goofed around together. Amy fell against a standing lamp, knocking it to the rug but not shattering it. The couch moved slightly out of position, complaining a little on its casters.

Henry had come home early today because his stomach was slightly upset, and the house, in the late afternoon, always seemed to be such a soothing place. He would walk in and see his daughters playing one of their complicated games, and he wished he could join them for the entire day. He had gotten used to being with them after the nights when Antonia had banished him and the girls upstairs. He had slowly learned, in those moments, how much he liked that enforced child time. It comforted him more than macroeconomic theory ever had. He'd never been particularly brilliant in his field, but instead he was hardworking, drawn forward since boyhood by some generic notion that he was meant to succeed. But truly, if the world had been different—if it had been a freer and stranger place— he might have said to Antonia, "You go off and do your work. I will stay here all day."

Those words, said even to himself, seemed sort of sad and pecu- liar; they sounded like the sentiments of a man in a midlife crisis. In the fall he would have to serve as department chairman; it was a position that rotated, and finally it was to be Henry's turn, but he dreaded the constant do-si-do of meetings, the intradepartmental memos he was supposed to send all the time, and the way he would have to take charge of that little duchy called the Economics Depart- ment, when all he wanted was to run his own household.

If he were in charge at home, then the house, at four-thirty in the afternoon, would already be alight with the first smells of food, as it had once been: Perhaps there would be lamb chops snapping with fat in the broiler or even the earthen smells of a chocolate cake. Children loved to be in a house in which a cake was baking; nothing made them feel more content. Yet his three daughters in the late afternoon of a school day were pretending to be at Jane Eyre's orphanage. The rooms they inhabited were chaotic and lively and slightly out of control. The rug bunched; someone would inevitably trip over it soon, he thought, but he didn't want to go in and straighten it, because then they would see him and stop playing and grow self-conscious. He wished so badly that he could be in the vicinity of his daughters' play more often, that it could just flourish near him without stoppage; he wished he were allowed to putter around among the girls' true nature, as ignored but central as a mother who stayed home all day.

For a long time, Antonia had seemed to enjoy that role, but then she'd been struck by new desires. As a result, his daughters had become more independent too, and this wasn't a bad thing at all, but Henry Lamb would have liked to step into the breach and cook those lamb chops, and straighten that rug, and do so much more, at least for a few more years, until the girls got too old and were completely lost to him.

Early on, he'd had an inkling of the ways in which he and Antonia were different from other couples. She had been a sexy, somewhat advanced girl from Halifax who had been enchanted by Henry's bookishness and leanness when they met there in the summer of 1958, when he was visiting his cousins after finishing up at the University of Toronto. "All the other men I know are boors," she had said as they sat in bathing suits on the rocky shore, and he had just finished explaining to her his interest in John Stuart Mill. "You're not."

At first he thought she'd said "bores," though later on he realized he had been mistaken. He might in fact have been boring to her; he bored himself sometimes. They had had sex in her parents' seaside house when no one else was home, on sheets that smelled saline from being hung out to dry in that coastal air, and he wondered if she liked it but could never find the bravery to ask. She certainly made a lot of noise during those sessions, rolling her head around and clenching her toes in a death grip, and it embarrassed him slightly, but then again most things did.

By 1973, married for thirteen years, he didn't think Antonia was interested in other men, but he didn't think she was very interested in him anymore, either. Partly, he'd done it to himself. When he found himself kissing Ginny Foley, the department secretary, at that Christmas party in 1969, it had been an accident, and an act of desperation. He had been so quietly unhappy within the narrow straits of his life at the time and was trying to find some way to salvage meaning from the world of the Economics Department.

There, then, was little redheaded Ginny. Even at the party she'd been at her desk, as always, and he had smiled at her benignly, then taken one of the sour candies that she kept in a jar, and said, "Hello, Ginny, I hope you can get away from your desk and have yourself an eggnog." He kept walking, and she followed him to his office. She stood in the doorway and said to him, "Professor Lamb, you know you're the only man in the entire department who treats me like a person." Then she took him by the shoulders and leaned up and kissed his mouth.

He had been shocked. He was sucking on her sour candy at the time, and his tongue and her tongue played a bit of ping-pong with that little orb, which cherrified the kiss and made it seem all the more salacious. It was as if Ginny Foley was a metaphor for all the pleasure and comfort that was missing from his existence at the university. The kiss reminded him of how little joy he took in most things. If only he could find a consciousness-raising group for men, then he would immediately go sit in some other husband's living room and tell everyone, "I wish I could just stay home and raise my daughters, and cook lamb chops and bake cakes, and watch my wife march off into civilization the way she wants to, and then watch her come home and listen to her tell me all about it."

But supposedly men did not need such a group. Men were happy with the way the die had been cast. They had held on to their power over the centuries; they ran departments to their liking, and they had long ago set the tone of the world, and though the women were taking the world back now, bit by bit, everyone would always be aware that the men had gotten there first and had laid down their big, primitive footprints.

In the car going home that night, Antonia had let him have it. To his horror, she had seen the kiss with Ginny Foley from the department hallway and had thought he was disgraceful. In her consciousness-raising group, she told him, they sometimes discussed the problem of infidelity and what to do about it. No, no, he had wanted to say. It's not like that. It's not like that at all. But he couldn't find the words to tell her this, and so he sat with her in the over-heated car, saying he was so very sorry and slowly working his way over the roads that stayed iced in Montreal all winter, and together they headed home.

There were to be no more cherry-tinged kisses with Ginny Foley; within a year she had married an electrician and moved to Saska-toon. Henry retreated into his work. Occasionally he returned home early from the university, such as on a day like today, and for just a moment he would catch the tail end of his daughters' rich and fully imagined inner lives. It was like being able to glimpse childhood, even as it evaporated.

"Jane Eyre, you are wanted in the schoolroom this very minute," one of his girls was saying to another. They were so beautiful, and he regarded them from the front hallway as if for the first time. Dur-ing their younger years, he'd been involved in committees and in political jockeying within the department, and in publishing articles, panting slavishly after that all-important gold ring called tenure. His girls treated him like a slightly remote figure. Amy used to sit in his study sometimes, in the space below his desk when he was in his chair, and she would grab at an ankle and hold on to it, and he never shook her away but instead sat there for longer than he'd meant to.

The world was changing, but not fast enough. Maybe soon a mother could go off and write all day without thinking of anyone or anything else, while a father could stay home and make a house smell like chocolate and play dollies with his daughters. But for now, as far as he could see, that couldn't yet happen. In this house, at least, there would be a halfway version, in which Antonia was sometimes excited or conflicted, and Henry was often sentimental or bored. Their three daughters seemed not to notice much of it. They were girls, still caught in the expansive amber of childhood. He stood for a moment in the front hallway and watched them play.

Chapter

THIRTEEN

A MY CALLED JILL frequently during the first week back from
her trip to St. Doe's, much the way that the two of them had
called each other when they were in college. Her voice was flat with
unhappiness. Jill remembered how, at exactly half their present age,
they had telephoned back and forth on dorm-room phones and met
for beers near midnight at a campus bar they liked where the walls
were carpeted and you could sit in a corner and lean back against
the spongy, unclean surface and say anything there was that had
to be said. You could sing your song of sorrow—a boy no longer
loves me; my mother is dead; I have no time to study for my Western Intellectual Tradition exam—and the other person would shake
her head or touch your shoulder or agree that life could be so hard.
They switched off being the one who told things and the one who
listened; neither of them was particularly needier than the other.
Although Jill, in those days, was still just a few years out from her
mother's suicide, she offset the trauma with her own quiet, methodi-
cal manner. Somehow, together, with their backgrounds so different

but their modesty and fidelity similar, Jill and Amy formed a duo. They met at all hours of the day and night, and they told each other things, and they never regretted what they had said. You could be a girl crying as you gripped a dented plastic cup of beer and leaned against the furred curve of a wall; and now, as a forty-year-old woman, your closest friend would not hold you responsible for that earlier incarnation.

Amy Lamb currently reminded Jill so much of that long-ago version of herself. Amy seemed, lately, like someone who had been formed and then unformed again. She had been tempest-tossed by Penny Ramsey, and it had hurt her; it still did. But now there was something else: She'd become sharply unhappy and angry with Leo, who had forged a few expenses, hoping to pick up some extra money. Maybe Amy was an innocent not to have known how common this practice was, and, though the cheating was small-time, it was still fraud, she told Jill, and its casualness shook her. She said she had always thought Leo was one of the good ones, that he was nothing like Greg Ramsey and those other piratic husbands.

Late at night on the day that she had found the receipts, Amy had called Jill. It was midnight, too late to get a phone call, but Jill didn't stiffen in the way that many people did when the phone rang at that hour, and this was for one reason: Her parents were both already dead. She'd long ago gotten those phone calls, the one about her mother so horrifying on that afternoon at the Pouncey School; the second one, about her father, years later and expected because he had pancreatic cancer by then. So really, as she lay in bed in the house in Holly Hills with Donald beside her and Nadia sleeping nearby, she had nothing much to fear when the phone rang at a time when it shouldn't have.

"Jill? I know it's late. I'm really sorry."

"What's the matter?"

Amy told Jill about the fake receipts that Leo had generated from their trip, and she said that he appeared to have been generating others for some time. "I found three of them that he hasn't yet handed in," she said. "The client gift and a drinks bill from the island, and a so-called client dinner from a Tuscan restaurant that we went to last month."

"So what was the client gift, really?" Jill asked.

"Oh, some little paperweight I bought my mother."

"How much was it? I'm just curious."

"Just over two hundred dollars," Amy said.

"Wow. That's a nice paperweight."

"It was pretty," Amy said, her voice slightly petulant, so Jill didn't pursue this.

Donald cracked open an eye and looked annoyed. Jill took the cordless phone down the wide, dim stairs of the house and sat in the dark of the den. Though Amy was so unhappy, it felt comforting that they were talking like this, and that the topic, for a change, was not Penny Ramsey. They were talking about marriage, and life, the way they had done when Jill lived in the city. "Oh, Amy, come on," she said finally. "Don't magnify this. Don't catastrophize."

"I'm not catastrophizing. It's how I feel."

"So what did you do with them?" Jill asked.

"The receipts? I left them there."

"I hate to sound blasé," Jill said, "but this kind of thing is pretty common in business, isn't it? Doesn't it happen all the time?"

"I suppose so. But Leo was always different. And please don't tell me that you think morality is a fluid thing, Jill."

"I wasn't going to say that. I wasn't even thinking it. But now that you mention it, I guess it's true. There are circumstances."

"But why would he secretly become this person who would cheat like this, even in this little, pathetic way? Or keep it from me?" asked Amy.

"Maybe because it's little and pathetic."

"I really have no idea of what he's thinking lately. We are extremely detached. Not that he even necessarily knows it."

"You have to talk to him," said Jill.

"I can't."

"Well, then I don't know what else to advise." There was quiet on the line for a moment. "Any word from Penny?" Jill asked finally.

"No."

"No?"

"I'm done with that."

"And what about the boyfriend?"

"He's apparently lucky. I called the framing department at the Met. They said he's supposed to go to some rehabilitation institute outside London. He'll be okay, but it'll take a long time. His aunt is taking care of him. I sent him some chocolates and a letter, but I didn't really know what to say. I don't even *know* him. I just told him that I was sorry about everything that had happened and that I hoped he got better soon. That kind of thing. The whole story has no real ending; it's so strange."

"This is the ending. It's just not satisfying, that's all. It's just not 'closure,' like people say."

Jill realized that she almost enjoyed the slow burn of piety she felt about Penny Ramsey, but it was followed by sympathy for Amy. It was as though Amy was a child who had left home despite her parents' entreaties that the world was a treacherous place. Now she had returned, broken and sad, because what her parents had said turned out to be true after all. When you reached the age of forty, Jill thought, you didn't need new friends. Apparently you *shouldn't* have new friends; they would only disappoint you.

"I think you should go to sleep," Jill said. "Talk to Leo about the receipts tomorrow."

"You should sleep too." Amy paused and blew her nose. "Are you still taking that Noctrem? I should get some."

"Yeah, every night. It really works. I'll give you a few."

"Thanks. You can be my dealer."

There was a pause. Jill might have taken this moment to suddenly say something to Amy about Nadia, to confess her anxieties about her daughter's intellect in a much fuller way than she'd ever allowed herself, but she couldn't.

"I know," said Amy, "that I've been a little obnoxious about the Penny thing. I realize you've been lonely out there, away from the city and all of us. And I never want you to feel, you know, abandoned by me."

"It's okay," Jill said.

"And I'm sorry for other things," said Amy. "Because you've been such a good friend, and I know you've been through a lot in your life. Your mother. And the whole fertility problem—"

"*Amy*. All is forgiven."

"You're sure?"

"Yes. I'm really sure."

They talked for a few more minutes, letting the conversation settle lightly down into the familiarity and safety of ordinariness. They both could have fallen asleep this way, staying on the phone and talking close until their voices slowed and stopped. Once, in college, they had done just that; Jill had awakened at dawn in the desk chair of her dorm room with the phone receiver pressed to her folded, hot ear, and to the sound of Amy's even breathing.

When they finally hung up now, Jill thought of how Amy was the only friend she wanted. Jill told herself this frequently. *No new friends.* This remained her theme as she made her way through the rest of her first winter in Holly Hills.

The morning after the phone call, Jill Hamlin traveled through the downtown area of the suburb in her car, along the broad main street that was flanked by shops and trees, on her way to pick up Nadia from the birthday party of a boy in her class named Liam Rostower. The street was still arched and crossed overhead with Christmas lights and wires, though Christmas and New Year's had passed. The town apparently kept its lights up until the last gasp of winter in the middle of January, at which point all indications of festivity would come to a halt, and workmen would stand on ladders unscrewing and removing jollity.

Jill pulled into a parking spot in front of the pottery studio at the shopping center where the party was being held. She entered Going to Pot, and saw several other mothers crowding the vestibule, some talking on cell phones as they struggled to hold on to their children's newly glazed vases or candy dishes. Going to Pot was a birthday mill; children at parties here were allowed to choose among four different generic ceramic pieces, which they would then be handed to paint and stipple and strew with glitter, and which would then be placed inside a roaring industrial kiln that was being stoked in the back room. At the end of the party, paper plates of birthday cake would be passed around, the birthday song would be hastily sung, the children would be reunited with their freshly glazed and fired creations, and then everyone would go home.

It was not possible, at Going to Pot, to fail. You didn't need to be artistic in order to bring home a passable piece of preshaped clay. Yet the creation that Nadia had made drooped to the side, unable to stand on its own, and Nadia's hands had flattened it so that the opening was only wide enough to contain, what? A single blade of grass? A hair?

All around them, children poked one another's jazzy little creations, then deposited them with their mothers. Jill watched as the other children, their load lightened, preened and coupled and tripled, heads close, having a great deal to say. The only one with nothing much to say was Nadia, who stood off to the side, not particularly unhappy but simply exhibiting a kind of stillness that was in itself troubling to Jill. She took her daughter by the hand and led her through the chattering field of children. No one noticed that Nadia, the new girl at school this year, was leaving the party. Her absence would be felt only as strongly as her presence had been.

That evening, Nadia's little vase leaned against a container of coconut rice on the dining room table where Jill, Nadia, and Donald ate take-out Thai food from Bangkok House that he had picked up on his way home from the train station. Nadia struggled with her chopsticks, holding one in each hand and bringing them together to wrangle a single noodle of pad thai. Her face was shining with oil. Donald noticed the piece of pottery and lifted it up, turning it slowly, then said, "Where did you buy this, Jill? It looks valuable."

Nadia stared at her father, sensing she was being put on, but he betrayed no humor. Donald was a kind father, and time after time he was able to express love for Nadia in a playful way that Jill just couldn't. "Mom didn't buy that, Daddy," Nadia finally said.

"Oh no? What do you mean?"

"I made it at Liam Rostower's birthday party."

"Excuse me?" said Donald, wiping his mouth and putting his napkin down. "I'm supposed to believe you made this?"

"Yes, Daddy," Nadia said. "I made it. Mom, tell him."

And so Jill was drawn reluctantly into the game, forced dully to confess to Donald that, yes, Nadia had made this vase. But why couldn't she just go along with it? Why did it bother her that Nadia was too old for such a game? Why did none of this banter between parent and child come naturally to Jill?

A few days later, at pick-up at the local public school, Jill walked through the groups of children until she saw her solitary daughter standing by the heating ducts. Nearby, two girls exclaimed together over some enormous fantasy novel called *Blindman and . . .* something. *Blindman and the Moorcutter? The Moorcatcher? The Moorchaser?* The fact that these first-graders could read such an advanced book startled Jill, and the fact that they could discuss it in an informed manner was equally alarming.

"I like the part where the Moorchaser gets the gold bullion," one of the girls said to the other. "And did you know there's a surprise ending? Blindman turns out not to be blind after all. Even though he was born without eye sockets, he had *tiny eyes* in his nostrils. He could always see everything the whole time."

"I love surprise endings," said the other girl.

"Can you sleep over this weekend?"

"I'll check the schedule."

There wasn't even anything particularly egregious about the exchange, but to Jill it was unbearable. With no adults watching, she bent down to the two girls and said, "Don't you think that book is a little *old* for you? You're only in first grade. Don't you think it might make some of the other children feel a little bit bad because they can't read it too?"

One of the girls looked terrified and ran away. But the other girl held her own. "You're Nadia Hamlin's mom, right?" the girl said, and Jill realized, from her red hair and slightly popping eyes, that she was Juliana Gregorius, daughter of Sharon Gregorius, creator of

Wuv Cards. Though all the children were dressed in casual school clothes, it was easy to see that Juliana was stylish and composed like her mother, and that Jill, in choosing this child to single out, had made a tactical error.

"Yes, I am," said Jill, slightly taken aback.

"No offense, but she will never be able to read this book," said Juliana Gregorius. Then she turned and walked away.

No one had heard the exchange, either the aggressive way Jill had spoken to a child or the child's devastating response. Of course, Jill was the inappropriate one here, but she would probably get away with it. Who would believe a six-year-old when she claimed that a perfectly respectable mother had approached her and told her she shouldn't read a hard book because it would make other children feel bad? There had surely been a misunderstanding. Jill felt slightly crazed here in the pick-up area of this school, but she was not done yet.

Her eyes probably looked wild as she made her way over to Nadia's first-grade teacher. But Mrs. Kelleher, a veteran teacher in her sixties, with hair like yellowed lamb's wool, had seen everything. She knew the score, and, of course, like most teachers, she preferred the girls who shone with possibility. Jill could see this now, as Mrs. Kelleher, a wide, thick-built woman, stood chatting with several of the mothers.

Only in the enclosed universe of a grade school could such a homely and pursed woman be popular; only here could she be the one all the mothers tried to suck up to. Jill saw how readily seduced Mrs. Kelleher was by the mothers of the more precocious children, and she compared this response with the weary look that Mrs. Kelleher now gave Jill as she approached. No matter what Jill did, she would be unable to seduce Mrs. Kelleher into loving her daughter.

But she had to find out about Nadia, one way or another, and she was in a very rare mode of confrontation, so it might as well be now. Without Amy around to practice on and possibly temper her words, she proceeded. "Mrs. Kelleher," she said, thrusting herself into the middle of the group of mothers. "Hi."

Mrs. Kelleher's eyes flickered back longingly to the other women.

"Hello," said the teacher, who was both an old pro and, Jill thought, kind of a cunt.

"I just wondered how Nadia was doing in class," Jill said.

Mrs. Kelleher looked Jill right in the eye, then came close, moving them both away from everyone else, and said in a low, confidential voice, "Mrs. Hamlin, I was going to call you anyway. I have begun to have real concerns about Nadia. For a while I thought it was just the adjustment to a new school and a new environment, but it's still going on. Have you thought of having her evaluated?"

So this was an afternoon of honesty, and it was breathtaking. Jill had asked for it, and there was even something relieving about it. The usual falseness and strain were gone. "Yes, I have," Jill said.

"I can recommend someone in town, if you'd like," said the teacher. "I'll e-mail you tonight."

With the briefest smile, Mrs. Kelleher turned back to the other mothers, and Jill heard her say something about how Liam Rostower knew all about the origins of Groundhog Day. "During Sharing Circle, Liam told the class that the tradition might have begun in the fifth century, with the European Celts believing that animals possessed supernatural powers. He was quite the expert." All the mothers grinned and smiled and popped up and down like groundhogs around the teacher.

A while later, sitting at the kitchen table with Nadia, Jill watched as her daughter ate her snack and struggled over her homework. One hand held a pink cupcake, squeezing it a little too hard, and the other held a pencil in a forced grip. Jill glanced down at the workbook, noting the dense paragraph of text on the page and the various questions that were meant to be read and then answered at the end:

1. Why does the farmer want to sell the old nag Gypsy?
2. Do you think it's fair?
3. What would *you* have done with Gypsy?

Jill knew that Nadia could barely read these words and would need her mother to hover above her and sound out each syllable in a way that would give both of them a reassuring but false sense that Nadia herself had been reading. She watched Nadia struggle for a while as the sky outside the kitchen window grew darker and the street lamp by the curb automatically popped on and the day shifted into evening, and soon Donald would come home on the train with the other men. They would hear his footsteps in the front hall and the rustle of paper as he thumbed through the day's mail on the front hall table. Then, giving her father a few courteous seconds to acclimate himself, Nadia would spring up from whatever she was doing and fling herself against him with wanton abandon. Donald, smelling of office and train and newspaper print, would gratefully accept the tackle.

Until then, though, Jill and Nadia would sit together at the table, and the story of the farmer leading his nag across a grassy meadow would remain an abstraction. The cupcake detritus that dotted the surface of the text would prove more compelling than the text itself. Nadia would apply a damp index finger to each crumb, then put it into her mouth, wistfully recalling the lost pleasure of the snack. But the trail of crumbs would always lead back to the farmer and the nag, in whose company Nadia Hamlin would be forced to live, perhaps forever.

So the sky became dark, and the farmer and the nag waited in the field. Jill, watching her daughter's baffled expression and tired eyes, finally said, "I think that's more than enough, honey, don't you? You've been working hard for a long time. Let's just stop."

"But there's more to do."

"It's okay," Jill said.

Nadia asked, "Did you used to do your homework with your mom when you were little?"

"Sometimes."

There was a pause, and then Nadia said, "Where *is* she again?"

"She died, remember?" Jill said, her throat sticking unexpectedly for her mother, even now, after all this time. The feeling just went into hiding and then reappeared at moments like this one, when you had to seem stoical and not full of sensation. "It was a long time ago," Jill told her daughter. "We've talked about that."

"Right," said Nadia. Then she said, in a matter-of-fact voice, "I had another mom too, once. But she couldn't take care of me, so you had to do it."

"I wanted to do it. I'll always want to."

Nadia kept looking at Jill gravely, and after a moment she placed a hand on Jill's hand, patting it. Then she said, "You're sure we can stop working now?"

"Positive."

Jill recognized her daughter's bravery and knew that it wasn't appropriate for her to have to be so brave—to need to suit up every day and face an army of children with manifesto-length novels about Moorchasers under their arms, and a teacher who didn't draw enough gratification from teaching her, and nearly a full hour at lunch when Nadia would sit ignored at the end of a long table, chewing a soft sandwich. Her eyes would give her the appearance of being lost as she sat at lunch in the cafeteria by herself, and in her strangely beautiful little voice Nadia would sing her folk song about the saffron sister tree.

The following Monday, Jill had Nadia evaluated. She took her to a testing facility in a small office building in downtown Holly Hills, where Nadia sat in a room with an enthusiastic woman named Mrs. Jantzen. After a few hours Nadia emerged looking tired; even Mrs. Jantzen looked tired. The tests had been too much, and school was too much, and everything was too much. It was impossible to miss this.

Nadia's test results were not surprising, though even so they provided a severe blow to the narcissism of a parent. Jill and Donald sat in a small room while Mrs. Jantzen explained the various areas in which Nadia had shown significant cognitive lags. She said the words without any blame or embarrassment; she was used to delivering news like this to parents. Nadia was not so unusual to her, nor was she "as bad as you think," Mrs. Jantzen said.

Mrs. Jantzen handed Jill the box of tissues that sat on her desk beside a paperweight with the words "Children are like snowflakes," and a pad of Post-its advertising a timed-release, pediatric-dose drug for hyperactivity. Jill blew her nose and let herself cry into a handful of tissues, and she tried to listen as the woman explained that Nadia might do better if she had a "shadow teacher," someone who could help her through the day and give her the time and attention that Mrs. Kelleher apparently could not. "And the good part is that it can be paid for by the state," said Mrs. Jantzen.

"That's the good part?" said Donald. "Great. I was waiting for the good part."

"You will have to petition for it," Mrs. Jantzen went on, unperturbed, "and probably even sue, but you will get your way in the end. It's a big pain in the ass, pardon me, but it's just the way it is."

"Are you saying we have to do this?" Donald asked. "That we are obligated to have her singled out in this way?"

Mrs. Jantzen shook her head. "No, Mr. Hamlin," she said. "Some parents prefer to put their children in a special school. That's a family decision, based on circumstances. But at any rate, you tell me she is struggling. And when I look at these results, I would have to agree. Why should Nadia have to struggle so much? It seems unkind to me."

In the car on the way home they sat silently. Jill was reminded of their many visits to the fertility experts years earlier, and how they had left those offices with a similar sensation of heartbreak. There was heartbreak everywhere: in losing a mother, in missing your closest friend, in wanting a child, in raising a child. But off at work all day, Donald was cordoned off from his daughter's limitations. When he returned home from the city at night, Nadia's loving nature was so appealing to him that she probably seemed to be the most articulate and unusual child on earth. Maybe he had even been serious about the beauty of her bud vase. Maybe he was so much in love with her that she shimmered with greatness, blinding him. This was a good thing, Jill realized, but it did not help right now, in the car, as Donald slipped his hand briefly into his suit jacket, against his heart, as though he'd been shot.

That night, he was as playful with Nadia as ever. He danced her around the living room and sat with her on her bed before sleep, and together they read a pile of picture books. Jill peered into the room and saw them going over some of the books they had read when she was three and that most of the other children had long ago discarded. For Nadia, these books were more than nostalgic; they were like life itself.

Jill went to call Amy. "It's me," said Jill.

"What's up?"

She paused. "Nothing," she finally said. If she began to talk about Nadia now, over the phone, she would become upset. So she would talk to Amy in person, not that it would do any good, for Amy knew only what it was like to raise a boy whose mind was capacious and honeycombed, filled with everything imaginable. "Nadia and I are coming into the city one day after school this week," Jill said. "I have to get her a spring coat. Can I see you then?" Amy said that she was still feeling bad, and that though it had been a week already, she hadn't said anything to Leo about his fake receipts. She was reluctant to make a date with Jill. "I'm not feeling very social," she said. "Oh, come on, Amy, it's just *me*," Jill said, and Amy relented.

The women arranged to meet on Thursday afternoon; Mason had a piano lesson then, and Amy said that if Jill wanted to, she could come sit with her during it, and they could talk. So Jill took Nadia with her on the train into the city, and bought her the spring coat she needed, and they met up with Amy at a music school in the East Nineties where children had been learning piano and flute and voice for over a hundred years.

The two women and the little girl sat together in the drafty anteroom, and around them swept shuddering scales, and the opening gambit of "Für Elise," and the theme from "A Charlie Brown Christmas," all of it seeming to represent childhood itself, so familiar was it and so frequently the province of a parent's desires rather than a child's passion. It would probably not have occurred to Amy that Mason didn't need to study piano. Did she think this solid, fact-gathering boy would grow up and become Noël Coward, with a crowd of good-looking young people gathered around him at a party, everyone singing old favorites? Many of the boys and girls of America were now as oversubscribed and overextended as executives. Their mothers were their secretaries, keeping track of the children's calendars, running slightly behind them as they went from piano lesson to fencing to papermaking to martial arts to the homes of other children and then back out into the world. Jill would not keep such a schedule with Nadia. She would not be part of this particularly American obsession, and she knew this now.

"We had Nadia tested," she began, and soon the spell of Amy's unhappiness and self-absorption seemed to lift temporarily as she listened to Jill's story. Nadia sat off to the side, her schoolbooks unopened on her lap. Instead of doing work, she was brushing the hair of one of her homely little doll horses that had—in addition to four legs, a mane, and a tail—long, blonde woman's hair and false eyelashes. Jill imagined a line from a commercial for the toy: *Does your little girl dream about riding horses but also about being a slut?*

"This must be really hard on you and Donald," Amy said. "I wish you'd told me about some of this, about the extent of all your worries."

The two women sat together with the music playing all around them. Nadia, Jill noticed, was now crouching on the floor, brushing the hair of her horse/woman, and as she did, she sang to herself. At first, she sang a song about "lucky landlubbers" from the children's TV show *Ahoy, Mateys,* and then something about the seasons changing that she'd learned at school, and then, finally, she sang her usual song: *"Rise, sorrow, 'neath the saffron sister tree . . ."*

Later, when Jill tried to re-create the moment for Donald, she was unable to tell it in a way that gave it the real resonance it had possessed at the time. Nadia was playing with her doll and singing to herself, and the music that had been rising and falling from the practice rooms suddenly stopped, as the teachers in those different cubicles coincidentally seemed to want their students to take a break at virtually the same moment. A lone harp was plinked for a few cocky extra notes, then it paused. The hallway of the music school was silent, except for Nadia's folk song. As Nadia sang, and as Amy and Jill sat there, a tall woman with black hair in a topknot walked by. She was a well-respected voice teacher named Anna Milofsky, a fifty-two-year-old Russian émigrée who taught here one afternoon a week as a favor to the school. On all other days she taught classes at Juilliard.

But Jill knew none of this yet. That information would come later. Now, Anna Milofsky went slowly down the narrow hall, carrying a libretto in her hand, and in the middle of the respite from sound coming from the practice rooms, she stopped.

Jill looked at her curiously, not understanding. Amy figured it out first. "Jill," she whispered. "She's listening to Nadia."

"Oh, get out of here," Jill whispered back, but weirdly it did seem to be true. Anna Milofsky was listening to Nadia singing her little song. *"Rise, sorrow, 'neath the saffron sister tree,"* Nadia sang.

"Excuse me, who is this girl?" the woman asked.

"My daughter, Nadia," said Jill.

"She's quite good. She has transposed the song into a minor key and then made some adjustments."

"I'm sorry, I don't know what you're talking about," Jill said, standing up from the bench. She and Anna Milofsky were the same height; usually no other woman was as tall as Jill.

"I am also amused by her wit," said Anna Milofsky.

"Excuse me?"

"Her song. She has made a new arrangement. She heard it one way, and she changed it so that it's quite different."

"We really don't understand," said Amy. "My friend's daughter sings all the time, and she sings this folk song a lot."

"We adopted her from an orphanage in Siberia," Jill explained. "My husband and I think maybe she learned it there, before we got her."

Only now was Nadia paying attention to the conversation taking place around her. She glanced up with some trepidation at her mother and Amy and at this woman who looked like a large, gentle bird with silky dark wings.

"This is not a folk song," said the voice teacher. "Is that what you think it is?" Both women nodded. "Oh my dear," she said, addressing Nadia. "I think you heard this somewhere else. Do you remember where it was, darling?" Nadia shook her head no, but her face was pink with pleasure. "I will sing the real version, which you cleverly transposed."

The voice teacher began to sing. The words of Nadia's song merely rearranged themselves in emphasis, the end of one syllable moving to become the start of another. Now, as Anna Milofsky sang, it was easy to see how everyone who had heard Nadia Hamlin singing had mistaken her words all along.

Nadia's version went: *"Rise, sorrow, 'neath the saffron sister tree."*

While Anna Milofsky's version—the real version—went: *"Rice-a-Roni, the San Francisco treat."*

So there was no saffron sister tree; there was no command for sorrow to rise. That melancholy, peaceful mantra, which Nadia had sung to comfort herself over the years, and which the women had chanted as they sat on their yoga mats, was now revealed as being something mundane. Jill made a sound that was like a moaning little cry. There was a sharp bit of a laugh in there too, because it was absurd to have imbued shy, hesitating Nadia with mournful and semi-magical unknowableness—to have made her into myth—when in fact she was plainly present, and Jill had been the one to wrap her in something that did not exist. All children were unknowns, Karen had said; they slipped in and out of knowability over time.

Nadia went down the hall to the water fountain with Anna Milofsky, the two of them talking a little about music. Amy took Jill's arm. "I know we all thought it was this beautiful, mysterious lyric," said Amy. "But look! It's something else, okay?" Jill didn't say anything. "Don't use those test scores against her, Jill. Just don't." But still Jill couldn't really speak. "Remember that day in the Golden Horn," Amy said, "when she was a baby and you asked me if I *liked* her?"

"Yes." Jill nodded, ashamed.

"She's got her things, definitely," said Amy. "Okay, so we know that now. And maybe she's got music too. Just don't be so sure about everything being the worst. Don't be so convinced all the time."

The music cranked up again from the practice rooms. Mason returned to his dutiful interpretation of Beethoven, but there was no evidence of soulfulness in his hands. The harpist down the hall wantonly pulled at a string. The hour was late, and the music teachers were likely yawning as they shepherded their students through the end of their lessons.

Nadia's song had only been a jingle from a television commercial; it was as American as could be. Nadia had heard it frequently in the apartment, certainly, when she was very little and Jill had planted her in front of the TV in her high chair in desperation, trying to find a way to entertain the child she didn't yet know at all and was somewhat afraid of. Nadia might very well have a difficult life, but apparently she had an unusual ear. Her song was no longer melancholy, and never had been.

F ROM TIME TO TIME, when he really thought about it, it bothered Donald Hamlin deeply that his wife was friendless. "I am not friendless," Jill insisted, but this did not assuage him. She mentioned Amy and Roberta and Karen, but he waved them away. His point was that Jill had no friends here in town, and although she did not want any, it was clear that she needed some, and quickly. The city seemed farther away, and the lives of the people there, while still vivid to her and filled with carefully described drama—Penny Ramsey's love affair and subsequent abandonment of her injured lover; Roberta's e-mail relationship with that girl she was bent on helping; Leo Buckner's low-level, everyday corporate cheating—were separate from Jill. Amy and the others were elsewhere, and Jill was here, in this town whose name maybe did sound like the name of a stripper, as Donald had once said, for it had a similar appeal: big, open-legged houses with wings and extensions; wide, seductive lawns;

all the parking spaces you could ever want; and yet you couldn't find substance or love.

Or, at least, you couldn't find them if you didn't want them. Jill knew there were women here she might like, but she still did not plan to look. She had developed, as Donald said, pathologically introverted tendencies in midlife.

"Locally, you are friendless," he persevered.

"You're my friend," she tried. "And you live locally."

"That is a very pathetic statement. You know what I mean."

"You don't exactly have many friends, Donald. And you don't know *anyone* in Holly Hills."

"True, but I'm a man. We have our poker friends, and we cling to our wives like koalas. Plus, I'm only basically here during the day on weekends. What am I supposed to do, start up a conversation with the other fathers at the bagel place? 'Is that poppy seed you've got there, buddy? Me, I've got sesame, and it's *still warm.*'"

The bagel place was a common destination for the men on Sunday mornings; they took their children with them in the car for company, and they lined up in the small, crowded store that smelled so wonderfully oniony, pointing to the different metal baskets, then walked out carrying a hot, lumpy bag and headed back home, their circuit completed.

"No, I don't imagine you starting up a conversation in the bagel place," Jill said.

"The primary difference," Donald said, "is that I'm fairly happy here, or anywhere, really, and you're not."

It was the primary difference, Jill Hamlin thought from time to time, between someone whose mother had killed herself and someone whose mother had not. But this distinction, like so many others, had been lost. Your personal history of pain, by the time you reached the age of forty, was supposed to have been folded thoroughly into the batter of the self, so that you barely needed to acknowledge it anymore.

When Jill finally made a friend in Holly Hills, the act of friendship was done almost against her will, against her better judgment, in secret, in darkness, in *sleep*. How strange this was, in retrospect. She was not looking to replace Amy Lamb, who would never have to be replaced. But even so, Jill Hamlin needed other people around her. She did not believe this, though, until she was forced to become aware of it.

One night, when, as always, she could not sleep, Jill took her usual dose of Noctrem, and then added another five milligrams for good measure. She walked around the house, checking doors and lights. It was midnight; everything was in order. She looked in on her sleeping daughter. Nadia had begun being "shadowed"—what an ominous word, as though she were being stalked by a pedophile—during the previous week at school, and so far the results were encouraging. For the first time all year Nadia had been able to keep up with the work, Mrs. Kelleher had said, and the teacher had sounded pleased; maybe she actually wasn't an awful person. Maybe she was just realistic and would look out for Nadia now that she knew she was getting the help she required. Jill, for her part, had become a kind of shadow-mother, and Nadia absolutely needed the big protective shadow that Jill threw across her. This week too, Nadia had taken her first singing lesson in the city with Anna Milofsky, who had invited her to be a private student, and she had enjoyed herself. Though Nadia had real talent, she was not a star like her namesake, Nadia Comaneci. She lacked the take-charge attitude of that other Nadia, the extreme self-determination, and the shockingly mature skill. Instead, she was just a girl, intently practicing.

"We sang scales," Nadia had said after the lesson, "and I am going to practice them every day in my room with an egg timer. Do we have an egg timer, Mom? Miss Milofsky says we should get one."

Nadia was on an upswing! Jill thought, and she supposed this ought to have been enough to get an anxious mother to sleep at night, but it was not.

Jill returned to the bedroom and lay down beside her husband.

"You're here," Donald said in appreciation. "My socially aloof wife. Quick! Get under the covers with me." She did, and they touched, striped pajama top to white nightgown, and the sensation, even through all that material and the veil of the double-dose nonbenzo-diazepine hypnotic Jill had swallowed, was arousing. They made love in the darkness of the silent house, and then she fell into sleep beside him.

What happened next was not something she would ever remember but instead would later have to piece together like the details in a detective story. She had only thought that she was asleep. She had thought this, much the way that the Noctrem user on that trans-atlantic flight—thinking she was filling in the British cryptic cross-word in the newspaper but instead actually drawing circles on her blouse with a magic marker—had thought the same thing. Actually, Jill was in a Noctrem-induced twilight state, and she rose from the bed at two A.M., still in her nightgown, bent down to put on a pair of running shoes, and then took her keys from the night table and walked downstairs. Her eyes must have been open, for she did not miss a single stair. She disarmed the security system so it would not go off when she opened the front door, and then Jill walked outside onto Jacob's Path.

She had never even seen her suburban street in the middle of the night, but it was incontestably beautiful with the curlicue wrought-iron street lamps on and the houses dark and almost hidden behind their shaggy cutouts of trees and bushes. Occasional houses revealed one single lit window, and in each case the color was unusual and delicate, whether it emanated from a perpetual golden surface light over a stove or the aqua glint of a tiny flat-screen guest-bathroom night-light, guarding the little soaps and hand towels and potpourri and serving no other obvious purpose. Lights on inside a house provided the sensation of lives lived. Even if you slept throughout the whole time that those lights shone, you still might like to have fallen asleep knowing that they were there.

Jill never understood why she had chosen 21 Jacob's Path.

Had she chosen, say, 23 Jacob's Path, she would have wound up at the door of the unfriendly Glesser family, who would probably have called the police. Later, Karen Yip would speculate that it was because 21 was a Fibonacci number. "Karen, I don't even know what Fibonacci numbers are," Jill had said. "I mean, I've heard of them, but that's about it." Karen told her that Fibonacci numbers—which formed a sequence, each one equaling the sum of the two preceding numbers: 0, 1, 1, 2, 3, 5, 8, 13, 21, etc.—notoriously existed liberally in patterns throughout nature in a fashion that was a wonder to mathematicians and to those of a spiritual bent. Perhaps, she said, Jill had simply been drawn to 21 in the same ineffable way. But the more likely explanation, Jill thought, was that the house, unlike all the other houses on Jacob's Path in the middle of the night, showed some movement in its front window, and perhaps Jill had noticed it.

Jill Hamlin, in her nightgown and running shoes, rang the doorbell of 21. There was no answer, and so she rang a couple more times. The chimes were deep and melodic, and finally a woman came to the door. She was slightly older than Jill, with brown hair that did not hold a hairstyle for long, and she was dressed in a T-shirt and green surgical pants. She and Jill had passed each other once or twice in their cars on the street, and they had nodded but had not stopped to introduce themselves. Alice Ettinger was barely around; the hours she kept were unpredictable.

"Hello," said Jill from the doorstep. The woman just stared at her. "I don't think we've met," Jill continued. "We live down the street." The words were spoken so innocently, and the woman considered the situation, trying to make sense of it.

"Look, I'm not sure you know this, but it's two in the morning," Alice Ettinger finally said, and her face had softened in the presence of this sudden strangeness, for she clearly thought Jill Hamlin was mentally ill or brain-damaged. "I think you should go home. Is there someone else in your house?" she asked slowly and gently. "Do you live with someone?"

"My family."

"That's good. Let's take you to them. They must be worried. Hold on, I'll get my coat. Stay right there, okay?"

The spell began to lift then; maybe the word "family" had served as a trigger antidote to the powerful drug Noctrem and its unpredictable, if rare, side effects. But by the time the woman came back with her coat, Jill had mostly returned to herself, woozy, shocked, and found that she was standing on the front doorstep of 21 Jacob's Path in the middle of the night in her nightgown. "Oh God," Jill said. "Oh God. I can't believe this."

"It's okay," Alice Ettinger said, slipping on her coat and stepping outside. "You're safe now," she said.

"No, no, you don't understand. I'm awake. I'm *awake* now."

"What?"

"That thing happened to me, I think. A side effect of Noctrem!"

"Noctrem? A side effect? You mean like that woman on a plane who thought her blouse was a crossword puzzle?"

"Yes."

"Or that other one who phoned the police because she'd shoplifted as a child? I read that article."

"Yes, yes!"

"Holy crap!"

They both began to laugh out loud. Alice Ettinger, divorced for ten years, her kids in college, a labor and delivery nurse who had come home exhausted only half an hour earlier after assisting at a birth at the local hospital, let Jill Hamlin into her house. They sat in the den, and Jill, recovering from her brief chemical trance, apologized repeatedly and expressed her horror and embarrassment at having simply rung the doorbell of the house of a stranger in the middle of the night. It was *insane*!

They would have various conversations over the rest of the lingering winter and into the spring. When the weather grew warm enough at the end of February, Alice and Jill drove to the town park and the recreation fields. They brought Alice's field guide with them, and they crouched down in the bushes, running their hands through greenery like women in a supermarket examining produce.

"Holly Hills wasn't a bad place to raise the boys, all things being equal," Alice said. "It's actually prettier than most people think. The developers will destroy all the nature in the end, but until they do, I consider it mine."

This suburb, it seemed, was jammed in places with plant life, and though most of the residents were busy with their jobs or kids and did not avail themselves of this, Alice, when she wasn't at the hospital, did. It wasn't that Jill's friendship with Alice Ettinger made her love the township of Holly Hills; she was still aware of both the slight hollowness at its center and the correspondent need that people here had to make something *happen*: a crafts fair in the parking lot of the mall, the painstakingly rehearsed and admirable local opera group's annual performance, which this year was to be Benjamin Britten's *Billy Budd*. But no place was idyllic; Jill also disliked the self-congratulatory nature of the city that lay glistening in the invisible distance. She was here for now, and she had someone else to talk to who was intelligent and likable and with whom she didn't feel as though she was just letting the rest of life fragment.

Jill told her about how she had planned to go into academia, and how, somehow, that hadn't happened. "Oh, interesting. My parents," Alice said as they went for a walk, "were both in academia, I guess you could say, but on the high school level. They were English teachers. They were like Mr. and Mrs. Chips. They always told us that if it were at all possible, we should try to find something we love doing, and preferably find it really early."

"That's smart."

"Oh yeah. Because if you don't, it's really hard to find it later on. There are so many crap jobs in the world. So many incredibly boring ones. But the good ones keep you there. I mean, I never heard of anyone who quit being an astrophysicist."

"You found a good one, right?"

"The hospital has been pretty good to me, generally. All of us in my family actually ended up doing something that we love."

"My mother did something that she loved for a while," Jill said. "She was an actress. She was even in the chorus of a Broadway musical."

And then she envisioned the young version of her mother that she knew only through photographs, wearing a toga, standing on a Broadway stage, doing, briefly, the thing she'd always wanted to do most, back in a time that itself now seemed as remote as ancient Rome.

Chapter

FOURTEEN

TO: ROBERTA SOKOLOV < *sokpuppet@earthlink.net*
FROM: BRANDY GILLOP < *Brandyg2311@aol.com*

Dear Roberta,
Hey, how are u? So I got my friend Chrissy who has a camera
to take the slides of my paintings, and here they are, sent to u
as an attachment. I think they came out alright but I am not
sure because I have never done slides of art before. Please just
remember Chrissy is not a "pro." (And neither am I.) I hope
they look the way u think they should. I know there's not a lot
here. But it's a good thing I am graduating from Lorton HS
this year because, guess what, they are completely getting rid
of art in the curriculum and replacing it with Business Skills
for the Workplace. Thank u soooo much for agreeing to take a
look at these.
xox
Brandy

TO: BRANDY GILLOP < Brandyg2311@aol.com
FROM: ROBERTA SOKOLOV < sokpuppet@earthlink.net

Dear Brandy,
It was so great to hear from you. Your slides came out really
well, I think. One of the paintings—the one of the old woman
in the rocking chair—feels a little generic, I'm afraid. If you
don't mind, I think I won't include that one when I send these
to someone. Now I just have to figure out WHO that someone
should be. The person I was going to send them to—the friend
of a friend, who runs a small museum in the city—is appar-
ently no longer reachable. (Long story...) So I will have to
rethink this whole plan. But I will ask around, and I am sure
that I will find someone within the next week or so. Please
remember, Brandy, that you are very young, and that while no
one is going to offer you a gallery show, someone might want to
offer you an internship. If that happens, I could maybe also ask
around about getting you a cheap apartment share in Brooklyn,
where all the kids like yourself live, and a job waiting tables, or
something. Stay tuned.

Meanwhile, all is well here; life is busy with husband
and kids and the chaos that is our daily life, but I will get back
to you as soon as I hear from the gallery person I end up send-
ing your slides to. Stay warm, say hi to your mom, stay away
from Tyler Parvell (ha ha, I know you will), and keep doing
your art.
xox
Roberta

When Nathaniel Greenacre called his wife from the television
station one afternoon and said he was coming home from work early
because he had something to tell her, she immediately thought all
the thoughts she had been primed over the years to imagine: He no
longer loved her. He was leaving. He was dying. Roberta saw him
dead, his long, gaunt body in a simple, unvarnished coffin. He would

probably want to be buried with puppets on his hands. "It's something good, babe," Nathaniel said, though he insisted on telling her in person. She could not remember him ever, over the course of their marriage, making such a dramatic gesture. There were no surprises with Nathaniel. Everything he did was usually understated, laconic.

By the time he made it back uptown on the subway and arrived at the apartment, she had to leave to pick up Harry and Grace at their schools, and so he accompanied her there, which he had never done before. "So tell me this thing already," she said as she walked with her husband in the chilly sunlight. "Don't drag it out. It's making me very nervous."

Nathaniel stopped on the street and turned her toward him, taking her wrists in his hands. "It's happened."

"What?"

"We were getting ready to do a remote, and then there was suddenly all this downtime because one of the anchors couldn't get back from the story about the fire on the ferry."

"What fire?"

"Breaking news. Forget it; no one hurt. So we were just sitting around on the soundstage, and I took out the puppets."

"Which puppets?"

"Nuzzle and Peeps, of course. I was entertaining the troops; doing a kind of slightly filthy version of my kids' act. And we're all there, the other cameramen, and they're kind of encouraging me, and I don't notice that someone else has come in."

"Oh God."

"Why do you say 'Oh God'? Who do you think I'm talking about?"

"I have no idea. It just sounds like a big moment."

"It was. It was Irwin Mester."

"The head of the network?"

"Right. He's standing there watching me do my act, and nobody tells me he's there, nobody stops me, and I'm really *on,* doing those voices. And the guys are all laughing a lot, and apparently Irwin Mester is laughing too. Then I saw that it was him. I'd never seen him before, but of course I recognized him from all the photos on the wall: Dear Leader. And he told me that my act was very funny, and he asked if I've ever done it professionally. *Professionally!* I had to restrain myself from saying, 'Oh, only every weekend for the last thirty years.' But he wanted to know if I was interested in talking to the people in children's programming. Apparently, they've been in fruitless discussions about trying to find something with 'crossover' appeal, and he thought maybe this was it. So he took me downstairs to the executives at children's. Irwin Mester took me himself! He went with me into their suite and interrupted a meeting. They were really startled. And he had me do Nuzzle and Peeps for them, right there. It was surreal. They were all sitting around drinking little bottles of water, and I'm standing there with my puppets, doing the voices. They started laughing. Oh, Roberta, we talked a lot, and they said I'm getting a show."

Nathaniel looked as if he were about to cry. She pulled him toward her and kissed him, and other people saw this moment and glanced over and smiled as they kept walking. It was a sudden instance of emotion just popping out of the day.

"This is incredible," Roberta said.

Nathaniel would come to describe himself as the person on the longest failure-to-success curve in the history of children's entertainment. He was fifty-two years old when he got his break. It was never supposed to go like this. Because he had not made it all those years ago, he was never meant to make it. He had been a failed person; they had each long ago stopped wondering and had each stopped striving. As soon as Nathaniel had taken the job as a cameraman, they had known that was the end of his puppetry dream. But now it wasn't.

"I have to call Wolf as soon as we get home," Nathaniel said as they approached Auburn Day. "He will be just fucking floored. I'm going to have to tell him he'd better smoke less weed and start practicing."

"What do you mean? He's going to do the show with you?"

"Of course. He's Peeps."

"I used to be Peeps," Roberta said with sudden intensity.

"But that was over a decade ago."

"Yes, I stopped when Harry was born."

"I know, but then when the kids got older you said you never wanted to do it again, you hated it, it wasn't who you were, and that was fine, babe. Wolf, he's my Peeps. He still doesn't mind all the crappy venues. Wait until he hears this; he's going to be making real money. And we are too. Lots of it, if it goes as planned. I can quit my day job. At least, I'll still be going to the network, but I'll be heading downstairs now. Goodbye, heavy camera that is ruining my back. They want to start putting this together fast. They're going to bring in some writers and a show runner; same guy who did *Ahoy, Mateys*. Boy, I guess I'll finally need an agent."

"I think I should do Peeps," Roberta persevered. "I was the *first* Peeps, Nathaniel, and we're married. Doesn't that give me an edge? Also," she added, somewhat pointlessly, "Wolf doesn't even have kids."

"That's not a prerequisite."

"He's a *pothead*," she tried.

"Look, I have to let him do it," said Nathaniel. "He's put in all this time."

He would not be moved. Wolf Purdy was a marginal person but he was Nathaniel's friend; he had been doing the voice of Peeps at libraries and in the auditoriums of YMCAs on weekends, intermittently, for a full decade. That had to be worth something. If a reward came to Nathaniel, then a reward would come to Wolf as well. Roberta, in wanting to be the voice of Peeps now that there would be some real gratification in it, knew that this was how the story went. She thought:

"Who will cut the wheat?" said the Little Red Hen.

"Not I," said the Duck.

"Not I," said the Cat.

"Not I," said the Dog.

"Not I," said Roberta Sokolov.

At home at night, Nathaniel, who almost never made phone

calls, monopolized the telephone, calling everyone he knew. The puppetry community was lit up with the fact that one of its own had gotten a sudden big break. No doubt there was bitterness emanating from some of the little apartments and houses where the other puppeteers lived, the spaces where men and women who forced the hollow skins of creatures onto their hands practiced all the time. "Fuck," a puppeteer could almost certainly be heard to say, after the usually melancholy and terse Nathaniel Greenacre telephoned to reveal his news.

"Fuck," Roberta said to herself as she listened to Nathaniel exclaim happily on the telephone in the distance while she helped their daughter, Grace, wash her hair in the clawfoot bath in the one small bathroom.

"What?" Grace said, whipping around, spattering water. "Mom, what did you say?"

"I said 'fug.' It's a word."

"I thought you were cursing. I thought you were cursing at Daddy."

"I wouldn't do that," said Roberta. She poured a plastic measuring cup full of warm water over Grace's head, where the hair came to wet points like multiple horns. Then suddenly, in her guilt, Roberta bent down and kissed that head, smelling it in all its neutrality and burgeoning essence of flower before the slow ruination began. All those art projects that Roberta had done with her children! All those many hours spent on craft, not art! She had enjoyed it; it had been *blissful,* it had been worth it, but now she bitterly felt yet again that she should have been out in the world doing art. The big male art stars of the late '80s and '90s hadn't spent their time cutting Clorox bottles into pigs with their children, or stringing uncooked macaroni onto thread. They'd had wives to do that, or nannies, or studio assistants.

Out in the living room now, she heard the sound of Harry playing a video game. *Pshoo, pshoo, pshoo,* went the sonic air rifles as they smashed apart the pulp of asteroids. Nearby, not minding the noise, Nathaniel kept talking to whomever he was talking to, explaining his new and unexpected great fortune, as if unable to quite believe it himself. He was immodest in his description of what had happened to him; he'd been waiting far too long.

Maybe there were no second acts in American lives, Roberta thought, but really, were there ever more than a few first acts at such a late age? The world did not look with excitement upon a fiftyish, easygoing, lined-faced, long-haired dad who had been plucked from obscurity based upon talent. Usually, the only time that someone old was allowed to make it big was when he won the lottery. Then, everyone loved the spectacle of the person who had never thought anything good would happen to him: the immigrant janitor beside his wife, tears streaming for the cameras as the couple hold up the six-foot-long check. Blind luck excited everyone. But the idea that you might still have a creative shot, even now, in your fifties, had no romantic tinge. Roberta, for one, looked upon her husband with a surprisingly cold assessment.

Of course, he wanted to have sex that night. He would probably be walking around with a continual boner for the next five years, she realized, or for as long as *Nuzzle and Peeps* was a hit. He would probably stay hard into syndication. "No," she said in bed after the children had been tucked into the bunk beds of their tiny room and the dishes had been washed in the sink and Roberta's hands still smelled of a detergent rendition of lemon-verbena. "I can't, Nathaniel. It's been a big day."

"I know. That's why, honey pie; I'm feeling good. We could have fun." He took her hand and placed it lightly on his penis the way a teenaged boy might do with a reluctant girl.

"Nathaniel, no," she said, and then, for effect, she left her hand there for one extra second, unmoving, unfriendly, as though to underscore her lack of interest and set into relief his inappropriate excitement. Immediately, she knew that she was being mean to him. He was just a pulsing, happy man, improbably patient and improbably rewarded at the end.

Where is *my* reward? Roberta thought churlishly, almost in tears. Where is it, when is it my turn?

"I'm sorry," she told Nathaniel, taking away her hand. "I know this is your big day. And I am really happy for you, and everything that's happening."

"It'll work out to be great for you too," he said. "If everything goes through, we'll be able to move out of here."

"What? We can't give up our apartment," she said. "It's *free*."

"But we can. We can just let it go. Tell your parents we've had a great run, but if it's okay with them, we're going to sell it and use the money toward an old house up in Harlem, where it's more real, and more lively. One of those historic brownstones you've always loved. And you'll be able to have a painting studio, not just a tiny dark corner. It'll all be good," he said.

"A painting studio? I am not an artist anymore, Nathaniel," she practically spat out.

"So you've been lying fallow. I was, too, and look what happened."

"No, *you* weren't lying fallow. You weren't successful, but you did the work. You supported us with your day job, and then you went out every weekend, stuffing those puppets on your hands and going to those libraries and schools and auditoriums. You just went and did it, but I didn't. I didn't go with you, and I didn't stay a painter, either. I didn't keep developing the way I was supposed to. I mean, I had talent, but I couldn't stay on track. I was going to do that Old Children series, remember? With Anne Frank and everyone else who died young? I don't know, maybe it was because my parents gave us the apartment."

"What do you mean?"

"We had to take it, and it let us have a life here. But maybe it spoiled me, and look, we've been living in this neighborhood where we don't belong. Everything's so expensive, and everything's a little dull and basically predictable." She paused and realized she was breathless. "I didn't go into art thinking it was a life-or-death matter. It wasn't like I had to paint my way out of a little town in South Dakota."

"Well, art isn't always about survival," said Nathaniel.

"I wouldn't know. I don't hang around with artists anymore. I love my friends, but we've been sitting in that coffee shop for so long." She paused. "We're like the Hopper painting *Nighthawks*. Except we should be called *Dayhawks*."

"You're so hard on yourself," he said, touching the edges of her hair.

Roberta felt herself soften at his desire to make her happy now, in the first light of his own happiness, which was perhaps the first unclouded happiness of his previously disappointing adult life. "I don't think living somewhere more interesting and diverse will inspire me," she whispered.

"But we'll have to see now," he said.

She did like the idea of getting away from the soporific routine she'd fallen into. They would leave here. She would burn for a long while at the insult of her husband's shocking ascent, but she would hide her jealousy from him and from everyone she could, for it made her seem like a bad person, and she wasn't bad. You weren't supposed to feel this way. You weren't supposed to feel it toward your own husband. He was supposed to be inextricable from you, and the two of you were meant to make your way through the world as a two-backed beast. She thought of Karen Yip, who out of all of them was particularly ardent and protective toward her husband. Karen had been repelled back when she'd heard about Penny Ramsey's affair. Women like Penny Ramsey, married to hustling, coarse men, were the ones who were meant to feel resentment toward their husbands, not women like Roberta, whose own husband was authentic, original, true.

Nathaniel should have let her become Peeps again for television; he should have given her that, but, primly, he would not. He would withhold it from her. He wouldn't be the one to inflect her day with meaning. Instead, he would give her a beautiful house in Harlem with a studio filled with light and the possibility of new, more interesting friends.

Immediately upon thinking about friends, Roberta felt guilty, and she e-mailed Amy and Karen right away and made plans to have breakfast tomorrow morning at the Golden Horn. She'd tell them Nathaniel's news there, and they'd be surprised and happy and even a little tearful. Shelly Harbison, if she happened to be in the booth, would probably scream. A year from now, Nathaniel would have risen to the top of children's programming with *Nuzzle and Peeps* and the dopey stoned Wolf, and Roberta would observe his success from her artist's studio in her house in Harlem, where she would stand at an easel, a paintbrush held inches above the surface of the canvas, still not yet ready to touch down.

> TO: ROBERTA SOKOLOV < *sokpuppet@earthlink.net*
> FROM: BRANDY GILLOP < *Brandyg2311@aol.com*
>
> *Hi Roberta,*
> *Just checking in! I know it's only been a couple of weeks since we wrote to each other, but u said u'd let me know who u decided to send the slides to. So I don't mean to be a bother, but if its alright it would be great if u could let me know. I've been working on a new series of paintings called "Behind the Train Tracks." Tyler Parvell got kicked out of school permanently for selling meth, by the way. I will definitely not miss him. But I do miss u.*
> *xoxxo*
> *Brandy*

On a night in late January, all the parents of the fourth-graders at Auburn Day came to school for second-semester Open House, one of the two evenings in the whole year when every parent, father and mother both, put in an appearance. They walked up and down the halls on their best behavior. Emptied of the boys, the school looked beautiful at night; the floors of the halls gleamed and the walls were thick with drawings and posters whose overarching theme was, according to an enormous piece of hand-lettered oaktag, Prehistoric Man. As the parents wandered along the hall, they each looked for their own son's particular contribution, following the chronological story of dumbstruck mankind trying to find its footing in the bleak and milky darkness of the nascent world.

All the mothers and fathers studied their sons' drawings and writings with a kind of depraved love and pride. Each illustration of cave people and each line of prose was exclaimed over, low in the throat. In the classroom a few moments later, the young male teacher made a few remarks about the curriculum, and as everyone got up to go meet the next teacher, there was a commotion from the side of the room, and Roberta turned to see the anorexic mother Geralynn Freund slumped down in her chair looking white, ghastly.

"Lie back," said an orthopedic-surgeon father.

"I'm so sorry," Geralynn Freund said. "I got dizzy. I think I got up too fast."

"When was the last time you ate?"

"Lunch, I guess."

"And what did you have?"

"I don't remember."

"Lie back," he repeated, and this time she obeyed. The other parents milled around uncertainly, but Geralynn said that she was completely fine, that they were making too much of a fuss, and that everyone should go. The father and a couple of other parents stayed, but all the others shuffled out of the room, talking in quiet, worried voices about her. Was there a friend they could contact? Her doctor? No, she'd said, she was fine, really, and soon she stood up and smoothed down the front of her pants legs and smiled a little, and left the room with the others.

The evening chugged on. The parents went to meet the math teacher, and the Latin teacher, and the science teacher, and then, briefly, the art teacher. Roberta watched, a little amused, as one of the most extreme businessman fathers squirmed in captivity while listening to the earnest art teacher say "pastel" and "homemade tempera paint" and the line ". . . and finally we'll be making our own Calder's circus." The father desperately began to finger the cold and silent PDA clipped to his belt, as if willing it to come to life.

In the hallway between classes, Penny and Greg Ramsey materialized. They looked the way they always did on the rare occasions when Roberta had seen them together. Standing here in a couple, they gave off neither friction nor distance. From farther down the hallway, Roberta saw that Amy saw them too; Roberta watched Amy glance over at them, then say something quietly to Leo. But if Penny Ramsey was aware that all these other wives and even their husbands knew the story of her love affair and its awful conclusion, it didn't come across. "Hi," Penny said to Roberta. "Good to see you."

Greg Ramsey gave a small smile. "Hey, how's it going?" he said. His collar was stiff, his silvery tie straight. He held his head rigidly as he and Penny walked to the science room. Probably he had never learned about his wife's lover; they were still married, after all. Or else maybe he knew everything, and they had struck a deal. But he certainly had no idea that all these women milling in his midst knew *everything*. Penny, beside him, didn't speak. The Ramseys were almost shocking in their lockstep serenity.

So many people seemed to have what they wanted, Roberta thought. So many people quietly took what they needed. I should be Peeps, she was reminded with renewed, angry despair. I shouldn't be punished. I should at least get to be Peeps, to be part of a hit show, to get to go to a really great job every day and feel the feeling that work can bring you. I could even be one of the lesser puppet characters: Crinkle, or Thistle. Nathaniel shouldn't keep me out like this. But it was his moment, it was his show, and he had politely told her as much. He wanted to do this without her. They were a team in their marriage, but nowhere else. Roberta watched as the Ramseys walked into a classroom at the end of the hall: Greg held the door open for his wife, his hand on the small of her back as she went inside, her face lifting as she prepared to greet the next teacher.

When the school presentations were over, the Sokolov-Greenacres, the Lamb-Buckners, and the Yips had dinner at Shin-ba, a Japanese restaurant around the corner from the school, where they sat at a round table in the front window. A candle burned in its globe in the center of the table, and everyone was slightly distracted by the clock and by the babysitters, who surely had their own eyes on the clocks at home. After all, this was a school night, a work night. The women turned away from the table briefly to call home on their cell phones. Their parallel, echoing conversations flared up: "Hi honey…" "No, I said nine-thirty, then no more video games." "All right, you can eat one, but no more than that.…Yes, put her on.…*Hello*, Sharmila!"

"So how was your winter break?" Wilson Yip asked everyone. "You guys go anywhere good?"

"That feels so long ago already. But nah, we don't do that kind of thing," Nathaniel said. "Not our style. We're shut-ins."

"But you won't be that way for long, I bet," said Karen leadingly, and then Nathaniel appeared unabashed as he spoke about his recent good news and about the development of his upcoming television show. Roberta watched as he revealed himself proudly, in person. Perhaps none of the others could imagine ever wanting to be a puppeteer, of all things, but they could definitely understand what it meant to desire success, and to be successful.

Everyone raised glasses of Suntory beer in celebration of *Nuzzle and Peeps*, which was "in heavy negotiations," as Nathaniel told them, his mouth shaping the words almost lustily. He was someone who had never before been "in negotiations" at all. He drank his beer and made a few slightly disingenuous remarks about how no one ever knew whether or not a show would make it past its pilot or whether it would be a hit even if it did. Then he participated in the conversation that Leo initiated, about intellectual property rights as pertaining to puppet characters and whether Nathaniel was adequately represented legally.

"You should call Ned Bertucci at Selker Dean," Leo said. "They do entertainment law exclusively. I could give you his e-mail."

If Nathaniel hadn't had his success, Roberta knew, then he would be sitting at the table in unconnected and beery silence. But now her husband had somehow gotten himself deep inside the private club of professional success; he had said the password, and the thick door had swung open, welcoming him in, and he was in a cool oaken room, sitting stunned but confident in a club chair.

They all talked about a few things that had happened in the news that week. They talked about "the way things were going" in the U.S., and here the conversation became despairing and melancholy. It was like secretly hearing the men sing the folk song "Donna Donna" that night in the woods, their voices reverent as they grieved for the death of the poor calf with the mournful eye.

"I often feel, lately, that we've lost control of everything in this country," Nathaniel said.

"I know, it's true," Amy agreed. "It's hard to think that, because then you have to face up to everything that's happened. Everything that's been done to this place."

"I was so patriotic when I was growing up," said Leo. "Whenever we would sing the national anthem, I would get sentimental. Now I feel so cynical about it."

"But if you face up to what's been done," said Wilson, "then it's like waking up from a bad dream—"

"—and the dream's still going on," Roberta said. "That's what you meant, right?"

"Right," said Wilson.

"Oh well, better have another Suntory, then," said Nathaniel. "Nothing else to do about it except get shit-faced. Oh, miss!" he pretended to call to the waitress.

There was mild laughter, then some attention was paid to the actual need for refills. Briefly, the men talked to the men, and the women talked to the women. This happened sometimes in the middle of a group meal; the table would suddenly self-select by sex. The men were talking about finances now, while the women dipped down briefly into various subjects: how Dustin Kavanaugh had apparently come out of the closet to his parents this week, announcing that although he was only twelve, he already knew he was gay, and how his mother, Helen, the powerful and selfless charity figure, had embraced him and said if he ever wanted her to spearhead a gay charity, she would, but that meanwhile she and his dad would just love and support him; how Hand-in-Hand Day had indeed been ripped from the school calendar, perhaps forever; how Jake Giffen had needed to use his

EpiPen on a field trip to a botanical garden, because his seatmate had eaten a bag of kettle chips cooked in peanut oil; how vermin of some sort—giant hard-shell cockroaches, one version of the story went; weevils, went another—had been discovered among the tubs of mango-chutney chicken salad and quinoa at night at Camarata & Bello, and the store had been shuttered by the Board of Health, much to the unhappiness and secret thrill of its customers, who loved and craved the food but had always felt like hostages to the fuck-you prices; how the mother of Jackson Pershing, whose bond-trader father had been killed in the World Trade Center, would be getting married in a few months to her son's former science teacher, Mr. Bregman, and how the boy's entire class was invited to serve as ushers at the wedding.

Wilson Yip heard the edge of the conversation about Jackson Pershing and was drawn back in. The other men came too; dinner conversations had invisible strands, which you held on to and followed. "That's great about Laura Pershing getting married again," Wilson said. "I knew her husband. He was a nice guy."

Roberta thought about how, back in the first few days after the attacks on the towers, all the restaurants in the city had been packed. No one wanted to stay at home by themselves; she and her friends and their husbands and kids had met up at restaurants for dinner. The kids ate chicken fingers and drank milk from cups with lids and accordion straws, while the parents mostly drank strong drinks and talked and talked. They were pressed together at their tables, all the TVs overhead with their traumatic visuals, everyone joined together in the face of something new and strange. We're all falling, Roberta had thought, and we're all afraid.

The people with jobs, she'd thought, had the relief of the office to go to after 9/11—the comfort of routine, and order, and the thrust of work: its depth, its concentration. Without those elements, you might feel lost and much more frightened. Though, of course, in a work environment you could get trapped in a stairwell; you could die there among the people you worked with instead of at home among the people you loved. Roberta's daughter, Grace, only one year old on that day, had been too little to understand what was happening, but her son, at three, had been frightened, or at least had absorbed his mother's fear and reflected it. At home that afternoon, for lack of a better idea, Roberta had gathered whatever she could find among the tubs of beads and pipe cleaners, and had sat down with Harry at the table and begun work on a gigantic crafts project. "Let's come up with the best project we can think of," she'd said. "Something really incredible."

So they'd decided to create an entire amusement park that after much thought Harry christened Fun Place, and for long periods of time they'd lost themselves in Fun Place, which in Roberta's imagination existed as the opposite of the smoking charnel house that was now downtown Manhattan. It had carried them through the days and weeks that followed, until Fun Place possessed a Ferris wheel and a carousel and a cotton-candy stand with actual cones of fluff held in the hands of Lego figures. One day they got tired of it, or no longer needed it, and so they stopped work on it. Fun Place, put aside, began a typical trajectory of decomposition, and then it was gone for good. But craft had gotten them through those first uncertain weeks.

In the restaurant now, the platters of sushi arrived, and everyone quietly admired the theatrical presentation of one another's food. "So," Amy said, "you saw the Ramseys tonight?"

"Yes. Gliding by. They look very much together," said Karen.

"The happy couple," said Roberta.

"Wait, what's this?" Nathaniel asked his wife.

"I'll tell you later."

"I think," said Amy, "that everyone's marriage is strange and private and some kind of secret bargain. And really, in the end, unknowable."

"That sounds profound," said Nathaniel.

"But I'm serious," Amy went on. "All marriages are like that."

"Not ours," Wilson Yip said. "Nothing dark or unknown there."

"I can confirm that," said Karen, and she took his hand.

Roberta, looking up at that moment, saw a figure pause outside the front window, where snow was starting to float down lightly in swaying strokes. It was Geralynn Freund in her big black shearling coat. She peered inside the restaurant like someone who longs to be sitting at a table with friends in candlelight. Suddenly she noticed Roberta, and it was like making eye contact with a feral animal; anxiety raced in both directions. Roberta waved her chopsticks, but Geralynn only smiled briefly, then turned away.

"Wait, that's that mother from tonight," said Leo. "The one who got dizzy."

"Right," said Amy. "Geralynn Freund. *You* know about her. I've told you."

"No you haven't."

"Yes, I really have, Leo. More than once." Amy sounded so irritated at him, almost angry, and everyone at the table noticed.

"Sorry. I don't remember."

"Of course you don't."

Leo abruptly stood up. "We should ask her to join us," he said.

Without seeking anyone's opinion he pulled open the front door, letting the night wind into the small, dark restaurant and making all the candles gutter in synchrony, as if they were on a birthday cake, being blown on unsuccessfully. Everyone at the table watched the surprising pantomime of big Leo and little Geralynn out on the snowy street; Amy looked at her husband as he pointed and gestured, but Geralynn shook her head with regret. Still he would not relent, and finally they all watched as she shrugged, and then he opened the door to bring her inside.

Someone carried over a chair, and Geralynn sat shyly among the couples. All she ordered was miso soup, and she barely put the small lacquered bowl to her mouth; it was as though she had ordered it simply to warm her hands. They talked about school, and the boys, and a movie that had just gotten good reviews, though the people at the table who had seen it insisted on not spoiling the plot twist for the ones who hadn't. Then, at one point, Roberta politely said to Geralynn, "So, what've you been up to?"

Geralynn put down her bowl and looked a little hesitant. "Actually," she said, "I've been really busy lately."

"With what?" asked Amy.

"Well, I know I used to see some of you at the gym," said Geralynn. The women tried to look innocent, as though they weren't sure they could remember ever having seen her there. "But I stopped going because of my situation," she added. Again, everyone tried to appear neutral, polite. "And then it occurred to me," Geralynn went on, "that, you know, there ought to be a special gym where people with eating differences could work out and not feel self-conscious or as if they had to explain their choices to everybody all the time." She shrugged. "So I started one. I've rented a space in SoHo, and I have investors and a client list, and we're opening in three months. When I started looking into it, I found out that there's a big, unexploited consumer base of women with eating differences. We're calling the place SlimGym." She laughed tightly. "I only hope we don't get sued by the beef-jerky people."

The women were shocked, impressed, a little bewildered; they congratulated Geralynn and told her that this was wonderful news. She gave them more details: Len Goodling, the full-time dad, was one of her principal investors. They had made the deal one afternoon during pick-up at the school, waiting for the boys to appear. They'd gotten to talking that day, and Len, who had apparently made a killing years earlier in cord-blood storage technologies, prompting him to retire at thirty-seven, was looking to invest in something new and also be a bit hands-on.

Later, after dinner was over, as Roberta and Nathaniel climbed the four flights of stairs to their apartment, Roberta was bothered by how casually Geralynn had used the strange phrase "eating differences." Uneasily, she knew that Geralynn was one of those people who didn't really want to be cured, that she seemed to be one of the women who probably logged on to pro-anorexia websites and posted self-righteous messages. Maybe this was actually going to be a so-called pro-ana gym, with members who all longed for their bodies eventually to resemble nothing so much as long twigs of dried beef jerky. Whatever the case, Geralynn seemed in charge, and, oddly, she did not seem lost.

As Roberta continued up the stairs to her apartment, she and Nathaniel passed a boxed set of cassette tapes called *Learn Italian the Maria Tornello Way* and a jigsaw puzzle of Big Ben, no doubt missing crucial pieces—a chunk of the London sky, perhaps, as if the atmosphere were a skin that could be punctured. To be anorexic, like Geralynn Freund, she thought, amounted to wanting to shed yourself of some of the imperfect mosaic of pieces that made you who you were. She could understand this now, for maybe underneath that desquamated self you would locate a new version. Roberta had been sitting around with her friends talking about their lives, and sitting with her children for so long now too, and yes, it had been wonderful, yes it had been essential, but now she wanted some of that time back. She wanted to have a roomful of paintings to show for it, even slightly immature and awkward ones like Brandy Gillop had. She wanted the feeling of propulsion that Brandy possessed.

She was ashamed of what she had done, or not done, really, to Brandy. The girl e-mailed her from Lorton, South Dakota, a couple of times a week, "just checking in," she said, or "wondering how things are going." Roberta was initially supposed to have passed along her slides to Penny Ramsey, although because Penny Ramsey was no longer Amy's friend, it wasn't doable. Then Roberta was supposed to have asked around and gotten someone *else* to send Brandy's slides to, except this was around the time that Nathaniel got his big break. Roberta had become distracted by Nathaniel and then resentful, and she had stopped dwelling on helping Brandy Gillop. She thought less frequently about helping her, and when she did think about her, it was with mild and unwarranted annoyance. So she had still done nothing with the girl's slides. They remained in a desktop folder on her computer. To her own mortification, she had done nothing at all for Brandy Gillop after promising her the moon, and she still couldn't bring herself to write to her now, even to say, "I fucked up," or "I was negligent," or "I was jealous because everybody except me seems to get up and do their art and find success, regardless of their circumstances," or, simply, "I have no excuses. I'll get moving on this right away."

Many people were out there planning and plotting their own futures. Even Geralynn Freund apparently had big—if disturbing—plans. Nathaniel and his agent were on the phone all the time; Nathaniel walked around the apartment with the cordless phone earpiece attached to his head like a businessman, taking notes while he asked questions like, "So what's their counteroffer? Is there any way we could get a little more at the back end?" Roberta's resigned husband was now alert and verbose and ambitious. He pushed ahead, demonstrating the notion that work could pave your entire life with meaning. Roberta thought of Nuzzle and Peeps, and she longed to pull them off her husband's hands, and off Wolf Purdy's hands too. While the men just stood in incomprehension she would cut the puppets up with a pair of shears, even though those puppets were probably soon going to make it possible for her and her family to live in a great house uptown. If she still didn't become an artist after they moved there, it would be nobody's fault but her own.

Every few days over the next six weeks Brandy Gillop, thinking of the future, e-mailed Roberta, asking her whether the slides had been sent out to anyone yet and then whether for some reason Roberta was angry with her. And then, finally, whether Roberta was in fact still alive. For why would this woman from New York City have shown such a great interest in helping her, only to suddenly become indifferent and disappear? *Hello?* Brandy would write into the ether. *Hello? Hello? Is this still your correct address? Are u there, Roberta? Hello?*

Chapter

FIFTEEN

Lorton, South Dakota, 2007

B ECAUSE THERE was no day or night inside the casino, Jo Gillop
did not know when to get tired. And because she didn't, she
found herself surprisingly alert and in good spirits most of the time.
Lots of girls disliked the casino, and in the break room they said that
they would rather be anywhere but here. One girl insisted she would
rather stand in the boiling sun and pump gas than stand in the cool
of this room and hand out rolls of chips, but that was crazy thinking. It was true that the men in their string ties and the old ladies
with the buckets of coins that they carried the way fishermen carried chum could be awfully depressing. But the casino was always
awake, cranking along with the sound of good cheer, and when you
were here, it was easy to forget about everything else in your life.

So now, on her shift, sitting on her stool behind the window,
Jo Gillop forgot about her ex-husband, who paid no child support

and never would; Jo had raised Brandy single-handedly for the past ten years. "Like a one-armed bandit," she had told her friend Ricki, who sat at the next window. Jo forgot about the fact that she had car payments to make and that her mother was deteriorating daily from Alzheimer's and was going to have to be put into a facility out in Vermillion, and who was going to come up with the money to pay for that? Jo also forgot about the way that Brandy had been cut loose by that woman from New York who had promised to help. She forgot all of this, and she forgot about the fact that the world was getting more and more expensive, not to mention violent. At night, when she came to work at the Kubla Khan Casino, she walked in through the employees' entrance and put on her red blouse and name tag and sat behind her window with a feeling of relief and anticipation.

The other girls were so nice. Everyone talked about their love lives: The younger ones told stories from the world of online dating and sex and no-good men, while the older ones, like Jo and Ricki, dispensed practical advice. Jo was done with men. She would have nothing to do with them ever again; it was too bad she wasn't a lez, she said, making the others laugh, scandalized, because that would have been just fine with her. Even the men who flirted with Jo here in the casino were of no interest to her; she was forty years old, and she didn't need that anymore. Everything she wanted in life she could get right here; the Kubla Khan was like an entire society. And Brandy was working here at the window on her other side, part-time.

Brandy had no interest in this place; it wasn't where she wanted to be, and surely it wasn't where she would be for very long. She hated the casino, and always said, "Mom, how can you stand it here? Look at these people. It's like a walking graveyard. Why don't they just kill themselves now and get it over with?" Jo sometimes had to tell her daughter not to feel superior, but it was the role of young people to be superior. The two Gillops sat side by side on their stools making change, which was so easy because of the new cash registers that were like computers and almost let you sleep as you worked, if that was what you wanted.

But Jo Gillop didn't want to be asleep. Her life had been a story of fuckups: She'd gotten pregnant out of high school and married the "father," the smiling dummy Roy Gillop, who of course had had no fatherly bone in his body, and things had gotten worse from there. So when Brandy got pregnant by that slick and stupid boy Tyler Parvell, Jo had cried and then begged her to go to Sioux Falls to have a procedure, even though Jo was personally sickened at the idea of it. Jo Gillop had had a tough life, and it was still not so hot, but coming to the casino every day was far and away the best part. In this bright and restless world, you were never bored; the men admired you, and the other girls were your companions, and you could always hear the cheerful music, the rough sorting of chips, and, every once in a while, the sudden excitement of coins falling against coins when someone in the distance hit the jackpot.

Chapter

SIXTEEN

T HE MOVING VAN was parked on the street in front of The Rivermere at a quarter to eight one morning in early February, with
various men in matching red T-shirts swarming it; briefly, there was
no way to tell whether the furniture was going to go in or out, and
then it became clear. Nearby in the driveway stood a young mother
in her thirties in a down vest with a couple of small kids nearby, trying to direct the traffic of their belongings. "Moving out?" Amy asked
automatically. The woman nodded. This was the widow in 14H, an
ordinary, pale ash blonde with the beginnings of dark roots. What
had Amy imagined: that the woman would be dressed in black all
these months later, that she'd be wearing a mantilla, that she would
wear her grief so openly that anyone could recognize it right away?

The other mothers in the building had been right; she hadn't
been able to stay here all that long and would probably now have to
go somewhere smaller, less expensive, maybe a suburb or town, even
briefly staying with a sister or parent. The widow in 14H stood in front
of the building on moving day in the way that a husband usually would,

trying to deal with the very busy, indifferent movers who spoke only Hebrew. "That box is upside down," she told them, but no one seemed to hear her. "Joshua," she called to a child. "Come away from there. You'll see all your stuff when we get there."

"Good luck," Amy told her. "Wherever you go." The woman smiled distractedly, nodded, then turned back to the deep opening of the enormous truck.

"That's the one whose husband died, isn't it?" asked Mason as he and Amy turned the corner onto the street.

"I think so."

The building, she had heard one of the other mothers say in the elevator last week, now had its own defibrillator, which of course would make the rent go up even more, the mother had added.

"Maybe she's getting remarried," said Mason. "Like Jackson Pershing's mother."

"I doubt it, honey. It's kind of soon."

"You would never get remarried, right?" he asked. For him there was only Amy and Leo, forever and ever, bound into marriage and family and immortality. Then, when she said nothing, he said, a little less surely, and almost to himself, "I know you wouldn't."

A month had gone by since Amy had found Leo's faked receipts, and still she had not told him she'd seen them. One day, a few weeks earlier, he had taken them from his desk. She'd let the silences between them lengthen more than usual, but it was unclear to her if he even knew this. Amy hadn't been able to stand Greg Ramsey for his insistence upon grabbing everything in sight, when really, as Karen had implied once, men like Greg were just doing what they were meant to do. But Leo had never seemed to have that kind of arrogance; he was decent, a worker bee, devoted to his family, and yet in an accidental moment in the study she had seen evidence of another part of him that she'd somehow never noticed before.

Tonight, though, there would be oppressive, enforced togetherness for Amy and Leo at the Kenley Shuber dinner-dance at the Waldorf-Astoria. Once upon a time, when she and Leo were both lawyers at the firm, this had been an annual event she actually looked forward to, if only because they got to put on evening clothes and drink a better quality of wine than they were used to. Then, when they went home at the end of the evening, she and Leo would undress and lie in bed, deconstructing what the other lawyers had said and how everyone had looked. They would make fun of a few of the overtly sucking-up associates, and Amy would be critical of a couple of the wives who had seemed, from the vantage point of one's late twenties, nice but dull.

Amy remembered finding herself in a brief conversation during the cocktail hour one year with Rita Pfarrer, the wife of one of the partners, and she recalled how Rita had talked at brutal length about a golf vacation she and her husband had taken to a castle in Ireland. Amy had looked past this wife to the other lawyers who stood tantalizingly in the distance. As soon as she could escape her she did, and she knocked back ice-cold Cosmopolitans in big martini glasses with her friend Lisa Silvestri, then stood with Lisa and Leo and the other associates she liked.

Rita Pfarrer was dead of colon cancer now, and Stewart Pfarrer had retired. The old guard was mostly gone, and the newer guard, which included senior salaried associates like Leo and his friend Corinna and some others, had begun its ascendancy. Lisa Silvestri had hung on, and unlike Leo had been made partner. She'd never married or had children; she'd made a series of choices, or work had claimed all her time, for at age forty she seemed on her own, occasionally calling Amy at the height of a weeknight, a school night, wanting to chat.

She was the first person Amy saw tonight when she and Leo entered the banquet room. There was Lisa, a tall, big-breasted, formidable woman in a black cocktail dress, standing with a few other partners and their spouses. Leo steered Amy over, and soon she was in the circle too, where she didn't really want to be. Now the men and a few of the women leaned in to one another and talked shop. The dance floor was dark and polished, and the band played the same echoey, listless songs she had danced to in college, while the lawyers and their spouses located their name cards and sat down. The large round tables created a wedding atmosphere, and Amy found herself between two lawyers she had seen at Kenley Shuber functions before but had never spoken to. One, Ron Devenish, was in his forties, thickset, bald, and distracted, and the other, Mark Canterburg, was young and courtly, or at least he behaved that way during the appetizer course, a small tureen of butternut squash soup.

From all around the room came the gabble of conversation, the clanking of spoons against china, the tentative sucking-in of too-hot soup. Amy noticed a young woman sitting a few seats over—the wife of one of the youngest associates, who had a baby at home—and she looked neither overly unhappy nor uncomfortable to be here. This evening was for her husband, she was probably thinking. Oh yes, it was extraordinarily boring, perhaps one of the most boring ways possible for humans to spend an evening, but it wasn't meant for *her,* it was meant for him. The young wife had nothing to prove, and so she took a long hit of her drink, pressed a waled curl of iced butter into her sourdough roll with a blunt knife, and then sat back calmly to drink and eat and look around the room. Far across the table Leo sat between one of the most senior partners, a man with wild, untended eyebrows, and his friend and colleague Corinna Berry, young, black, pretty, her body like a blade inside a night-blue sheath. Leo's head was moving back and forth, as though each of the lawyers satisfied a different need in him. He turned to the old partner and appeared boyish and sonlike, and then he turned to Corinna Berry and just appeared happy. Even through the blockade of the floral centerpiece, with all its shoots and tendrils and oversized blooms, Amy could recognize her husband's momentary pleasure.

But over here, on the other side of the flowers, Amy sat between two lawyers in a kind of funk. Devenish took it upon himself to speak to her first. After it was established that she was married to Leo, there was a brief, dull volley with a dead ball about the status of recent litigation, and how the Pittsburgh case—"the salmonella defense"—was going. Then, when it was revealed that Amy too used to work at Kenley Shuber, the lawyer regarded her with sudden mild interest.

"So where do you work now?" Devenish asked.

"Nowhere," she said.

"Ah," he said. His eyes dashed past her, then quickly dashed back, as if realizing he had been reflexively rude and trying to cover it. But she'd seen the eye dash, just as she had seen it many times before in the city. If you had a career here, then you were given a chance to stump for yourself. People were relieved when you were able to say that you did something. Without the cloak of a profession, there was no way to judge you and come to some hasty decision. If you said you did nothing, though, the person's eyes might dash past you, over to someone who did something and who could be assessed and talked to with ease. Here and in L.A. and perhaps in London and wherever else there were important jobs and the feeling of a stirring economy, utility often beat quietly inside friendship, and you quickly assessed the way that the other person might be helpful to you, even at a distant point in the future.

Now, at dinner, Canterburg hadn't heard Devenish's question, and a moment later, after Devenish returned to the robotic eating of his dinner, Canterburg tried his own version. "So what do *you* do, Amy?" he asked heartily, as though it was an original question.

"I eat bonbons all day," she said.

Canterburg looked at her for a long moment. "Oh my God," he said. "I would do that in a minute."

"You would?" She was confused by what he'd said; no one had ever expressed such a desire to her.

"Oh yes," he said. "I am so burned out, you have no idea."

"I was kidding."

"I know," he said. "But I wasn't." He smiled, and she, surprised, smiled too, and they started to settle into talking, but all of a sudden Amy looked up and saw that Corinna Berry had grabbed Leo's hand and was taking him onto the dance floor. He seemed incapable of refusing her this, and he looked helplessly at Amy and shrugged.

She dispassionately watched Leo dance with this slender young woman; he was an inadequate dancer, and Amy had learned this on one of their earliest dates. His skill had never improved, and so dancing was not a part of their life together. It wouldn't have occurred to her to try to get him to dance with her tonight; she didn't want to stand close to him or talk much to him. But she saw that he didn't look unhappy at all as he moved around on the floor like a bear with a young woman trapped in his paws. He looked awkward but content, he and Corinna leaning into each other, laughing and whispering. Lisa Silvestri was watching them too, and Amy knew her old friend must feel sorry for her.

By the time the plates of prime rib had been cleared away, Canterburg and Devenish had moved their chairs slightly back from the table and were talking only to each other behind her head. A woman from an adjacent table joined them. Amy listened a little, understanding virtually all of what they said, but realizing that, though sometimes the conversation seemed to gather itself up and become lively, there were many tired, end-of-workday, generic moments. The three corporate lawyers sitting together seemed intermittently engaged and bored by their own talk. Mostly they didn't speak about the subtleties of the law, the beauty and specificity of legal language, the intricacy of a case that kept them up at night. They talked about the upcoming weekend retreat and about billing clients. The woman said she had become a billing *machine,* and that soon she was going to start billing her children for the time she spent playing Clue and Boggle with them.

Amy remembered going for the job interview at which she was asked about that legal software, Juxtapose BriefScan, and how hopeless she'd felt when it became clear that she knew nothing about it. She'd long lost her old debater's bravado, too. Instead, like so many people she knew, she'd sought satisfaction around the edges, and time had slid past, and until recently she rarely had been idle and often in fact had been very busy. That life could be so *boring,* of course, she thought, not unlike the way a job could easily be boring. It seemed to her now, looking around this huge ballroom of corporate lawyers and their spouses, that work did not make you interesting; interesting work made you interesting. She realized only that she came down on the side of purpose.

That night in bed, stripped of their dress-up clothes, Amy and Leo lay on their backs in their pajamas, side by side. He belched slightly and touched his stomach. "That prime rib is just sitting there," he said. "And I feel like I drank too much."

"You could have told them not to refill your glass," she said with mild disgust.

Leo was already turning away on his side. He might have been Devenish, she thought. Leo was indifferent to her too, by virtue of having a fixed place in the world, a good answer to the question of what he "did." But he wasn't superior. She might be limited, but he, in his small and maddening and ordinary way, was immoral. It was unplanned, but Amy put a finger on his shoulder and said, "I have to ask you something."

Leo turned around in bed. She waited a second and then she just said it. "What was the story with those receipts?"

"What?" asked Leo.

"The receipts in the desk last month. The ones from St. Doe's— the paperweight I bought my mother, which you called a 'client gift,' and I think the bar bill from the island, and a receipt from that Tuscan place we went to."

"Amy," he said, "you haven't worked in a really long time, so you don't know."

"Tell me, then."

"It's not a big deal. And that client gift—it was a couple of hundred dollars."

"Yes. '*Two hundred tirty-tree* dollars.'"

"What?"

"Among everyone we know," she said, "you were the moral one. At the Japanese restaurant on curriculum night, *you're* the one who invites Geralynn Freund to join us. You just do these things. It's you. But then you go and do *this,* and what am I supposed to think?"

"Everyone does what they need to," said Leo. "I'm like the last one to know this. Otherwise, it's just too hard to get by. We are so deeply in debt, and you want so many things."

"*I* want?"

"Yes! You want! A weekend spa trip with Jill. Sending Mason to private school. And, of course, that ridiculous trip to St. Doe's, where you spent thousands of dollars of our money. Including that paperweight."

"You said the trip was fine. And we used mileage and credit card points," said Amy.

"Mileage, yes. Credit card points, no. What did you think, this elite place that nobody's supposed to know about takes credit card points?"

"So why did you say we could go?"

"Because I knew you really wanted to. And basically you take care of everything outside work, and I felt bad, and wanted to give you this. You wanted me to say yes; you left it wide open so I could say yes. But I am just working so much, and it's never enough."

"Someone could find out about the receipts, couldn't they?" she asked.

Leo shrugged. "It's possible, not likely. But yes, it's happened at other firms."

"So those receipts are just floating around in somebody's file somewhere? Was it the first time?" Leo didn't say anything, and Amy said, "What is wrong with you?"

"What is wrong with *you*?" he said. "You want to be in this marriage, but you also want to be this child. Not knowing things, except every once in a while when you absolutely have to." He looked away from her, then looked back sharply. "We could not afford that trip," said Leo. "We really cannot afford our life. Those receipts do nothing, do you get it? They are my pathetic way of trying to be resourceful, when in fact there *is* no way." Then Leo's mouth rearranged itself into a grim little line. "I can barely support you and Mason," he said. "I can barely do what I'm supposed to do."

Amy's heart was fast now. "We can put Mason in public school," she said. "It wouldn't be the worst thing. And it would help a lot, right?"

Leo didn't say anything; he just kept looking at her. "All right, then. I'll go back to work," Amy finally said. "Not just a volunteer job, like I was thinking about. A law job. I'll do T&E somewhere, if I can."

Leo nodded, as if he knew she would say this. "It's not so bad," he said gently. "You've wanted to work. You've been ambivalent about still staying home. You always talk about it, and then you don't do it, and I figured that one day you really would."

"Yes," she said, her voice starting to waver, "but I didn't want it to be like this. Under duress. I don't know how to get back into things. I don't even know how to use Juxtapose BriefScan!"

Leo appeared confused. "Why would you? It was discontinued two years ago. We use Comprehend Corporate Litigator now. CCL."

So much time had passed that the dazzling new software from that job interview was now *old hat.* She herself was so old hat that it was absurd to think she could just come back. But she would have to. She'd sit with Leo in the tiny study at the Sven desk, and he would show her how to use Comprehend Corporate Litigator, and how to interpret the monthly statements that were jammed crudely into their mailbox like ransom notes. She would read their credit card statements in detail, including the penalties that gathered, and she would see just how deeply in debt they were and would understand what they were up against. Looking at the numbers at the bottom of the bills, she'd know that they weren't abstract figures but were real and unmanageable.

Amy would sit in that study—finally the word "study" would have meaning as a name for this room—and she would start to read her old legal textbooks and some of the law journals that Leo kept bound on the shelves, and after a while she would have remembered enough from her previous life as a lawyer so that, although she wouldn't be at all caught up with everyone else, she would at least be somewhere in the crowd, struggling, taking the subway during rush hour, lying in bed at night with clients in her mind, all of them dancing in a circle and keeping her awake. God, she would have to wear panty hose again every day, she realized.

"Do you think anyone will hire me?" she asked Leo in a small voice.

"Ah, probably. Not for a lot of money, and not somewhere that's so-called good. But there are a lot of firms."

She nodded, accepting this. "At the dinner tonight," Amy said, "when you were dancing with Corinna Berry, I have to say that really depressed me." Then she asked, "Why don't you want to sleep with me anymore? Am I completely unappealing to you sexually? Am I like a crone? Like a cow? Just the mother of your child, and so I'm desexualized?"

"That's ridiculous," Leo said. "It hasn't got anything to do with you. We've just gone off a little," he tried, kindly.

"It's more than that."

He paused. "All right, sure, it's a lot of things, I guess. It happens all the time, and it's as common as anything. As common as those receipts," he felt he had to add. "But there's another part too: I don't know if you've noticed, Amy, but I have put on twenty-one pounds this year. I'm like a whale."

"You are not." But she thought about the cookies he ate each night before he went to bed; recently, he had purchased a box of shaggy coconut Girl Scout cookies from the daughter of a colleague. Amy recalled the "chocko" Bing-Bongs he had brought home from St. Doe's and had placed on a plate by the bed the night before, and the pastries that were laid out on platters at his office in the mornings.

"Yes, I am," he said. "And the idea of having sex and of you seeing this stomach rising up above you like the sun, well, it makes me want to die. I look like my father," he said. "I'm a middle-aged guy who looks like Murray Buckner, who ran the magazine stand in the Strode Building. Now how did that happen to me?"

"It happens to everyone."

"It doesn't happen to you," he said. "You get to stay home and take care of everyone and everything, including yourself. You're basically holding back time."

"Oh, is that what I'm doing?" she said. "I don't think so."

It was the longest conversation they had had in a while. There would be further conversations about all of this; they would carry Amy and Leo through the weeks and months. Much of what they said would be repetitive. At times Leo would be interested in the conversation, and often he would not. When she spoke about Mason's school or about how much she missed Jill or about how Roberta was moving to Harlem and they would see each other far less frequently, she saw that he did listen but that there was effort involved. He couldn't help the fact that he was only partly compelled by the world she had fashioned over the past ten years since she had left work and Mason had been born. That world could be absorbing yet was also pulled along by a current of tedium, and everybody knew it.

Children had a lot to do with it; they were the most fascinating part of it all, but mostly only to their own parents or, depending on the particular aspect, sometimes only to their mothers or only to their fathers. You stayed around your children as long as you could, inhaling the ambient gold shavings of their childhood, and at the last minute you tried to see them off into life and hoped that the little piece of time you'd given them was enough to prevent them from one day feeling lonely and afraid and hopeless. You wouldn't know the outcome for a long time.

"I have to go to sleep now," Leo said finally. Then he added, "If I was able to stay home all day, I'd lose weight."

"But you would go out of your mind."

"Maybe," he admitted. Then he said, "I really don't mind my job, you know. I actually like it a whole lot more than you think. I like the days when I get to go to court. I like talking to the judges. It's always really interesting there."

"I know," she said.

"If I stayed home, I'd read a lot of Thomas Mann. I'd read the one that I never got around to reading. The very long one."

"They're all long."

"How did Thomas Mann find the time to write such long books?" Leo asked. "Nobody has that kind of time now. The entire world is so impatient."

He moved close against her and she could feel the convexity of his stomach. He was right, it was bigger than usual. "I could help you lose weight," Amy offered.

"Thank you." He kissed her head. "If it works," said Leo, "and I stop hating my physical self so much, I think we can resume as planned."

"So you're not thinking of having an affair with Corinna Berry?"

"Corinna Berry is sleeping with Lisa Silvestri."

"Lisa? *Really?*" She was amazed at this secret shift. Leo nodded. But then Amy realized that she hadn't received one of those evening calls from Lisa recently, and she also remembered how Lisa had sat watching Leo dance with Corinna tonight. Lisa, she understood now, had not been watching Leo at all.

"But even if that weren't the case," Leo said, "of course I wouldn't sleep with her. Why, would you have an affair? You mean you're like Penny Ramsey?"

"No," said Amy hotly. "I am not."

"Good," said Leo, and he pulled her on top of him in the way that he sometimes used to, so that at first she seemed as light and flexible as a paper airplane, and then, as she arranged herself on him, she became heavier, forceful, weighting him down.

Something would happen; it was imperative that it happen now, if only to create a line of demarcation between not-sex and sex. They were both full of food and drink, and the air seemed kitcheny, overly warm. She could smell wine on him and lifting off herself too, and it was as though they belonged together in their slightly ruined and filled-up state. As a teenaged girl, Amy had loved boys who were similar to her: unthreatening, slight, and narrow; she could imagine kissing them forever. She'd eventually exchanged all of that, but she'd never known she would exchange it for a middle-aged man who lay helpless, his body part bear, part man, part air mattress. She lay on him softly, and he kissed her in the full way he did back when they were young coworkers, co-conspirators. He kissed her without distraction but with the concentration that was required now in order to show that you were not distracted. This was middle-aged sex, married sex. Maybe it wasn't the last hurrah of the body. There would be more of those, but how misguided they'd been to think that what had come before would last for the duration.

In the middle of your life you should have as much sex as you could, Amy Lamb knew, and do it now, don't wait. It was an emergency disguised as a luxury. Leo kissed her faster now, and the wolfish sounds he made were like the ones he sometimes made in his sleep, dreaming. She buried her mouth under his arm, where the pheromones situated among the soft wires of hair inexplicably drew her in.

Love was stronger than reluctance, or at least you had to make it be. You had to do everything you could to return the husband to the wife, and the wife to the husband; to pull her on top of him with mouths open and the door locked, and a child sleeping somewhere on the other side of it. Nothing was connected anymore to the urgency of young love or to the possibility of sex flowering into family. Leo did what he knew she wanted him to do, his head lowering between her legs in the way a husband recalls what a wife likes, and then does it, bringing her those flowers or that certain kind of chocolate. She got up on her elbows and watched him briefly.

They had given up on sex in the same way they had partly given up on marriage, but here it was again in all its shifting weight and preferences. Amy lay back. She held on to his hair, as she had sometimes done in such a moment over the years. "I'll need Rogaine," he had once said, early on, after she had pulled so hard that he had felt a sickening follicular tug. But of course his hair had stayed intact. Even his retired father had a full head of hair, though its shoeblack color had turned to gray. Amy held fast to Leo's hair, and she thought how tenacious they both were. "I'm going to come!" she said in a slightly operatic voice, as though he wouldn't know this was the case. He always knew, just as she knew the same about him a few moments later. It was as if, in sex, they were forever describing all the action to a third party who could not see or feel anything. For some unknown and perhaps evolutionary reason, they often announced themselves in this primitive and warning way.

Then, at the end, they were both thirsty; he padded out to

bring them water, knowing the path through the apartment in the darkness. The cup he brought her was an old plastic one that had belonged to Mason years ago. Amy saw the words *Ahoy, Mateys,* which were now half worn off like a rub-on tattoo. This had been married sex, followed by a drink from the old, fading chalice of their little boy, whose own essence was even now in his sleep rubbing off and changing, and was no longer what it had been. *Why Mommy crying?* Mason had asked her when he was very little.

Husband and wife lay in their bed high up in The Rivermere in the middle of the night, their party clothes still cobwebbing the two chairs in the room. It was a weeknight, much too late for them to be awake, but they were awake anyway. The plastic cup was warm from the dishwasher, but the water they drank was cold and delicious.

S PRING ARRIVED, though the snow stayed on the ground longer than it should have, and the streets of the city were strategically spread with puddles and pools. The boys jumped into them, annoying their mothers, and an old woman in The Rivermere skidded on the curb outside the building and broke her hip. Slowly the days lengthened and lightened.

Out in Holly Hills, the township awakened into the new season. The air was highly pollinated, and watery-eyed mothers watched their children run around the backyards and up and down the wide streets. Jacob's Path exhibited its particular beauty, and the realtors cruised through the neighborhoods with potential buyers, offering patter and pointing. All the lawns had been tended and the bushes sculpted, and Donald took Nadia around their property with a pair of electric clippers, letting her try them herself. "She'll cut her hand off," Jill said as she watched them go. "She can't use electric clippers."

"She'll be fine," said Donald with certainty, not even looking back. Nadia ran ahead of him into the grass.

In May, Nadia performed at a small recital in the city that included the voice students of Anna Milofsky. It was held on a Saturday in a borrowed classroom at the Juilliard School. The other students were all teenagers: boys in jacket and tie, and lithe girls in strapless dresses, their hair drawn back off their emerging women's faces. Nadia wore a sashed green velvet dress that she had chosen herself at a children's store in the Holly Hills Shopping Plaza, though her mother was slightly perplexed by the choice, the insistence on *green,* until Nadia started to sing the unannounced second of two songs:

> "Alas, my love, you do me wrong,
> To cast me off discourteously.
> For I have loved you well and long,
> Delighting in your company.
> Greensleeves was all my joy,
> Greensleeves was my delight,
> Greensleeves was my heart of gold,
> And who but my lady Greensleeves."

Her voice was slightly tremulous and too small in the drafty classroom, but her pleasure at singing was transparent to everyone listening, and this was obviously the most persuasive reason for lessons. Donald lowered his camera and forgot to take pictures; he and Jill were made submissive before their daughter.

Later that night, after a celebration dinner at a Szechuan restaurant on the West Side that they used to love, they got into the family van and began to drive home. Nadia was already overwound and sleepy, and her head fell against the seat, her hand still holding the program from the recital, now curled. In darkness the family left the city that had once belonged to them, and on the highway the buildings receded like objects being discarded one by one. Goodbye, Chrysler Building, Jill Hamlin thought; goodbye, Citicorp Center; goodbye, Empire State Building. Goodbye, unmentionable ghosts of those once-unloved towers, made lovable in their loss.

When they had first moved to Holly Hills and Jill had feared she'd made a mistake, Amy had said to her, "Think of this as a specific part of your life. It doesn't have to be forever. Anyway, who can think in terms of forever? Think of it as one chapter in a biography written about you: Chapter Eight—Jill Hamlin: The Suburban Years."

This was what Jill thought of now in the car, for these were the suburban years. The city was all light and silhouette; Holly Hills even at Christmas could never compete with the massive effect. But the city also seemed both crazily inhuman and human. How could people *live* like that, on top of one another, always running, so competitive, always looking toward the next thing? And how could people live any other way, so separate and alone in their individual houses and delineated, proud plots of land? It seemed that everywhere you went, people quickly adapted to the way they had to live, and called it Life.

One day recently, Jill's neighbor Alice Ettinger had invited her to come watch a delivery at the local hospital, and Jill, though squeamish about the blood and the pain and the drama of the experience, had accepted. She thought of herself as she looked at the young, frightened woman in labor on the half-cranked bed, shivering in a gown peppered with teddy bear icons, an epidural taped to the white flesh of her back, preparing herself for the improbable task. This was what I never got to do, Jill thought, and she watched tensely as that woman pushed and pushed the baby out into the suburbs and the world.

Holly Hills, Jill announced to Donald one day, was not hell. There was no holly, and there weren't many hills, but still, *Holly Hills is not hell*. Say it five times fast. With Nadia more involved in school, Jill began to get to know a few other local mothers. They started to call the house, and slowly Jill unfurled. She never made friends with Sharon Gregorius and that group of women who had been involved with Wuv Cards, though, oddly, that business venture would eventually become a great success. Six months from now, the four mothers who had been at that first, stressful planning luncheon would appear on the Home Shopping Network holding up their greeting cards, and the orders, astonishingly, would rapidly come in.

What struck Jill mostly about life here was that she did not compare it with life in the city as frequently as she used to. The city seemed as if it no longer required her presence, the way that once, in her human arrogance, she had felt it did. The buildings would stay, God willing. The lights would blur together, and the subway below would make it all tremble like glassware on a shelf. Jill and her family would be gone for a long time, perhaps for good, though they would come back to visit frequently. There were yoga classes, and lunches with Amy. She and Amy might never live in the same place again, she knew, until they were old and their husbands were dead and they shared a cottage somewhere by the sea. Once a week after school now, Jill took Nadia on the train to sing for Anna Milofsky in a room at the music school. Jill sat outside in the hallway, a place where mothers always sat.

Sometimes she read a history book; other times she looked over her daughter's homework or made notes with a stylus on her Black-Berry about a new speech therapist she had meant to call for Nadia or a math tutor who she had heard was wonderful. Sometimes she was busy and engaged, and other times she was so tired she imme-diately fell asleep. Once, during a fifteen-minute nap in the middle of Nadia's voice lesson, Jill dreamed that she was a girl again herself, playing field hockey at the Pouncey School, flying across the field with her stick in hand, heading toward something in the distance that she couldn't yet see.

In the mail one day, Jill received a letter from Pouncey inviting her to come to the seventy-fifth reunion of all the past winners of the Vivian Swope Prize, given to "A Graduating Senior Who Dem-onstrates the Most Promise." She accepted, and though Donald thought it would be a great weekend trip for all three of them, after thinking about it she said no, she thought she might want to go by herself.

There in New Hampshire on a Saturday afternoon at the begin-ning of June, all the promising girls, long turned into women, gath-ered on the green. The afternoon was clear, just as it was in their memories of school, but now the air had a kind of loamy, almost fecal tang to it, which was not what they remembered. Memory is snobby, a magnet picking up only the choicest filings: sunlight, breeze, ageless buildings, the brick scrubbed and woolly with ivy. The day was beautiful, but still it smelled embarrassing in a way, as though they themselves were responsible. In fact, a nearby wheelbarrow of fertilizer was the locus of that smell. A stranger couldn't know and might not have cared that once, long ago, these women had trod all over this lawn.

Their footsteps had been much lighter then. Their feet had been smaller, narrower, and not yet swelled from years and years of bad but irresistible shoes and from the onslaught of pregnancies, after which most women shoot up one whole shoe size. The actual shoes had been different over time too: penny loafers, pumps, Pappagallos, buffalo sandals, and briefly those anvil-shaped, cloddish things called Earth Shoes, and then, eventually, penny loafers again, because most things in the world are circular, even footwear.

If only being young traveled such a circular route. If only a girl, practically cracking apart with promise, could grow up and live her life, feeling a healthy supply of pleasure and a modest amount of disappointment and then, just when it seems as though it hadn't been worth it—just when she begins to inhabit a kind of dour existential awareness—she becomes young once more. Miraculously, she becomes as clean and hopeful as the pennies she once worked into the slots of her shoes.

The women on the grass would never again be girls, but their sense of girl life, at least here at the Pouncey School in Weyburn, New Hampshire, on the first weekend in June, was vivid, fertilized. They had come from various parts of the country to be here, taking smallish planes to the airport or traveling by car or bus from the cities and suburbs and occasional rural towns in which they lived. They had circled this date on their calendar months earlier, though each of them had other upcoming appointments that were more pressing: MAMMOGRAM: 10:15 (NO DEODORANT OR BABY POWDER), or BOOK GROUP. FIRST 320 PAGES OF SWANN'S

WAY. The weekend visit to Pouncey, however, was a beacon in the future all spring. Rains fell in different regions of the country. Spouses fought. Children turned their eyes to whichever screens persuasively glowed, and the persuasion was always similar, anywhere in America.

The Swope winners waited with anticipation to return to the place where they had been young and promising and had been given a serious education without limits, and were told to *soar,* and where once they had never even heard of a mammogram—had thought it was, maybe, like a telegram? Where once the skin of their body had encased very little fat but had held mostly the collection of those hanging bags that were your organs, as pink and bright as party balloons that no one would ever see.

Jill had driven six hours north on June 3 and had parked in the faculty and visitors' lot, right by the new gym, which she vaguely remembered had been built several years earlier after an aggressive capital campaign. Back in the 1980s, Jill Hamlin's era, the girls had gone to ballet class in a small gym with a dark wooden floor and, weather permitting, had played field hockey out on this very lawn. Someone was always spray-painting orange goal lines on the grass, and yet the grass itself had lived to tell the tale.

The gathered group of Vivian Swope winners gave off no particular impression, as they were of such different ages. The older ones looked a bit alike; there was that waist thickening and the dulling of the hair, which a good salon could spin into gold. The youngest ones, graduates from the late '90s and even later, looked exceptionally chic and might have been mistaken for current Pouncey students, the ones from Belgium or Dubai whose parents had sent them across oceans with steamer trunks to study here at old Pounce. They exchanged business cards, and probably some kind of networking took place, and it was highly useful, though really, when women networked with one another, they knew that elsewhere, men were doing this same thing and that the men's networking would likely lead to greater amounts of money and more access.

"Margie Allenberg, Naples, Florida, class of '63," a thin, tan, tennisy woman said, walking up to Jill with an outstretched hand. The women from all the different eras exchanged names and geographical locations and also, because it actually seemed appropriate in this context, asked one another what they "did," and what they had done with their lives. What they had done with all that promise. One was a vice president in charge of marketing for a hotel chain; one was a physician with the U.S. Navy; another taught anthropology at the University of Michigan; and several of the very oldest ones said that they were retired teachers or librarians, or that they were homemakers. A woman from the class of '92 said she was a dominatrix and then began to laugh shrilly and said she was just kidding, she really designed sportswear. One of the women close to Jill's age was a veterinarian, one worked part-time, and another said that she was right now between careers.

Jill, when asked, told another woman, "Actually, I'm basically a shadow-mother."

"Pardon?"

"My daughter has some learning issues. We had to hire a shadow-teacher for her at school, but I think I'm sort of a shadow-mother. I have to be around a lot, arranging things, and so, you know, I'm there."

Jill took out a photograph of Nadia, and the woman said how pretty she was. Jill would be a shadow-mother for a couple of years more, she knew. Eventually she and Nadia would each have to move on, but that would be a while from now. Jill imagined going into the storage area in the furnished basement of their house, finding the box marked "Course wk., NYU," and thinking about what it would be like to rewrite her dissertation after all this time and maybe try to publish it as a nonacademic book, as Donald had once suggested. There was still a bottomless readership for books that had anything to do with the Civil War. The basic ideas in the dissertation were sound, if underdeveloped. She would have to open up the writing, to see where it would go if she didn't have a thesis committee looking over her shoulder. Was the dissertation itself corroded into bread crumbs or something resembling human remains? In all likelihood it was still there, intact. She would take a look at it one day when she worked up the nerve.

Jill had easily given up those seminar rooms, first—briefly—for Tilt-a-Whirl Productions, and then for the long and unscrolling state of everything that came afterward. It was hard for anyone to stay fixed and certain in life. Many years down the line, so many people were not where you had thought they would be. Selby Rothberg, the former head of Tilt-a-Whirl, had gone on to run a major movie studio, where she was responsible for several summer hits until she was forced out in a kind of overnight coup. But it wasn't simply about sexism, someone suggested; it was now also about ageism. Selby Rothberg had aged out of the system and had been replaced with a smiling, cool baby shark named Caitlin Verstappen, who would do the bidding of the Japanese shareholders of the studio's mother company. No one seemed to know what had become of Selby Rothberg. It was said that she was writing her acidulous Hollywood memoirs, though it seemed too late for such a book to interest many people; other, similar books had been written long ago, in a time when people had the leisure to care about that subject. Someone else had heard that Selby lived on her payout in a crumbling house in Malibu and that she was involved in animal rights. Many women had claimed her as their mentor over time, perhaps without her knowledge.

Jill's advisor, Michael Dearborn, had died of AIDS-related complications in the mid-1990s, before protease inhibitors were widely used. She'd learned this from the alumni bulletin she received each month even though she'd never gotten a degree. Oh, her handsome bearded mentor, gone from the world in that pile-up of young men. The long view over time of anyone's story was surprising but inevitable, and inevitably sad.

"You know," Jill said to Amy recently, " I think I was probably depressed back in the days when I was having trouble writing my thesis, and I just didn't know it."

"It can run in families, right? A genetic predisposition?"

"Yes. You know how they always say that when a parent kills herself it's like she's leaving the door open for the child? And then that door is always open?"

"For you it's shut," Amy said. "Click. I have just shut it."

"No," said Jill. "Nadia shut it." They were quiet. "Do you realize that if I'd gotten my Ph.D. back then, by now I would probably have been teaching college for fifteen years? That would be my life. 'Professor, can we go over my paper now?' 'Why yes, Sally, come in.'"

Here on the lawn at the Pouncey School, when the women were done exchanging stories, someone said, "So what do you think she would have become?"

"Who?" someone else asked.

"Vivian Swope."

They all took a few minutes to imagine what might have become of that original promising girl with the silk hair ribbon if she hadn't been killed on a school outing in 1931. She could have been a pilot, one woman conjectured; it was said that she was very adventurous. A biologist, said another. Poet. Costume designer. Housewife. Nun. They kept talking as they headed toward the Westaway Refectory, where they used to consume fried flounder and a variety of puddings, and where soon they would sit and eat and keep talking until the kitchen staff told them it was time to close up for the night.

N o one had been all that surprised when Roberta Sokolov had announced that she and her family were moving to Harlem. People heard "Harlem," and they stiffened slightly, thinking you were moving where you really weren't wanted, or that you and your children would be unsafe. Neither seemed wholly true, though Roberta wasn't sure. She knew she wanted a big change. You just had to know the good streets, she told her friends. You had to get to know the neighborhood. Her friends had given her a farewell breakfast at the Golden Horn, with gifts for the new house, and she had cried a little and said, "I will really miss this whole thing, being mothers together all these years," but it seemed to her afterward, as her feelings of sentimentality diminished, that she could leave the other women behind without a tremendous amount of regret. She would be pulling her kids out of their private schools and putting them in a new charter school not far from their new home that, while only a year old, had a very good reputation. It was ironic, she knew, that back when she and Nathaniel had no money, their kids had gone to private school, and now that they had money, their kids were going to public school.

In the weeks before the move, Roberta went through her belongings and separated out the things that she no longer wanted. These she took into the hallway and placed on the windowsill of the stairwell, the way tenants sometimes did in that building. There, then, were the books she had owned but had never read or had already read and would never read again; a bottle of very expensive moisturizer that Karen Yip had once bought for her as a birthday present, its seal still unbroken; one of Roberta's parents' old centerpieces from St. Patrick's Day, with its now rock-hard sugar shamrocks and tiny leprechauns hiding among the shredded green tissue paper, which Roberta had felt too guilty and emotional about ever to throw away. Suddenly she had courage. Everything not essential was shed before the move.

Then, finally, the family was installed in the new house on Strivers' Row, the historic street in Harlem. The place was beautiful, and though there was still a good deal of renovation to do, she loved it there. Her children had their own bedrooms, and Roberta had an art studio, as Nathaniel had said she would. But while it was not really a surprise to her—instead, it was more of an expected sadness—still her artwork hadn't taken form in the muscular way she had hoped. At first, after Harry and Grace were off in their charter school, Roberta tried to paint. Then, after a few weeks of hesitation and paltry efforts, she thought, *Fuck it,* and gave it a rest.

Wandering around the new neighborhood, trying to find a drugstore and a place to get coffee in the morning, Roberta had come upon a flyer on a lamppost asking for volunteers at a women's health services agency on 128th Street called Essential Care. She called, and they gave her a job answering telephones; the place was understaffed and, according to the director, had "one foot on a banana peel." The paid workers—all women—in the office of EC often complained at length about the low salary and the unrewarding nature of the work, which often involved trying to get adolescent girls with STDs or extremely old women to go see a gynecologist for the first time ever.

It wasn't that the dismal offices of EC appealed to Roberta at all, or that she felt real affection for the other people who worked there. Officiousness was a common trait among the staff; maybe it was a defense against the onslaught that always took place in this medical office: the clients crowding the dingy waiting area, demanding service as they poked their heads in through the small slot behind which a receptionist warily sat.

Roberta worked there in a volunteer capacity at first and then eventually for pay. Part-time at first and then, finally, though she had not planned this, full-time. Soon she was doing everything at EC: answering phones and giving advice and making referrals, behaving in a manner that was sometimes officious but more often just kind and tired. She occasionally heard herself saying to a frightened woman who'd come in, "Just get the mammogram. It's better to know than not to know, don't you think?"

Work rose up in the same inexplicable way that her art had receded, except once in a while, on the weekend, Roberta went into her studio and fooled around a little with a charcoal pencil or a thin brush and a glass of milky watercolor water. Neither of her kids ever asked if they could use the studio for storing their bikes or having a sleepover, or wondered aloud whether that space really needed to be called "the studio," when it was clear that Roberta rarely used it as one. Maybe Nathaniel had warned Harry and Grace away from ever saying anything to their mother that would make her feel bad about the fact that her painting hadn't gone well since they'd been living here, just as it hadn't gone well when they'd lived in their tiny walk-up apartment.

She was touched by their sensitivity to her, though it was possible that she'd imagined the whole scenario. Children were narcissists, after all, and perhaps her children never thought about her art studio and how strange it was that their mother was rarely in it. Or maybe it never occurred to them that art was something that some lucky people did full-time; after all, being a working artist was so hard. You had to be disciplined all the time, and almost no one in the world was able to earn a living from art.

Lately, she was rarely in the house at all; with Nathaniel's television success, and Harry and Grace doing after-school programs at their disorganized but diverse and so far not-bad charter school, and Roberta working full-time at EC and overtime on some days when they were understaffed, the house sat, fully alarmed and defended, in its own sunlight during the afternoon, without anyone there to admire the preserved and recently painted moldings or the little rectangles of green and violet stained glass or the high ceilings or the gently curving banisters. It was like a craft project that, over time, would start to falter and nobly collapse, but this wouldn't be discernible for many, many years. At night, the family converged and stomped around, tired, overworked, full of complaint and anecdote, and then they sat at the table in the grand dining room and ate the take-out that someone had brought home, and told one another about their day.

ACROSS THE COUNTRY in Lorton, South Dakota, Brandy Gillop came home from the casino and paced the small living room of the apartment, giving a cool, critic's assessment of her most recent painting that sat on an easel. It was good, she decided, but not great, though she wasn't particularly skilled at knowing when a painting worked or didn't. That woman in New York City had just shitted all over her, and that was typical of the human race. People always disappointed you; this was something you could count on, and you shouldn't ever forget it. Roberta Sokolov had been a big tease, and the dream of New York City now seemed like a big tease too.

Roberta had once told Brandy that she'd always hoped to do a series of portraits of some kind; it had something to do with children growing up, she remembered. Brandy thought about doing her own series of portraits now. She could call it The Disappointment Series, she thought, but then right away she had a better idea; she'd call it People Who Fucked Me Over, and she'd use dirt colors and thick, angry strokes. She would paint disgusting, ugly portraits of Tyler Parvell and her uncle Roy and her father, of course, and Roberta. She would need a thicker brush than the one she had. She made a note to herself to go out later and buy one.

KAREN YIP'S PARENTS, Chu Hua and Jun Tang, flew in from San Francisco and stayed for a full week late that spring, exclaiming once again at the opulent life that their daughter and son-in-law lived, and bringing bags of Chinese lychee gummies for the twins. No one could say for sure what a full enough life was; everyone's standard was different. Karen still went for job interviews, treating each one as spectacle, enjoying getting dressed up in a fine suit for the occasion and hearing about the work that was currently being done at the firm, and in what way she would possibly "fit" into all of it. She had been uncommonly brilliant at statistical analysis, and though she hadn't worked since the twins were babies, every interviewer inevitably offered her a job.

"We can really imagine you here," the interviewers said. "We think it would be a mutually beneficial arrangement."

They wrote down a figure on a piece of paper and slid it across the table to her. She loved that sexy, dramatic moment, the *shoosh* of the paper being moved. The figure was always impressive; her worth had remained high even over these years of absence. But inevitably she said no, the job wasn't right for her, she did not think it was a perfect fit after all. Wilson didn't care at all if she worked or not; he liked hearing about the interviews and the offers and the specs of the companies, but it was up to her whether or not she went back. One day, she supposed, she might find a job that impelled her away from the soft freedoms of her daily life; it was possible, even statistically likely, that she would. But there was no need for it. She wasn't impatient with the way her life was going, and they had enough money, and she didn't care what anyone else thought.

For now, at night, with her parents asleep downstairs in the guest room, her twin sons asleep across the hall, and her husband Wilson asleep beside her, Karen simply let herself be pelted with numbers, which surrounded her and accumulated in drifts and columns, adding up.

D RESSED IN MATCHING orange vests, two kindergarten fathers walked round and round the streets of the neighborhood. "What are we looking for, exactly?" one asked.

"No idea," said the other. "Mayhem, I guess."

They laughed a little and made a few remarks about safety walk: how it seemed useful in theory, but how it probably never made a difference. The men were both thirty-two years old. One of them also had a baby at home, though he had left her with a sitter so he could come out and do safety walk at his older son's school. His wife was a psychopharmacologist with a successful fledgling practice. Did the people of the city get more and more troubled with each passing year, given the anxious circumstances of their lives, or was his wife simply a wonderful doctor? He really had no way of knowing.

He'd been the features editor of a newsmagazine until their second child was born, and then he and his wife had had a discussion, and they agreed that he would take off two years to stay home with the baby. Two years, and then they would do day care; they had enough saved up to make this plan possible. At times he thought about the office: the particular smell that it had had, something clean and metallic, which didn't exist anywhere in his home. It was the smell of *paper clips*, he had decided once, with longing, after the baby had spit up a gruel of milk and strained lamb on his shirtsleeve.

But mostly, though, he knew that if you longed for what you did not have, then you would be one of those unhappy people you could find anywhere in any setting, the ones who couldn't appreciate what they had as long as they saw something they did not have. He thought of his wife sitting in her office, leaning forward in her chair with her prescription pad at the ready, while someone in the chair across from her sobbed. His wife took the burden of that patient's pain, and though he admired her for doing this, he was relieved that it was not his burden. He had no deadlines at the magazine anymore, no crazy art director to deal with. He thought now of the baby, hoping she had gotten a good nap today. When she didn't nap, her schedule was screwed up for the rest of the day and night. He also thought about his son, who right at this moment was staying after school for karate class, his legs kicking and his arms whirling, shouting *"Hi-yaaaaaaa!"* to another little boy, who would shout it right back.

The two fathers said hello to the mothers who streamed by on this pretty, calm street in the middle of the afternoon on what would have been a workday once and was, at least for now, something else.

A T NIGHT, in midtown, at a scientific research institute funded by a European conglomerate, the lights of an office were still on, though almost all of the scientists had gone home. Isabelle Gordon, string theorist, stood at a green blackboard talking to her colleague Martha Scarpino. Their words went back and forth as Isabelle wrote out an equation that was so long that the nub of yellow chalk just disintegrated between her fingers as she wrote. But she was on a roll and didn't want to stop; so she kept on going, uninterrupted, writing with her fingertips in the air above the blackboard, continuing the equation for Martha, who followed along, nodding rapidly.

Both of them were unable to turn their brains off like light switches; they had this in common. They also had in common a belief in the likelihood that their shared primary interest, super-string theory, would turn out to be a valid theory of everything and that one day this would be universally accepted. Until then, it was just a question of plodding along, gathering data, making your case at conferences, standing at a lectern and delivering a paper in a small but forceful voice, and also standing at a blackboard at night, writing an equation until the chalk dissolved. Isabelle Gordon didn't mind being just a flouring of yellow chalk dust herself, or a vibrating object that thought about everything constantly and liked designer shoes and loved her children and her husband madly, crazily—as much, she had told her son Ty once before bed, as she loved D-branes and gauge bosons and Calabi-Yau manifolds. Yes, as much as that, which, they all knew, was really saying a lot.

BUT LOVE did not have to be the thing that everyone at work aimed toward, arrows poised. Amy Lamb knew this early on into her new job. For five months now, she had been working as a lawyer in general practice. It had taken a long time to find an acceptable position. She'd answered an online ad for a women's law firm that had seemed wonderful initially, but when she went for the interview it soon became clear to her that the young woman behind the desk thought Amy was far too old to work there. It was a great insult. Though she got herself a couple of interviews cold, it was actually through Lisa Silvestri's connections that Amy found the job as one of four attorneys at a modest storefront law office downtown called Stellan Frankel Bern. The other lawyers, two women and one man, all in their thirties, were convivial enough, and seemed to have lives outside their job. Most of her cases were standard T&E, work that Amy would never burn to do or regard with great desire. Yes, what a shame it was, she thought now, silently addressing her mother, that she hadn't found something she really loved and was brilliant at in time to chase it down. But still it was a relief to earn money, and it was sometimes a surprisingly significant pleasure to find that most of the particulars of legal language and instinct had held fast over the years after all. And she also felt it was a pleasure, an honor, weirdly, just to be working. On Monday mornings, the lawyers lingered briefly in one another's cubicles, asking about the weekend, dawdling a little before giving themselves over to another week.

Amy and Leo now took turns taking Mason to school in the morning. Leo disliked having to skip the gym every other day, and he worried that he was arriving at his desk far too late, but he found that it wasn't a tragedy and that his clients would manage if he arrived at a more reasonable hour. Amy still looked forward to the days when she took Mason to school; she had been doing it for so long that it had become part of what she expected. Sometimes the mornings were hectic and unpleasant. She had a meeting with a client first thing and could not afford to be late, yet she couldn't get Mason out of bed.

"DO YOU KNOW HOW IMPORTANT IT IS THAT YOU GET UP RIGHT NOW?" she would cry to him, but maddeningly there would be no answer.

Sometimes, he simply could not find whatever book he was reading; it was certainly not one of the *Blindman* series anymore. The long novels of Rachel Millar had finally been abandoned in favor of another series, by an Englishman named Sebastian Sunderland, whose *Starfish Island* trilogy involved an underwater cave populated by creatures who had the ability to regrow severed limbs at will and breathe perfectly in the silent depths of the ocean. *Blindman and the Moorchaser: Book the Third* had been placed on a high shelf in Mason's room; he would likely never look at it again until the day when he became a father reading to his own child.

One morning when they were about to leave the apartment for school and then for work, Amy could not find her briefcase. "Oh God, where is it?" she repeated. "Where did I leave it? Oh, this is bad."

"What's going to happen, you'll be marked unprepared?" Mason said.

"I'm serious; it's important."

Mason produced his electronic object finder, which, she had recently learned, he had programmed to include his mother's most essential belongings too, ever since she had gone back to work. He pressed a code into the plastic device, and they both waited. Momentarily there came a corresponding, faraway, android voice.

Your-brief-case-is-o-ver-here, it said, and she and Mason ran through the apartment in search of the sound.

There, in the bedroom, under a pile of silky clothes that she had worn yesterday and had neglected to put away, so tired was she last night, was her briefcase, with the brown leather surface and the golden metal clasp that made a gratifying noise when the nub was pressed into its groove.

Your-brief-case-is-o-ver-here, the object finder repeated, and she picked up the briefcase and opened it, checking the contents, seeing that all the papers were there, all the directions for the day. *Your-life-is-fi-nite,* the object finder told her. *No-one-knows-a-ny-thing. But-do-not-stop. Do-not-fal-ter. Do-not-wait. It-is-late-in-the-day-but-I-think-there-may-still-be-time.*

O N THE AFTERNOON that Amy deposited her first, fairly modest paycheck, she went into a small bookstore near her office and bought Leo a copy of *The Magic Mountain.* Slowly, over the weeks, she began to notice that the red satin bookmark moved from page to page like a hand on a clock, collecting heft behind it. Leo was tired at night, but she watched him make his way through the book she had bought him. He had lost a little weight, but particularly with his reading glasses sitting on the bridge of his nose, he did look like his father. But she looked like her mother, and there were worse fates than that.

Penny Ramsey remained mostly an absence. On the rare occasions when Amy saw her on the street, Penny was with Holden or her teenaged daughters, and once she was with Greg. Or else Amy was with Mason, and the two women simply smiled and said hi, how are you; how are the kids; how's school going for them; how's the museum; I hear you've started at a law firm—is it going well? And then each of them barely waited for the answer. But always Amy imagined that one day she would see Penny alone, and she would say something to her of significance. It had been over a year now, yet that still hadn't happened.

Could you tell me something, please, Amy would ask: Was our friendship real back then? Did you actually even like me at all? Did you love Ian? Did you love your husband? Do you love him now? Wasn't that whole thing crazy? Do you even know what became of Ian, finally?

Amy had lost track of Ian Janeway; he'd never replied to her letter, not that she'd expected him to. Sometimes she imagined him in London, still recovering and obsessive and hopelessly lost, unsteadily making his way up the stone stairs of the National Gallery assisted by two metal canes, each step sending jags of pain humming through the thirty-three vertebrae of his spine.

As it would turn out, Amy Lamb saw Penny Ramscy alone one day at the end of that spring. It was during the evening rush hour in the subway below Penn Station. Amy was walking quickly in a crowd toward the trains after work, when she glanced into one of those brightly lit, nonfat frozen-dessert stands to which women are often drawn, needing a vague trace of sweetness at the end of the day. Penny Ramsey was perched on a stool in the tiny space, taking a few hurried spoonfuls of milk, sugar, chemicals, and air from a cup. A briefcase and a good, candied-looking pocketbook were at her feet, and in her left hand was a sheaf of slides that she was holding up to the light.

Amy would have said something to her; it was all so long ago already, and neither of them thought about it much, and she wasn't angry with Penny anymore, and it wouldn't have been a big deal. But Penny, she could see, was working. She was working even now, after hours, sitting at a frozen-dessert stand, because work often expanded and lapped over the edges of anyone's day. Penny was thinking about something that had nothing to do with Amy or Ian or being a friend or being in love or walking away from her injured, overexcited lover. Actually, she was thinking about mid-nineteenth-century bromine daguerreotypes, and whether she ought to build an entire exhibition around them at the museum, and Amy felt it was only right to leave her alone. She watched as Penny Ramsey looked and looked at those slides in a long moment of concentration. Then Penny dropped her cup into the trash, picked up her briefcase and pocketbook, and slipped off among the crowd of people heading for all the different trains that flowed like separate rivers from this single station.

IN THE GOLDEN HORN on a Monday morning at the very end of the school year, the owner, Adnan Veysel, said to a waiter, "So where have the ladies in the back been? I don't see them very often." The waiter, young, uninterested, shrugged and proceeded to spray a table with blue liquid from a bottle, then wipe it away and place buntings of napkins and silverware on its surface.

"Maybe they went to another place," the owner said in answer to his own question. He had noticed that the back booth was less frequently full in the mornings at the start of the school day, or at least that the women who came and sat here lately were not the same ones he had been seeing for years. He saw some younger ones these days, with baby carriages and strollers. Their voices often sounded excited, and they had so much equipment that they practically decorated the booth with it. Over time he would probably start to forget about the regulars; this new crowd would become the new regulars.

But now, though, he still thought about the women who until recently had come here most mornings. He had never known any of their names, and he saw them only briefly when they first walked in, and then perhaps from above, if the place was particularly busy and he ended up bringing them their water glasses or even their orders. He recalled looking down at the tops of their heads and the parts in their hair as they sat and he stood. He thought of them as the ordinary-looking brown-haired one who always smiled at him right away; the very tall and pretty blonde one—she'd already stopped coming here so much earlier, but he still remembered her; the slightly thick-built one with the nose; and the Asian one, who always figured out the bill. Different women had joined them from time to time, but it was the four originals who no longer came very often.

He might see one of them sometimes, or maybe another, but they didn't appear consistently anymore, or in a group. In the past they had always lingered after the breakfast rush. They overtipped the waiters, he'd noticed, leaving amounts of money that seemed to have nothing to do with how much food they had actually ordered.

But as he thought about it now, he decided that he could not believe they had gone somewhere new; it just didn't seem like something they would do. He imagined that they felt a kind of loyalty toward the Golden Horn, as if it were their school or their house of worship, and that this feeling had held them in place over such a long stretch of time. For his own reasons he was glad that it had. But now the world, he thought, had taken them. He knew that this could suddenly happen. One day you just woke up, and there was somewhere that you needed to be.

ACKNOWLEDGMENTS

I am grateful to many people for their generosity, advice, and good conversation. These include my mother, Hilma Wolitzer, my friend Deborah Copaken Kogan, who has been so smart and encouraging, and Stacy Schiff, Cathleen Schine, Martha Parker, Erin Cox, and Grey Hirschfeld. Many thanks to my amazing agent, Suzanne Gluck, and to my wonderful editor, Sarah McGrath. Finally, my gratitude goes to my family: my loving sons, Gabriel and Charlie, and my husband, Richard Panek, for all his essential help.